Some reviews of

CLOSING

'Hugely readable'   *Woman*

'Set in post-GLC London and the unemployment-
ravaged North East, dealing with Thatcherism and
feminism, idealism and pragmatism, *Closing* really is
one of those "novels for our time" and as such is
profoundly unsettling ... Zoe Fairbairns displays a
fearsome apprehension of our modern anxieties.'
Fiction Magazine

'A wonderfully saleable mixture of ideas and humour
that has Best Seller stamped all over it.'
Women's Review

'First class entertainment ... a strong, good-humoured
and sardonic plot that gives full value for every penny
of its price.'   *Irish Times*

D0544396

Closing

Zoë Fairbairns

Closing

A Methuen Paperback

A Methuen Paperback

CLOSING

British Library Cataloguing in Publication Data

Fairbairns, Zoe
Closing.
I. Title
823'.914[F]   PR6056.A48

ISBN 0 413 14690 1

First published in Great Britain 1987
by Methuen London Ltd
This edition published 1988
by Methuen London Ltd
11 New Fetter Lane, London EC4P 4EE
Copyright © 1987 by Zoe Fairbairns

Printed and bound in Great Britain
by Cox & Wyman Ltd, Reading

Acknowledgements

The people who did most to help me write *Closing* are Elsbeth Lindner, Fiction Editor of Methuen London Ltd, and writer John Petherbridge, with whom I live. I thank them for giving so generously of their time, wit and wisdom.

Many saleswomen, salesmen, sales trainers and others have helped me research the background for the book by allowing me to interview them, sit in on their courses or just follow them about. None of them appears in the book, and neither does any other real person or business. Any resemblances are coincidental. Thanks to: Louise Alsop, Robin Boston, Rosie Boycott, Gillian Brett, Helen Burrel, Ozzie Byers, Helen Carr, Deirdre Dine, Andy Evans, Isabel Fairbairns, John Fairbairns, Sylvia Fairbairns, John Gall, Tom Golbourn, Debbie Hickman, Sue Kennedy, John Landau, Theresa Lloyd, Sara Maitland, Ken Meadows, Michael Meynell, David Mitchell, David Moody, Sue O'Sullivan, Joan Pearce, Peter Pearce, Ruthie Petrie, Tamsin Powles, Lorna Quick, Michael Reid, Carol Sarler, Ian Scott-Parker, Dan Smith, Deirdre Spencer, Carole Sweet, Steve Tandy, Angela Truell, Elizabeth Willis, Jeanette Winterson.

Thanks too to Michael Thomas, my literary agent, for many years of encouragement and help; and everyone at Sunderland Polytechnic where I was Writer in Residence during the early stages of writing the book.

Part of *Closing* grew from my short story *Relics* which appears in *Despatches from the Frontiers of the Female Mind*, edited by Jen Green and Sarah Lefanu, published by The Women's Press (1985); Collindeane Tower, where some of the action of the novel takes place, first appeared – in rather different circumstances – in my novel *Benefits*, published by Virago (1979).

Zoë Fairbairns

You Need It

I

As a rule, Gina Heriot liked driving; but she was not liking this. It was a Monday evening in early January. After a mild Christmas, snow had, to everyone's surprise, been falling all over Britain since morning. The rural Surrey road along which she was travelling was unknown to her, twisty and dark. Little avalanches tumbled down on to it from the slope on the left; on the far side was a sheer drop of uncertain depth.

Snowflakes beat hypnotically against Gina's windscreen like malevolent insects with stings that could penetrate and blind. A long tail of traffic had built up behind her, lights goading her to increase her speed, but she would not. Ahead towered a Stalton Industries lorry, its blue tarpaulin inadequately roped down. If they were careless about that, they might be careless about securing the load too, whatever it was. Stalton Industries was a large chemicals company. Gina's boyfriend Oliver worked for them, as it happened; he was an assistant sales manager in their pharmaceuticals division.

Since Gina could not, with safety, overtake the Stalton's lorry, she intended to keep her distance. But a car from behind nipped into her stopping space, forcing her to brake. She put a cigarette into her mouth but did not light it. The idiot driver overtook the lorry and plunged on into the darkness. He achieved this without mishap but Gina stayed where she was, entranced still by the snow and the flapping of the lorry's tarpaulin. *Can I sell you people some rope?* she would tease Oliver when she saw him at the end of the week. *That's R-O-P-E, it's quite useful for stopping things falling off the backs of lorries. . . .*

At last, to her great relief, the lorry started to signal an intention to turn right towards what looked like a farm track. She did not envy the driver the task of manoeuvring his unwieldy vehicle down it, but that was his problem. The lorry moved to the centre of the road, leaving sufficient space for Gina to pass on the left.

When she was halfway along the lorry's length she realized that it was starting to swing back towards her.

She noted this with interest. Her brain had gone into slow motion. *Aren't people funny?* she thought.

She was too committed to stop. There was nowhere for her to go. The lorry was all around her with its familiar Stalton's logo – 'Another Delivery to British Industry'. She punched her horn. Her eyes met the eyes of the driver of the lorry, white in his mirror. The lorry plunged right. Fortunately nothing was coming, but the lorry went into a skid. The tarpaulin burst and something fell towards Gina like a wall, missing, but crunching under her tyres. By the time she had regained control of her car and parked it as far off the road as possible, which was not very far, the lorry had disappeared over the edge of the right-hand side of the road. Distant cracking and banging sounds suggested that the lorry had fallen a fatally long way. But a quick glance told her that the vehicle had come to rest against some handily placed trees, and the noise was that of its load being shed. She could not see what the load was.

Her first impulse was to get the fire brigade. She was herself a chemistry graduate, and a sales representative for an industrial plastics company, and she knew that a Stalton's lorry on its side should be treated with great respect. The lorry bore no special signs to warn of a toxic or inflammable load, but this was not a guarantee. Whatever danger the driver might be in, trapped in his cab, to have Gina or some other hero climb in and share it with him would do nobody any good.

But other cars were stopping, their drivers and passengers rushing altruistically forward, down the slope towards where the lorry tilted against the trees. 'Keep away, keep away!' shouted Gina, covering her mouth with her scarf, feeling something burn her skin, hoping it was only snowflakes. 'You don't know what he's got in there.'

'But the driver – '

'Call the police and the fire brigade. The fire brigade first.'

'There's a man in there – '

Not all the cars were stopping. Some drivers preferred to pretend they had seen nothing. They whizzed by without reducing speed, zigzagging between bystanders.

'Has anyone got warning signs?'

4

'There's a man in there – '

'But you can't help him.'

The driver of the lorry untangled himself from his seat belt and clambered like a spider from his overturned cab. 'Thanks a million,' he snarled at Gina. 'I'll do the same for you some time.'

'Are you all right?'

'No thanks to you.'

'What are you carrying?'

'Mind your own fucking business.'

'What are you carrying, you ill-mannered berk?'

'Acrylic sheeting. Next question? Dangerous stuff, acrylic sheeting, that's why people double-glaze their houses with it – ' She was relieved, but his rudeness and his assumption of her ignorance infuriated her. Any sympathy she might have felt for the fright he had suffered, and for the loss of his load, had disappeared. *Not carrying it now, are you?* she thought.

He was staring angrily down into the dark valley. He was not hurt. He was just an ordinary oaf who had wanted to get home and had driven carelessly to achieve this. Who did not want to get home? He might even be drunk. *Just an ordinary Stalton Industries oaf*, she would tell Oliver: *like you*. She turned her back on the oaf, wishing him joy of his acrylic sheeting, hoping that it was all either smashed, like the bit she had run over, or inaccessible down steep slippery slopes. *Another rural English valley double-glazed by Stalton Industries . . . .*

He picked up a piece of the material that was scattered on the road – a piece about the size of a paperback book – and put it roughly into her hand. 'Go on, take it to Friends of the Earth, get it tested. "Shouldn't be allowed on the roads . . . " '

'*You* shouldn't, that's for sure!' He had been mimicking her voice, or at least he obviously thought he had; Gina knew that she did not really have a plum in her mouth. 'That was one of the worst pieces of driving I've ever seen, you could have killed me – ' As if to render unbelievable the fact that the accident had been his fault, he began to get organized with great efficiency and calm. He sent for help, cleared the road of acrylic as best he could and rewrote the story of what had happened for the benefit of anyone who would listen.

'You saw her! Overtaking on the inside – '

'You were indicating right!' Gina cried. 'You were going right!'

'I should push off if I were you. I haven't read your numberplates.'

'Haven't you? Well, I've read yours, mate, and I know your company well.' His slur on her driving and his suggestion that she might have some connection with an organization like Friends of the

5

Earth were outrageous but easily dismissible; more disturbing was the impression he had given to bystanders that she had been indifferent to the possibility that he might need rescuing from his cab. She wanted to explain to them that the first rule after an accident involving chemicals was to stay clear until the exact nature of the hazard was known.

She sat in her car, shaking, fiddling with the piece of acrylic with one hand, smoking a cigarette with the other, waiting for the police. Even before the accident she had been late for where she was going. The police came. She gave them her particulars and her account of what had happened. To her own ears her voice sounded as strange and alien as what she was saying: it might have been a news bulletin about a stranger. She proceeded on her way, turning right at the next junction. She was going on a course. The starting time was 6 pm. It was 8.30 now, but she drove slowly, watchfully.

Rainbows of Christmas lights glowed along the windows and verandahs of the Donian Hotel, a former Tudor coaching inn, now modernized with low, snugly curtained annexes and a conference centre. The sign in the lobby said: 'The Donian Hotel welcomes START Selling – Women!' and an arrow pointed the way.

'They started at six,' said the receptionist.

'I know. When do they break for dinner?'

'They've just had it.'

'Damn,' said Gina. 'Look, I'll leave my luggage here and go straight in.'

'Rather you than me,' said the receptionist.

Gina decided to take a drink in with her, to steady her nerves. She entered the conference room through swing doors. She had hoped that she would be at the back, but she seemed to be in the wings of a small theatre, with access to the auditorium only possible via the stage.

The speaker was saying, 'Today's householders want their bathrooms to express their personalities. It may be the smallest room but it should be a fun room.'

Gina tiptoed past her, mouthing 'Sorry.' The audience of about thirty women was arranged in semicircular rows of tables and chairs, a nameplate on each table. Gina spotted her own name and made for it.

The speaker concluded her remarks on bathrooms, at which point it became clear that she was not the main speaker but one of the course delegates, doing a self-introduction. The main speaker, Daphne Barclay from START Selling, said, 'Thank you, Mrs Fraser. I'm sorry that you were interrupted.' Gina smiled that she was sorry too.

'Are you Mrs Mickleston or Miss Heriot?'

'Heriot.'

'And are you on a sales training course or a pub crawl?'

Gina looked at her gin and tonic with embarrassment. Perhaps it was not quite the thing to have brought it in with her. She was about to apologize when one of the women laughed. She could not tell who it was, but she recognized the laugh as the laugh of a nervous underling at the new boss's first joke. It was a hedging-your-bets kind of laugh, an insurance policy. Gina despised such craven behaviour. Daphne Barclay was, according to the START Selling literature, twenty-six, only a year older than Gina, and several years younger than many of the others here, as far as Gina could tell. So why did they let her intimidate them?

'I've come for the course,' said Gina, speaking politely, sitting tight.

'Then we'd better give you a round of applause for getting here!' Everybody clapped.

'Now, Miss Heriot, if you could just take your drink back to the bar, I'm sure they'll look after it for you. Don't be long. This course began at six, and you don't want to miss any more of it, do you?'

Angry and embarrassed, Gina left the conference room. She drained her drink, went to the bar, sat down and ordered another.

2

The wheel turned and the cage went down the shaft into the mine. The wheel turned the other way and the cage came up again. Tom Mitchison, the model-maker, stepped back, satisfied for now. He had been working all day on this, with scrap metal and driftwood from the beach and wire for the pulleys. He was eighteen and had his own business.

His girlfriend Shelly, who was seventeen, sat sewing clothes for the stiff wooden dolls which, half-made, lined the shelf behind her. Chris, a former school friend, turned the handle on the new model. He was Tom's age and, like Shelly, unemployed.

Shelly said, 'Don't break it.'

'Break it, I hardly touched it. Is this all it does? Go up and down?'

'You've not finished it yet, have you, Tom? There's going to be wagons and coal and a railway – '

Tom sighed. 'If I've time.'

'And what'll you be asking for it? Or do you leave that to the sales department? What am I bid for this beautiful, er – beautiful, er – ?'

'Oh shut up, Chris,' said Shelly.

'You'll not know your mam when she gets back, Tom. She'll be selling you last week's newspaper for more than you paid for it.'

Tom ignored him. 'I think that's me for the day.'

'Coming out tonight?' said Chris.

'We might, later. I've got my Auntie Pat coming round to cook my tea.'

This had been arranged last night when START Selling had rung up to say there was a free place going on one of their courses and would his mother like to take it up? She had appeared delighted –

'I never thought I'd be accepted, did you, Tom?' – and then she had flown into a panic over the short notice. She had gone round to her sister's, who had come bustling back to indulge in her favourite occupation: telling people what to do. Auntie Pat had helped his mother to choose what clothes she should take with her, packed them into one of her own suitcases, taken them all out again and ironed them. 'I'll look after Tom. He can have his meals with us.'

'There's no need for that,' he had said. 'Shelly'll come round.'

His mother and his aunt had exchanged glances, and his aunt said, 'I'll come in and cook for him. I'll keep an eye on him.'

His mother always insisted on what she called certain standards being maintained while he lived under her roof. This morning, when he was saying goodbye to her, having helped her carry her suitcase and bags of models to the Sunderland bus station to catch the coach going south, she had asked him to give her his word that he and Michelle (his mother always referred to Shelly by her full name) would not do anything while she was out of the house that they would not do while she was in it.

He had stared through the smeared glass of the bus terminal at the teeming snow and the darkness of the still-early morning. The coach had looked as frail as one of those tiny aeroplanes setting off in the early days of transatlantic flying. 'You'd think they'd've sent you your train fare.'

His mother had laughed at this. 'Give, give, give, that's you all over. Why should they? They've given me a free place.'

'There's probably something in it for them.'

'There's something in it for *us*. That's all I care about.'

'They probably think you've got some flash car.'

'They can think what they like. I want your word, Tom.'

She had wanted his word, so he had given it.

'Coming up for tea, Shell?' he said, as Chris shuffled off into the snow and darkness outside the workshop.

'Won't your aunt mind?'

'''Course not. With a bit of luck, she'll go home early. Don't want to go out, do you?'

'Not with him,' said Shelly, making a face in Chris's direction.

'He's all right.'

'Can't he say anything nice? It's lovely.' Gently she fingered the model colliery. 'He's just jealous.'

Tom understood his friend better than Shelly did. Chris had not had a job since leaving school, but then Chris, unlike Tom, had left

9

school without qualifications. Tom remembered bitterly what his own CSEs (in woodwork, metalwork and history) had qualified him to do. For eight months he had stood at the end of a conveyor belt in a paper mill waiting for enough packages of paper to arrive to fill a trolley. When the trolley was full, he had had to wheel it either to a store room or to a lorry. Then he would wheel the trolley back to the conveyor belt and start again.

There had been variety. It had not always been the same kind of paper. Sometimes it had been typing paper, sometimes drawing paper, sometimes computer paper. You could tell what kind of paper it was from the shapes of the packages.

He had put his back out and been laid up for twelve weeks.

He had liked his next job. He had loved it. He had been on the general maintenance team at the Waylands Open Air Industrial Museum. He would still be there if he had had his way, but it had only been a short-term youth training project.

Waylands was a monument to the days when the north-east of England had counted for something in the world: an industrial centre that had been looked to for all the new discoveries of what could be done with coal and steam and iron. Working there among the heavy old machinery, Tom had felt strangely close to his father, a fitter in a shipyard, who had been killed in a road accident when Tom was a baby. He had stayed on for a few weeks after the end of his placement on the youth training project, as a member of the Friends of Waylands Volunteers, but it had irked him to do for nothing what other people got paid to do, what he himself used to get paid to do, and he had drifted off, drifted into a life of lying in bed half the morning, visiting his mates, having them visit him, signing on, going to the library to read the Situations Vacant, knowing full well that by the time he had applied for them they would not be vacant at all. More to amuse himself than anything else he had started making copies of the machines he had worked with at the museum, and the next thing he knew, his mother had started on at him to join the Enterprise Allowance scheme. The government would give him forty pounds a week to come off the unemployment register and make models. It had sounded fair enough to him.

He put his arm round Shelly to keep her warm as they tramped from the garage that was his workshop towards the flats. He felt no benefit from his coat. He had had it on all day. Snow rose over his shoes, three-year-old trainers, but it did not matter. He had no sensation in his feet. They might have been amputated, he might be limping along on bleeding stumps. The wind seemed to be blowing darts of snow straight into his bones. He was very skinny, though he liked his food and ate as much as he could get. That was one thing about being cooked for by his aunt: she had been warned off giving anything that looked like charity to her sister's family, but when she cooked, she cooked. For as long as he could remember, the women in Tom's life had urged him to put a bit of flesh on. This advice had come from his two elder sisters as well as his mother and his aunt, and, more recently, successive girlfriends. He did not mind the attention, but he was happy as he was. He thought his gaunt cheeks and long sticks of limbs made him look sexily vulnerable and slightly dangerous. Shelly had once said that his hip bones were as sharp as knives. He had asked her if she were complaining, and she had said, 'Not really.'

'Who's this coming in, Scott of the Antarctic? Oh, hello, Michelle, pet, how are you? Take your shoes off, I've just done that floor. Did you get those dolls finished?'

He winked at Shelly and mimed *nag, nag, nag*. 'All right if Shelly stops for tea, Auntie Pat?' His aunt said of course, there was plenty. The air in the kitchen was warm and fragrant with the smell of something meaty.

'I'll run you home later, Michelle. This is no night to be standing around waiting for buses. I hope Ann's arrived safely. Tom, go and wash your hands. Just get the knives and forks out of the drawer, Michelle.'

He padded to the bathroom in his stockinged feet. He noted new toothpaste, new soap and a pack of twenty toilet rolls from the Cash and Carry. His aunt sailed close to the wind as far as giving charity was concerned . . . but what were a few toilet rolls one way or another when Tom and his mother were already in debt to Auntie Pat to the tune of a thousand pounds?

A thousand pounds was what you had to have in the bank before you could be accepted on the Enterprise Allowance Scheme. 'It's just to prove you're serious,' his mother had explained, failing to see what was so funny about it. 'If you can't put your hands on a thousand pounds and nobody'll lend it to you, you probably haven't got what it takes to run a business.' She had been quoting the chartered accountant she had met at a Self-Employment Day School at the civic centre in Newcastle. Tom himself had had to go on a short course on business management as a condition for getting his allowance, but he had not paid it much attention as his mother was going to look after that side of things. For some complicated reason to do with her widow's pension his mother was not herself eligible for an Enterprise Allowance; but the Newcastle Day School had been open to anyone.

They had considered trying to borrow the thousand pounds from a bank, but his aunt and uncle had stepped in with a loan from their savings, saying, 'Let's keep it in the family.' He had not realized that this would make his aunt think she had bought shares in his life, though he should have.

Washing his hands, he wondered how Chris had heard about his mother going on the course. He had not told him. He had not had the chance. This time yesterday his mother herself had not known that she was going. She had applied months ago, but she had forgotten about it and so had he. Now he supposed the entire neighbourhood knew. He found the whole thing disturbing. He did not even know what a sales training course was, or why his mother thought she needed one. Most of the things he had made so far she had sold quite easily to friends and neighbours by word of mouth, so if she came back as a fast-talking foot-in-the-door type, what did she think she was going to sell? Rubbish, that was what: rubbish like the wooden dolls he was supposed to be making in her absence, the ones his aunt had asked about. They were quick to make, their limbs were rigid, they did not move, they did not do anything, they did not *work*. Mitchison's Working Models was the name of the business, and his mother wanted him to spend his time making things that did not work. He blamed the accountant for a lot of this, the accountant whom his mother never missed an opportunity to quote: 'Our accountant says you've got to have the right proportion of low-cost items in your range.' 'Our accountant says one of the worst mistakes family businesses make is not to cost their labour.' 'Our accountant says you've got to keep proper time sheets.' *Our accountant says roll over and put your feet in the air.* Tom had not yet met 'our accountant' but he did not like the sound of her.

Shelly oohed and aahed with bliss as Tom's aunt packed her plate with food. He liked to hear Shelly making sounds of bliss. He wondered what the chances were of dissuading his aunt from driving her home.

'This is delicious, Mrs Sturrock.'

'Auntie Pat's a one-woman famine relief agency.'

'I don't know where you put it all,' said his aunt, pleased.

'I've often thought the same about you.'

'Don't be rude,' said Shelly. His aunt was on the large side, unlike his mother, unlike Shelly.

'I take no notice, Michelle. I hope Ann's all right. She said she'd phone when she got there.'

Tom had had his transistor on in his workshop, for company before Shelly and Chris came round. He had heard but had not taken in the weather reports and traffic warnings. He had not thought to apply them to his mother's journey south. Now he felt anxious: the blizzard was not a local one, it was all over the country and motorists were being advised not to make unnecessary journeys. A look passing across his aunt's pasty face made his throat constrict, for it was one of his mother's looks. Normally they were as unalike as two women could be, but sometimes fleeting evidence would appear of the blood-tie.

He had been fatherless for as long as he could remember. But occasionally he seemed vaguely to recall a moment of loss, the fading out of a face, rather as his mother's face was fading now from his aunt's features.

It happened before, it could happen again, he thought.

'I'll phone my dad, he'll pick me up,' said Shelly.

'No need for that,' said Auntie Pat. 'I've got a bit of clearing up to do and I promised Ann I'd look over the accounts. Then I'll run you home. I'll not be in the way – '

'Ga – ga,' said Tom. 'Mama.'

'What did you say, Tom?' said his aunt.

'Cut my food up, Auntie Pat.'

'I'll cut up more than that – '

Shelly giggled, getting his meaning. His aunt did not get it, so he explained. 'You treat me as if I'm two years old, I'll act two years old. What do you think, we can't do it in the daytime?' He was surprised at himself. He did not normally speak to his aunt in such a way.

'It's no concern of mine what you do or when you do it. But I told your mother I'd look after the flat and that's what I intend to do.' She was as good as her word. After she and Shelly had done the washing-up, she disappeared to Tom's mother's bedroom to look over the accounts. 'I hope she freezes her bloody tits off,' said Tom.

'Are you warm enough in there, Mrs Sturrock?' called Shelly in a voice of great concern.

'I'm fine, thank you, pet.'

'If she drives you home, get your brother to bring you back,' Tom suggested.

'Very likely,' said Shelly. 'Don't do that, she'll hear.'

'Not if we do it quietly. We'll put the telly on, to cover your shrieks and moans.'

'The main news this evening,' said the television, 'is – '

The panic that he had driven away by fondling Shelly returned, and he waited for it: *The main news this evening is the pile up on the M1 in which a coach carrying –*

' – is the Prime Minister's speech to the Confederation of British Industry in which she said – '

'No news, then,' Tom scoffed. If there had been a serious crash it would have come first, surely?

'I'll just hear this,' said Auntie Pat, appearing in the doorway.

'See?' Tom mouthed at Shelly, stealthily withdrawing his hand. 'She's been listening.'

His aunt sighed: 'She's got guts . . .'

Tom saw his mother's guts spilled over a snow-covered road.

' . . . say what you like about her policies.'

The phone rang. Tom picked it up; it was his mother, reversing the charge, but his relief did not last long before it became clear white rage. She was stuck in a telephone box. She was pretty sure she was only about three miles from the Donian Hotel but the snow was falling so heavily and she had so much luggage that she could not proceed on foot. Her coach had been delayed on the motorway, she had missed her connecting coach in London and had had to take a train followed by a local bus. The bus driver had misheard where she wanted to go and dropped her at the wrong place. . . . She kept laughing at her plight, stuck in a phone box with no coins to phone the taxi company whose card was on the wall, nothing but a suitcase and bags of Mitchison's Working Models. . . . She would give him the taxi number and would he please phone and tell them to come for her? 'All right, Tom? I know I'm a fool, not to have the right change . . .' She laughed again, but he was not laughing. He was seething. Who the fuck did these southern bus drivers think they were to say his mother did not speak clearly, who the fuck were START Selling not to make proper arrangements for her travel. . . . 'Keep calm, Mam. I'll phone the hotel, they can come and pick you up.'

'No, Tom, why should they, the taxi – '

He took command. Shelly and his aunt were looking at him with anxiety in their eyes. He waved masterfully for them to turn the television down so that he could hear himself think. He got his mother to describe exactly where she was. She read from the emergency services card, insisting that he should phone the taxi company and not the Donian. He phoned the Donian, using the number his mother had left for use in case of emergencies. He kept being put through to the wrong people. 'I don't know her bloody room number. She hasn't got a room number, she's not there. *Listen to me*. You've got a course on, right?'

'START Selling, yes.'

'I want to talk to the feller in charge.'

'You mean Miss Barclay.'

'Miss Barclay then.'

'Miss Barclay doesn't really like being interrupted while she's teaching. Can I get her to call you back?'

Tom's response to this was such that the anxiety on the faces of the watching women turned to shocked laughter in Shelly's case, and panic in the case of his aunt, who obviously thought it would be no more than he deserved if they hung up on him.

But they did not hang up on him. They went and did what they had been told. They took their time, but they did it.

'Good evening, this is Daphne Barclay. Who am I speaking to, please?'

'Shelly, I told you to turn the TV down!' he roared.

'It's down as far as it'll go, Tom,' she said, holding his hand to calm him.

Of course it was down. He ran his hand over his eyes, realizing his mistake: in his agitation, he had connected the picture on the screen with the nerve-jangling voice on the phone and thought he had been put through to Margaret Thatcher.

He had often wondered whether anyone had ever told Margaret Thatcher, really told her, where she got off. Used Denis to do it, before she became Prime Minister?

'How may I help you?'

Denis ought to have done it, in words of one syllable. And if he had run out of words, he could have sent for Tom, and then the nation and the world would have owed the two of them a debt.

3

Gina Heriot was sipping her third gin and tonic when the hotel telephone rang. Reception had been very quiet up till now, as if nothing were happening in the hotel except START Selling – Women! She was alone in the bar, depressed, angry and frightened, trying to read a giveaway newspaper from the local tourist board.

'MURDER WEEKEND', said the headline. *I could be dead*, she thought. *I could be dead now. Not next year, not in an hour's time, but now, this person who I am could be having her first taste of the experience of being dead. What's a Murder Weekend?*

You could go to a hotel – not this one, she noted with relief – and enact a whodunnit, written specially for the occasion by a famous, though unnamed, novelist. You had to be careful when you went for walks on the cliff top and watch out for anyone slipping white powder into your champagne. You had to lock your door at night and pull back the sheets and examine the bed before you got into it.

People would pay for such things? Gina might be dead now. Stalton Industries might have been trying to murder her, to stop her pinching their customers. She did not often succeed in doing this, but it filled her with glee when she did. *Obviously your people heard I was going on a course*, she would tell Oliver: *and thought, Christ, we don't want her turning into an even hotter shot than she is already. So they decided to run me off the road.* She shivered.

Murder Weekends were enormous fun, said the tourist newspaper; but not for the faint-hearted.

She could be dead now. Where would she be, what would she be? The spirit of a young, vigorous, optimistic person like herself would not be snuffed out like a flame. Whatever happened to the body –

even if nothing remained of it – the spirit would, she was sure, stay around, howling in outrage: *I can't be! I was going along quite normally! Why me, why not him? Is this justice? I have appointments to keep.* Her heart ached with self-pity, and dread of how frustrating it would be. For it would happen. It had not happened today but one day it would happen. She would die, just like everybody else. And it would be like being in prison, knowing that your loved ones were being made miserable by lies being told about you, knowing that your affairs were being mishandled, but unable to do anything.

J.R., Bobby, I'm dead. (Gina's employers were two brothers, Roy and Alex Franson. Everybody called them J.R. and Bobby.) *My order pad's in my briefcase. I might have spelled that buyer's name wrongly, could you check . . . ? Oliver darling, I'm dead, it wasn't my fault, I haven't made a will but Mummy will know you're to have everything.*

Gina's eyes filled with tears and she lit a cigarette. Through the tears and the smoke, the hotel receptionist appeared.

'Excuse me,' she said timidly. 'Aren't you going into the course?'

'I'm not in the mood for ritual humiliations.'

'She always does that when people are late.'

'That's her problem,' said Gina. 'She should grow up.'

'Thing is,' said the receptionist, 'I've got this man on the phone who wants her to go and pick his mother up.'

Gina laughed. 'Where from?'

'She's stuck in a phone box.'

'She might wish she'd stayed there.'

'Thing is,' said the receptionist, 'I don't suppose you could go, could you? It's only three miles down the road. And then I wouldn't have to interrupt Miss Barclay while she's teaching.'

Gina started to agree; then she remembered she had been drinking. She was, as it happened, just as good a driver with two and a half gins inside her as she was without, but why should she risk her licence just to save Daphne Barclay from inconvenience? 'I'm not getting in my car again tonight,' she said. 'I'm sorry.'

'I'd go, only I'm on duty.'

'Of course you are, why should you? It's not your problem, it's Daphne Barclay's.' The receptionist looked as if she might cry. 'All right,' said Gina. 'I'll fetch her, I don't care.' She strode towards the conference room, opened the swing doors and stood between them. 'Sorry to interrupt,' she said loudly, 'but you're wanted urgently on the phone.' She did not wait for an answer but returned to the bar, sitting where she could listen.

'Good evening, this is Daphne Barclay, who am I speaking to

please? Yes, it must be very worrying for you. Yes, I do understand how you feel. Yes, I can tell that you're angry. Yes, of course you would. Could you repeat that? Oh, I thought you did. No need to apologize, I'm on my way to collect her.'

Gina sat with eyebrows raised and shoulders hunched, hiding behind the back of her chair. Daphne Barclay walked round and stood in front of her, petite and coquettish in her tightly belted blue wool frock and her very high heels. Her face was quite childlike, made up to look as if she wore no make-up, curtained by chin-length chestnut hair, straight and shiny as water; her mouth was the mouth of a spoiled brat.

'No,' said Gina.

The spoiled brat turned into a friendly adult. 'I'm sorry?'

'I'm not getting into my car again tonight. I've been in an accident.'

'What? That's terrible. I didn't realize, why didn't you say? Are you all right?'

'Yes thanks. I'm fine.'

'Has a doctor had a look at you?'

'It's not necessary.'

Daphne Barclay's brow furrowed. 'Do you know, I'm not so sure about that. You don't look well at all. Were you hit? You could have internal injuries that – '

Gina had had enough. 'I'm not hurt, I wasn't hit, I'm just a bit shaken and I'm not – '

'And I made it worse,' Daphne Barclay sighed. 'I knew I'd upset you with that round of applause. I always start my courses off by getting delegates to give themselves a round of applause for being there, and I don't want latecomers to miss out. Well, all right,' she admitted confidentially, 'I suppose there's an element of wanting to embarrass the person so that they won't be late again. Maybe I shouldn't. Do you know what you ought to do now? You ought to get straight back into your car and drive.'

Gina was not fooled, of course. The concern over the accident and the near-apology over the round of applause were clearly synthetic. The suggestion that she go for a drive to get her nerve back was so transparent that it was funny. Here was a very manipulative woman, one who clearly understood the principles of using anger and charm to get her way, lacking only in subtlety. Doubtless that would come with experience, and then she would be unstoppable. For now, though, Gina was not fooled. Interestingly, Daphne Barclay appeared to have met her match in the man on the phone, calming him, but in the end acceding to his demand that his mother be collected from her phone box. Perhaps he was a bigger bully than Daphne was. There was no way that Gina would have allowed herself to be bullied or tricked into running this errand. What had decided her to go was concern for the lost woman herself, trapped and freezing while Daphne enacted her rituals of flirtation and assertiveness. If it would be contemptible to be taken in by this kind of thing, would it not be even more so to allow it to prevent one from doing a kind act? Daphne might eventually have gone, but only after exhausting all other possibilities, and with very bad grace.

Gina was going, not because Daphne wanted her to but because she herself wanted to. It was, as Gina's teachers would have called it, a Christian act. Gina was bigger than Daphne, and kinder, and that was why she was going. At least, that was the way she explained it to herself, driving through the snow, feeling nervous, and grumpy, and a bit of a fool.

She found the phone box and waved and beckoned to the figure cowering inside it. Gina did not want to get out of the car to open the boot; she signalled that the woman could put her luggage on the back seat, and hoped that she would not need any help.

'I'm sorry,' she gasped, dumping a suitcase. 'There's more –' And she darted back to the phone box. Gina sighed and got out to help her.

The phone box was full of carrier bags from supermarkets. Gina wondered if she had got the right person. This might be a stray meths drinker. But the name the woman gave – Ann Mitchison – was the one Daphne had mentioned, or approximately so. Ann Mitchison was not the type Gina would have expected to meet at START Selling – Women! She might not be a meths drinker but she was distinctly housewifey.

Why 'START' Selling, anyway? she thought irritably. She knew 'START' was a mnemonic – Sales Techniques And something or other – but even so: START Selling. What did they think she had been doing?

And why women?

'Your good deed for the day,' said Ann in a northern accent, when everything was safely aboard and they were driving along.

Gina could not have put it better herself.

'Thanks,' said Ann.

'No trouble.'

19

'I hope my son wasn't rude.'

'I didn't talk to him. My name's Gina Heriot.'

'Oh. I thought you were Miss Barclay.'

'No, I'm not.'

She did not want Ann to smell the gin on her breath, so she kept her face firmly forward, concentrating on her driving, and encouraged Ann to do all the talking. Ann did not need much encouragement. She talked in shy, compulsive bursts. She apologized for being a nuisance, for bringing Gina out on such a night. If Gina had not come so promptly, she might have been buried under the snow, like a flock of sheep she had seen disappearing before her eyes. 'I thought they'd move, but they didn't seem to mind,' said Ann. Gina said, 'I expect they're used to it,' and asked Ann about her business. Ann said she was not really in business, it was her son. He made models; she just sold them and did the books with the help of her sister and their accountant. She was afraid this course might be a bit high-powered for her, but she had been offered a free place and thought that she might as well come. Gina said she had not known that there were free places. Ann said that her accountant had arranged it: an impressive woman was Ann's accountant, apparently, full of good advice for which she knew how to charge: '£50 per hour plus VAT! I said, "Hold on a minute, I think there's been some mistake, I thought it was free." She says, "It's free *today*, Mrs Mitchison, I'm just telling you what I would be charging so you'll know to make the most of me. £50 an hour for talking to people – " '

You'd be a rich woman, wouldn't you? thought Gina.

'I'd be a rich woman. It was this day school for people setting up in business. She was one of the speakers, she said, "What do you think is the most profitable line to get into in the north-east these days?" What do *you* think, Gina? Guess.' Gina could not. *What on EARTH have I come to?* she was thinking. *This woman's an amateur.* 'Shopfittings,' said Ann. 'She says, everyone thinks they can run a shop. They go into shops every day of their lives, they played shops as bairns, so they think, where's the big problem? So they spend all the money they've got, and some they haven't, on fancy shelving and computerized checkouts and the shopfitters sit back and count their money and wait for the shop to go out of business. Then they come in and do it for someone else.'

'She sounds a proper ray of sunshine, your accountant,' said Gina.

'She says it's not her job to be a ray of sunshine. She says she's a paid professional pessimist. She says to me, you tell me what you're thinking of doing, and I'll tell you why you can't do it. I say, I've no intention of opening a shop. My son's a skilled craftsman and I'll sell his models to anyone who'll buy them, but he doesn't make enough to fill a shop. I'll go door to door. She says, all right, I think you can do that.' Ann reached over the back of the seat and took a wooden merry-go-round out of one of the carrier bags. It looked like something from a Victorian fairground. Gina made admiring sounds, wondering if she was expected to buy it.

As they came within sight of the Donian Hotel, Ann said nervously, 'What have I missed?'

'Don't know. I've missed it too.'

'I'm sorry.'

'I mean I was late too. Look, if you've got any sense – '

'What?'

'I mean, if you take my advice you'll go straight to your room and get out of your wet things.' Having been conned into rescuing Ann, Gina felt protective of her and did not want her subjected to Daphne's sarcasm when her resistance was low. 'Have a hot toddy sent up and join the course in the morning.'

'I don't want to miss anything,' said Ann.

'Swot,' said Gina affably. She helped Ann take in her carrier bags. That wooden roundabout was rather sweet. She might buy it before the end of the week, to give to one of her nieces or nephews.

4

'This,' Miss Barclay was saying, 'is a full-time course. I don't know what you talked about over dinner, but you should have been selling to each other.'

Dinner, thought Ann. *I wonder if I get any dinner.* She edged towards her seat. Gina had warned her that she would have to cross the platform to get to it, but the way Ann saw it was that if she was going to get into trouble for being late she might as well get it over with.

'You are all here in your companies' time, don't forget that. From now on you're only off duty when you're asleep, and even then you should be dreaming of products and presentations. A surprising number of delegates in the past have said that they dream about *me*!'

I can see why men would, thought Ann. Miss Barclay was a nice-looking lass, about the same age as Ann's second daughter. In fact she seemed very nice generally; Ann could not understand why Gina had refused to come in for the end of the session.

'I have not asked them *what* they dream about me! But don't be surprised if I do turn up in your dreams, because I shall be there: checking up.'

Ann reached her seat. 'Mrs Ann Mickleston', it said. 'Mickleston's Working Models'.

'Would someone give these out for me please?' Ann wondered if she ought to offer, to earn her keep as she was on a free place. But one of Tom's mottos was: 'Never volunteer.' Fortunately someone else started to distribute the pile of plastic wallets, embossed with the START Selling crest.

'Each of you has five hundred pounds to spend. My goodness, that woke you up, didn't it? Sorry it can't be in the currency of the realm, but it *is* the currency of the course. You must spend it all. Unspent notes do not count as part of your final total. Sign the notes as you spend them to ensure there's no cheating. *Don't laugh.* Buy from the delegate who sells well; who convinces you that, whatever the product is, you need it. I know some of your products cost more than five hundred pounds, some a good deal less, so it's up to you to take bulk orders, or accept part-payments, deposits, do whatever you'd do. At the end of the course we count up and see who's made the most money. And now I see we have a newcomer.'

'I'm sorry,' said Ann.

'We all are,' said Miss Barclay. 'You've missed the self-presentations, Mrs Mickleston, so you'll have to find out about your fellow delegates by listening to them extra carefully.'

'It's Mitchison.'

'I beg your pardon? Speak up, please.'

'My name. It's Mitchison. Sorry, but – '

Miss Barclay picked up a small box and, continuing to speak, brought it to Ann and placed it on the table in front of her. 'First thing tomorrow morning, you and Miss Heriot can do *your* self-presentations.' Ann opened the box: it contained plastic letters, with which she assumed she was supposed to correct the spelling of her name on her nameplate. 'Where *is* Miss Heriot?'

'She . . . um. Wanted to get changed out of her wet things.'

'And you didn't?'

'I'm sorry. I didn't want to miss anything.'

'There's no need to be sorry, Mrs er. None at all. I like your attitude, I like it very much. Well, good night, everybody. I commend the hotel swimming pool to you as a way to start your day, but it will not be accepted as an excuse for lateness. Eight thirty sharp. For breakfast I can recommend the haddock.' Miss Barclay swept out.

The class members – delegates seemed to be the word – took longer to leave, chatting to each other. No one talked to Ann and she felt too shy to make approaches, so she studied the nameplates to see who everybody was and what they sold. They were all much younger than she was, but she had expected that. There was a Mrs Katie Fraser from a bathroom furnishings company and a Mrs Alice York from a travel agency. Others were in insurance, computers, pharmaceuticals, kitchenware and publishing. Some company names she did not recognize. Teresa Beal – not Miss or Mrs – was from *Atalanta* magazine, which Ann had never heard of. Teresa Beal herself reminded Ann of somebody – somebody she had seen on television, perhaps.

Ann was cold, wet and hungry. The restaurant was closed. She wondered if there might be a chocolate machine somewhere, or peanuts in the bar. Some of the women were going to the bar for a nightcap, but she did not want to spend money on drink and she would feel a fool just asking for peanuts. And anyway, they had not asked her to join them. She went to her room.

It was more than a room, it was like a little flat. It had its own bathroom with a shower and a bidet and hand-basin as well as a bath. There were enough towels and soap to keep a small family clean.

There were two beds, bigger than singles but not quite doubles. If they had wanted her to share the room, perhaps with someone else on a free place, she would not have minded, but the gift card with the bunch of flowers on the dressing table made no mention of a room-mate. It just said that the manager and staff of the Donian Hotel welcomed Mrs Ann Mickleston, delegate to START Selling – Women!, and hoped that she would enjoy her stay.

She experimented with the lights. They could be 'dim', 'bright' or 'very bright' in various combinations. There were tea- and coffee-making facilities, a telephone, shoe-cleaning equipment, laundry bags, a writing desk, two armchairs, a television and a fridge. She opened the fridge hopefully, but it contained only drink. The price list taped to the door was only slightly less terrifying than the room service tariff, which told her that she could have a club sandwich sent up if she wanted, with chips and a fresh green salad.

Her indecision over this put her in mind of her accountant, and she decided to write to her on hotel paper to thank her for making the suggestion that had brought her here.

'Dear Miss Hutton, I am writing to inform you that my application to attend a START Selling course was successful. As you know, there is no charge . . .'

Miss Hutton always wanted to know what things cost, and she wanted receipts kept to prove it.

' . . . but I have kept a careful record of my travelling expenses . . .'

Would a sandwich be an allowable expense? The test for whether an expense was allowable against tax was whether you would have bought the thing if you had not been in business. She would certainly not be eating a sandwich at this price if she were not in business.

If in doubt, enter it as an expense, Mrs Mitchison. I will keep you on the right side of the law, never fear.

24

When she paid for the sandwich, she would presumably be given a receipt.

She could always tell Miss Hutton that it was for newspapers and magazines.

It was late but she decided to phone Tom to say that she had finally arrived. He had sounded quite worried earlier, as if he were the one who was stuck in a phone box. To save money she went to use a call box in reception, but one of them only took cards and the other was out of order. She returned to her room.

Tom sounded suspiciously wide awake.

'Are you alone?' she said.

'Mam –'

'All right, pet. I trust you.'

'Thanks very much,' he grumbled. 'Did Miss Lloyd come and pick you up all right?'

'Miss Lloyd?'

'Lloyd, Barclay. I knew it was a bank.'

'Tom, you didn't say anything to her, did you?'

He laughed. 'I did it all by sign language.'

They were edgy with each other: missing each other, she supposed. They were not used to being apart. She told him about showing Gina his merry-go-round in the hope that she might offer to buy it. 'No luck, though. I don't think we're supposed to sell things to each other, not really.' She told him about the game they were supposed to be playing, pretending to sell things with monopoly money.

'So it's all fun and games, is it?' he said, sounding resentful.

'That's right,' she replied, moving her face away from the phone. 'Hey, you,' she said. 'I told you not to put the champagne there. Put it next to the other bottle and get rid of those empties.'

He did not laugh. Perhaps it had not been very kind of her to joke in such a way. She decided to mention a bad point. 'Never mind champagne, I could eat a horse.'

'Haven't you had your tea?'

'Dinner,' she said. 'Din-nah. Dinnah was served, but I missed it.'

'But your meals are included. Get Miss Barclay to rustle up a steak.'

'I could have a sandwich sent up, but –' She told him what it would cost.

He was outraged. 'That includes the plate and the cutlery, right? You're entitled to something to eat, Mam. Full board included, that's what it said.'

25

'I know, but this is room service. This is different.'

'Pay for it, then,' he said recklessly. 'You saved on not having a taxi. Treat yourself.'

'I might. Did Pat come round all right?'

'Aye. She's been buying bog rolls again.'

'Well she's not to.'

'Shall I get her to take them away again?'

'Good night, Tom,' said Ann firmly. 'You be polite to your aunt.'

She unpacked her things. She had panicked a bit, being sent for at the last minute and not knowing what to bring in the way of clothes. Pat had said, 'That's nice, take that,' and Ann herself had said, 'But I prefer this,' and she had ended up bringing nearly everything she owned that was halfway decent and not in the wash . . . but it all looked rather lonely in the huge wardrobes and the deep drawers. On the dressing table she set out some of the models: the merry-go-round, a horse-drawn milk float and a Noah's Ark whose animals went in and out if you turned a handle.

The milk float reminded her of cheese and puddings and her own hunger and she dialled the number for room service. After all, for the rest of this week her food would be free.

'Reception.'

'Could I have room service, please?'

'There's no room service, I'm sorry, madam.'

'But it says twenty-four-hour room service here.'

'I'm sorry, they've just gone off. We're short-staffed at the moment.'

She boiled water in the kettle and made herself a cup of tea, adding all three of the foil-capped pots of milk. She added sugar as well, though she did not usually take sugar. She filled the long green bath with water and lay in it. She kept topping it up. The hot water went on and on. If she were not so hungry, she would be basking in luxury.

There was nothing to clean the bath with when she had finished, so she managed as best she could with one of the hand towels. The room was very warm and she walked about in her nightie, not needing her dressing gown. She caught sight of herself looking rather glamorous in the smoky-coloured mirror. She had one last look in the fridge, but there really was nothing to eat. She made herself another cup of tea, black because she had finished the milk, and climbed into bed with it. Discovering a remote-control switch for the television, she settled back to watch the end of the late-night film.

5

Teresa Beal was up early, looking for the swimming pool. But she found her way barred by scaffolding, and Daphne Barclay looking disconsolate in a tracksuit. 'Apparently they're replacing the sun-roof.'

'Oh, shame,' said Teresa, though she was not surprised. The whole hotel seemed to be undergoing refurbishment. Her room had smelled of paint and there had been ladders covered with dust-sheets in the corridor outside. 'Straight into breakfast, then,' she said cheerfully.

'It's that way,' said Daphne firmly, walking off the other way.

All right, thought Teresa. *I wasn't going to inflict myself on you.*

Actually she had been planning to sit with Daphne, if she could. She wanted to ask her why this was a women's course. It was not like any other women's event that Teresa had ever been to. She had not expected it to be; she might have been disappointed if it had been, she had not come here to be collective and correct. She had come here to learn how to sell, and with that in mind she was only too happy to acquiesce in the clear division between teacher and taught, to enjoy the smooth-running efficiency, to do as she was told and not to think too much. That was all perfectly okay. But what she wanted now was some indication that START Selling had put on a women's course for some reason other than to fill up a block booking at a quiet time of year.

The dining room, when she went for breakfast, only confirmed this impression. Last night's Christmas decorations were coming down, and the staff doing the job were making no effort to be quiet about it. The number of laid tables suggested that no one was

28

expected except the START Selling women. And Ann Mitchison, with whom Teresa shared a table, apologized for eating so much but she had had no dinner and there had been no room service.

Ann was nervous about her impending self-presentation. Teresa urged her not to be. 'You just say your name, a bit about your business and what you're – '

'What I'm hoping to get out of the course, I know,' said Ann miserably. 'What I want to get out of the course is to be able to stand up and speak, only I've got to do it before I've got it, if you see what I mean.'

Teresa saw and tried to think of something encouraging to say. 'Well, we'll all be on your side.' She assumed her fellow delegates would be, but really she knew little about them. They had all got up one by one yesterday and said what they sold, who they worked for: Katie Fraser sold bathroom fittings to builders' merchants; Alice York was a travel agent based in Milton Keynes, shortly to be transferred to Lanzarote to sell villas; Chris Catling sold office equipment . . . but none of them had said why, or what they had done before, or how they felt about their jobs. One or two of them had managed to slip in references to how many children they had, but Daphne Barclay had not allowed any dwelling on such matters, urging them to stick to the point.

Daphne herself had stuck rigidly to the point. 'I'm expecting you to give me your undivided attention for the rest of this week. Some of you probably think I'm still wet behind the ears. You have a perfect right to know by what authority I speak.'

An impressive curriculum vitae had followed. Daphne Barclay was of proudly entrepreneurial stock. Her parents were successful businesspeople in their own right. The use of the phrase *in their own right* had amused Teresa so much that she had missed hearing the precise nature of the Barclay family business. *In their own right* suggested that Daphne did not want it supposed that her parents throve only in so far as they had managed to produce her. Nor had Teresa caught the name of the institution from which Daphne held a diploma in Sales and Business Management. Clearly these points had been made only as formalities. More important was the range of goods and services which Daphne had, at one time or another, sold, and the range of buyers with whom she had dealt. Such a variety of jobs in the past of one so young (financial services; instant coffee; veterinary pharmaceuticals) might be thought of as an embarrassment, suggesting as it did rather a lot of hiring and firing and bad decisions, but Daphne had made it sound as if all her decisions had been good ones. She had been accumulating experience to equip her (it had been implied) for this day. Her most recent job had been with a firm of estate agents. It was while there that she had been offered employment with START Selling, a member of whose staff had bought a house from her and been kind enough to say that he found her skills and manner irresistible.

As a START trainer she had given courses to people who worked in travel and tourism, industrial disinfectants, personnel services, fire safety equipment, camping gear, fork-lift trucks... her audience could, in fact, name it, and Daphne Barclay had some experience of selling it.

Taking their cue from this display of what might be called positive thinking and might be called boastfulness, the women had mentioned no problems, insecurities or doubts. (And Teresa had been the same. She had not mentioned problems, insecurities or doubts either, and her fantasy of sticking her hand up and asking whether Daphne had any experience of making feminism saleable had remained a fantasy.) The nearest they had got was in answering the question: 'What do you hope to get out of the course?' They wanted more efficiency, more self-confidence, improvements in their call-to-sale ratios. But they had not said why they thought they were not efficient or self-confident, or what would happen to them if their call-to-sale ratios did not improve. In short, Teresa did not know any of the things about them that she would normally expect to know, having spent an evening among women. Dinner had been a shy and stilted affair in the half-empty dining room; Teresa had established that none of the women had heard of *Atalanta* magazine until now, and then she had shut up. Someone's suggestion that they all go for a drink at the end of the session had raised Teresa's hopes, but the bar had closed early. And in any case Daphne had by then put a ban on casual or personal conversation; they were to buy and sell with toy money; and if they dreamed, they were to dream of Daphne herself.

Teresa thought of all the people she knew who would say that they had told her so.

'Who do you work for?' Ann asked politely.

'*Atalanta* magazine.' *Am I supposed to sell her half a page?*

'I don't think I know that one.'

'It's a feminist magazine,' said Teresa, as she had said last night to no response whatever. 'What I'm hoping to get out of the course is a more businesslike approach to selling advertising and selling the magazine itself. What's known as the post-feminist era – ' she heard herself burbling on, watching for the nearest cliché and striking out bravely towards it, unnerved by the polite indifference before her. She did not feel like telling the whole story; Ann Mitchison, like the other women, had never heard of *Atalanta*, so why should she care what happened to it?

Saleswomen were drifting into the dining room and standing in line to choose their breakfasts. There was no sign of Daphne, as there had been none last night at dinner. Did she make a point of eating apart from her delegates? Did she dislike them? Encountering Teresa in the corridor near the swimming pool this morning, she had seemed ill at ease and had fled from what might have turned into a conversation between equals.

The dining room's wide windows gave on to dazzling vistas of snow, frozen hard and glinting. The sky was blue in the disconcerting way of too-blue eyes. Teresa was remembering another restaurant, a cosier one, in Soho; she was remembering going to lunch there with Greg Sargent, puzzled by his invitation because they had already had lunch this year.

'I'm going to make you an offer,' he said, closing the door of the private room. 'If you accept, the news will be released by us at the appropriate time. If you refuse – and please don't feel you've got to, just to prove that you're a woman of principle because I know that already, otherwise I wouldn't be asking you – if you refuse, I want you to forget it was ever suggested. I shall deny it in any case.'

Teresa said calmly, 'Isn't that what they say when they offer someone an OBE?'

He started ladling out gazpacho (having sent the waitress away in order, it was implied, that his hospitality might be more personal and more private), refusing to be put off his stroke by her flippancy. He cocked one of his famous eyebrows, as if Teresa had just raised an important point. 'Yes,' he said. 'No one's allowed to snub the Crown publicly.'

'You know all about it, do you? Good gracious, Greg. Are congratulations called for?'

He passed her her soup in an earthenware bowl, looking like one of his own publicity photographs. Whenever he went into a new enterprise (and no one knew quite where he would turn up next: the Our Ways logo moved through commerce and industry like an oil slick in uncertain waters) Greg liked, as founder and managing director, to be pictured doing that enterprise's work: ironing a pair of Our Ways jeans, kick-starting an Our Ways motorbike; scooping brown rice into brown bags in an Our Ways supermarket. Gossip columnists called him the millionaire radical. He preferred to be known as the radicals' millionaire. 'Don't be such a damn fool,' he said. 'Are you going to listen to me or not?'

'I'm listening.' She was looking too, absorbed by the sight of his expert fingers on the ladle as he served himself. Nineteen years ago, as students, they had been lovers. That passion had been extinguished by the waters that had flowed under various bridges since, and she was glad she no longer felt anything for him, for how otherwise could they have a matey lunch once a year (or twice, in this case), hurling friendly abuse at the way each of them had turned out – *you used to be so nice!* – and parting with no more than a single, luscious, mouth-to-mouth kiss to sustain them until next time? Still, she was entitled to look at his fingers.

'It's about that magazine of yours,' he said.

He always called *Atalanta* that magazine of hers. She always replied, 'It's run by a collective.'

'Yes, but you own it.'

'On paper, perhaps.' She sprinkled her soup with chopped onion and cucumber. 'I thought the last issue was rather good, didn't you?'

'Excellent,' he agreed politely, though it had not been. 'But I've been wondering what's happened to this month's. You should put a bomb under your subscription department...' Teresa was the subscription department, as he well knew, '... you don't want to alienate faithful subscribers like me and Brenda. How many other married couples do you know who have a copy each?'

'Spot of bother at the printers. How *is* Brenda?'

'What sort of response did you get to the appeal?'

So that was what this was about! Teresa was more relieved than embarrassed. She had thought they were heading for far deeper waters than her failure to thank Greg and Brenda for their encouraging letter and their thousand-pound cheque.

'Not bad, considering it was the second appeal this year. We, er, thought donors wouldn't want us to use up resources sending out receipts, but in your case, with such a generous... we should have...'

'What's the score, Trees?'

Teeth gritted, she said, 'Can't you guess?'

'Probably, but why should I with the owner sitting here?'

'I am only the owner on paper,' she reminded him. She paused while the waitress changed the plates; then she told him that, pleased though *Atalanta*'s printers were with the progress made towards the settlement of *Atalanta*'s debt to them by the proceeds from the appeal, the printers' bank, sadly, was leaning on them; and they needed another ten thousand pounds before they would print the next issue. 'And they're holding on to our artwork, just to encourage us. You know this already, don't you?'

'Do you remember what I said when you got that money from the GLC?'

The Greater London Council had for some years been giving grants to feminist projects, of which *Atalanta* had been one. The Greater London Council had now been disbanded by the government.

'I don't remember you saying anything,' said Teresa.

'It must have been Brenda I said it to,' said Greg, as if it did not matter all that much. 'If I were in the government – this government, I mean – and I had something as subversive and powerful as the women's movement to deal with, know what I'd do? I'd give it money. Money it didn't have to earn by pleasing the punters. I'd let it keep the money long enough for it to forget *how* to please the punters – let it get fat – and then I'd take the money away.'

'Fat!' Teresa thought of the malnourished, grey little news sheet into which *Atalanta* had declined.

'Fat,' Greg repeated. 'Fat and smug. Fat on ideology and self-righteousness. Do you know what Brenda says? She says, "God, this thing's boring now" and puts it on the pile. She doesn't read it. I do, though. I'll miss it if it goes.'

'Even as we speak a donation may have arrived which – '

'You can't run for ever on donations.'

'Why not? We always have.'

'You need more advertising.'

Annoyed by his patronizing tone, Teresa said, 'Why didn't I think of that? If you've asked me here to book six months of double-page spreads of women's bums in your jeans – '

'Once!' he shouted. 'I tried that once, and you've never let me forget it – '

'I was going to say, the answer's yes. Ssshh, Greg. I'm sorry.'

'Don't sshh me, it's my caff.'

'Sorry, sorry, sorry.' She squeezed his hand. He took it away. 'Go bust,' he said. 'See if I care. If that's the way you talk to your advertisers – people who want to help you – it was a damn silly idea in the first place.'

'What was?'

'That I buy the title, clear the debts and see if it can't be run properly with benefits to all concerned, not least the readers.'

She had known, of course, that this was what was in his mind. She had been playing for time, not wanting to hear him actually say it, not wanting to have to answer.

'Under whose control?' she asked.

'There would have to be an editor.'

'Who? *Who?* Would everyone in the collective be kept on?'

'I'd want to keep you on.'

'What as?'

'Business manager.'

She laughed bitterly. 'You must be mad. If I were any good at business management, this wouldn't be happening.'

'You haven't been given a chance,' he said. 'I'm willing to give you one, and I'm going to start by sending you on a course.'

6

If she was going to have to do this self-presentation, she might as well make the most of it. At twenty-five minutes past eight, Ann left the breakfast table and went to her room to collect the merry-go-round. Her plan was to hold it up as an example of the kind of thing Tom made.

A chambermaid was already in there, making the bed.

'Sorry,' said Ann. 'I just wanted to get this.'

'What is it?'

'Well, it's just a toy really.'

'It's lovely, isn't it?' said the chambermaid. She admired all the other models that were set out on the dressing table.

'Sorry if they're in your way.' Ann put them quickly into a drawer so that they would not be.

'My little girl loves things like that,' said the chambermaid. She seemed very friendly and Ann would have liked to stay and chat with her about her little girl, but she did not want to be late again.

She went into the conference room and sat down with the others. She put the merry-go-round on her table, then thought better of it and put it under her chair. Nobody else had anything on their desks except pens and paper and she did not want to draw attention to herself. With a bit of luck, Miss Barclay might forget about the self-presentations.

'Good morning, everybody!' Miss Barclay was beautifully turned out again. She was wearing a blue suit with a silky blouse and a necklace and earrings that looked like tiny icicles. Her hair shone as if she had just washed it. She seemed in better humour than she had been last night. 'Did you all sleep well? Enjoy your breakfast?' There was an uncertain, embarrassed silence; but Miss Barclay did seem to want her questions answered. She performed a yawn, groaning and stretching. 'Like that, is it?' she said. Everyone laughed at her, and she laughed back at them. 'I'll try again. Did you all sleep well and did you enjoy your breakfast?'

'Yes,' said a few voices. 'Yes thank you.'

On Tom's principle of never volunteering, Ann had not joined in. Now she thought she should have: to test her voice.

Miss Barclay's voice was lovely: melodious but firm. There was nothing unwomanly about it, but you knew not to argue with it. 'You think you're tired now,' she teased. 'You wait. But I mustn't alarm you. On START Selling courses we work hard, but we play hard too. Did any of you try the haddock?'

Someone said – rather audaciously, Ann thought – 'Do you own the local fish shop, or something?'

'I beg your pardon?'

'Nothing, just a joke.'

'I see. Well, let's not waste any more time. You've all come here because you want to learn to sell better, but I have a special piece of news for you, to help you start the day in the right frame of mind. It's this. You have *already closed* the most difficult and important sale of your career. You have sold yourselves.'

Did Teresa Beal let out a long sigh, or did Ann imagine it?

'You have sold yourselves to your employers, as salesmen and potential salesmen. You have persuaded them to invest in you by sending you on this course. It's not just your fee. It's your salary for the week, too, and the cost of the business you won't be bringing in while you're here. It's a lot, isn't it? But you're worth it. Your employers know you're worth it. We started yesterday with a round of applause for ourselves for being here, but let's not leave your employers out. *They're* not living it up this week in a first-class hotel, they've got to go to work. So let's have a round of applause for them, for recognizing your worth – thank you – and let's resolve to make the most of every single – good morning, Miss Heriot.'

'Sorry,' said Gina, rushing in. 'Had to get some petrol.'

'If I were you, I'd stick to gin.'

This got a laugh, which Gina took in good part.

'Punctuality is the courtesy of kings,' said Miss Barclay, but she did not pursue the matter.

Ann could have killed Gina. Miss Barclay had not so far mentioned the self-presentations of last night's latecomers, but Gina being late again might have reminded her.

'On the table in front of you, you will each find a START Selling memo pad, with the compliments of START Selling. I want you to make a list of everything you've bought since you arrived here yesterday evening. And why. Not a long essay, just notes. Go.'

Ann thought: *I'd've bought myself a sandwich, given the chance.*

Someone did not understand the question and said, 'You mean drinks, things like that?'

'Just do what I said. I said it perfectly clearly.' Everybody wrote. Miss Barclay picked on someone, Katie Fraser, bathroom fittings. 'What have you written?'

'I had a lemonade out of the minibar, if that's what you mean.'

'It's exactly what I mean. Minibars in hotel rooms are an example par excellence of the right product in the right place. If you'd had to send down for it, you might not have bothered.'

If she'd had to send down for it, she wouldn't have got it, thought Ann, hoping never again to know the hunger of last night. She had felt such a fool. The hotel must have been full of food. She just had not been able to get at it.

Miss Barclay was still talking about minibars. ' . . . and people who like to tipple quietly all night can do so without drawing attention to themselves. I don't suppose that applies to *you*, Mrs Mitchison, but what have you bought since you got here?'

'I haven't bought anything.'

'Haven't you? Didn't you have breakfast?'

'I thought it was paid for.'

'Did you all hear that? She thought it was paid for.' Ann thought she might be sick, but it was all right. 'Mrs Mitchison has drawn our attention to a very important point.' Had she? 'The person who *consumes* a product and the person who *pays* for it are not necessarily the same.' Ann wondered if she would be expected to queue up separately for her meals from now on. 'But they are both equally important to us and we must keep them both in mind from now on. We are all buyers all the time, just as we are all sellers. START Selling did not choose this hotel for you without examining all the facilities, including the catering. When you go back to work next week and your colleagues ask you about the course, we want you saying, "The food was great." Of course we don't mind if you say something nice about the tuition as well. Miss Heriot, what have you bought?'

'Petrol.'

'Petrol! Why did you buy petrol? Are you hoping to make a quick getaway if the pressure gets too great?'

'My car goes better if it has petrol in it.'

'You may think this is pathetically obvious,' said Miss Barclay, 'but if I had in my possession the amount of money the average salesman loses by failing to see the obvious, I could retire. Where did you buy your petrol?'

'At the filling station over the road.'

'Why?'

'It was the nearest.'

'Thank you! Just like Mrs Fraser's minibar, then! The right product in the right place!' Miss Barclay flung back the cover of a flip-chart with a loud crackle. Darting across the page with a felt-tip pen, she wrote:

> REASONS FOR CHOICE
> 1. Right product
> 2. Right place
> 3.

'Mrs York?'

Alice York said that she had bought a *Daily Mail*.

'Why?'

'Er . . . well, because I wanted to read it, I suppose.'

'You could have read the *Daily Express*. You could have read *The Times*.'

'I always buy the *Daily Mail*,' Alice explained.

'Habit, then, good,' said Miss Barclay. She wrote:

> 3. Habit
> 4.

She said, 'Would that life were always so simple, that we could all have buyers who used us rather than the competition out of *habit*! Because it is easier to buy from us than not to! That should be your goal, and you will achieve it with START. Miss Laburn, how about you?'

Gwen Laburn had bought herself a pair of tights to replace a pair she had laddered. Miss Barclay wrote 'Emergency' as the reason for buying. Some of the women had had wine with their dinner ('Luxury'), and Chris Catling said she had put 10p in a box for the Lifeboats, she did not know whether that counted. 'It depends why you did it,' said Miss Barclay. 'Are there any sailors in your family?' 'Well, I've got a dinghy,' said Chris Catling, and Miss Barclay wrote:

'Insurance'. Another woman said she had bought a postcard and a stamp, but Miss Barclay said that that came under the heading of the right product in the right place since there was no post office nearby. Ann was starting to feel awkward; she seemed to be the only person not to have bought anything.

'. . . The *Guardian*,' said Teresa Beal. 'For its politics.'

Miss Barclay turned to write – 'Politics', presumably – but she made a dot and stopped. 'You mean the *Guardian* is the newspaper that you prefer?'

'For its politics, yes,' said Teresa.

'And for its news coverage? Its features? The crossword?'

'I buy it for its politics mainly.'

'Is there no other newspaper with whose views you agree?'

'Well, the *Morning Star*'s a bit soft on Soviet armaments – '

'Putting that to one side, you might equally well have bought the *Morning Star*?'

'They didn't have it,' said Teresa.

'Your first choice was unavailable, then, so you bought your second.' Miss Barclay wrote 'Second choice when first unavailable' and continued in this vein until she had written up ten reasons for choice. 'Let's see if we can bring this all together and find out what it means. I'm surprised none of you mentioned making telephone calls.'

'I phoned my son,' said Ann.

'Why? Why didn't you send a postcard like Mrs Phillips?'

'I thought he might be worried and I needed to – '

'Pardon?' Miss Barclay cupped her hand round her ear and looked excited.

'I thought he might be worried – '

'Yes, yes, you thought he might be worried, you said that but what did you say after that?'

'I wanted – '

'No. That is *not* what you said. You said you – ?'

'I phoned my son.'

'That's what you *did*. But what did you *say*?'

'I told him I'd got here all right – '

Miss Barclay was losing patience. 'I am not asking you what you said to *him*. That is no concern of mine. I'm asking you to repeat what you said to me and the rest of the class just now. You *must listen*. All of you. Good gracious, if you won't listen to yourselves, why should anyone listen to you? You have two ears and one mouth. Use them in that proportion.'

Teresa came to the rescue. 'You said you needed to do something, didn't you, Ann?'

'Ye – e – ess!' Miss Barclay looked pretty again and stopped shouting. 'Thank you, Miss Beal. Thank you, Mrs Mitchison. You *needed* to communicate with your son immediately – because he was anxious about you – and you bought the service provided by Telecom because that was the service that *best met your need*!

'All of you,' Miss Barclay continued after a drink of water, 'are top-quality material. You are in your present jobs not just because your employers chose you but because you chose them. It follows that you could move more or less whenever you wanted to, and work for the competition.

'It follows, since you have not moved, and since you are people of integrity and knowledge, that your product is the best available. You would not be selling it otherwise.

'Your buyer, therefore, needs it.

'Know your buyer needs it, but do not tell him. Not in so many words. No one likes sentences that begin "You need . . . " "You need a filling." "You need to lose weight." "You need a clip round the ear."

'So, don't say it. Don't say "You need it." Convey it. Convey it by means of the three Ps.

'Your presence.

'Your product.

'And . . .' But before Miss Barclay could say what the third P was, the fire alarm went off.

7

' . . . Questions!' said Daphne, when the fire alarm had stopped. 'Probing, persistent, polite, pertinent questions! The right question for one set of circumstances is not necessarily the right question for another set of circumstances. Imagine you are me . . .'

Gina did not really want to imagine herself as Daphne, but she had to admire the stage management. What better way to divert attention from the fact that the third 'P' was 'Questions' than to have the fire alarm go off?

'Imagine that your product is sales training courses. What questions would you put to a sales manager to help focus his mind on his need for your courses?' Gina stood up. 'Yes, Miss Heriot?' said Daphne tolerantly.

'Would you like me to go and see if there's a fire?'

'I'm sure we'd be told if there were.'

'We have just been told. That was a fire alarm. I think I'll go and check, if you don't mind.' Gina walked out on the probing, persistent, polite, pertinent questions. If she had set off the fire alarm herself, she could not have timed it better. She needed to phone her boss. She had missed him at home this morning and resigned herself to waiting until the coffee break. But he should be in his office by now.

Workmen were replacing the carpet tiles in the telephone booths in the lobby, so she went to her room to phone. 'Roy, it's Gina.'

'Gina. How's it going?'

'Tacky,' she said. Then she remembered that sending her to START Selling – Women! had been Roy Franson's idea. 'Really interesting, I'm learning a lot. You won't know me when I get back. Now listen.

Guess who nearly ran me off the road last night. You won't be able to so I'll tell you.' She described her accident.

Roy Franson sounded concerned. 'Are you all right?'

'Yes, but that's not the point. The point is that whoever was waiting to take delivery for that acrylic is still waiting for it and deeply dischuffed with Stalton's. I thought you might want to let Dennis know.' Dennis was the Franson & Franson representative for the south-east.

'Fine, I'll tell him. Thanks, Gina. Fire away.'

'What?'

'Who's the buyer?'

'How would I know? But it seems to me that whoever it is can't be a million miles from the scene of the crime, I mean the driver wouldn't have been going a long way in weather like that, would he? He'd have rung up and told them to wait till tomorrow . . .' she giggled, 'or longer, as it turned out. And it's the depths of the country so there can't be that many places. Dennis could just drive around and look. And I'll take a cut of his commission.'

'I don't think I'll send him out specially, Gina.'

'Oh.'

'But thanks for being so keen.'

'Keener Gina, that's what they call me.'

'Back to your course then, keener Gina. Not that it sounds as if you need it.'

'Oh, I wouldn't say that,' said Gina. She put on her best Texan drawl. "Bye, J.R.'

"Bye, Gina, honey,' he replied.

On her way back to the conference room she said to the receptionist, 'There isn't a fire, is there?'

'No, they were just testing. Was she cross?'

'Cross? Daphne? She just chewed up a light bulb and carried on as if nothing had happened.'

'Thing is, I was supposed to tell her they'd be testing it, only I didn't like to interrupt.'

Back in the conference room, the project was still to think up questions to put to a sales manager to focus his mind on his need to send his team on a course.

Gina decided to be good. ' "How many salesmen do you employ?" ' she offered.

'Yes, we've already had that one,' said Daphne. 'Could someone tell Miss Heriot what we decided about "How many salesmen do you employ?"?'

One of the insurance women said, 'It's all right but it's a bit of a boring question to start off with and it doesn't really focus his mind on his needs.'

'Thanks,' said Gina, and the other insurance woman added, 'Also, you're setting yourself up for the smart aleck response, which is "Too many." ' Again Gina said, 'Thanks.'

'Could you ask who trains them now?' asked Ann Mitchison.

'Much better,' beamed Daphne. Ann Mitchison could do no wrong, it appeared. Her humility gave her favoured status. She seemed to have recovered from last night's ordeal. It must have been terrifying for her, to be marooned like that, watching sheep disappearing under the snow. Gina hoped she thought it was worth it.

Then she thought, *SHEEP! Farmland! Unexpected snow! Some farmers like to put up shelters for their livestock.*

'There are three possible answers,' Daphne intoned, 'to "Who trains your sales force now?" The first is "Nobody." Nobody trains them. They don't say that, of course. They say "I train them myself" or, "They pick it up as they go along" or sometimes they say, "Salesmen are born, not trained." What they mean is, nobody. You come straight back with your second question, which could be – ?'

' "Are you sure you're getting the best out of them?" ' said the travel agent.

'Good. And you go on from there. Let's think about the sales manager's second possible answer, which is that he sends his team to one of your competitors for training. What are you going to say to that?'

'Ask him if he's happy with the service they're providing.'

'Yes. Go carefully here, because he knows what you're after. Selling to salesmen – or sales managers who used to be salesmen – is the most difficult job of the lot, they've heard it all before, they've been on courses. *Don't run down the competition.* It creates a bad impression, makes the buyer defensive, after all you're suggesting he's made a bad choice, aren't you? Let him work it out for himself. . . .'

That Stalton's lorry must have been going to a farm, thought Gina. *I wondered what he thought he was doing, trying to turn right down a dirt track. And then he must have thought better of it, which was why he –*

'Now, if our sales manager doesn't train his team himself and doesn't send them to the competition, there's only one possible answer to the question, "Who trains them now?" It's the worst of the lot. It's, "You do, you fool." If that's his answer, then you've really blown it. You might as well hang up your order pad for good. Or summon the nearest secretary and beat her brains out for not briefing you properly.' Daphne mimed doing this with a ruler. 'Did you say something, Miss Beal?'

'Yes. I don't see why you're telling us to blame someone else for our own mistakes.'

'You can beat your own brains out if you prefer,' said Daphne. 'There are two kinds of questions, closed questions and open questions. Closed questions are those that can be answered yes or no, open questions encourage the buyer to talk about himself, his company and his needs. Miss Heriot, *where* are you going *now*?'

'I've got an appointment.'

'Your employers didn't mention any appointment when they enrolled you.'

'They don't know about it.'

'Miss Heriot, at the end of this week I'm hoping to be able to present you with a diploma confirming that you have attended this course. A great deal of weight is attached to these diplomas in the world of selling. Your employers will be expecting you to return with one, but if you persist in being late or absent – '

'Look,' said Gina. 'Please. Let me explain. I didn't get the chance to introduce myself last night. Can I do it now? My company . . .' Gina relaxed into her standard introductory spiel. She tried not to be wooden about it, but she had said it so many times. Daphne looked none too pleased at having her session hijacked, but she seemed intent on keeping Gina in the room. 'If people like Stalton's are the hypermarkets of the industrial plastics industry, Franson & Franson are, if you like, the corner store. We can't compete on size, but we're personal and very reliable. We try harder. We do nearly fifty per cent of our business by being people's second supplier – the people they turn to in an emergency, or when their main supplier lets them down. So we have to keep on our toes. We can't afford to let an opportunity slip.'

'That,' said Daphne, 'is true of all of us.'

'But it's why I can't sit here being taught how to sell while I'm losing an order!' Gina had planned to walk out on these words, but Daphne's mention of the diploma held her back. In Gina's view a START Selling diploma was worth about as much as a START Selling five-pound note, but Roy and Alex Franson might not see it that way if she returned to them diploma-less. *Back to your course, keener Gina.*

44

They were nice men, easy to work for most of the time, but Alex especially was given to occasional rages. He was famous for them. 'Please. Let me go.'

'I would prefer you to stay,' said Daphne. 'But you're not a prisoner. Do whatever you think best, and take the consequences.'

Deflated and miserable, Gina sat down. As a token gesture of defiance, she looked at the clock. It was nearly coffee time, not that that would be any use. Coffee time was fifteen minutes. She might go out at lunch time, though, and miss lunch. 'I'm sure you'll find you've made the right decision,' said Daphne, magnanimous in victory, adding: 'Thank you. And thank you for your self-presentation, and thank you for reminding us that we haven't heard Mrs Mitchison's self-presentation. I'm so sorry for leaving you out, Mrs Mitchison. Would you like to do yours now, and then we can take a break.'

Ann Mitchison went out to the front, her face full of fear. 'I'm sorry if I upset things by arriving late, and I want to thank Gina – Miss Heriot – for picking me up, and Miss Barclay and START Selling for letting me come on the course.' Gina felt slightly embarrassed, and smiled in what she hoped was an appreciative and encouraging way. 'If someone had told me this time last year that I'd be here, I wouldn't have believed it. But that was before I heard of the Enterprise Allowance Scheme.'

'It is a marvellous scheme, isn't it?' said Daphne pleasantly, when Ann appeared to run out of words. 'What is your product?'

'Mitchison's Working Models. They're hand-made working models.'

'Models of what, exactly?'

'Anything. You name it, and Tom – that's my son – will make a model of it.'

Daphne prompted gently: 'Is that one of them?' She was looking towards Ann's place. 'Hiding under your seat? We'll be coming later to how we present our products, but in the meantime it's safe to say that we should never hide them under our seat. Why don't you bring it out and show us?'

Ann fetched her merry-go-round and put it on Daphne's table. She twirled it. The different colours of the horses spun into each other. 'They all come off, you see,' said Ann, removing two of the horses. 'And you can put them back in different places.' She smiled hopefully. 'This one's ten pounds.'

'Charming,' said Daphne. 'Very charming indeed, Mrs Mitchison. Thank you.' And she dismissed them all for their break.

*

At coffee everyone wanted to look at the merry-go-round and take a turn at twirling it and removing the horses. Gina had seen it already, so she sat apart, looking out of the window, frustrated by the thought of her lost order, irritated by the sound of workmen banging somewhere in the hotel. When she had driven across the road this morning to fill up her tank – wherever she was, Gina always liked to have a full tank – the road had been slippery, and she doubted that it was any better now. Not that that would prevent her driving out to find the farm if that was what she decided to do. But it might stop Stalton's from rescuing their lorry and what remained of their acrylic; it might stop them sending a replacement load. Franson & Franson drivers were made of sterner stuff, and so were their representatives. They had to be. Somewhere out there was a very cross customer, and other people's cross customers were bread and butter to Gina, and the people with whom she worked.

8

Sexually disappointed, he had slept badly, dreaming an alarming dream of birds' wings, roaring water and wheels turning. He woke up with the image of a complex machine vivid in his mind. Waiting for his aunt to come in and make his breakfast, he sat up in bed and drew the machine.

As soon as he had drawn it, he recognized it.

'This could be the answer to the world's energy problems,' he told his aunt, as he ate his egg and sausage and toast.

'Oh aye,' she said. 'What is it?'

'Once you start it moving, it'll move for ever.'

'Isn't it time you started moving?'

'I think I'll have a try at making one.'

'After you've done the dolls.'

Tom enjoyed explaining things. Some of his favourite times, when he worked at the museum, had been when visitors stopped to ask him questions. 'You've heard of A. J. Ribson, the Victorian engineer?' he would say, knowing full well that the visitors would probably not have heard of him. 'He invented the winding gear you've probably seen at the pit.' The museum had its own colliery, reconstructed with real machines, brought in from the region's worked-out coal-fields. 'And the steam hammer at the foundry. It's not generally known that Ribson was a bit of a magician as well. He used to put on shows. Of course, to a lot of people, magic and the new engin-eering were one and the same. When you call something magic, it just means you've not understood the principles it works on.'

He himself did not fully understand the principles of the peacock fountain, but he explained anyway and his aunt listened. 'He made it for a mate of his, a mill-owner. You've got a hollowed out peacock, and a tank of water, and siphon pipes, and weights. If you get it right, the water goes up the pipes and in through the peacock's backside and out through its mouth. The tail opens and closes through hydraulic pressure. And it'll go on for ever. I could do a miniature one.'

'And who's going to buy it?'

'I'll leave that to the sales department.'

Out in the hall post rustled and she waddled off to fetch it, giving him a chance to have a look at the local paper that she had brought with her. 'CAB DRIVERS SAY NO TO ONE-WAY SYSTEM.' 'HETTON VICAR HITS OUT AT "MIND-BEND" CULTS.' 'STUDENT RAPED IN PLAY PARK.' 'It's a wicked world we live in,' said his aunt over his shoulder, handing him a letter. 'It certainly is,' he agreed, reading it.

Dear Sir or Madam,
Thank you for your application. All the advertised vacancies have now been filled but we will keep your name on file and contact you should anything suitable occur.

He said, 'Great news, Auntie Pat. They're going to keep my name on file. Filed under "Sir or Madam".'

'Who is?'

'Never heard of 'em,' he said, though he dimly remembered applying.

'What are you doing, applying for jobs? You've got a job.'

He supposed he had. He did not feel employed, even though his dole had stopped now that he was on Enterprise Allowance. He just felt that his name had been moved to a different register within the Department of Health and Social Security. He was still broke and at home. He was still being ordered about by women: his mother, his aunt, Margaret Thatcher and 'our accountant'.

His aunt tore open an envelope. She said, 'It's addressed to the business,' as if she thought that explained why she was allowed to open other people's post in other people's homes.

' " . . . in payment for the windmill, which my grandson is absolutely delighted with . . . " ' She laid three five-pound notes on the table. 'There you are, Tom, another satisfied customer. They shouldn't send cash through the post, though. Ann should tell them that.'

He picked up the notes. 'We can have a night on the town.'

She put out her hand. 'Thank you, Tom.'

'We don't have to declare it.'

'I think we'd better keep things straight in that department, or Miss Hutton'll be on to us.'

'She's not worth the paper she's written on. What's the good of an accountant who won't let you fiddle?'

'She's not that kind of accountant.'

'More's the pity.'

His aunt looked as if she did not disagree, but said that she would enter the payment into the account book anyway.

'And I'll take it to the bank,' he said, pocketing the money.

'I'll do that,' she said. 'You've got your work to do.'

'I have to go out anyway.'

'What for? Anything you need – '

'Research,' he said loftily.

'That's one thing I can't do for you.'

'You're a grand cook, though,' he said, giving her a hug and a kiss on the cheek. He got ready to go out. She came grumbling after him with the paying-in book. 'Make sure you get it stamped,' she said.

One of the best things about the museum was the moment of arrival. You got off the bus and walked for ten minutes down a lane. Sometimes this would be chock-a-block with visitors' cars, but if, as he fantasized now, he were arriving for an early shift, it would be magically quiet except for the sounds of the farmyard, and it would be easy to imagine himself stepping backwards in time.

It was like that now because of the weather: the ground was covered with slush, and more snow threatened. Many of the exhibits were housed indoors, but the term 'Open Air Museum' deterred visitors who did not know this, a fact that did not bother many of the craftsmen, who regarded visitors and their questions as a bit of an intrusion. 'Is the iron hot?' they had been known to ask Hughie the blacksmith, as he hammered away, scarlet in the face, at a piece of metal urgently needed by the tram-fitters; and Hughie would grit his teeth and confirm that it was. Or they would stick their fingers into the potter's clay, to find out whether it was soft. Others would help themselves to souvenirs: screws and tools from a factory work-shop, or pieces of stone from where skilled stonemasons were reconstructing a row of pit cottages with materials rescued at great expense from demolition.

He bypassed the admission turnstiles and climbed through a hedge into the farmyard. A dairymaid whom he knew greeted him, winked at him and looked the other way. She wore a long skirt and wellies, and carried a pail of steaming milk towards the creamery where it would be churned into butter for sale at the museum shop. After the farm, the next exhibit was the railway station and the steam-fitting sheds. He stopped to watch a gleaming locomotive of black and green being jacked up to have its coupling rods changed. He stood unnoticed among a group of boys of his own age (his replacements on the youth training programme, he assumed) and watched the skilled men tinkering knowingly with their beautiful engine. Most of the skilled men were in their sixties or older, and volunteers: retired or redundant railwaymen, or enthusiasts with a hobby who, far from expecting payment for indulging their obsession, would gladly pay the museum for the privilege if they had to. Tom recognized old friends among them but they were too absorbed in their work to notice him, standing or squatting round the engine, discussing it in soft voices like vets attending a huge injured animal. He would have liked to stop for a chat but he knew better than to interrupt.

He walked on, feeling lonely, past the station waiting room where a log fire burned, supervised by Ed, the stationmaster, in a Victorian frock coat. Tom and Ed exchanged waves through the window. Ed was another obsessive, a right nutter: he lived for the museum. He lived *at* the museum, caretaking with his wife. In Tom's day it had been rumoured that Ed was so much in love with the museum that after dark, when everybody had gone home, he took his wife out among the exhibits and screwed her on top of the coal trucks or under the Ribson steam hammer in the foundry.

Tom found that he had turned automatically towards the site office, to clock in. He retraced his steps, heading towards the library, part of which was housed in a green shed with a sign in curly script: WORKING MEN'S READING ROOM. 1^D PER DAY.

He was pleased to be recognized by Keith, the archivist. They exchanged news, and Keith told Tom that he was right to set up in business on his own. After all, nobody ever got rich by working for somebody else.

Tom told him he wanted to look at the Ribson papers. Keith looked doubtful. Unless he were very much mistaken, the Ribson papers were out on loan to Oxford University. Tom doubted this, and pressed him tactfully. He had often heard Keith telling visitors that such-and-such a document was at Oxford, or Edinburgh, or the British Museum. More often than not, Keith just wanted it known that his stock was in demand among the mighty of the land. He wanted it acknowledged that he was indispensable. 'Have a look for us, would you, Keith?' Tom pleaded. 'If I go in the archive myself, I'll never find what I want.'

Keith scurried off to look. No one other than himself was allowed in the archive, as Tom well knew. Princess Margaret herself had not been allowed in, when she came to look over the museum and open the refurbished Co-op. She would ignore the No Smoking signs, Keith had predicted. She would set the place on fire.

He ambled slowly between the rows of wooden benches and tables, waiting for Keith's return. He was alone in the reading room, save for the ghosts of the working men of the past who, exhausted by their labours, would nevertheless pay their penny a day and sit here hour upon hour, pursuing the learning that they had never got at school, or keeping abreast of world events in the newspapers.

Keith brought two fat files, tied up with ribbon: cuttings and documents and drawings. Tom went through them with awe and excitement. He had to keep reminding himself not to get distracted from what he had come for, which was the plans for the peacock fountain. He found them, started to make notes, then asked Keith if he would do a photocopy instead. Keith grumbled that the photo-copier would damage the documents, but Tom went on at him until he agreed.

He stared at a photograph of A. J. Ribson, with his long Father Christmas beard and his twinkling eyes, half wise, half mad, full of secrets. The greatest secret of all (Tom read now, in a page from an 1870's newspaper) was Ribson's Automaton: Sally.

Sally was a four-foot doll that used to sit on Ribson's knee and talk. That was easily achieved, but then, according to reports, Ribson would set Sally on her feet and she would walk across the stage, seeming to be powered by nothing stronger than her inventor's voice. The scientific correspondent of the newspaper had challenged Ribson to let him examine Sally and report to his readers on what he found. Ribson had agreed, throwing the event open to the general public at three pence a time. They had come in great numbers, as had expert engineers and Fellows of the Royal Society. They had expected to find Sally attached to Ribson's fingers with wires thinner than the eye could see: or else something inside her, magnets or mice or even a midget making her move. They had found nothing and had confessed themselves dumbfounded. And the mystery of Sally's workings had never been solved, said Keith, handing over the plans for the peacock fountain: for Ribson had left clear instructions that Sally was to be destroyed on his death, and if he had made any

51

notes or drawings on how he had built her, they had never come to light.

Armed with his plans, Tom went next to look at the fountain itself. The image that had appeared in his dream had been of a working model, the peacock swinging its tail to and fro and spitting out water with disdain. But today it was still, the water was turned off and the whole mechanism was encased in plastic sheeting to protect it from the weather. Tom lifted a corner of the plastic sheeting and took some measurements, just to be sure that the reality of the construction corresponded with the plans. He had never been so close to the peacock's face: it was about the same size as the face of a small dog and there was something of Ribson himself about the eyes. *I know something you don't know*, they said.

And Tom thought, *We'll see about that.*

If it's true about Sally, you must have made her somehow.

I'll copy everything you ever made, and one of these days I'll know your secret.

What a man, he thought. *Turning the wheels of the Industrial Revolution one day; conjuring tricks the next.*

If Sally was a conjuring trick.

Well, he fooled the Royal Society. I wish I'd been there.

He wandered around the museum a bit more, then got the bus back into town and went shopping. He bought glue, screws, glass piping and a small tin of paint, peacock blue. Then he went to the bank, marvelling at how they expected you to queue up for the privilege of handing over your own money.

His aunt did not appear to share his view of it as his money when he went home, after an afternoon spent in his workshop carving a chunk of pine from the beach into the shape of a peacock.

'What's this seven pounds fifty?' she raged, looking at the paying-in book. 'Fifteen pounds is what came this morning and fifteen pounds is what's gone in the accounts.'

Casually he produced the receipts from the hardware shop. 'Legitimate business expenditure,' he said. 'Ask Miss Hutton.'

'Oh,' she said.

'No need to apologize,' he said. 'Genius is always persecuted.'

9

Teresa had not sold *Atalanta* to Greg Sargent. The other members of the collective would not hear of it. There were five of them and they spoke with one voice, lining up against Teresa, to whom accepting Greg's offer seemed inevitable. *Atalanta* was a women's magazine. To have it owned by a man would be a contradiction in terms. Yes, even a man like Greg Sargent who (they took Teresa's word for it, for the sake of the discussion) was an avid reader, a generous donor, a member of CND, an equal opportunities employer and a big spender at the Silver Moon Women's Bookshop in Charing Cross Road.

'What's the alternative?' Teresa asked.

'Look, he can only have two reasons for wanting to do this. Either he means to control it, and that's not on. Or else he just wants to sit back while women do the work, and make money out of it.'

'Okay, but what's the alternative?' Teresa persisted. 'We can't pay Big S what we owe them.' Big S were *Atalanta*'s printers: radical, friendly, sympathetic, but with problems of their own and therefore insistent.

'There's fifteen years of women's labour gone into making *Atalanta* into something he wants to own,' said Carla, who was twenty.

'Sixteen years,' corrected Teresa, who was thirty-nine. 'What's the alternative?'

'And the readers, what about the readers?' said Beverley, who was Carla's lover and older than Carla: she was twenty-two. 'If Greg Sargent wants to set up some pseudo-feminist magazine, we can't stop him. But not with our name.'

'I bet he's after the mailing list,' said Abida. 'That's all he wants.

53

He wants to sell his bloody jeans and we wouldn't advertise them, so – '

'If I don't – ' Teresa stopped. 'If *we* don't sell to Greg, what do we do?'

There was silence. She tried again. 'Suppose it's a straight choice between selling to Greg and folding. Which should it be? Let's all write down our answers so we won't influence each other.' Pieces of paper were passed round, written on and collected up by Teresa, who said, stricken, 'Five to one, then. Do you really mean this, all of you? You'd really rather have the magazine disappear than take a chance on Greg?'

'But is that really the choice, Teresa?' said Mary.

Teresa passed her the accounts book. 'You tell me why it isn't.'

Mary knew a lot about Greek mythology. 'Atalanta herself,' she said, 'was tricked into marriage by the promise of a golden apple. But some versions say that rather than let the man fuck her, she turned into a lioness and bit him in half.'

Teresa's enrolment for START Selling – Women! (the course Greg had intended to send her on) was part of the process of turning *Atalanta* into a women-owned, women-controlled lioness, unmolested and commercially strong. Sending her on the course had been controversial. The others had thought the fee a great extravagance in the circumstances. Teresa had replied that on the contrary it was absolutely essential in the circumstances. They were all going to have to sell as they had never sold before. 'Granted,' they had said, 'but what does sales training *mean*?' 'I don't know,' Teresa had replied, 'but if Greg was willing to spend money on it, you can rest assured that it means something.' They had taken this point but still felt there were better uses for the money. The problem had been solved by Teresa's parents, who had paid Teresa's course fee as a Christmas present-cum-donation.

Rather than sell the title to Greg Sargent, the collective had agreed temporarily to compromise on other principles. There would be no more collective working or long meetings until the magazine was back on its feet. Everyone was given a task, and she would (it was agreed) bloody well do it. The GLC was gone but other grant-giving bodies survived. They must be approached with renewed energy and a more impressive product. Beverley would redesign the magazine's pages, making them as zappy and eye-catching as possible, even if this did mean leaving out the occasional chunk of words. Carla would set up interviews with famous women, not all of whom need necessarily be on record as feminists, and their pictures would be taken to go on the cover. Mary would make one final trawl for donations, concentrating on those women who, having started out with *Atalanta*, had gone on to higher things, glittering careers at the Equal Opportunities Commission, for example, or best-seller writing, or reading the news on television. Mary would also come down like a ton of bricks on people who owed *Atalanta* money. Abida would arrange as much free publicity as possible, fly-posting, and wheedling free puffs from sympathetic journalists. Teresa would sell advertising in perfect freedom: for the duration of the emergency, nothing would be turned away.

'Nothing?'

'Nothing. Well – if it's something really awful, you'd better bring it out for discussion – '

'We've agreed there's no time for that,' said Abida crisply. 'Teresa must make her own judgements. We all must, and if the others don't like it, tough.'

'Is this a collective or a junta?'

'It's a junta. What about distribution?'

Atalanta had always boycotted the major distributors, on the grounds that they also dealt in pornography. *Atalanta* had relied on local groups, subscriptions and alternative bookshops. Now Teresa was sent to make enquiries. The distributors were less than enthusiastic, but she would work on them. 'I think we can make a virtue of necessity here,' she told the others. 'Subscriptions are better, we get the money in advance. And we'll make the local groups pay in advance too, and we won't accept returns.'

'They'll never wear that.'

'They'll have to. Tell them it's an emergency and we'll give them a big profit margin. If you'll pardon the expression.'

One last thing remained. Big S, the printers, must be prevailed upon to carry on printing and to reschedule the debt. Teresa was given the job of persuading them to do this. 'Thank you very much, I'll enjoy doing that,' she said.

'Well, you are the owner, after all.'

'I didn't realize you knew.'

'This is an emergency.'

Yes, yes. Martha and John Pixley, who owned Big S, knew all about the emergency. Who knew better than they did? *Atalanta* was not the only Big S client in trouble. Martha and John wanted to help. Third-generation socialists, they had set up their company specifically to service community publishers. They had two price structures. Their rich clients subsidized their poor ones. Their terms to *Atalanta* were as generous as they could possibly be. Nothing would give them greater pleasure than to write off the *Atalanta* debt altogether, but . . .

'I'm not asking you to write it off. I'm asking for a breathing space.'

'What do you think you've been having?'

'I know. You've been fantastic.'

'And we want to go on being fantastic. To you and the labour movement generally. But we've got problems of our own. Don't put us in this position, Teresa. Can't you spread the risk, at least? Can't you get a bank loan?'

'They laughed me out of the office.'

'Can't someone lend it to you? Look, get a loan for half of what's outstanding, and we'll carry the rest for six months. We'll go on printing you and you can pay as you go.'

And this was what was agreed. It was not perfect – it involved Teresa borrowing £5,000 from her parents. For the time being they could afford it – her father had just retired with a lump sum – but it saddened Teresa to ask for it. It made her feel dependent. It embarrassed her and she did not tell anybody. She suspected that her relationship with her parents was a source of speculation and some scorn among her acquaintances. If a grown woman lived with her fit parents it usually meant one of two things: exploitative parents or a daughter who dared not fly the nest. These were, of course, stereotypes. It was interesting how people who made it their life's work to resist the placing of stereotyped assumptions on private relationships, still raised their eyebrows when she said she lived with her parents.

She did not live *with* them, of course; just in the same building. Their house had a granny flat, and as the granny in question had died before she could avail herself of it, renting it out to Teresa, who was always hard up, had seemed the obvious thing to do. What was the alternative? Rent it out to a stranger, whom Teresa's parents might not like, and have Teresa go and rent other, probably inferior, accommodation from another stranger, whom *she* might not like? That would be ridiculous. Teresa lived independently and had her own front door. She liked her parents as individuals, and they liked her. They would have been friends even if they were not related. They supported her aspirations and activities. They were the secret rescuers of *Atalanta*. They wanted no credit for this, and Teresa was happy to keep it dark, hinting that the money was her own, a life assurance policy, cashed in early. It was a loan. On that, Teresa was in no doubt. It was as important to her that she repay her parents as it was that she do the right thing by Big S and keep *Atalanta* afloat. So even though some of the content of START Selling – Women! was inimical to *Atalanta*'s philosophy, and some was irrelevant, and some frankly ridiculous, her head was down and her notebook full. Could a radical magazine, an ideology, a moral system, be sold in the same way as an insurance policy, a home-made toy or a time-share villa in Lanzarote? For the rest of this week she was suspending her scepticism and believing that it could.

10

'You Need It!' cried Miss Barclay at the start of the second morning. 'I've Got It! You Can Have It! And Closing! These are the four essential stages of every successful sale. Recite them to yourself on your way to making your call.'

Ann muttered along with the others: 'You need it, I've got it, you can have it, and closing.'

'Not like that! You *Need* It!' Miss Barclay mimed driving a car. 'I've *Got* It!' She stepped out of the car and brushed fluff from her shoulders. 'You *Can Have* It!' She knocked at a door and stepped through, smiling, briefcase in one hand, visiting card in the other. 'And Closing. Don't be rigid about it, of course. It's there to help you, not restrict you. Think of it as a military drill. You are your companies' frontline troops. You are well prepared and know your job. Sadly, though, the enemy also knows his job. I speak metaphorically. Your buyer is not your enemy, he is your friend, but he does not always play by the same rules as you, so you must keep your wits about you and concentrate.

'You Need It. We did that yesterday. We talked about the buyer's needs, the buyer's perception of his needs and the ways in which we can focus his mind on his needs. Our main topic today is I've Got It. Having established his needs, have we got what he needs? Not approximately, but precisely? Of course we have – we wouldn't be calling on him otherwise. He may not, at first, agree with us. We deal with that tomorrow. You Can Have It. And Friday is for Closing. Closing the sale. That is our reward and that is what we must work towards.

'The Closing smile is not earned lightly. I haven't said much to you so far about sales aids, though I will be mentioning various display materials which you can buy from START at specially reduced rates for diploma holders. But the most important sales aid of all cannot be bought, or sold. It is this. *Smile*. A smile is the shortest distance between two people. Smile when you arrive, smile as you ask your questions, smile as you present your product. Smile while you dial. The first session this morning is about use of the telephone.'

Two tables had been set up at the front of the conference room, with a telephone on each. The telephones were wired up to a tape recorder and a loudspeaker. Sandra Liffey, who sold cookware at parties in people's homes, was called out to sit at one of the tables. Ann was called to the other. 'Don't look so terrified, Mrs Mitchison – '

'Sorry.'

' – there's nothing to be scared of, you're just the customer for now.' Miss Barclay slapped her little hand over her own mouth and rolled her eyes in mock horror. 'Did you all hear my mistake? *Just* the customer, indeed! Don't let me hear any of you saying that, not even in fun. The customer is the most important person in the world. You are the most important person in the world, Mrs Mitchison.'

Ann straightened her shoulders.

Sandra Liffey picked up her phone.

'Smile . . .' said Miss Barclay softly.

Ann's phone rang. She picked it up.

Miss Barclay said: 'STOP! Do you want your customers to think you're sitting by the phone waiting for it to ring? Let it ring three times and answer on the fourth.'

Ann did this. She smiled. She said, 'Hello?' Her *hello* rasped round the room on the loudspeakers. Miss Barclay did not seem to like it either. 'STOP! What does that word "hello" mean? Nothing. I don't want to hear it. Give the name of your business when you answer the phone, your own name, and then ask how you may help.'

Sandra Liffey said mildly, 'I don't phone businesses, I phone housewives.'

'And how do you know that this particular housewife isn't in business too? Ideally you would know, of course, because you would have researched your calls before making them. But what if your boss gives you a list of what he assures you are red-hot prospects and then disappears to an important conference without telling you anything about them?' Miss Barclay winked. '*You* know the kind of important conference.' She mimed taking a swing at a golf ball. '*Do not disturb*. Happens all the time, doesn't it? Mrs Mitchison, would

I be right in thinking that you don't have separate telephones for business and personal use? There's nothing wrong with that when you're starting out, but it's doubly important to answer in a business-like manner. How do you know this isn't a customer? And if it's a personal call, saying the name of the business will make it clear that you haven't time to chat.'

Ann tried to imagine what her friends would say if they rang her up and heard, 'Mitchison's Working Models, Ann Mitchison speaking, how may I help you?'

Still, if that was what you had to do. . .

Miss Barclay came across and indicated that she wanted Ann to give up her seat so that she herself could sit in it. 'Try again, Miss Liffey, and be ready for anything.' Ann stood aside, feeling like a spare part. Sandra Liffey dialled again, smiling. Miss Barclay answered on the fourth ring. Ann wondered whether she was supposed to return to her seat or wait. 'This is START Selling,' said Miss Barclay in a tinny voice. 'There's no one in the office to talk to you at the moment so this is a recording. Please leave your name, telephone number and reason for calling. Beeeep.'

Sandra Liffey banged her phone down. 'I hate those things. I'll call back.'

'The right response for the wrong reason,' said Miss Barclay. Ann shifted her weight from foot to foot. 'We can none of us afford to be afraid of technology. But *never* – any of you, I'm speaking generally now – never leave a message on a tape for a cold call. Can anyone tell me why? Firstly, no one's at their best on a tape unless they've got a prepared patter, and if you're going to use a prepared patter you might just as well write it down and send it. The purpose of the call is to make personal contact, isn't it? If you say the wrong thing, it's there on the tape for as long as the prospect wants it. The only sensible message would be to leave your name and a request that he call you back, but why should he? He doesn't know you. Even if he does, you're losing the initiative. He may call you at an inconvenient time, though of course there should be no such thing as an inconvenient time to receive calls from a customer. More likely, he won't call back at all, and then what do you do? Leave more messages? They may be hours, even days, apart, but when he returns and plays them one after the other, they're going to sound like his wife nagging him. *Call me back. I've told you five times. Call me back.*'

Ann looked at Teresa. They were not supposed to have private conversations during the meal breaks, but as part of the selling game Teresa had made clear that the magazine she worked for was a feminist magazine and she was a feminist. She did not like Miss Barclay's sexist jokes. Teresa was certainly looking annoyed, though whether because of what Miss Barclay had said or because everyone was looking at her to see if she would protest, Ann could not tell. She was still sure that she had seen Teresa on television. She must ask her.

'And another thing,' Miss Barclay continued. 'That taped message was very bad.'

'It wasn't mine,' said Sandra Liffey.

'No, I made it up as an example. Too wordy. Never say there's nobody in the office, it's obvious and it's regrettable. Don't draw attention to it. Just ask him to leave his name and number. Which, as I say, he won't do if he's got any sense.'

Someone interrupted and said, 'My company sells answering machines, and I can't accept that.'

'Fine,' said Miss Barclay, turning towards the woman who had spoken, Chris Catling. 'You can be next. Where are you off to, Mrs Mitchison?' Ann had decided to return to her seat. 'We haven't finished with you yet! Let's see if Mrs Catling can sell you an answering machine.'

'So glad to have caught you in at last Mrs Mitchison,' said Chris Catling smoothly. 'Does it ever worry you, the amount of business you may be losing by leaving your phone unattended?'

'Good,' said Miss Barclay.

Ann decided to be a bit cunning. 'It's the kids,' she said. 'They run me off my feet. Still, we'd not be without them, would we?'

'Indeed not, Mrs Mitchison, but – '

'Have you got children yourself?'

'Yes, two girls and a boy, but what I – '

'Same as me! How old are they?'

'The girls are twelve and fourteen and the boy's nearly ten – '

'Birthday coming up, then! Have you thought what to give him?'

'Well, he's very interested in – '

'Don't tell me, computer games. It's another world these days, isn't it? How about something different this year? I've got a model steam engine that I think your lad would love. It's a working model, hand-made to scale, only one of its kind – '

'As a matter of fact,' said Chris Catling, 'trains are rather a hobby of his.'

Beautiful, thought Ann. *She walked right into it. I'm getting the hang of this.*

Miss Barclay said 'Stop!' and Ann waited modestly to be praised. 'Did you all hear Mrs Mitchison talking herself out of that sale?' Ann blinked. Miss Barclay fiddled with switches. The air filled up with a loud hiss. ' . . . run me off my feet. Still, we'd not be without them, would we?' What was wrong with that? Her voice sounded a bit foolish but that might be the recording. What she had said was all right, ordinary conversation to break the ice, one woman to another. ' . . . have you thought what to give him?' Ann's voice was replaced by Chris's: 'Well, he's very interested in . . .' Ann's own voice cut in: 'Don't tell me, computer games!' and she understood.

'Sorry,' she said.

Miss Barclay was not going to leave it at that. Her eyebrows had disappeared into her hair. ' "Don't tell me. *Don't tell me!*" What kind of nonsense is that, asking a good selling question and then interrupting with "*Don't tell me*"? Never do that! Don't ask a question if you don't want to know the answer, and never interrupt a buyer while he's answering. Keep your mouth closed. Shut your trap. Weld your teeth together. Put a padlock on your tongue and put *this* – ' she produced a zip fastener, ' – on your lips. Otherwise we end up with something like this.' Once again she played the terrible tape. 'How about something different this year? I've got a model steam engine – ' 'She hasn't established that a model steam engine would *be* something different, has she? If she had waited – *listened* – she might have discovered that the Catling child is already *obsessed* with steam engines! That you can't *move* in the Catling home for the son's steam engines! And if Mrs Catling hears the words "steam engine" again she'll scream, because Mrs Catling's idea of something different is a nice clean educational computer game! All right, Mrs Mitchison?'

'Yes, Miss Barclay. Sorry. I talk too much.'

Miss Barclay sighed and did not deny it.

'I thought I was supposed to be selling her an answering machine,' said Chris Catling.

'So did I,' said Miss Barclay. 'You'll never sell anything to anybody if you let the customer steal the initiative like that.' And she sent them off for their break.

Ann said to Teresa, 'Don't think I'm being rude, but haven't I seen you on television?'

Teresa replied, 'You might have seen my sister.'

'Who's your sister, then?'

'Marion Henley.'

'You're Marion Henley's sister?'

Others heard and came over: 'Marion Henley's sister!'

Ann asked, 'What's she like in real life?'

'Have you got a sister?' Teresa retorted. 'What's *she* like in real life?' The sharpness in her voice told Ann that it had been the wrong question, some jealousy there, perhaps; but there was no stopping the others.

'How did she get into that?'

'She was a reporter before.'

Ann spotted Chris Catling on the edge of the circle and decided to push home her advantage with regard to the steam engine. 'How long has your son been interested in model railways, Chris?'

'For ever,' said Chris.

Teresa was still being besieged by questions and comments about her newscaster sister. 'I don't suppose it's as easy as it looks.'

'Marion says it's very difficult, she says there's a lot more to it than knowing how to read.'

Ann persisted with Chris. 'Does he make them himself?'

'Christ, yes. Unless he covers his bedroom with glue for some other purpose.'

'Well, you wouldn't have that problem if you bought one ready-made.'

'What I always wonder is what they're saying to each other during the music.'

'I know, it looks very cosy, doesn't it? You feel you shouldn't interrupt.'

'Send me a catalogue,' said Chris to Ann.

'I've got one upstairs.'

'Great, I'll look forward to reading it.'

'I mean I've got one of my son's engines.'

Chris laughed and said to anyone who might hear: 'She's not going to drop it, is she?'

'We're not supposed to.' Ann went to her room and fetched the engine. She cleared a space on a table and showed how it worked. Everyone admired it.

'All right,' Chris sighed. 'How much is it?'

'Fifteen pounds. It's hand-made.'

Chris Catling took three pretend five-pound notes out of her START Selling wallet, signed them on the back as Miss Barclay had instructed on the first evening, and handed them over. 'Now, how about buying one of my answering machines in exchange?'

II

The rest of the day was taken up with Product Presentation: Features, Benefits and Perfect Selling Sentences. Selling had a grammar all its own, apparently. A Feature was a fact about a product, a characteristic. Features of *Atalanta* – Features of any magazine – included size, number of pages, target audience, frequency of publication, price. Features were neutral, neither good nor bad. The point was to express them as Benefits. A Benefit was the interpretation that the salesperson chose to place on the Feature. This would vary, depending on the person being sold to, so this was where technique came in.

A Perfect Selling Sentence contained a Feature, a Benefit and a reason why the Benefit would enhance the buyer's life. In the case of Alice York's holiday villas, for example, a Perfect Selling Sentence would go something like this: 'It's a hundred yards from the beach' (factual, neutral, verifiable, a Feature) 'so you don't have to take everything with you when you go for a swim' (a Benefit, provided that you had established in advance that the buyer liked swimming) 'perfect for family holidays!' (Life Enhancement.)

For a home contents insurance policy, it would be: 'The annual premiums are index-linked' (Feature) 'which means that replacement values are always covered.' (Benefit.) The Life Enhancement was 'peace of mind for you and your family'.

For Ann Mitchison it was 'Hand-made by a skilled craftsman, so different from mass-produced toys in shops, let your child be the envy of his friends!'

A reference to the buyer's family seemed to be mandatory in the Life-Enhancement section, Teresa noted.

She decided to give it a try.

'It's a feminist magazine, implacably opposed to patriarchy, hours of reassuring reading for your husband and sons.'

No, Teresa. Stop messing about. You're here, aren't you?

'It's the authentic voice of the women's movement.' *Correction.* 'It's *an* authentic voice of the women's movement. It's been at the forefront of campaigns that have been won, but it doesn't rest on its laurels. Not like some. It nips away at patriarchy like a gadfly, and . . . and you'd just better buy it or you'll wake up one morning and it won't be here.'

And then what? *And then what?* Of the six collective members, five had said that they would rather see *Atalanta* collapse than have it taken over by Greg. Their arguments had been perfectly cogent, but they had shaken Teresa and filled her with grief. This shock and grief had continued even when Carla and Beverley and the others had made it clear that they considered the choice to be a false one; that they intended to see to it that *Atalanta* was neither taken over by the Our Ways empire nor forced into liquidation; that they were prepared to make hitherto-unacceptable compromises to ensure this. The fact remained that if they failed – and Teresa was not contemplating failure, but *if* – five out of six members of the *Atalanta* collective would, like Catholic virgins and martyrs, prefer death before dishonour.

This realization had confirmed for Teresa the existence of a gulf between her and the other collective members, a gulf far deeper than could be accounted for by the fact that she was old enough to have been their (teenage) mother. Their commitment to *Atalanta* was strong, but it was not, as it was with her, exclusive. *Atalanta* exhausted Teresa, and she was never more than a spectator on the sidelines of other projects, a day-tripper to Greenham Common, a standeraround with bunches of flowers when women like Mary emerged, grey-faced but beaming, from their week in Holloway Prison, a sympathetic listener to accounts of what the strip club's bouncer had said, and tried to do, to Carla on the anti-pornography march. Abida and Beverley were as active in anti-racism campaigns outside *Atalanta* as they were on its pages; Mary drove the minibus for a women's get-you-home service on Saturday nights . . . all of them, in short, had other fish to fry and, sad though they would be without *Atalanta*, they would not be bereft. They believed that there were other things, just as important, and they lived that belief. They lived in a world of campaigns that waxed and waned, triumphed, were defeated, were reborn, or just outlived their own usefulness . . . they had not hitched

65

their youthful wagons to this one particular star and allowed themselves to become middle-aged with it.

Teresa might once have been able to say that a feature of magazines like *Atalanta* was that they alone fought for women's rights. She could not say that now, not when nearly all the glossy women's monthlies carried their quota of articles on rights at work, day-care, male violence, even lesbianism, and a goodly proportion of those articles were written by women who used once to be mainstays of *Atalanta*. They had moved out, moved on, kindly giving their shares in Atalanta Magazine Ltd to Teresa. (Their successors had not wanted to be shareholders, they did not believe in it; it was only a formality anyway, and they trusted Teresa not to pull rank.) Teresa had not moved on. She had sat tight as her generation passed. *Asset stripping*, she had called it, usually only to herself but sometimes out loud. 'You were an asset,' she told her sister Marion. 'And now you've been stripped.' It was all so unfair. A thing was built up out of commitment, idealism and free labour. Conventional society pretended to stand aloof. It had not been standing aloof at all, of course; it had been monitoring progress, waiting to see if this women's lib business would catch on. As soon as it caught on, ideas and key people had been poached, privatized. 'You've been poached, privatized.' 'No I haven't,' said Marion in her famous voice. 'I'm just taking the struggle elsewhere. No point in demanding equal opportunities if women won't take them. Don't tell me you wouldn't have done the same. . . .'

Marion did not add, *given the chance*. Teresa had not been given the chance, no one had tried to poach or privatize her.

'And anyway,' said Marion, 'I'm a role model.'

The START Selling women had heard of Marion. They had not heard of *Atalanta*.

The START Selling women were to spend Wednesday evening dividing into their syndicate groups (*breaking down into workshops*, Teresa called it to herself, defiantly), jointly (*collectively*) putting together a sales presentation for one member of each group.

The hotel management regretted that the central heating in the syndicate rooms was off. It was undergoing its annual maintenance check. The bedrooms were still warm, though, so they met in the bedrooms. *Atalanta* was chosen as the project for Teresa's group, so she felt obliged to offer her room. She would have preferred not to do this. It was not that her room was untidy, on the contrary, its state was excellent, for the very good reason that her lover Sam (so new to her life that the dew was still on him; she had met him at an office party on December 17th, and they had had a very happy Christmas indeed) had said that he would see if he could get away and join her for a night. 'I love hotels,' he had said. 'We can pretend we're having an affair.'

It was unlikely that he would come. 'Don't worry if I don't,' he had said. He was a freelance graphic designer and the pattern of his life was dictated by his unpredictable workload. Teresa certainly was not going to attach any great meaning to it if he did not show up. But it would be just her luck to have him come tonight. She left a note for him at reception, welcoming him and telling him that on no account was he to try and find her room. He was to sit in the bar and wait for her. 'It's very unlikely that he'll come,' she told the receptionist casually. 'But if he does, could you give him this? It's *very* important. I mean, if he comes it is, but he probably won't.'

'I see,' said the receptionist.

Teresa just hoped that the hotel's staff shortages would not send the receptionist off early, leaving Sam to wander the corridors and barge in on the syndicate discussion. The START Selling women might be impressed by his youth and beauty, but they would not be impressed by a feminist having a lover who felt free to interrupt her while she was at work. Daphne would hit the roof. Daphne would be touring between the rooms, visiting at unpredictable intervals.

The syndicate group settled in the room. Gina Heriot said that she would be chairman. One of the other women asked whether that should not be *chairperson*. She gave Teresa a mischievous look as she said this.

'My main concern at the moment,' said Teresa, 'is to find a distributor. I'd like to put together a presentation to convince a distributor that we're worth handling.'

'Okay,' said Gina. 'We'll all be difficult distributors. Fire away.'

Teresa passed round copies of *Atalanta*, the first of the new, improved issues to be produced in the shadow of Greg Sargent. Gina said, in a well-mannered, head-girl sort of way: 'This looks very interesting, Teresa. Why haven't I come across it?'

'Because we haven't got a distributor.'

'Oh, right, yes, silly me. Why haven't you got one?'

'Partly because we haven't wanted . . . well, we've been a bit rude to them in the past, I'm afraid. And they say we're too small, too inefficient and not really worth their while.'

'Chickens and eggs, then,' said Katie Fraser, who sold baths. 'You'll always be too small if you're not professionally distributed.'

Claire, who had made the remark about chairpersons, said, 'Why do they think you're inefficient?'

'We have been. But we're working on it.'

'That's it then, isn't it?' said Gina. ' "We try harder." That was one of the best advertising slogans ever. Who was it? No point in pretending you're the biggest when you're not, so make a virtue out of not being. I use it all the time, you should have heard me yesterday trying to persuade a farmer to build acrylic shelters for his sheep – '

She had gone off in her lunch hour, apparently, convinced that she had identified the person for whom the Stalton's load had been destined. She had been wrong, but she had tried. By God, she had tried. She had not succeeded, but she had taken the farmer's name for future reference, and he had taken hers.

Teresa coughed.

'Sorry, Teresa. We were talking about you.'

'Yes,' said Teresa. 'Another reason why the big distributors are hostile to us is that they're mostly men.'

'I don't see why that should be a problem,' said Gina. 'You're not asking them to read it, you're asking them to sell it.'

'Anyway, it's going to be a bit less anti-men, isn't it?' said Ann Mitchison, looking up from her copy and speaking for the first time. 'You said . . .'

'That's one of the ones that's supposed to be a bit less anti-men,' said Teresa, and Ann said, 'Oh. Sorry.'

'Why all this anti-men stuff anyway?' Claire demanded. 'I mean, there's nothing feminist about this course, is there? Thank God. I mean, I'm sorry, Teresa, but I'm not a feminist, I've never needed to be, and there it is. It's just a course.'

'Yes. I had noticed. If you ask me, the reason why they haven't let men come on it is because they'd make a fuss about the conditions. All the banging about, fire alarms going off – '

'Well, there hasn't been so much banging about today, has there?' said Ann in a conciliatory way. 'They've had to stop work on the swimming pool roof because the stuff didn't arrive. The chamber-maid told me, she's ever so nice, she bought one of my models for her little girl . . .'

Teresa waited for this to stop. 'Our circulation's just getting ready to take off,' she said, but Gina, in the chair, was not listening. She was staring at Ann with a gleam in her eye. 'What did you say? Repeat what you just said.'

'I said she bought one of my – '

'You said the stuff hadn't arrived for the sun-roof! The manager, I have to see the manager!'

'He's probably off duty,' Teresa warned, but Gina was out of the room before the words had left her lips.

'Let me tell you about some of the interviews we've got planned,' said Teresa. 'In the March issue, we're hoping to do – ' The door opened; Teresa flinched with hopeful fear that it might be Sam, but it was Daphne.

'How are we getting on? Who's chairman, or perhaps I should say chairp – '

'Gina,' said Teresa.

'And where is Miss Heriot now?'

'She's, um, gone to have a look at the swimming pool.'

Daphne was in high good humour. 'I hope she doesn't make the mistake of diving in. There's no water in it, and no roof either.'

Whether it was the informality of the setting – meeting in bedrooms like earnest undergraduates – or whether unpredictability of mood was part of Daphne's policy of keeping everyone on their toes, Teresa did not know: but Daphne seemed enormously charming this evening, and very relaxed. She sat on Teresa's bed and curled her legs under her, removing her shoes and tucking her skirt round in a way that was so meticulously modest it was quite touching. She gave forth her accumulated wisdom on magazine distribution with her usual air of being the only person in the room who knew anything about it, but there was a warmth in her words which Teresa had not noticed before, and she started to wonder whether Daphne might have a special interest in *Atalanta*. Whether she might be a feminist *manquée*. *Very manquée indeed*, Teresa argued back with herself; *I could overlook all the hes and salesmans, but not the cracks about nagging wives and stupid secretaries. On the other hand ... what do I know about what Daphne's gone through to get to where she is? She's the only woman in the* START *Selling team ... their prospectus calls her 'this newest jewel in our crown'. What does she think of that? What does she think of us, of me? I must be more tolerant.*

Daphne's advice echoed Gina's words – the distributors were not being asked to read *Atalanta*, they were being asked to sell it. Daphne pointed out that between the moment when the proofs left the hands of the proofreaders and the moment when the customer took her copy of the magazine out of her shopping bag, all the important decisions about it would be made by people who had not read it.

That included the customer herself, who would not have read it before buying it. Presentation, then, was all. What distributors would be looking for was a magazine which could be seen, at first glance, to cry *You Need It!* to the shopper, and to cry it loudly enough to be heard above the clamour of competing *You Need It!* from the other women's magazines. The cover would have to be cheered up, said Daphne. The price would have to be reduced, it was the most expensive magazine on the market and one of the thinnest. What about a free gift on the cover, some perfume or something? And what about assuring the distributors that their efforts would be backed up by national advertising? 'You get the idea?'

'Yes,' Teresa sighed. 'Thank you. . . .' It was nearly time to finish. 'Thanks, everybody, for your suggestions. One last thing. Forget about distributors for now. Just be, well, you. You've all got a copy to look at, would any of you like to buy it?'

There were seven women in the room, counting Daphne, not counting Teresa.

Ann Mitchison said, 'I'll have a copy. In fact, I'll take a year's subscription.' She signed her name on the back of a START Selling ten-pound note and handed it to Teresa, returning the magazine at the same time.

Three of the other women started to do the same.

Trying to hide her disappointment, Teresa said, 'It's all right, you can keep them. I brought them to give to you.'

Daphne said softly, 'That wasn't very sensible, was it? Now you'll never know if anyone would *really* have bought a copy.'

Teresa stared at Daphne, perched on her bed like a little girl in her stockinged feet. Daphne said, 'If you want people to pay for something, for heaven's sake don't let them see you giving it away.'

Teresa said, 'Would you . . . ?'

'Not if I can have it free, no. Why should I?'

Apologetically Teresa took back the copies from the women who had been told they could keep them. 'Now,' she said, 'would anyone like to buy, really buy, a copy of *Atalanta*? Daphne?' It was the first time Teresa had first-named her in her hearing.

'No, thank you,' Daphne replied.

12

His aunt was still ironing his shirt as he finished his tea, but by the time he had shaved and had his bath, the shirt was laid out on his bed along with his dark maroon trousers, freshly pressed with the creases the way he liked them. His mother could not have done them better.

He got dressed, arranging his collar as best he could to emphasize his large and manly larynx in his skinny neck. He used to be self-conscious about his larynx, until Shelly said it was sexy. He did up his trousers over his flat stomach, anticipating the sensation, as he closed the zip, of opening it again, or having it opened, in the not-too-distant future.

He leaned towards the mirror and drew back his lips to check his teeth. He had good, strong, even teeth. He was proud of them, he took care of them. He cupped his hands over his mouth, went 'Ha – !' and sniffed the result. He smelled only toothpaste but he sprayed his mouth with breath freshener, just to be sure.

You could say what you liked about sex, it was still the best free entertainment going, particularly now that he had got beyond the persuading stage with Shelly, and she had got beyond the pretending she didn't want to stage. She had a hunger to match his own.

He was not sure that she always enjoyed it as much as he did, though she said she did. Anyway, he did his best.

'Seen my coat?' he asked his aunt.

'It'll be where you threw it when you came in.' She turned from the sink and admired him. 'Where are you off to?'

'Youth club,' he said. 'It's a new one that's opened, me and Shelly thought we'd give it a try.'

'What time will you be back – ?'

Oh Christ, he thought.

' – because I may be gone, so you'd better take your key.' She reached into her purse and took out a five-pound note. 'Have a drink for me,' she said.

'Auntie Pat, you shouldn't.'

'Give it back, then,' she said. 'Go on, enjoy yourself.'

His first disappointment came when her mother opened the door to him. He had assumed that Shelly's mention of a youth club over the phone had been code for the fact that her parents were going out. He did not think that Shelly was any more interested in youth clubs than he was.

Shelly's mother seemed settled in for the evening, watching television and sewing. He chatted to her while he waited for Shelly to get ready. He hoped he was not going to be frustrated again. Sexual frustration was one thing he could not stand. It made him wild, as Miss Daphne Barclay had discovered on Monday night. It was as much his frustration that had led him to speak to her in the way he had, as his concern for his mother and his fantasy that Daphne Barclay was Margaret Thatcher incarnate. And when she had taken the wind out of his sails with her 'How may I help you?' and 'I can tell that you're angry' and he had ended up apologizing and begging ('No need to apologize'), he had felt as he always felt when he wanked himself off: disgusted. *Where's your pride, man?*

The alternatives to sex being wanking or frustration, he failed to understand why people made such a fuss about it. It was one of the few activities of which it could safely be said that all normal people – all normal animals too, for that matter – did it from time to time. That, and breathing. He tried to imagine it: *Now I don't want you and Michelle getting up to any breathing while I'm away.* It did not do anyone any harm. Shelly was on the pill.

She came in, wearing a short blue skirt that he could not remember having seen before, and a top made from some sort of glittery material. She always managed to look fresh and nice, in spite of being on the dole. She had done something new to her hair which emphasized the elfin quality of her pretty face, but she had very little make-up on. This pleased Tom. He hated fighting his way through layers of make-up.

'What's this club you said you were going to?'

'It's a new one, Mam. It's on a barge on the river.'

'Don't be late, then. Eleven o'clock, what do you think?'

What do you think? Tom was not fooled. If Shelly's mother said eleven o'clock, eleven o'clock it would be. His heart sank.

Shelly shivered as they waited at the bus stop, and he put his arms round her. Today's fierce wind had blown away most of the snow, but it remained in small grey pockets. Frost glinted in a hardening film on the surface of the road, and cut through the soles of his shoes into the soles of his feet.

' "It's a new one, Mam," ' he teased. ' "It's on a barge." '

She slapped him playfully. 'It *is*.'

'Get away.'

'One of my friends told me about it.'

'You really want to go to it?'

'What else is there to do?'

He sighed heavily. 'Aren't we going to Barbara's?'

Barbara was a friend of Shelly's who lived alone with her eighteen-month-old son in a council flat. She sometimes let Shelly and Tom use the flat.

'You can't just make use of people, Tom.'

'She doesn't mind.'

'She does. She's my friend, and I know.'

He knew he was beaten. He got the message. She did not mind doing it, she liked doing it, but she wanted it confirmed that it was not all he went out with her for. If they were supposed to be going out, then out was where she wanted to go. 'The youth club, then.'

'It's free,' she said pointedly.

'All right, all right, I've got money. Let's go for a drink first, eh? A quick drink at the Palmerston and then we'll go to your barge.' She looked sullen but said nothing. He started to hum 'A Life on the Ocean Wave', stopping when the bus came.

Chris was in the Palmerston, as Tom had hoped he would be, and so was a group of girls having a hen party. The bride-to-be wore a huge top hat made of silver foil. Her dress was covered with streamers and sequins and headlines cut out of newspapers: 'NIGHTS OF PASSION'. 'HONEYMOON HORROR FOR TEENAGE COP'. 'GIVE ME A BIG ONE'. In her lap was a cucumber with a pink ribbon tied round the end. From the looks of things she had been drinking since opening time, and so had her friends. ' "Dinah, Dinah, show us your leg – " ' they sang, and Chris joined in with gusto: ' "A yard above your knee." '

'Oh shut up, Chris,' said Shelly.

73

'What? What? That's lasses over there, singing that. Why shouldn't I?'

'It's a private party,' said Shelly. 'Mind your own business.'

'What are you having, Chris, another half?'

'A pint in there, thanks, Tom,' said Chris, draining his glass and setting it down before him.

'Shelly?'

'Port and lemon.'

When he got back with the drinks, Chris and Shelly were going at it hammer and tongs. 'What's this about you'll not marry her, Tom?'

'Eh?'

'I said nothing of the kind, Tom,' said Shelly, turning pink. 'I just said it's perfectly possible to go out for a drink before your wedding without behaving like that, and if I did it – *if* I did it, I said –'

'Have you not done it yet then?'

'Leave it out, Chris.'

'Any advice you want from your uncle Chris –' The song changed. ' " – as she slipped between the lily-white sheets with nothing on at all!" Not embarrassing you, am I, Tom?'

'He's drunk. I'm going.'

'Sit down, Shelly.' She sat. 'Chris, if you –'

'I know when I'm not wanted, man.' He took his drink and lurched towards the hen party. 'If you want to get a bit of practice in before the big night, pet –' he said to the bride, who turned her back on him.

'We'll go in a minute,' said Tom to Shelly.

'Tom, I didn't say that, honestly I didn't.'

'Of course you didn't,' he said, but he wondered. He wondered if she wondered. He did not normally stay long enough with one woman for her to start wondering. This was partly because he liked variety and partly because it was not fair to them, to let them start wondering. He had no plans for getting married. He had a lot of living to do first, and a business to set up.

'It's much too soon for us even to think about getting married,' she said. It was obviously on her mind. What was that saying about protesting too much?

'Where's this youth club of yours, then?' he said.

From the height of the great iron bridge they could see it quite easily, cosily lit in the gaping darkness of the estuary, but it was hard to work out how they would get to it. They would either have to make their way through a series of fenced-off yards belonging to builders' merchants, or go through the recreation ground which covered the site of the shipyard where Tom's father used to work. They decided on the recreation ground, though Shelly was anxious. 'There was a lass raped here.'

'You'd better stick with me, then.'

To take her mind off weddings, he suggested stopping for a go on a swing. He held her on his lap as he thrust his long legs back and forth to make the swing rise higher and higher in the burning air. It was a low-slung swing and when it came down he had to be careful not to graze his feet on the ground. All the moving about made her squeal, though not, he thought and hoped, entirely with fear.

'Hey, Shell. Let's give the youth club a miss, eh? We can go back to my place. Auntie Pat will have gone by now. Eh?' he whispered, fondling her. The swing came down, she leaped off and he followed.

Access to the youth club was along a narrow gangplank. It was covered with sand but still slippery. A few other people were waiting to get on, and they had to take turns. Fast music thudded out from a group inside the barge, whose name, painted on the side, was RIDEEMUS.

The group sounded pretty second-rate to Tom's ears. They were probably friends of the manager's, and could not get gigs anywhere else.

'Have you got your membership?' asked the girl on the door, who was dowdy and plump with straggly hair and a long skirt and thick stockings.

'I thought it was free,' he whispered to Shelly.

'It is free, but we have to have membership,' the girl on the door explained. 'Fire regulations. The last thing we want to do is fall foul of the authorities, when we're only here to say hello to the young people of Sunderland.'

'Where have you come from?' Shelly asked politely.

'We were in Middlesbrough before, and Hull. We travel around and stay where we feel welcome, and we want to start by making *you* feel welcome.'

'Jesus,' said Tom.

'Jesus wants you to have fun,' said the girl with the straggly hair, nodding with great earnestness.

13

'Name? Address? Occupation?'

'Company director,' said Tom.

Shelly nudged him and looked as if she might contradict, but she herself was grabbed and questioned. Tom's interviewer (for that was what it was like, an interview) was a girl and Shelly's a man with a floppy jumper and spots.

'Company director, eh? You're doing well for your age, Tom.'

Further down the queue, someone was saying, 'A barman, eh? That must be pretty interesting, Bill.'

'Unemployed, eh, Terry? I don't suppose that's much fun. We'll have to see if we can help you through our Job Finding Project.'

Tom's interviewer called over: 'We've got somebody here who's a company director.'

'Oh *really*? Do you have any vacancies?'

'It's a family business.'

Shelly's look said: *That'll teach you to show off.*

'Didn't offend you by asking, did I?' said Tom's interviewer. 'We want to be of service to the young people of Sunderland.' She paused for a moment before saying Sunderland, as if she had had to work out where she was.

'What is this?' he muttered to Shelly as they walked towards the music. She took off her coat, put it on a bench and tidied her hair with her hands. He had been mistaken about the group: the music was coming from a tape which sounded home-made and out of date.

No one was dancing, and Tom did not fancy starting it off. The light was dim, but the effect was dreary rather than romantic. The place seemed bigger inside than out: like a barn. Drinks were being served: lemonade in plastic cups. 'What is this, Sunday school?'

'I don't know,' she said. 'This girl I met at the library said it sounded good.'

'Hang on a minute. An hour ago it was a friend of yours said it *was* good. Now it's just some lass you met in the library – '

'All right, Sherlock Holmes. She said it was free.'

'Come and have a drink,' said one of the organizers. 'Orange, lemonade, ginger beer – ?'

'Got any beer beer?'

'No alcohol, I'm afraid.'

'Jes . . . I know, I know. Jesus wants me to have fun.'

'I'll have a lemonade, please,' said Shelly.

'And your friend?'

'He'll have the same.'

Other couples arrived and stood around looking as bored and astonished as Tom felt.

'Aren't you going to ask me to dance?' said Shelly.

'Let's go and have a proper drink, Shell. We don't have to go home if you don't want to.'

'Leaving already, Tom and Michelle? We haven't said hello yet.'

'Hello.'

'Hello, my name's Judith. I've been with Rideemus for a year and I really enjoy travelling round the country and meeting other young people.'

'Are you something to do with the church?' said Shelly, trying not to giggle at Judith's earnest face and blind-as-a-bat glasses.

'Well, yes and no. We're a new group, though we are on good terms with the established churches. One thing we do believe in is having a good time; is it all right, Michelle, if I ask Tom to dance?'

He shot Shelly an imploring glance, but she giggled and gave him a push and there he was in the middle of the floor with Judith shifting gracelessly from foot to foot.

Shelly started dancing with a shaggy man in overalls.

Judith said, 'Do you come from a religious background? Do your parents go to church?'

'My dad's dead.' He did not normally volunteer this information to strangers.

'Oh, I'm sorry. Was it recent?'

'Come on, Shell. Dave and Angie'll be wondering where we've got to.'

If she said, *Who?* he would wring her neck.

'Well, we'll let you go – ' said Judith.

'Thanks.'

' – otherwise you'll say we kidnapped you. But you've got to come back. We're having a day conference on how young people can raise the spirits of a depressed town.'

'That sounds interesting,' said Shelly, with her hand in front of her mouth.

'Sounds great,' said Tom.

'Goodbye,' said Judith, seeing them along the gangplank. 'Laugh with the Lord.'

'Eh?'

'Laugh with the Lord,' said Shelly, and the two of them fled up the river bank in hysterics.

'All right, Shelly,' he said, when they had recovered. 'I give in. I'll never mention sex again. I'll not even think about it. And you'll never take me to have my soul saved – '

She shook her head, still laughing. 'I didn't know, Tom. Honestly. I didn't know that was what they were.'

'Are you sure? This wasn't your idea of a joke?'

'*No.* This girl at the library – '

'You can give her a punch on the nose from me.'

'Your face when Judith asked you to dance – '

'Yeah, all right,' he said. 'Come on, we're going home.'

' "I'm a company director," ' she said, mincing about, looking proud.

It was just after half past nine, which gave them a good hour, allowing for Shelly to get home by eleven. Given the choice he would like longer than an hour to spend on it, but they were not being given the choice.

'If the neighbours see us, will they tell your mam?' she said, as they climbed the icy steps to his flat.

'What if they do?'

'I hate all this skulking about. As if we were doing something wrong – '

'We'll not be doing anything wrong tonight,' he said heavily. 'She's still there.'

'Who?'

'Auntie Pat. The light's on. The bloody guard dog's still there.'

'Oh well,' said Shelly.

'She might've left it on for burglars.'

'We can go in and see.'

'Aye, but if she's there we can't just walk out again, can we? Once we're in, we're in.' He grabbed her hand desperately. 'We'll go to my workshop.'

'No, Tom –'

'What? I only want to show you my peacock fountain.'

'Your what?'

'Once it gets moving, there's no stopping it.'

'All right,' she said, following him.

He had worked all day on the peacock fountain, forgetting the dolls his mother wanted finished before her return, forgetting his half-finished colliery, in his fascination as he carved the bird and cut and bent the glass tubing, softening it in the flame of his gas burner.

His mother had promised to buy him proper power tools as soon as the business could afford it, but today he had been content, working as Ribson had worked.

Just before he went in for his tea, he had set the mechanism going in a trial run. It had worked. His heart had quickened at the realization that he had got it right, his model worked. The water went up and down in the siphon pipes, the peacock's tail opened and closed, the bird swung round in perpetual motion. . . .

But he had forgotten to stop it.

He should have poured the water away, but he had left it and it had frozen, frozen the perpetual motion into stillness. The peacock was stuck in an iceberg. He had not yet painted its face, but he could see it glaring reproachfully at him, its throat and its backside clogged with ice. He cursed.

Shelly said, 'Don't you have any heating in here?'

Carefully he picked up the water bowl with its burden of fragile machinery. He set it down on the paraffin stove. He lit the stove. 'Don't worry,' he murmured. 'We'll soon thaw you out.'

14

Oh, some sex at last, thought Teresa. *I haven't had sex since Christmas. As soon as Daphne shuts up about You Can Have It, I can go to my room and do exactly that. That is NOT WHAT I MEANT. It's not a commodity, it's not an IT, it's him, Sam, he's here, he's come to me when I thought he wouldn't, he's abandoned his deadlines and driven through the snow to be with me in a hotel because he thinks it's sexy for us to pretend we're having an affair.*

WHAT DID HE MEAN BY THAT? Why does he need scenery?

Hush, he's here. What stronger sign than that could I want, could there be? He's upstairs in my room waiting, raiding the fridge, pouring me a whisky and soda. He might be in bed with all his clothes off.

Or even the bath. GET ON WITH IT, DAPHNE.

'Nobody,' said Daphne, summing up, 'no salesman ever won an argument with a customer. The only time you should even contemplate contradicting a customer is when his Objection is based on a genuine and verifiable error of fact. Miss Heriot, for example, was told by the manager of this hotel that the acrylic sheeting that had been delayed in transit from Stalton's was of a grade unobtainable elsewhere. Miss Heriot was able to point out, politely, that the exact same material was available from her company, at a lower price.'

Gina grinned, showing her gums.

Oh jolly good show, Gina, thought Teresa. She was frankly awed by Gina's unquenchable enthusiasm for her pieces of plastic. If Teresa herself were to be involved in a road accident with a rival – she searched for an equivalent, the ad manager of *Marxism Today*, perhaps, or *Cosmopolitan* – and even if that person were to be beastly to her about it afterwards, si e doubted that her first impulse would be to go haring off after *Marxism Today*'s, or *Cosmopolitan*'s, lost business.

But then that was probably why Gina was what she was today – a high-flyer, if ever Teresa saw one – and why Teresa was what *she* was. *Still, high-flying isn't everything, you know, Gina. You may have stolen a customer from Stalton Industries, you may be all set for a bonus from your grateful boss . . . but is your lover upstairs waiting for you?*

'Acknowledge the Objection. Let the buyer know you hear him. And then what? Mrs York?'

Alice York stifled a yawn. They had been Dealing with Objections all day. 'Use questions to turn Objections into Benefits.'

'Can you give me an example of how you might do that?'

'Suppose I had someone who was interested in a villa but thought it was too expensive. I'd ask him how much he was expecting to pay. Then I'd subtract that from my asking price and point out all the Benefits he'd be getting for such a small amount.'

'Yes, good,' said Daphne, who appeared to be winding down. 'And if you can express the amount in terms of something he wouldn't think twice about paying for – a gallon of petrol a day, or a packet of cigarettes, if he smokes – so much the – yes? Did I see a question?'

'What if he can't afford it *at all*?'

Teresa was dumbfounded. All week she had been trying to screw up her courage to introduce the occasional question of ethics into the class discussions. Most of the time she had kept quiet, deterred by the apparent lack of interest in such matters. Wouldn't it have to be this evening that Ann Mitchison came up with a subversive question, fundamental and therefore time-consuming?

'Why would you be offering it to him if he couldn't afford it?' Daphne enquired.

'You might not know,' said Ann.

'Research Your Calls, Mrs Mitchison.'

'You *might not know*.' If indignation was making Ann brave at last, good for her, but did it have to be this evening? 'People keep up appearances. They might want nothing better than to buy a special toy for a bairn's birthday, but – look, I'm sorry to bring this up, and I know it's getting off the point, but where I come from – I mean, you might know you can talk them into buying the model if you try, but for all you know it's either that or new shoes.'

'Then it's up to you to be better than the shoe salesman, isn't it?' said Daphne.

Teresa tutted and let out a short, sharp breath. But that was all she did. She was not here to fight everybody's battles, was she? Soon they were dismissed to go to bed.

Oh God, he's so lovely, she thought, making the most of the moment before she would enter the room and see him. *I know I won't keep him for long, and I won't make difficulties when he finds someone his own age. I won't make a fuss as I turn into old friend and confidante.*

Maybe that's what he's come for, to tell me he's already found someone. He was with her last night and now he's come to tell me. OK, I'll say. OK, I understand. Let's have tonight and then that'll be it. And it won't be long before my hunger fades into what it was before, a wanting so faint that it hardly remembers what it was that it wanted . . . which is better, really.

The bedroom was empty.

He was in the bath, all six foot three of him, draped about like an octopus . . . or a rugby player. He had the build of a rugby player but he was not one, thank God. He made a modest gesture with a face flannel. 'I don't want any,' he said.

'Any what?'

'Whatever you're selling.'

'Tell me,' she said, perching on the edge of the bath. 'What *do* you want?'

'I haven't got any money on me.'

'You haven't got any anything on you, except soap.' He stood up and wrapped her in his long wet arms. 'You'll catch your death of cold,' she said. 'Let me dry you.'

He said, 'Yes, Mummy,' and she dried him.

'I'm dry now,' he said.

'Not quite.'

In the case of all bodily parts that they had in common, his were bigger than hers. This was unusual for Teresa, whose lovers in the past had tended to be of a build slighter than hers, and to say things like, 'Teresa, I love to curl against you.' Greg Sargent used to say that. Greg, in his day, had been a great curler-against, little squirt that he was. He, and others like him, had found it hilarious to ask to borrow items of Teresa's clothing – gloves, hats, slippers – and then declare them too big. There was none of that with Sam, the original giant panda. *Where did I GET him?* she thought, and she remembered: the Saturn Press Christmas party, at 20:17 hours precisely, he had come tipsily towards her through the crowd to say,

'I wanted to tell you. I love the way you say Gorbachev when you read the news.'

'You're never going to let me forget that, are you?' he said now.

'Not until you say something worse.'

'How about this?' he said. *Here it comes*, she thought. 'Can you lend me some money?'

'I knew it. How much? How long for?' To mask her relief she was pretending to be indignant. She was overdoing it, though, so that he would know she did not really mind.

'Ten pounds? Till next week?'

So I'll see him next week.

'What's mine's yours,' she yawned.

'Gee, thanks,' he said. 'Seriously, I'm sorry. I hate to do it.'

'That's a relief,' she said. 'Help yourself from Mummy's purse.'

It cost her nothing to make allowances for his age. She found an excitement in his urgent clumsy vigour that more than compensated for the satisfactions that a slower approach might have given her. He was insecure, though; he kept apologizing. 'Don't,' she said. 'I love . . .' *it? you?* ' . . . the way we make love.' 'But I keep thinking I'm not doing it right,' he said. 'There's no such thing as doing it right,' she told him. She wanted to add, *We've both got lots to learn and lots of time to learn it in*, but she did not want to presume upon his time.

They had brandies out of the fridge, and he said, 'How's the course?'

'What course?'

'Aren't you here on a course?'

'Am I? Ah yes, it's all coming back . . . what aspect of the course interests you most?' She gave him a bright smile.

He closed his eyes. 'I don't know, Teresa. I'm beginning to wish I hadn't asked.'

'Thing is, you should never answer a question until you've found out what the questioner wants to hear. I mean, you might say "How's the course?" and I might say "Very entertaining" and you might say "*Entertaining!* I'm not paying out good money to have my sales force entertained, that's what their wages are for." You need it, I've got it, you can have it, forget it.'

'Don't you have normal conversations any more?'

'Do you like having normal conversations?' She thought she had better stop this soon. She did not want to discourage this other endearing aspect of him, the way he always wanted to know about what she had been doing, and remembered what she said, this genuine curiosity that went beyond letting her speak until it was his turn again. She must not tease him too much, he did not seem to object but he might be seething inside.

'Get your *Atalanta* here!' he barked. 'As a special bonus this month all the pages are numbered consecutively – !'

'Oh shut up. We only did that once.'

'What, numbered them consec –'

'It's very positive,' she said, trying to be fair about the course. 'She starts from the premise that if it wasn't the best you wouldn't be selling it.'

'What? *Atalanta*?'

'*Atalanta*, anything. Your designs . . . seems to me the women's movement could do with a bit of that. Half-hearted entrepreneurs are always in the wrong. The devil's got all the best tunes.'

'The devil being Daphne Barclay?'

'Possibly . . . I haven't sussed her out yet. On the face of it she's a right pain, but there may be something deeper . . . that may be wishful thinking, but I'll tell you this. We could do with a few like her on our side.'

'I'm sorry I didn't come last night,' he said. 'Were you worried?'

'Me?' said Teresa, who had not slept.

'I had to finish a book jacket. Rush job.'

'You don't have to explain, Sam.'

'I know I don't, but I want to. It's awful when you're in love with someone and they don't turn up. You imagine all kinds of things . . . well, you probably don't, but I would.'

'I did,' she said.

'What did you imagine?'

'That you'd gone off me.'

'I haven't. Have you gone off me?'

'No.'

'Good.'

'Good.'

'What the hell are you doing?' she shrieked, waking in the dark, reaching for the light, and the phone. 'Oh . . . it's you.' She rubbed her eyes. 'Sorry . . . sorry, I . . .'

It was 6.00 am and he was half dressed. *Walking out, eh?* She had expected it. She had not expected to find him going through her handbag, though. She certainly had not bloody well expected that.

'But you said,' he said in bewilderment. 'You said help yourself.'

'Did I? Oh yes, I remember . . . you should have done it last night, I woke up and saw you and I thought . . . where are you off to?'

'I've got an early meeting. I want to miss the traffic. Didn't I say?'

She could not remember what had been said and what had not, except that he had said that he was in love with her. And now she had shouted at him for the first time. 'Is ten pounds enough?'

'Yes thanks, I just have to sort things out with Big S.'

'Big S, eh? I thought you said they were usually quite good about paying.'

'They are. They sent me a cheque for a hundred pounds for doing some layouts for them and it bounced.'

Teresa was wide awake. 'When did this happen?'

'I got the cheque back from my bank yesterday morning. Refer to Drawer. So now I'm overdrawn on my overdraft till I get – '

'Big S bounced a cheque? Jesus.'

'It's probably a mistake. Big S wouldn't do that.'

'They wouldn't do it on purpose. But what if their bank knows something we don't know and isn't honouring their cheques?'

'Going bust, you mean?'

'I mean just that. Half the left in London has been trading on Big S's good will . . . Jesus.' Teresa started to get dressed.

'Curtains to my hundred pounds, then,' said Sam. 'What are you doing?'

'My heart bleeds for your hundred pounds. *Atalanta* owes five thousand pounds to Big S.'

'Oh God . . . I didn't make the connection . . . you'll have to pay it.'

'We can't pay it. We haven't got it. If Big S have got the receivers in, they'll close us down too. Can you wait while I pack? I've got to come to London with you.'

'I wasn't going to Lon – sure, I'll take you to London, if that's where you want to go, but aren't you panicking?'

'Panicking!'

'Don't shout, you'll wake everybody up. Suppose you're wrong, suppose it's just a cockup.'

'Suppose it isn't!'

'Suppose it isn't, suppose you're right. Nothing's going to happen before Monday, and if it does, let the others take care of it. You do rather assume you're the only person who can handle – '

She was throwing things into her suitcase. He was trying to calm her down, she knew that he was being helpful and reasonable, if she wanted him to drive her to London he would miss his own appointment to do so. He just thought – he just wondered whether she might consider – that it was a bit silly for her to miss the last day of the course, which she had paid so much money to come on, when there might be nothing she could do in London, indeed, nothing that needed doing.

15

I'm going to tell her, thought Ann. *Free place or no free place. I'll speak my mind. Up to you to be better than the shoe salesman indeed.*

She doesn't know, of course. I'd pity her her ignorance if there weren't too much of that kind of ignorance, if it didn't do so much harm.

Tom was right about the train ticket. Well no, all right, it was kind of them to give me the free place and all my meals and I've no right to ask for more. No right to expect it. But he was spot on when he said that people like Miss Barclay have probably never heard of not being able to afford a train ticket. Never heard of having to think twice before buying a pair of new shoes for a bairn.

I'm going to tell her, and if she thinks I'm rude then that's what she thinks.

It was the last morning. Ann was packing before breakfast. In some ways the week seemed to have gone very quickly, yet her miserable arrival seemed years away. And the person she had been when she arrived was like a stranger. She had apologized to Gina for bringing her out, apologized to the class for disturbing them . . . she had been like a broken record, *sorry, sorry.* Well, Miss Barclay's crack about the shoe salesman had put a stop to that once and for all. By the time Ann had finished with Miss bloody Barclay, she would be the one to do the apologizing.

She went to the dining room for breakfast. All week she had felt uncomfortable at meal times. The hotel food was very good, she had never had such an opportunity to make a pig of herself and not count the cost. Sometimes, not feeling hungry, she had eaten little and

87

regretted the waste. But even when she had wanted to eat a lot, she had held back, and not just for the sake of her waistline either.

She had not wanted to appear to be taking advantage. She had not wanted to be thought of as a scrounger, a freeloader, the sort of person of whom it was said, *Give 'em an inch and they'll take a mile. They're never grateful.*

Ann was grateful all right. But there were limits.

She helped herself recklessly to muesli, kedgeree, croissants. She was looking for Teresa. Teresa had made a face last night when Miss Barclay had made her comment. She might be an ally. She might join Ann in her protest. It would come better from two of them. But Teresa did not arrive for breakfast.

Miss Barclay did not come to breakfast either, but then she never did. She did not seem to think that Ann and the rest of them were good enough to eat with. When should Ann confront her? The cowardly thing would be to leave it till the very end, and then there could not be any comeback.

Comeback? What comeback could there be? Ann had thought she might be in the running to win the competition – pretending to sell with START money – but that was childish. Might Miss Barclay withhold her diploma? Tom would laugh like a drain if that happened, particularly when he heard the reason. They could deprive her of her diploma . . . but she had been here, hadn't she? They could not take that away. She had learned what she had learned. She must have learned something, mustn't she, if she was sitting here now planning to tell Miss Barclay where she got off.

It's very important to me, she would say, *to make a success of my son's business. And I know that because I've been here. I'm going to be more efficient and more, what's the word, assertive. And I'm ready to work hard and make adjustments and push myself to do things I thought I'd never do. But one thing I will never do, Miss Barclay* (she would say) *is to use one of your hard-selling tricks on someone who wants what I've got to offer but can't afford it.*

That was what she would say. The only thing she had to decide was when. The session would begin in ten minutes. Miss Barclay would be in the conference room now, looking over her notes. Ann should go to her right away. She had finished her breakfast, so what was she waiting for? Miss Barclay was no older than Ann's daughter Debbie.

'Ann!' cried Gina. 'Where are you going, I want to ask you something.'

Ann sat down, relieved and furious.

'I certainly owe you,' said Gina, swallowing large mouthfuls of melon. Gina had no inhibition about going for the most expensive things. Once, standing behind Ann in the carvery queue at dinner, Gina had heard Ann ask for beef and had said, 'Spoil yourself, you can get beef at home. I'm having duck.'

'What do you owe me?'

'The other night, when we were in Teresa's room. If you hadn't mentioned about the swimming pool roof, I'd never have made the connection.'

'What – ?'

'It's like one of those legends, isn't it? When the hero goes off searching for something and then a wise old wizard points out that it's here, at home, under his nose.' Gina laughed. Gina laughed a lot, nothing knocked Gina off her perch. She was another one who got what she wanted by assuming she would get it. Ann smiled politely, hating herself. She had nothing to smile at. She had let the moment slip. She had been all keyed up to go and talk to Miss Barclay, she had let Gina distract her from doing it and now she knew she never would do it.

' . . . so in return,' Gina was saying, 'I'm going to buy one of your models. Really buy it, I mean, none of your funny money.'

' "In return?" '

'Well, no, not like that. I mean, I thought I would when you first showed it to me, that roundabouty thing – '

'As a favour?'

'No, of course not! I want it. I *need* it. I want to give it to my niece.'

'Thanks for your kindness,' said Ann. 'But I'm not in business to receive favours, and neither's Tom.'

'Money in a man's pocket,' began Miss Barclay, looking up from her notes at eight thirty precisely, as if the night had been a minor distraction, 'shows society's appreciation of his worth.' She started playing with a new set of gadgets. She had had gadgets for every session, flip-charts, videos, wired-up telephones. This time it was flat metal stick-men which she fixed to a magnetic board. Into the hand of one of the stick-men she put a flat bag marked '£'. 'When a man chooses to exchange that money for goods and services – ' The goods and services were represented by a box in the hand of the other man. Ann wondered what Teresa was thinking of all this *man* business, but her place was empty. ' – When a man *buys*

89

something – ' the box and the money bag exchanged owners ' – he is passing that appreciation on. He is saying to the other man, "I will contribute to your livelihood because you have provided me with what I need." '

Yes, but –

I must talk to her. I'll never forgive myself if I don't.

'What could be more moral than that?' said Miss Barclay, chilling Ann with the thought that she had read her mind. 'But the English language is hard on salesmen, hard on us. Sellout. Soft Sell. Hard Sell. Sold down the river. Sold his soul to the devil. None of the colloquial uses of the word "sell" are very flattering, are they?

'And if someone asks you if you've – ' Miss Barclay hunched her shoulders, nibbled an invisible cigarette butt and put on a working-class accent ' – "'eard the one about the travelling salesman", you know you are not about to be treated to a tale of honesty, social responsibility and sexual continence. Why is this, do you think? Why is the world so hard on us, this world that buys and sells all day every day to keep its lifeblood flowing? Ladies and gentlemen, I have been selling sales techniques to salesmen since I was fourteen years old and I am proud of it. I sleep well at night and hold my head high during the day and so should you. You are the breadwinners for the rest of society. Nothing happens until somebody sells something.'

There was truth in that, Ann supposed, grudgingly. Tom could make models till he was blue in the face but if she did not find customers for them they would have nothing coming in.

'Closing is a much misunderstood expression, and some of my colleagues in the sales training profession must take responsibility for that. Some sales training programmes might lead you to believe that Closing means this.' She produced a large mousetrap and sprang it shut on to her finger. Everyone winced. Miss Barclay smiled; she had only been pretending. 'The closing of a trap. To others it means this.' She opened the door and let it fall shut, pretending to turn a key. '*Closing* the door. *Closing* off of other options. Closing the means of escape. But that is not the START Selling way. We do not see customers as prey to be trapped or prisoners to be prevented from escaping. If they want to escape, we have not been doing our job. He needs it, you've got it, he can have it. And so we move on to Closing. Wait . . .' she said, as if they had all been about to go somewhere. Miss Barclay wrote 'CLOSE' on the flip-chart. 'Close,' she said, pronouncing it with a soft 's', speaking very quietly as if to Ann alone. 'Close, *cloze*. It's the same word, isn't it? Closing means bringing the buyer and the product close. Closing does not mean pre-empting the buyer's right to make his own decision. It is the final stage in a process whereby he finds that there is only one decision that he *can* make.'

Closing meant making the other person do what you wanted them to do. Ideally, that meant buying something. But you could not expect always to close on a sale, Miss Barclay said. In that case you must close on something else. If the person said they wanted to think about it, you must close on a promise that they would see you again when they had thought. If they said they wanted to talk it over with their boss or wife, you should close with: 'Would you like *me* to talk it over with your boss or your wife?' You must Always Be Closing, ABC. And you must ask for the order. If Miss Barclay had in her possession the amount of money lost by salesmen who did everything perfectly and then forgot to ask for the order, she could retire. And another thing. Once you had closed, you should keep quiet. Get the signature, take the money and then get out. Otherwise you might find yourself talking yourself out of the sale, like the shop assistant from whom Miss Barclay had once been all set to buy a rather expensive dress, until the assistant had said, 'The marks on the sleeve will come out when you wash it.' Miss Barclay had not noticed any marks. Ann sighed for the shop assistant, then she sighed for herself. Her huffy response to Gina's offer to buy the merry-go-round had been a perfect example of talking herself out of a sale. If Miss Barclay ever got to hear about it, Ann would be immortalized as a START Selling example.

16

The Simple Close, the Reflex Close, the Answer-a-Question-With-Another-Question Close. ('When could you deliver it?' 'When would you like us to deliver it?') The Alternative Close, the Might-As-Well Close. ('You might as well have some of these, mightn't you? Now that I'm here.') The Now-or-Never Close, the Double Bluff Close, the Double-Double Bluff, the Self-Fulfilling Prophecy Close for upwardly mobile customers. The I-Know-You're-Not-Going-To-Fall-For-One-Of-My-Closes Close, for use when selling to salesmen. The Old Pals Close, to be employed sparingly on people who owe you a favour, which should be everybody. 'The company's got a big push on this one, how about helping me out and taking a dozen . . . ?' Ann's arm was aching from writing all this down, but she had to. After coffee, they were going to practise.

She decided that she would apologize to Gina and let her buy the merry-go-round. (The I'm-Sorry Close?) When the break came she went to her room and fetched it out of her suitcase.

Crossing the lobby she met Miss Barclay who was carrying her own cup of coffee back towards the conference room. Without slowing her pace, Miss Barclay nodded at the merry-go-round and said, 'Charming. Charming, Mrs Mitchison.'

'Miss Barclay. Could I have a word with you?'

Miss Barclay stopped walking and looked back over her shoulder. 'Yes?'

'It's . . . a bit private.'

'You'll have to join me in the conference room, then, won't you?' She obviously did not like the idea of having her break interrupted, but Ann had done it now.

'It's about what you said last night.'

'I said a great many things.'

'About the shoe salesman.' Ann's heart was starting to fail her. She was regretting having brought the matter up. Miss Barclay would make mincemeat of her. So she was surprised by the level of firmness in her own voice. 'I mean,' she said, 'I mean, I'm not sure I understood what you meant, about what to do when you realize the person you're talking to can't really afford . . .'

Miss Barclay was examining the merry-go-round. 'It's exquisite,' she said. 'How did your son get his training?'

'He's self-taught.'

'You must be very proud of him.'

Ann had never seen Miss Barclay at such close quarters. She had noted how young she was, and had marvelled at her poise and confidence. But now she saw a sort of vulnerability in her: she was pale under her thin layer of make-up, and her eyes, though beautifully blue, were blank and clouded with tiredness. And she would be tired, Ann realized for the first time. She had been working all week, giving of herself, never resting except when she was sleeping and she did not look as if she did very much of that. Ann and her fellow delegates could let their minds wander; Miss Barclay must concentrate. Ann was reminded of her daughter Audrey when she had her first baby: her happiness had competed in her face with a sort of horrified disbelief that it was possible to be this tired and to have to keep on going anyway. Anyone who was that tired might let slip a tactless remark.

'It was about my son that I wanted to ask your advice.'

'I have no experience with sons, Mrs Mitchison,' said Miss Barclay, as if she wished she had. 'Or daughters.'

'You see – it's been so useful this week – '

'Has it? Has it really?'

'Oh yes. Everybody – '

'Never mind everybody.' Miss Barclay smiled with a touch of friendly impatience. 'Never mind them. Has it been helpful to *you*?'

'Too helpful,' said Ann.

'I had to fight hard to get you your free place, you know. There was no shortage of applications, but yours was the one I had the feeling about. Did you say "too helpful"? What did you mean by that?' Miss Barclay seemed curious rather than indignant.

'I've sold Tom's models before this week. But I've never been organized about it. Or determined. If people bought something, I'd think they were only doing it to be nice. If they said no, I'd feel I shouldn't have asked.'

'Never feel that. Don't ask, don't get.'

'I'm not going to feel that from now on. I can hardly wait to get home and put it all into practice. I feel I could go out and sell a hundred merry-go-rounds before breakfast. And that's the trouble, you see. I'm going to be selling them faster than Tom can make them.' This sounded like a complaint, disloyal. 'Tom's a perfectionist.'

'I can see that.' Miss Barclay was playing with the merry-go-round. 'But he can supply the designs, and you can get them mass-produced. That's the way employment is created.'

Ann should have known that Miss Barclay would say something like this. 'He'd be so hurt.'

'You're going to have to be a little bit tough, Mrs Mitchison. Forget he's your son. He's the production department.'

Ann sighed and decided to have another try at what she had been intending to say to Miss Barclay about the shoe salesman. 'The thing is, when people can't afford – '

'Have I thanked you for raising that point last night? It's so important. I was a bit surprised that no one objected to our little joke about the shoe salesman. Middle-class people can get very self-righteous about that kind of thing, can't they? To appreciate the gritty humour of the poor, you have to have known poverty yourself. And, well . . .' Miss Barclay closed the door and lowered her voice. ' . . . this is very unprofessional of me, I shouldn't discuss delegates behind their backs, but I think you and I are the only people on this course to have known poverty. I think the others are used to being comfortable, very comfortable indeed in some cases.'

'You mean Gina?'

'Let's not name names.'

'Sorry.'

'You and your son,' said Miss Barclay, 'people like you, people like *my* parents, who taught me everything I know about selling, though *they* never went on courses, free or otherwise . . . people like you will be the saving of this country. Thank you for coming on my course.'

'It's me should thank you.'

'Your success is the only thanks that I require. What was it that you wanted to see me about?'

'What?'

'I've been breaking my own rules and doing all the talking. You wanted to see me about something.'

Deeply embarrassed, Ann looked for a way to get out of the conversation. Her eye fell on the merry-go-round. 'I'd like to give you this.'

'That's very sweet of you, Mrs Mitchison, but I can't let you – '

' – it's a thank you present for letting me come on your course and for being so kind to me.'

' – it's one of your samples!'

'Of course, I'm sorry, I didn't think. I'll get Tom to make you one and send it to you. A new one.'

Miss Barclay laughed. 'Don't misunderstand me, I'm not offended that you should offer me a sample as a gift, far from it, I am more touched and moved than I can say. But the course isn't finished yet, you know. There may still be orders that you can take with it.'

'Sorry, I didn't think.'

'So you can give it to me at the end. How sweet of you.'

The coffee break was over and the others were drifting back. Ann took the merry-go-round to her place and sat down.

To practise Closing they were to get into twos. One was to be the salesman and the other a difficult customer. They could assume that the salesman had already done You Need It, I've Got It and You Can Have It. Now the salesman must ask for the order and go on asking in different ways until the customer gave it. Once the salesman had obtained the order, they should swap over, and then they must move on to a different partner. 'A bit like an Excuse-Me dance,' said Miss Barclay, who would be walking round listening.

Ann got Alice York as her first partner and easily persuaded her to buy a milk float. Ann just said, 'Would you like one?' and Alice said, 'Yes, please.' That was a Simple Close. Alice then told her that if she signed the forms right away she would get her villa at a special-privilege price. (The Now-or-Never.)

Ann felt like putting up a bit of resistance. 'There's not much point in me owning a villa if I can't get to it.'

'I'm glad you raised that point,' said Alice. 'We do, of course, have our own airline, with half-price flights for owners.'

One of the women from the pensions company was awaiting her turn and overheard this. 'Don't set foot in one of her planes without life assurance.'

'Get out, I'm in possession,' said Alice. 'Mile for mile, it's cheaper than the bus. How about time-share, two weeks in November?'

Ann said, 'November's my busy time.'

'You could let your staff use it in November.'

'What staff?'

'The staff who, if you had them, would free you to fly out to your villa in Lanzarote whenever you wanted.'

'If I had one.'

'If you had one. Come on, Ann, give me a break.'

Ann laughed. 'All right.'

'Two weeks in November it is, then?'

'November? No, I want it all the year round. I'm going to retire to it.'

Alice York moved on and Ann bought an old age pension for herself and set up lifetime savings plans for her grandchildren. She was starting to feel sad at the thought that it was nearly over, that she would probably never see these women again. And next week, the Closing, or not closing, would begin in earnest.

'This one'll be a doddle,' said Gina. 'I've already told you I want to buy that roundabout thing.'

'Well, what can I buy from you?'

'STOP!' cried Miss Barclay, passing. The room fell silent. 'I have just heard the most beautiful sound.'

Now what? thought Ann irritably.

' "*What – can – I – buy – from – you?*" Isn't that what we'd all like to hear? Wouldn't it be marvellous if we could hear that every day? But we don't, do we, and it's just as well from my point of view because if your average customer went about saying things like that, I'd be out of a job. Carry on.'

Gina said in a singsong voice, 'Daphne's made a funny. It's a bit end-of-termish today, isn't it? How about some polystyrene packaging for sending breakable stuff through the post?'

'The thing is, Gina, I'm sorry I flew off the handle before – '

'Don't mention it. Me and my big mouth.'

'And I'd love you to have the merry-go-round, only I've just said I'd give it to Miss Barclay.'

'What?'

'I'm sorry.'

'No need to be, it's yours, do what you want with it. I'll have something else . . . but what did you give it to Daphne for?'

'I don't know,' said Ann. 'I was just talking to her and I gave it to her.'

17

Yes, thought Gina, moving on to make a fool of herself pretending to sell pipe-grade PVC to Alice York in the hope of thereby enhancing the plumbing in her villas, *yes, you were just talking to her and you gave it to her. I was just talking to her on Monday night, informing her that no way was I going to turn out in the snow to pick you up from your phone box and next thing I knew I was picking you up.*

I know her type. Iron will and fluttering eyelids. In a world full of idiots you are the only person who understands me, now do me this little favour, would you?

Caveat emptor, *fair enough. That's the business Daphne's in, we're all in, and a mug's a mug. But* caveat donor *... What a dirty trick, she ought to be ashamed.*

'Hey, listen to this, Alice.' Gina told Alice what Ann had told her. Alice did not seem to see the problem. 'If she wants to give it to her ... I wonder if I'm supposed to give her a villa.'

'Well, that's the point, isn't it? She wouldn't freeload off *us*.'

'See what you mean ...'

'Ann can't afford to be giving things away.'

'If she's done it, she's done it.'

Gina put to Alice her idea, which was that there should be a collection to buy the merry-go-round from Ann. Then they could give it to Daphne as a present from all of them. Alice agreed and Gina moved on to the others, interrupting their Closing to make her suggestion. It annoyed Gina, to whom the course had been an insulting and infantile celebration of the obvious and the banal, to find herself in this role. But at least Ann's books would balance. When Gina presented the *fait accompli* to Ann over lunch, she did so with care and tact. She said that everyone was dreadfully upset that Ann had been the only delegate to think of giving Daphne a present. Ann would be doing them a favour if she let them contribute. Ann only hesitated a little before agreeing.

Daphne's valedictory address began with a kittenish admission. 'I'm afraid I've played a little trick on you. When I gave out the START Selling currency on Monday evening, I may have given the impression that there would be a prize for the person who traded with it most successfully. Well, you may keep the money as a souvenir of your week with us, but prizes imply winners, and winners imply losers, and the purpose of the game was to keep your minds on the matter in hand. On a START Selling course, we are all winners!'

'Prizes, prizes,' chanted Gina under her breath. 'We want prizes!'

'Before I take my leave of you and give you your diplomas, I want to tell you a little story. It refers to my own beginnings in the world of sales training. It refers to a remark I made earlier, which I was surprised nobody took me up on. I said that I had conducted my first sales training course at the age of fourteen. Did none of you find that surprising?'

We were struck dumb with amazement, Daphne.

'It's rather a sad story, but it has a happy ending. A girl at my school was involved in a terrible accident and was told that she would never walk again. We decided to rally round to buy her the best wheelchair on the market, to enable her to live as normal a life as possible.

'My father and mother – who together have been my inspiration and example throughout my life – came up with a marvellous idea. It was that the Parent Teacher Association should give – lend, I should say – a ten-pound note to each class in the school, for us to invest and trade with as we saw fit. A bit like that Bible story – '

'The Parable of the Talents,' said Gina, who had been educated at a convent.

'The Parable of the Talents as you so rightly say, Miss Heriot. Sadly the Parent Teacher Association was not in a position to offer eternal salvation as an incentive, but they did promise an engraved plaque. In addition, of course, we had the satisfaction of earning money to help a person dreadfully disabled at a tragically young age through no fault of her own.'

I'm going to be in tears in a minute, thought Gina.

'Well, what did we do? What *didn't* we do? We had jumble sales and raffles and garden fêtes; we were sponsored to do all kinds of things. My class were kind enough to elect me as business manager, and I decided that we would concentrate on baking and selling cakes. Isn't that a bit obvious?, I hear you say.' Nobody had said this. 'The best ideas are often obvious, they become obvious because they are the best. Not for nothing have hot cakes become a byword for easy selling. That was clear to me even then.

'I divided my class into cooks and salesmen. Salesgirls, I should say, we were all girls. I chose the best-looking, best-turned out girls to form the sales team. And I sent them out to local offices during their tea and coffee breaks . . . by prior arrangement, of course.'

Wearing their school uniforms, I suppose, to cheer up the dirty old men. Gina looked round for Teresa, whom she thought might appreciate a note to this effect, but Teresa was not there and Gina realized that she had not seen her all day.

' . . . Wearing their school uniforms, and spotlessly white domestic science overalls. And among the many things I told them was that they must not mention the fact that they were selling the cakes in aid of a good cause.

'Does that surprise you? It surprised them, but I told them I would be down like a ton of bricks on anyone caught soliciting donations. I have nothing against donations, but it wasn't the point. The point was that we had identified a need and now we were meeting it.

'You know how people in offices love cakes? You know how it's always somebody's birthday?' Daphne paused in her story to perform one of her little shows. She was a desperate salesman in a phone box trying to get through to his office: ' "Listen, they want four thousand of the Mark Twos but only if we can deliver today . . . " ' Now she was an office moron eating cake. ' "Don't bother me with that now, we're having tea . . ." Office workers *love cakes*. They *need* cakes. Without cakes they cannot function. That is why we in the sales force have to work so hard to support them. I *identified a need* and sent my team out to *meet that need*. And that, I think, is where we came in. Others in my school thought of selling cakes, but they restricted themselves to selling in the playground, whining about good causes. We got out of the playground and recognized that meeting people's needs is the only good cause there is. Where *is* Miss Beal?'

Nobody knew.

'Extraordinary,' said Daphne. 'I particularly wanted her to hear this too. Never mind. The end of the story is that we bought the wheelchair and our friend came back to school and has led a full life ever since.'

'Yes, but who won the plaque?' said Gina.

'Who do you think?'

Not you, Gina thought. *Otherwise you'd have said.*

'Get Out of the Playground, Believe In Your Buyer, Smile While You Dial and Always Be Closing. You Need It, I've Got It, You Can Have It . . . and remember to keep your fingernails clean.' From anyone else this would have been a self-parody, but Gina still was not sure how seriously Daphne took herself. 'It has been my privilege to train you this week. I see you all as successful salesmen, or salespersons I suppose I should say. The only thanks I require is that you should prove me right. . . .'

Gina rose to her feet. 'Before we finish, I'd just like to say, on behalf of everybody, thank you, Daphne, for a very stimulating week, and an entertaining one too. If you ever get sick of sales training, we'll all come and see you on the West End stage. And we'd like to give you this small token of our appreciation.' She presented the merry-go-round with great solemnity, adding firmly: 'From all of us.'

'From all of you?'

'From *all* of us.'

'How sweet of you,' said Daphne, and she handed out the diplomas, her lips tight with suppressed emotion.

'They've spelled my name wrong,' said Ann sadly, looking at her diploma. 'Mrs Ann Mickleston.'

Everyone was milling around in the lobby, saying goodbye, exchanging cards.

'Tell Daphne, she'll send you another one,' said Gina.

'It's probably my fault, I'd better not.'

'How is it your fault?'

'Well, there was a card in my room when I arrived and it said Mickleston. I didn't say anything, so I've only myself to blame.' Gina shrugged. It was none of her business but it seemed a pity: she doubted that the walls of the Mitchison home were adorned with all that many diplomas. 'How are you getting home? Can I drive you to the station or anywhere?'

'There's a bus to London from the end of the road at five.' It was twenty past four now.

'Someone'll drive you to London. Who's going to London? Ann needs a lift.' Several offers were forthcoming. Gina got Ann fixed up, then said, 'Listen, Ann, I've been thinking. Does your son take commissions?'

'You name it, my son'll make a model of it.'

'Great. That's what I thought. You know I call my bosses J.R. and Bobby? And you know J.R. has a model of a derrick on his desk?'

'A – ?'

'You know, that thing that looks like an electricity pylon. It's part of a drilling platform. You do watch *Dallas*?' Ann said that she did. 'Could he make something like that? I'd love to give it to Alex as a joke – a joke on him, that is,' Gina added hastily, fearing that she had once again said the wrong thing, 'because he loves to play the big tycoon. Could your son do that?'

'He'd love to do it. He doesn't know it yet, but he'd love to.'

'I'll pay you in advance,' said Gina.

'I don't know how much to ask you for. I'd have to get him to cost it. How big would you want it?'

'Just something to sit on his desk. Let me give you a deposit.'

'Well . . . he might have to get some materials. . . .'

'Sure. How about ten pounds?'

'Five,' said Ann.

'What kind of a Close is that? Let me give you ten, then if there's any change you can send it with the model.' Gina was glad she had made her peace with Ann – she was sorry to have offended her – and she did genuinely want to have the model derrick to give to Alex. They said goodbye and wished each other luck. Ann went off with the woman who was driving her to London. The car park was emptying rapidly, a flotilla of Ford Escorts and Volkswagen Polos heading out towards the bypass. Gina made one final visit to the swimming pool annexe to make sure that everything was all right with the acrylic sheeting which had arrived yesterday afternoon following her urgent phone call. 'You'll know who to call another time, won't you?' she told the foreman. 'Franson & Franson, Gina Heriot. Remember the name.' She decided she had better get going, she had friends coming round that night.

18

Gina lived in Hampshire, in a small bungalow in a village on the edge of the New Forest, bought on a mortgage with help from her parents when she left Oxford. She drove fast until she reached the forest, then slowed down on account of the ponies.

Patches of snow shone out through the trees; a dark mist was gathering like smoke. A sports car passed her on a bend, forcing her into the side of the road – *Jesus, not again!* She hooted her contempt. Night was coming down fast and she struggled not to be hypnotized by the small square of pale light ahead of her. She thought she saw feathers of new snow, but they might just be falling from the trees.

This was her first long drive since the accident. She had been all right when she had gone out on her abortive search for the farmer, possibly because she had been mischievously exhilarated by the idea of escaping Daphne and putting one over on Stalton Industries all in one go. Now, though, in familiar territory, driving became more routine and, paradoxically, more frightening. She hoped she would get over this. 'Your people are too clever to kill off the competition,' she would tell Oliver. 'Just scare us out of our wits so we can't drive.'

Pimple, the Dalmatian Gina shared with the family next door, flung himself at the car in an ecstasy of welcome. Sharing him had been a compromise between having no dog at all, and having one who must frequently be left alone or put in kennels. Lee, next-door's eight-year-old, had come up with the name Spot all by himself; but the adults had been unanimous that they could not bear the embarrassment of shouting 'Spot!' in a public place to a Dalmatian, so they had compromised on Pimple.

'Get down, you madman!' Pimple licked Gina's face, breathing out the smell of a boiled sheep's head. Julia, Gina's neighbour, did not approve of tinned foods, even for dogs. Julia was thirty-five, ten years older than Gina. Most of Gina's women friends were older or younger than herself. The people she knew of her own age tended to be men.

Pimple's feet were muddy and Gina had a lot to do, so she sent him back next door and let herself into her own warm home. Julia had been in, turning up the central heating and picking the post off the floor. It stood on the hall table in three exciting heaps, testifying, along with the wound-on tape of Gina's answering machine, to how greatly she had been in demand during her absence.

It was madness to have invited people round for tonight, but typical. They would be here in an hour. Gina switched on her routine. She lit the sitting room fire, which she had laid before setting out on Monday. Julia had taken a carbonade of beef out of Gina's freezer to defrost, and there was French bread, various sorbets and ice creams, and plenty of wine. Her friends were used to the makeshift parties she gave to welcome herself home after a week away. 'It's like entertaining when you've got decorators in,' she would say. 'Everyone thinks it's heroic of you to do it at all. They don't expect much, so they're not disappointed.'

She unplugged the answering machine and took it into her bedroom, to listen to while she changed and unpacked. She put a UB40 tape on as well, softly, for background.

'Gina? It's Mummy. Are you away? I suppose you must be. I didn't phone for anything in particular, just a chat, phone me some time, would you? The number is . . .' Good old Mummy, law-abiding to the last. The tape said, 'Please leave your number' so she did. Gina stopped the tape and went for a quick shower. She came back and put on a pair of black woollen culottes with silver buttons, wondering if she would need a jumper under her green silk top. It would spoil the profile . . . she left the jumper off, the silk might feel chilly against her skin at first, but the pleasures of her own hospitality always raised her temperature by a few degrees.

'Gina. Here's a voice from the past that you might not recognize at once. Sister Brede, dear; we're having a careers evening and we always like to have at least one old girl on the panel, so we wondered if you . . .'

Gina put out her tongue at the tape. She had done well at school, though she had not enjoyed the regimentation, the intimacy, the personal intrusions. If asked at the time, she might have said she liked school, there being nothing to compare it with; but she had adult life to compare it with now, and there was no contest. She caught sight of the tip of her tongue and felt embarrassed; pretending she had just been licking something from her lip, she tried to recall some specific grievance against Sister Brede, something to justify the childish gesture. She could not. All she could identify was a general, restrospective resentment of the way Sister Brede and her kind had appeared to stand guard over the limits of the possible, leaving their charges to find out for themselves that there was more. It was as if school had been a trap, from which Gina had only escaped by extreme cleverness and good fortune. An unworthy thought: Gina had had a damn good education, Sister Brede had known what she was about. She was (or had been, at least) the only nun in the community with scientific training. She had supervised two young lay teachers, both of them male. When Gina went by the school at weekends, she often used to see lights burning in the science block. This would be gleefully reported back to the other girls on Monday, and there would be speculation as to which of the two young men Sister 'Fast' Brede had in her clutches. Gina knew now that it was much more likely that the nun regarded the labs as her private territory (a thing she was not supposed to have) and fled there to escape the snobbery of people who flaunted their ignorance with pride, who gushed, 'Oh, you're so clever. No, no, *you* change the plug. I don't know a *thing* about science.'

Gina got this too, of course. She had had a lot of it at university from friends who were doing arts courses . . . sociologists. Gina used the term 'sociologist' indiscriminately of all adherents of the liberal arts and the humanities. *I don't know a THING about science.* Her reply to that – usually unspoken – was: *How can you bear to be alive, then? The question split into other questions: How can you bear to drive your car, fly in aeroplanes, squeeze detergent into your washing-up bowl or do up your parcels with Sellotape without knowing – asking – wondering – where all these conveniences come from? How can you use words like pollution and additive in self-righteous tones when you hardly know what the words mean?*

Did the Friends of the Earth and people like that light their offices with candles? Did back-to-nature hippies abhor the use of personal stereos? How could they cop out of the marvellous world in which, like it or not (and they did like it, whatever they said) they lived?

It would be amusing to go back to school as an honoured adult.

' . . . let me know as soon as possible, please, dear. If you are otherwise engaged, we'll find someone else.' Gina chuckled. What

Sister Brede meant was: *Don't think you're indispensable, dear. Just because I want you to do something for me but can't force you, don't get too big for your boots. Don't imagine that the world revolves around you!*

The charge of imagining that the world (or possibly just the school) revolved around oneself used to be an all-purpose snub, a response to offences ranging from lateness or talking to gum-chewing and theft. The other girls treated it as a bit of a joke, using it on each other, but Gina used to have a peculiarly deep dread of it, and so had been a good girl and worked hard. And she had received her reward, three excellent A levels and a place at an Oxford college which had desegregated itself just in time to receive her.

Sister Brede's message was repeated three times on the tape, with increasing irritation. Gina felt nagged. 'I'm grown-up,' she said aloud, putting on eye shadow. 'You can't talk to me like that. I've got my own house.'

How could she have her own house? She was fifteen and Sister Brede could talk to her in any way she chose. The brittle voice on the tape had rolled ten years away like magic.

'Miss Heriot, this is Alan Morant from Kingston Personnel. We met last June at the ECN do. There's something I'd like to talk over with you, will you call me this evening?' Gina remembered no Alan Morant, but Kingston Personnel sounded interesting. Was she being head-hunted? She had heard of it – furtive phone calls to one's home number, mysterious references to 'one of our clients' – but it had never happened to her before. As a final-year undergraduate she had been short-listed by ICI but ultimately turned down by them. She had consoled herself in her disappointment with the knowledge that a small company like Franson & Franson would be a useful source of experience. Had ICI now seen the error of its ways? Well . . . she would take her time over her decision.

'Gina *dear*. I am trying to finalize the programme for the careers evening.'

Pure perversity, thought Gina. *She thinks it's out of pure perversity that I haven't got back to her.*

'Alan Morant again, Miss Heriot. I take it you're away, but I'll hope to hear from you soon.' He had left his home number, but she resisted her curiosity; her guests could arrive at any time, and it would not create a good impression if she had to interrupt Alan Morant to welcome them. She tapped out the number of the convent on her phone. A voice she did not recognize told her that Sister Brede was unavailable. Gina imagined her pottering around her labs in the quiet of Friday evening, having left instructions that she was not to be disturbed. She had once told Gina (in Gina's final term, when such confidences were permitted, it being too late for subversive use to be made of them) that she allowed herself on occasions to miss her religious devotions because she regarded scientific study as an act of prayer. 'We seek out the mind of God behind matter. The tide of secular science has turned, Gina; even committed materialists are now admitting that there are things that reason alone will never explain. . . .' Fine, but the explanation did not have to be God, did it? Not the God Sister Brede worshipped. Sister Brede believed what she had to believe; it would be unbearable for her if, as old age approached, she found one of the disciplines of her mind explaining away the other.

Gina left a message that she would be delighted to speak at the careers evening. She hung up without clarifying whether the arrangement need be confirmed. Sister Brede had threatened to look for someone else . . . but Gina's knowledge of what her contemporaries were doing, as listed in the Old Girls' Newsletter, told her that there was no one as suitable as she was. She wrote the date in her diary.

A hand cupped her breast; another had her by the shoulder and was forcing her round. She screamed and turned: 'Don't *do* that!'

'Sorry, I thought you'd have heard me come in.'

'You said you might not be coming.'

'I said I'd do my best. Oh God, Gina, I *am* sorry, it was meant to be a joke. Look, you'd better sit down, your heart's going like a – '

She dashed Oliver's hand away. 'A joke! Why do you think it's funny, why do you think it's clever, you know I'm scared of people breaking in – ' She let him take her in his arms, but delayed the moment of yielding to the sensations of softness that the shock and relief had given her. He was due for more punishment before she let him see how pleased she was that he was here. He was an inch shorter than she was, and twenty-eight days younger, but he could still baby her. His body was thin, but wiry and hard from the tensions of his job at Stalton's and the frequent squash games that he hoped were a remedy. He was much more of a worrier than she was. He said this was because managing people was more difficult than selling things. But this, in Gina's view, was sociologists' talk. She was just more relaxed by nature, when people were not trying to kill her, or pretending to. She was not relaxed now. She continued to tell him off, though she wanted to stop. He smelled of offices and petrol, cigarettes and sweat. He was tired, and his face was pinched with repentance over his thoughtless trick.

'You can give back your key.'

He fell to his knees. 'Oh Gina. Not that.'

'Well. You can lay the table, then.'

He agreed at once, which relieved them both. 'How many for?'

'Six.'

'The whole gang, then.'

'Six people are not a gang. You might not have come. You know I like to whoop it up on Fridays.'

'Yes, but I wanted to be alone with you. . . .' He glanced at the answering machine. 'Anything interesting?'

'Few things. What are you smirking at?'

'Pleasure at seeing you.'

'What's going on?'

'Does something have to be going on just because I ask if you've had any messages?'

'It's not your people, is it? Oh, go on. I'm not being head-hunted by Stalton Industries?'

'It's not that funny.'

'It is, it is, wait till I tell you . . . it's really you, is it?'

'My lips are sealed,' he said.

'Oh, come on. You have to tell me.'

'I'm keeping right out of it. Politics. I heard the petroleum products division were looking for somebody and I told them you were the obvious choice, if only because you keep pinching our customers. They said, "If we decide to approach her, we'll use our usual agency, Oliver." Pompous twits. Do you like the idea?'

'I think it's hilarious.'

'They are looking at other people, of course,' he said, hurt.

Gina went to the kitchen to finish getting ready for her guests. *Stalton Industries, all is forgiven.* She felt as exhilarated and proud as if the job had been offered to her and she had accepted it. Fond though she was of the Franson brothers, she had never seen them as more than a stepping stone. She laid the table. Oliver was having a shower. When he emerged she said, 'What would *you* feel about it?'

'Great,' he said. 'Stalton's have finally noticed the date and they're quite good about couples. Try to move them together, and so on.'

Gina was grinning into the oven. 'Even unofficial couples?'

'Well, if you hadn't invited the world and his wife to come round this evening . . .' The door bell interrupted him. Gina went to welcome Julia, Terry and Pimple from next door. 'He insisted on coming, sorry about the feet,' said Julia, meaning Pimple.

'Go in and get warm,' Gina ordered. 'We'll be with you in a minute.' She raced back to the kitchen. 'You were saying?'

'You want it now?'

'Yes.'

'Would you like to get married?'

'You mean if I get the job?'

'No, you twit. Anyway.'

'Yes.'

As soon as all the guests had arrived, Gina and Oliver made their announcement. They were roundly told off for not having said in advance that this was the occasion. Terry said, 'Haven't we got some champagne in the fridge?' and Julia went next door to fetch it.

I've Got It

19

'Let's give ourselves a round of applause for being here!' cried
Daphne to a roomful of taxi drivers a few miles from the Donian
Hotel where she had just finished START Selling – Women!

This was her evening class. She called it that to herself, though
it was late afternoon, really, before the drivers' busy time. It was a
little freelance job. Strictly speaking, START Selling employees were
forbidden to freelance, but Daphne was not bothered about that.
The job had arisen out of a recent incident when, her own car being
out of commission, she had travelled to the Donian by train and taxi.
On arrival she had been surprised by the failure of her driver to
offer her a card. She had telephoned the taxi company's head office
to express her surprise. She had suggested that the company's drivers
might benefit from sales training. The company had balked at the
price of a residential week, but had come to a private arrangement
with Daphne for a single evening.

'And we'd like to give your customers a round of applause for
getting there too, wouldn't we?' she ad-libbed. 'But they won't get
there, will they, if you sit there yawning like that. What goes up must
come down,' she beamed forgivingly. 'And anyone who goes to a
hotel in a taxi will sooner or later leave in one. Whose will it be?
Let's make sure it's yours.' She spoke for two hours on promptness,
courtesy, card-giving, helping with luggage, smoking and the importance of guarding one's tongue when conversing with colleagues over
the two-way radio. 'You may think it's amusing to hear old George
refer to his previous passenger as a miserable old bag, but what
impression is that going to make on *your* passenger?' She explained
about probing, polite, persistent, pertinent questions. 'If the question

can be answered in the negative, do not ask it,' she said. 'It's not, "Would you like me to collect you and take you back?", it's, "What time would you like me to collect you?" '

The cab drivers sat stunned, tired, she supposed. (What did they think *she* was?) They would have done better to come on a full course but there it was. A mean employer was a mean employer, a false economy a false economy. She set them some role-play exercises but they performed sullenly, refusing to enter into the spirit. Her own spirits fell, she watched the clock. She collected her fee and left.

Daphne was entitled to two Executive Weekends per year at the Pastures New Health Farm, at her employers' expense. Discovering this when she joined the company, she had resolved to save up her weekends for the summer, but when they told her that she would have to teach START Selling – Women! she had decided to have one after it, to give herself something to look forward to.

'We expected you earlier, Miss Barclay,' said the receptionist when she arrived.

Daphne offered no explanation. She smiled and waited for her key.

'Your employer said you'd be here by six thirty. You've missed your consultation, I'm afraid.'

Daphne felt herself drawn towards sarcasm – at £100 a day plus VAT clients should know better than to inconvenience staff – but she decided not to bother. 'Don't disturb the consultant now,' she said. 'I can see him in the morning.'

'Do you have any smoking materials with you?'

'Just my hookah,' said Daphne, who did not smoke. 'My pipe.'

'Any foodstuffs or alcoholic beverages?'

'No.'

The receptionist, a clear-skinned girl of about twenty, looked playful. 'And what have you got in your briefcase?'

What did she suppose, fish and chips? 'Company papers.'

'We do ask guests,' said the receptionist, 'not to do any work during the Executive Programme.' She pointed to a row of locked boxes. 'This is your personal safe and I'm going to ask you to leave your briefcase in it. The safes are supervised at all times. You keep one key and the manager has the other.'

Astonished into obedience, Daphne handed over her briefcase. 'How do you know I haven't got yards and yards of computer printout in my other bags?'

The receptionist smiled, showing the best set of teeth Daphne had ever seen outside her own mouth. 'We know that you know that it is in your interests to participate fully in the programme. If you cheat, you cheat only yourself. And there's this letter for you.'

The biter bit, thought Daphne in amusement, for was that not exactly what she had said, in different words, to Gina Heriot when she had wanted to play truant? A porter appeared and wheeled her luggage away on a trolley. She did not like leaving her briefcase, but she had done it now. She had not actually been intending to do any work over the weekend – apart from writing up her course report and one or two other small things – but it was just as well to keep temptation out of her way. What she needed was a complete rest. She followed the porter, glancing at her envelope as she went. She did not recognize the handwriting, or the rich black ink which gleamed as if it were still wet; but it must be something to do with work, for nobody else knew she was here. The postmark was London.

Pastures New seemed to be like a hotel, more luxurious than the Donian and a good deal cosier. But then a Salvation Army dosshouse might seem cosier than the Donian that Daphne had just endured, with all the banging about and mess and not being able to go for a swim. It was no wonder that she felt so tired, after a week without proper exercise. She had made her displeasure clear to the Donian manager (or rather the under-manager, the manager being on leave) and intended to include in her course report a recommendation that START Selling send a firmly written complaint. In the meantime she would make up for her swimless week with long sessions in the Pastures New pool, which she glimpsed through a glass door on her way to her room.

Also on her way to the room she saw a number of people wandering about in dressing gowns and slippers, which she found odd. Warm and informal the place might be, but one had one's dignity. *It's like a hospital*, she thought. *A hospital for people who aren't ill.*

Dear Miss Barclay,

Finding myself unexpectedly in London this week, I had hoped to have the opportunity of meeting you personally to express, on behalf of START Selling International, a warm welcome to our world-wide community of professional sales trainers.

My disappointment at finding you out of town is equalled only by the satisfaction it gives me to know that only a short distance from where I sit writing this letter, you are giving of yourself deeply and with dedication in pursuit of our shared goal: the spreading of the START Selling message throughout the business community of England and ultimately the world.

This knowledge fills me with personal warmth.

Will you give me your permission to pay a brief visit to the Pastures New Health Farm when you are there at the end of the week? In considering your answer, please believe me when I say that I claim no right to intrude upon your leisure. It is as a fellow human being that I request the opportunity to initiate what I sincerely hope will be a lifelong friendship between us, rather than as world president of START Selling International.

Cordially,

J. LINDBERGH STANLEY.

But for the fact that the letter was handwritten, it could have been done on a word processor, with all the appropriate gaps filled in. Daphne blew a quiet and delicate raspberry. These people, with their long sentences. *Personal warmth. Deeply and with dedication.* Still, the letter was personal to her and it pleased her. *Will you give me your permission?* She wondered what she was supposed to do if she did not give her permission, not that there was any question of that. *As a fellow human being.* What nonsense. Nice nonsense, but nonsense for all that. If Lindbergh Stanley wanted to see somebody, he saw them. *A fellow human being.* What else would he be?

A concept, Alistair had called him once. Alistair was Daphne's immediate boss; he had recruited her. *Lindbergh Stanley's not a man, he's a concept.* This remark of Alistair's referred to the fact that in fourteen years at START Selling UK, Alistair had never met Lindbergh Stanley. Presumably he had now, so that would make him happy. It was just Daphne's luck to have been away when the world president made one of his rare visits. Luck? Luck nothing: it was deliberate, she was convinced of it. Alistair was her friend but everyone else at START Selling UK was bitterly jealous of her and would have seen to it that she was not around when Lindbergh Stanley was, lest she outshine them in his eyes. *Well, eat your hearts out*, she thought. *He's coming to see ME.*

The monthly bulletin of START Selling International often carried reports of Lindbergh Stanley's tireless visiting of his subsidiaries throughout the world and messages from him (warmly congratulatory, or gently but firmly disappointed), but she could not recollect ever having seen a photograph. This alarmed her slightly, for how would she recognize him? He would introduce himself, of course. He had not said when he would come, so he would not expect her to be waiting. He would ask for her at reception and she would be fetched from wherever she was. This thought alarmed her more deeply, for what if he had already been here? What if, expecting her to come direct from the Donian after START Selling – Women!, he had been asking for her while she was giving an unofficial freelance session to the cab drivers?

The receptionist would have said. . . .

Unless she had been told not to, by a Lindbergh Stanley made furious by the unaccustomed experience of finding that one of his employees was not where she was supposed to be. . . .

Seriously worried now, Daphne decided to telephone Alistair at home. He would be able to advise and reassure her. If he had been with Lindbergh Stanley during the week, he would know something of his plans. Daphne looked round the room for a telephone, but on the bedside table where it ought to be there was only a bunch of flowers and a notice, taped down under a sheet of plastic.

In line with our policy of providing a complete break from work-related stress, we have removed telephones from the rooms of guests taking part in the Executive Programme. Thank you for your co-operation.

20

A note found under her door when she woke in the morning regretted that it was not possible to bring her any breakfast until it had been established what diet she was on. If she would care to make her way to the consultants' reception area, she would be seen as soon as possible.

She had had a disturbed night, with Lindbergh Stanley appearing to her in various incongruous and anxiety-provoking guises, and she was relieved when her consultant turned out to be a woman.

'What is your goal in coming to Pastures New?'

'I've had a difficult week,' said Daphne. 'And now I want a complete rest.'

'Active rest,' said the consultant, 'is what we are all about.' She took Daphne's blood pressure and a brief medical history. Brief it could only be: Daphne was never ill. She wondered what the consultant's qualifications were for doing all this. Anyone could wear a white coat and call themselves a consultant. Daphne was a consultant herself.

'Any specific health problems?'

'I hear a lot about burnout,' said Daphne. 'It worries me.' She said this because she guessed that it was what the consultant wanted to hear. She guessed that if she were to complain of a real ailment requiring real treatment, the consultant would be rather put out. Burnout was not, in Daphne's view, a real ailment. It existed, if at all, as an excuse for incompetence, like PMT or dyslexia.

'You don't look as if you need to worry about that,' said the consultant. 'Do you have plenty of hobbies? What do you do when you're not working?'

'I swim,' she said. 'I go to see my parents.' She smiled. 'I go to health farms, when I get the chance.'

'Hop up on the scales.'

Daphne awaited the consultant's verdict with interest. By every standard known to her, she was underweight. But since the tariff was an inclusive one, it was obviously in the interests of Pastures New that she eat as little as possible.

'We'll put you on a cleansing diet.'

Bravo, thought Daphne. *I must remember that one.*

'And your masseuse will do something about your thighs.'

'I beg your pardon?'

'Well, your weight's fine but it is rather in the wrong place, isn't it? Have you tried Celluluze?'

'Is it included?' said Daphne suspiciously.

'No, it's extra.'

Daphne turned it down with relief. For a moment she had thought that the consultant had been giving it as her professional opinion that Daphne had fat legs. Now she realized that the consultant had simply been trying to sell her something. The consultant moved on to describe the various treatments and facilities that were included in the programme. After breakfast, Daphne could have a blanket wrap followed by her massage. The gym was at her disposal, as were the swimming pool, the weight-training room, the tennis court, the golf course and the jogging track. There was croquet, yoga, eurythmics and relaxation. 'And conversation,' said the consultant finally. 'A change is as good as a rest, and one of the things we pride ourselves on at Pastures New is the wide cross section of society from which our guests come. We have a special Executive Programme – '

'Yes, I – '

' – for tired businessmen, and one thing we tell them is that they mustn't get into a huddle and talk to each other. They must *mix*, so if a strange man sits at your table at lunch, that's what he's doing: mixing. Oh.'

Daphne waited.

'I see you're on the Executive Programme yourself, Miss Barclay.'

'I would have mentioned it if it had occurred to me that you didn't know.'

The consultant became defensive. 'We do usually see executives on the Friday evening when they arrive. We do ask employers to send them in time for that.'

'Is it back to square one, then?' Daphne asked.

It was not. The real source of the consultant's embarrassment turned out not to be her failure to identify Daphne as the sort of executive to whom employers thought it worthwhile to give perks of this kind, but the resultant necessity of admitting that there was no Executive Programme as such.

'You mean everybody's programme is the same?'

'On the contrary, Miss Barclay, everybody's programme is individually tailored to –'

'But the Executive Weekend is purely a marketing concept?'

'You'd be very much mistaken to think that, Miss Barclay, we –'

'There's nothing wrong with it,' said Daphne. 'I think it's a very good idea.'

She was given a slip of paper that said she could have half a grapefruit and a bran biscuit for breakfast. These could be served in her room if she liked, but she was up now so she went to the dining room instead. It was empty except for a waiter whose badge identified him as Gary and a man in a tracksuit drinking coffee.

Daphne sat at the next table, and she and the man in the tracksuit exchanged smiles.

'Daphne Barclay, START Selling,' she said.

'Now, now, none of that,' said Gary.

'I beg your pardon?'

'At Pastures New we're not START Selling or Marks & Spencer's or Metal Boxes . . . we're just ourselves.'

'I'll have my breakfast now, please,' said Daphne, giving him the slip of paper.

'Scouts' honour you won't talk business while I'm gone?'

'Load of bollocks,' said the man in the tracksuit. 'Saving your presence.' He flapped his wrist. ' "Scouts' honour you won't talk business while I'm gone?" ' Bill Groves, Groves' Breweries. What kind of selling did you say you were?'

'Sales Techniques and Resources Training. START Selling.'

'Well, if I haven't started yet, it's too late now,' said Bill Groves.

'What makes you say that?' said Daphne, trying to remember something she had heard or read about Groves' Breweries recently.

''Morning, Roderick,' cried Gary along the corridor to an unseen person as he brought Daphne's breakfast.

'That looks like food to me,' said Bill Groves. 'Have you got friends in high places or what?'

Daphne started on the grapefruit and offered Bill Groves the biscuit which he ate furtively. Daphne herself was not very hungry.

An enormous boy in a towelling wrap appeared in the doorway, clutching a box and a board. 'Chess, anyone?' The high-pitched unbroken voice came grotesquely from the huge, misshapen body.

'Chess?' roared Bill Groves. 'It's not chess you need, Roderick, it's twenty laps round the jogging track.' He went over to the boy and started punching him, quite hard, Daphne thought, but Roderick made no attempt to protect himself or escape. 'Look at all this stuff! If you're five pounds lighter by this evening I'll see about playing chess with you.' Roderick shrugged and shuffled off with his box and his board. Bill aimed a kick at his rear end. 'We're old mates, me and Roderick. He's always here.'

Daphne had never before had, or heard of, a blanket wrap. Now that she was having one, she wished she had held out for a sauna instead. In a sauna, the sweat ran off you. Here she lay in a pool of it, immobilized in hot electric blankets and sheets of polythene. What if Lindbergh Stanley were even now asking for her at reception? It would take ages for her appearance and morale to recover from this.

'How are you feeling, Miss Barclay?' asked Sue, who wore a white overall and at whose elbow there was a telephone, a telephone with an outside line unless Daphne were very much mistaken.

'Trapped,' she confessed.

Sue loosened the blankets. 'Better?'

'A bit, but . . . well, to be honest, I feel slightly hungry.'

'I'll turn you down.'

'If you could just fetch me one of those bran biscuits?'

'Thing is,' said Sue, 'if guests don't lose weight, we get into trouble.'

Daphne spoke firmly to Sue, who scurried off. Daphne started to haul herself out of her wet, sticky cocoon, which retained her shape even after she had left it. She picked up the receiver of the telephone and started to dial Alistair's home number. It would be odd to talk to him without any clothes on.

She did not get to the end of her dialling. A voice said, 'Switchboard?'

Daphne smiled with wry submissiveness at the invisible operator and crawled back into her blanket wrap. She was only just in time: Sue returned with the consultant, who said, 'Your diet has been carefully worked out to meet your needs, Miss Barclay. Please don't ask staff to encourage you to break it.' Daphne closed her eyes as if she had no idea what the consultant was talking about. Five minutes later, Sue unwrapped her and sent her off for a cold plunge.

*

She guessed that golf would be a popular activity among her fellow executives, so she signed up for it. But when asked what her handicap was, she was forced to admit that her experience of golf was limited to crazy golf in the recreation grounds of childhood. She was given a personal lesson by the PE instructor who kept saying 'Good. Very good.' Daphne did not feel very good, she felt clumsy and suspected she was not being properly taught. It was important for a teacher to be encouraging, but that did not mean praising what was not worthy of praise. She decided to perform a stroke deliberately badly, to see what he would do. 'Good,' he said, smiling vaguely. 'Very good indeed.' A group of men were returning from distant holes, deep in conversation. Daphne was looking forward to lunch time.

She found herself at a table with two housewives and the daughter of one of them. The housewives were discussing illnesses, and the merits of different remedies.

'In Russia they chew sunflower seeds, in America they chew gum. In Russia hardly anyone wears glasses, but nearly all the Americans do.'

'That's because the Russians can't afford glasses,' Daphne explained, but there was no stopping the housewife and her theory: 'There must be something in it.' She changed the subject. Referring to her daughter who sat gnawing the stalk of a cherry, she said, 'She's losing it more quickly than me.'

'Well, but she's got more to lose,' said the other housewife.

'She's on a harder diet than me. I can have a baked potato tonight if I'm good. She can't.'

The woman who was not the girl's mother said, 'Is it very painful for you?'

The girl said nothing. The mother answered for her: 'She might as well get used to it.'

Daphne could not understand this obsession with food. After her week at the Donian she was grateful for the opportunity to cleanse her system. She finished her own small but satisfying meal and pushed back her chair. 'I'm off for a swim,' she said, and went to sit with Bill Groves and his friends. She was disappointed to find them gossiping about the other guests.

'Place is full of Arabs.'

'Where?' said Daphne, who had seen no Arabs.

'Oh, they don't eat with us,' said a man called Tim Clark, who worked for a bank. 'They don't have anything to do with us, they think we're unclean, they have a special wing. Unclean! See that woman in the jacuzzi this morning in her pyjamas?'

'The Sultana, you mean?' said Bill Groves.

'I wouldn't mind a sultana myself,' said Tim. 'Or a currant. How are you doing, Daphne? Have you cracked yet?'

Daphne found all this talk remarkably childish. The nearest town was only two miles away; if they wanted more to eat than they were getting, they could go there. If she herself decided to go there – to buy food, or to make a phone call – nothing would stop her. She would not leave, of course, lest Lindbergh Stanley arrive in her absence, but that was her personal decision. People seemed to regress here: to behave as if they enjoyed the idea of being children under the rule of a strict nanny.

'I do already know how to swim,' she told the instructor who was on duty at the pool.

'Just do lengths, then.'

'Isn't there a clock?'

'It's ten past two.'

'Not that sort of clock. A timing clock, to pace myself.'

'Take it easy,' said the swimming instructor. 'Try not to be competitive, not even with yourself. You're away from all that now.' Daphne started to swim up and down. It was probably just as well that she could not time herself. The swimless week at the Donian had stiffened her limbs, the results would be disappointing. At the shallow end, Bill and Tim and the other men were being taught how to swim. Daphne found it difficult to believe that they did not know already. She supposed that, given the chance of having their limbs moved into correct positions by a blonde instructor with a good figure, they had forgotten.

'Don't overdo it,' the instructor advised Daphne, when the men were all holding on to the bar to kick their feet. 'Have you ever learned survival floating?'

'What is it?'

'It's a technique for self-preservation in case you're shipwrecked, or fall out of a plane.'

'I'd better learn it at once.'

'Without a life jacket, right? You might think the best thing is to lie on your back or tread water, right? Wrong. All you'd need is to have a wave break in your face when you're breathing in, panic, and curtains. This way you control your breathing and only breathe when you decide it's safe. It's very relaxing.'

Daphne found it difficult rather than relaxing. She was expected to hang like a jellyfish, her back arched, her head and limbs dangling below the surface of the water, her lungs inflated. She was supposed to concentrate on blowing bubbles until the time came for her to raise her head, look round for waves or rescue vessels, inhale and recommence the cycle. She could not control her breathing as well as she would have liked. Perhaps this was because the shipwreck scenario was so incredible. Such a level of helplessness was beyond her imaginings, and outside her experience.

But she persisted – if a thing was worth doing, it was worth doing well – and got better. The instructor had been right: survival floating was relaxing, she could go on for ever. She lost all sense of time, all interest in it, in her blue, softly humming world. The Pastures New regime was a sensible one, she decided. Fascinated, she watched her own blurred body, trim and graceful in her turquoise costume.

Another pair of legs appeared, a body, a man. He trod water next to her, disturbing her reverie. She wished he would go away. It occurred to her that what she was doing was rather undignified, from a spectator's point of view, so she stopped and looked at him. He offered his hand. 'Tommy Croxley,' he said, adding the name of an electronics company.

'Daphne Barclay, START Selling.'

'Someone said you wanted to use a telephone.'

'Have you got one here? My goodness, aren't they making them small these days?' Survival floating must be making her light-headed; she had not meant that as it sounded.

'In my car,' he explained.

'That's very kind of you,' she said.

'It's all part of the service,' he winked.

21

'I'll show you how it works,' said Tommy Croxley, getting into the car beside her.

'I'm sure I can work it out.'

'It's a bit complicated.'

'Really? The Telecom model isn't.' She smiled at Tommy as he got out of the car. She closed the door. He waited outside, shivering against the wintry landscape. He had not brought his coat.

'Alistair? It's me.'

Alistair laughed. 'I knew they'd have their work cut out keeping you and a telephone apart.'

'Ve haf vays. How are you? Now listen. That article in Media Week about Groves' Breweries. Can you get it? November, I think.'

'Daphne, I'm at home.'

'That's why I phoned you there. It's in your purple folder, the one you always have. I remember you putting it in.'

Alistair sighed and went off to look for it. Daphne tapped her fingers, which became still as she saw in the mirror a green Jaguar sliding into the car park and out of her field of vision. She wound down the window of Tommy Croxley's car. 'Could you do me a tiny favour?'

'What?'

'Could you just nip into reception – it's warmer there – and sort of *hover*? That might be somebody for me and I don't want to keep him waiting. Oh, Alistair. Have you found it?'

'Yes, Daphne. How was the course?'

Daphne wound up the window. Tommy walked off, looking cross. 'The real star,' she said, 'was the scholarship girl. She was brilliant, actually. Insisted on giving me one of her samples as a present, which was sweet of her, and then she got the others to pay for it.'

'Sounds as if I was right about her then,' said Alistair, who had pressed Ann Mitchison's case for a bursary against Daphne's preference for a woman who sold fire extinguishers. 'And you were wrong.'

Daphne sniffed. 'You'd better have the present then. A wooden roundabout. The horses come off. You can give it to your grandchildren, sounds as if you've got them with you.'

'I have, yes. What did you want to know about Groves'?'

She detected impatience and was hurt by it. She had expected him to be alone, which he usually was at weekends, or so he said. He was divorced, and his grandchildren came only rarely. She wanted to share with him her little thumbnail sketches of delegates. It was part of their private debriefing ritual after courses. 'Then there was one of these people who take it as an affront that they've been sent on a course in the first place. Much too busy chasing real orders to sit and learn . . . well, it's up to them, I suppose. They've paid.'

'And did she?' said Alistair.

'Did she what?'

'Find any real orders?'

'Am I right in thinking that Groves' are planning to give their retail outlets a face-lift?'

'Er . . . yes.'

'And have we offered to train their staff?'

'Yes.'

'And are we going to?'

'They haven't decided yet.'

'That's what I thought. Thanks, Alistair.' Tommy Croxley was returning across the car park. 'Did he ask for me?'

'I don't know what he was asking for. Chap was an Arab.'

Daphne wound up the window. 'Lindbergh Stanley's not an Arab, is he, Alistair?'

'I wouldn't have thought so, why?'

'Didn't you see him? I thought you had a visitation this week.'

'So that's what it was,' said Alistair. 'All I saw was a flash of light, I thought it was the wiring. How did you know he was here?'

'Ve haf vays. Don't say you didn't see him. You must have seen him. He's sent me such a sweet note. He's coming here to see me either today or tomorrow. How odd, that he didn't make time to see *you*.'

'I've been out of the office a lot.'

'Never mind. I expect he'll come again.'

'Sounds to me as if there's been a misunderstanding,' said Alistair, with just a touch, Daphne thought, of smugness. 'Last I heard, Frank was taking him up to Scotland for the weekend to shoot some unsuspecting animals and talk about the new video. I had to change his ticket from Heathrow to Edinburgh; he's flying home at midday tomorrow.'

Daphne suppressed her rage. What Frank had done – Frank Grant was the managing director of START Selling UK – was absolutely in character. Frank would have heard of Lindbergh Stanley's plans to visit her and headed them off with an alternative attraction. 'Ah well,' she said, and then, to show that it was of no consequence to her how Lindbergh Stanley spent his leisure time, returned to gossiping about START Selling – Women! 'I must have said "salesman" once too often for the bleeding conscience of the women's movement, she walked out. And another thing, Alistair. The Donian's really going downhill. They practically had the roof off. I was embarrassed. We ought to get a rebate.'

'We are getting one,' said Alistair.

In the same second that she put the phone down, Tommy Croxley opened the door and slid into the driving seat. 'Where to, your ladyship?'

'I beg your pardon?'

'I thought we were going for a drive.'

'Oh, but I don't want to miss yoga,' she said.

'Yoga is not competitive,' said the yoga instructor. 'There's no such thing as a prize for yoga, right? It's not supposed to hurt or strain you. If it hurts, you're doing it wrong. You'll find this pose easier if you do it up against a wall.' Some of the men moved to positions by the wall and the instructor helped to arrange their limbs. She left Daphne in the middle of the room, bent sideways in what she herself considered to be a perfect triangle. There might be no such thing as a prize for yoga, Daphne reflected, but some people were clearly better at it than others. Roderick, for example, the fat boy who had been looking for a chess partner, was a pathetic sight. Daphne tried not to look at him. She could not understand how anyone could let themselves get into such a state. She blamed the parents.

'Fine, Roderick, don't force it,' said the instructor. She came up behind Daphne and put her hands on her shoulders. 'That's fine, nice open chest. My goodness, you're tense. Are you breathing?'

Of course I'm breathing, Daphne wanted to snap. *But Lindbergh*

Stanley was in town, and I missed him. She had enquired at reception, but nobody had asked for her.

The instructor demonstrated a shoulder-stand. She went round the room discreetly telling the women that they should sit this one out if they were having their periods, because of risk to the Fallopian tubes. Up Daphne went, her legs high and straight, her toes pointed. 'If you're getting a feeling of congestion round the eyes, come down at once.' Daphne's entire face felt full of pounding blood, but she refused to come down before the others did. At last the instructor said that they should all come down. Daphne watched her demonstrate sitting poses through a haze of dizziness. 'Most of you will find it easier to do this one with a cushion, so help yourselves.' The pose involved kneeling down, spreading one's calves and sitting between them. Everyone went to fetch a cushion but Daphne was determined to manage without. 'I think you have to have a specially shaped backside to do this one,' said the instructor. 'Very good, Daphne. Very good, Roderick.'

In the evening after dinner Daphne sat in the lounge, staring into the fire, composing her course report in her head. She would have preferred to do this on paper, but it was not worth all the aggravation and foolishness of having the Pastures New staff trying to stop her. Tommy Croxley suggested a game of table tennis, but her eye was on Bill Groves, who was playing chess in the corner with Roderick. As soon as they had finished, Daphne wanted to talk to Bill about his chain of off licences. Daphne did not understand chess and had no way of knowing how close they were to the end of their game. There seemed still to be a great many pieces on the board, and although Roderick kept saying 'Check!' in a squeaky, triumphant way, nothing ever seemed to happen.

She wandered across.

'What do you reckon, eh, Daphne?' said Bill, without looking up.

'I don't know anything about it,' she said, perching on the arm of his chair. 'Let me watch and see if I can pick it up.'

'His king's in check from my pawn, see,' said Roderick.

'I could take his pawn,' said Bill. 'But I have a feeling that I'd be walking into something.'

Roderick looked enigmatic and deeply excited.

'I don't want to intrude,' said Daphne, 'but can I book you for a quick chat afterwards, Bill?'

'I think I'm going to resign,' said Bill. He laid one of his pieces on its side. 'You may be a fat oaf, Roderick, but you're bloody good at chess.'

'But you could have got out of it! You could, you could! Look, I'll show you, you can have it again – '

'No, no, the best man won,' said Bill.

'Congratulations, Roderick,' said Daphne, wandering away with a smile. Bill followed to join her in the armchairs by the fire. Roderick sat on, absorbed in playing the game as it might have gone.

22

INT. DAY. SUPERMARKET. DIM CHECKOUT GIRL WATCHES
WITHOUT INTEREST AS FEMALE SHOPPER APPROACHES WITH
TROLLEY AND UNPACKS IT ON TO COUNTER. TIN OF TUNA
FISH FALLS TO FLOOR OUT OF SHOPPER'S REACH BUT WELL
WITHIN CHECKOUT GIRL'S IF SHE COULD BE BOTHERED
WHICH SHE CAN'T.

SHOPPER: Excuse me.
CHECKOUT GIRL: I'll get someone to pick it up. (Rings bell.
Stares into space.)
SHOPPER (tired of waiting): It doesn't matter. I don't really
want it.
CHECKOUT GIRL: Make up your mind. (Presents bill for other
items.)

SHOPPER PAYS AND LEAVES, MINUS TUNA FISH.
SHOT OF TUNA FISH BEING RETURNED TO SUPERMARKET SHELF
BY MEMBER OF STAFF.
SHOT OF SHOPPER BUYING TUNA FISH ELSEWHERE.

VOICE OVER: Just as the first principle of medicine is that
the treatment should do no harm, so the first principle of
salesmanship is that the salesman should not turn business
away.

MUSIC. TITLES: 'TIME TO START SELLING.'

'What do we think of it so far?' said Frank Grant to the script meeting which he was chairing. Present at the meeting were Daphne, Alistair, four other START trainers, the producer-director from the video company and a freelance scriptwriter who sat on the edge of his seat looking as if he expected to be stabbed.

Daphne looked straight at him and smiled warmly. 'I think it's *marvellous*.' Having read the entire script she had one or two suggestions, but she knew that you should never criticize a person without praising them first.

VOICE OVER: Let's see how that could have been handled.

SHOPPER DROPS TUNA FISH ON FLOOR.

CHECKOUT GIRL: My fault, sorry. (Gets down on floor, retrieves tin, showing a bit of leg. Keys in price, puts tin with shopper's other purchases.)
SHOPPER: Thank you.
VOICE OVER: On a START Selling course your staff will learn how Manners Maketh Money.

'Just one small thing.'

'Just one small thing from Daphne,' said Frank.

She did not care for his tone – it suggested that everyone in the room had been expecting her to raise difficulties, the only point of uncertainty being when she would begin – but she ignored it.

'When the checkout girl gets down on the floor, isn't it a bit undignified?'

'It only says "shows a bit of leg" Daphne, not the whole thing.' Frank laughed at his own joke and everyone else joined him.

'I'm not talking about that,' said Daphne. 'I'm talking about the implication that the salesman should grovel. Why should she say, "My fault, sorry," when it wasn't? Unless she actually knocked the tin out of the customer's hand, she shouldn't say "my fault". She can still be nice about it, but can't she say "whoops" or something like that?'

Frank turned to the scriptwriter. 'How do you feel about "whoops", Tim?'

'Whoops it is,' said Tim, making a mark. Daphne gave him one of her most intimate smiles, and moved on to her second point. 'I think there's a missed opportunity here. This is off the top of my head. But listen. All right, the checkout girl can pick up the tin. I'll give you that. But what if there's a dent in it? So she says . . .' Daphne had started out speaking quite slowly as her idea took shape, but she was getting into her stride now. ' . . . she says, "I'll go and get you another one." And she comes back with two tins. The one the customer thought she wanted, and another one that might be better.'

A few thoughtful nods greeted this suggestion, and Alistair said, 'Hmmm.' But the scriptwriter said, 'And what do we leave out?'

'I beg your pardon?'

'You've just added a scene. Fine. It's your film. But the length is the length I was asked for and if you're going to add a scene you're going to have to take one out and I was just wondering which one you had in mind, that's all.' The scriptwriter shrugged and sank into his chair. This, Daphne supposed, was artistic temperament. She and the rest of the START Selling team had been called here to put in their ideas, to brainstorm. If it was generally agreed to add a scene – and Daphne had only been speaking off the top of her head, but if it were to be agreed – then the technicalities of that were the problem of the production company, she would have thought.

'Shall we move on?' said Frank.

Daphne raised her eyebrows and resolved to sit out the rest of the meeting without further comment. It occurred to her that Frank himself had probably had more than a hand in the writing of this script. She marvelled at managers who would use up staff time in meetings at which the only staff contribution that was acceptable was praise for the creativity of the managers who had called the meeting.

> SHOT OF SALESMAN READING A BOOK. HE LOOKS EARNEST BUT NOT TOO BRIGHT. HE FORMS THE WORDS WITH HIS LIPS AS HE READS.

> VOICE OVER: Larry O'Loosey has an intellectual approach to his job. He doesn't need to go on courses, he's read it all in a book.

> CLOSE-UP OF BOOK TITLE: *SELLING? THERE'S NOTHING TO IT.*

> VOICE OVER: Larry sells domestic security equipment. Or at least he tries to. He knows that it is important to go where the need is and that he shouldn't waste the customer's time. He knows that this is true because he's read it in a book. Let's see how he gets on.

> EXT. DAY. LARRY APPROACHES FRONT DOOR, KNOCKS. LITTLE OLD LADY OPENS DOOR ON CHAIN.

LARRY: Good afternoon, madam. I'm glad to see you've got a chain on the door. It shows you're security conscious.

OLD LADY (very suspicious): Yes?

LARRY: But you can't leave the chain on the door when you go out, can you? With one of these . . . (Demonstrates lock with chain which can be fixed from outside with a key. Pretends to tamper with it, whereupon siren goes off.)

OLD LADY STAGGERS BACK CLUTCHING HEART.

LARRY: If it shocked you, think what it'll do to a burglar. Just open the door and I'll fit one of these for you in five minutes.

OLD LADY (recovering): Have you got any identification?

LARRY PRESENTS VISITING CARD WHICH HAS SEEN BETTER DAYS. OLD LADY GRABS THIS AND SLAMS DOOR. SHOT OF HER PHONING THE POLICE.

VOICE OVER: On a START Selling course, your team will learn that theories are not enough. Role-plays will teach them to respond with flexibility to the needs of the individual customer. Let's see how it should have been done. We'll keep Larry out of sight for a start.

SMART, ATTRACTIVE YOUNG SALESWOMAN APPROACHES FRONT DOOR.

VOICE OVER: *That's* better.

SALESWOMAN: I'm glad to see you've got a chain on the door. It shows you're security conscious.

OLD LADY STARTS TO REMOVE CHAIN.

SALESWOMAN: No, please. I know I'm not a burglar, but you don't. (Demonstrates product.)

OLD LADY: How long would it take to fit?

SALESWOMAN: Five minutes. May I make an appointment for our engineer to call?

OLD LADY: Well . . .

SALESWOMAN: Would Thursday be better, or Friday?

OLD LADY: Friday.

'No,' said Daphne. 'I'm sorry. I don't think she should say it only takes five minutes to fit. Who's going to have confidence in a security appliance that only takes five minutes to fit?'

131

'Good point, Daphne,' said Alistair.

The scriptwriter sighed. 'These things do only take five minutes to fit. I have done my research.'

'But it's not a benefit. It may be a feature but it's not a benefit.'

One of the other trainers, whose name was Charles, put his hands flat on the table. 'I've got it. The old lady says, "How long will it take?" and the salesman says, "I've known it take as little as five minutes, but it might be longer. We don't want to skimp." '

'Got that, Tim?' said Frank to the scriptwriter, who noted it down. 'Good point, Charles.'

Daphne fought back. 'When the engineer – engineer? Wouldn't it be better to call him a locksmith? – anyway, when he's fitted the lock, he can say, "Sorry it took a bit longer than we thought; that's because you've chosen such a good-quality wood for your door frame, durable and – " '

'But people don't *talk* like that, Daphne!' cried the scriptwriter, as if in great pain.

' – show appreciation of the customer's good judgement – '

'We weren't going to show it being fitted anyway, were we?' said Dan.

'It'll cost you, if you want another actor.'

Frank said sarcastically, 'Never let it be said that we let money stand in the way of using one of Daphne's ideas. Shall we move on?'

The video was to end with a shot of the START Selling team all together. 'Like a football team?' said Alistair.

'Yes,' said Frank. 'Daphne can hold the ball.'

'It will be my pleasure,' she said.

'You ought to decide what you're all going to wear for the final shot,' said the producer-director.

'Jackets and ties, I think,' said Frank. 'You can wear that grey thing of yours, Daphne.'

'Yes, that's one possibility.'

'I said, you will wear that grey thing.'

'I think you can rely on me to dress suitably.'

The producer-director looked at his watch and stood up. 'It's your film. You can all wear leotards with feathers up your arses for all I care. I just think the picture's going to be a bit unbalanced if Daphne's wearing, well, no offence, but something like what she's got on at the moment.'

'I think she looks very nice,' said Alistair. Daphne appreciated this, for she agreed with him: her silk skirt of acid green and co-ordinated top were recent additions to her wardrobe.

'We're not talking about looking nice, we're talking about looking like a team,' said Frank. 'I want you wearing that grey thing, Daphne.'

She wondered what would happen if she said that she no longer had the grey suit to which she assumed he was referring. She was to realize later that she would have been wiser to say this, or even to say nothing, to appear to acquiesce and then, if she chose to come dressed otherwise than in the grey suit, to pretend that she had forgotten or misunderstood the instruction. Frank would hardly send her home to change.

She would, in short, have been wiser to let the matter drop, but she did not. She had a deep detestation of being given orders. Requests were different. She could work as well as anyone could as a member of a team. No one understood better than she did that different members of a team had different responsibilities. A manager was entitled to manage. But not this way. *I want you wearing that grey thing.* Were Daphne in Frank's shoes, she would have said, *You look very nice in grey, Daphne. How about that smart suit?* Daphne remembered other times in her life when she had suffered from the arbitrary bossiness of people whose ideas were wrong, peculiar or unjust, but who nevertheless had the power to impose them on her. She remembered the petty humiliations of childhood. She remembered coming second in the school trading competition. She had in fact come first, but the school had changed the rules.

'You're ordering me to wear the grey suit, then?'

'Yes, Evita, I am. We're a team here, not a team plus Daphne Barclay. You won't drop dead if you don't stand out in a crowd for once.'

Grins spread round the room. Even Alistair's lips were twitching. She remembered the school announcement. ' . . . and Form 3A have come second. Well done, 3A!' 3A had come *first.* The others had cheated by not sticking to bona fide trading. They had accepted donations.

You won't drop dead if you don't stand out in a crowd for once. Daphne knew exactly what this was about. It was about professional jealousy. It was about the tendency of START Selling clients to ask for her by name. Imagine a manager being jealous of his own staff. It was pathetic.

23

'Frank, I'd like a word.'

'What is it?'

'I –'

'Yes, Daphne. If someone had told me that you had one word left to utter on this earth, "I" is the one I'd have expected it to be.'

Daphne blinked. 'Could you repeat that?'

'You heard. Just teasing. Sit down. Is this going to take long?'

'Nobody knows better than I that managers have sometimes to discipline staff.'

'Eh?' said Frank.

'But I do not think that disciplinary interviews should be conducted before an audience.'

'Did I give you a bollocking?'

'You said things which were, in my opinion, quite uncalled for. You called me names in front of strangers.'

'When I decide to give you a bollocking, you'll know.'

'You shouted at me.'

'Shout back, then.'

Daphne felt drained and defeated. A proper manager would deal with her complaint in one of two ways. He would either defend his conduct or apologize. Frank Grant just laughed at her. It was intolerable to be laughed at when she had not made a joke. From the security of his authority, he said, *Shout back, then*. Did he not realize that she nearly had? Did he not realize that this was what worried her, that if she once started shouting at people who treated her unfairly or stupidly, she might never stop? She fought to control her panic and rage.

'Why did you call me Evita?'

'Go and see the show and find out.'

'I should like to make a formal request that you call me by my name and no other.'

'Request noted,' said Frank.

She sat quite happily through the first act. She would never admit this to Frank, but she might have overreacted. If being called Evita meant that the men in the START Selling team identified her with the vivid, unstoppable Señora Perón, she had perhaps been wrong to take offence.

But in the second act, her gorge rose with horror. Evita died. She suffered and withered and died. The make-up artists had outdone themselves. Evita's eyes sank into her face, her bones pushed forward. Evita staggered towards her goal – the presidency of her country (she claimed only to want to be vice-president, but Daphne knew what she was after) – as if through a tangle of ropes of pain, ropes that broke on the sharp edge of her will only to reunite themselves like mythical snakes and grab her more tightly. Lest there be any misunderstanding of what all this suffering represented, old newspapers were flashed up on a screen, their headlines indicating that top cancer specialists from the USA had been brought in to attend upon Evita. Evita did not live to rule her country. She was defeated by her illness and her enemies. Her enemies sang taunting songs around her death bed, reminding her of her failure. They listed her unfulfilled ambitions. She plucked at her sheets. She died, her body was embalmed, the audience clapped.

Daphne did not clap. And Alistair's applause stopped when he saw her face.

'I'm surprised they didn't get hold of the X-rays,' she said, sitting immobile as the theatre emptied. 'I'm surprised they didn't show those as well.'

Alistair looked ashamed. 'I see what you mean. That was a bit sick, wasn't it? But you liked the music?'

'And that's what you were laughing at?'

'Me?'

'You laughed when Frank called me Evita. You all did.'

'No one meant it like that. Come on. Everybody has nicknames, I hate to think what mine is.'

Daphne had never heard Alistair referred to as anything other than Alistair. She was still looking at the stage, aware of his guilty presence at her side. She was thinking about the pain she had just witnessed.

'I plucked up all my courage to ask you out,' he sighed. 'And all I've done is upset you.'

'If something like that were to happen to me, they'd clap their hands.'

'Daphne, listen. May an old man give you some advice?'

She said warmly, 'I don't see any old man.'

'Being liked isn't part of the job. It isn't part of any job. Just do it as well as you do it and you'll be respected. You are respected.'

'But not liked.'

'Do *you* like *them*?'

'Not particularly.' This was hardly the point. 'I don't go around calling them – well, I can't think of a famous man who had a horrible death and had a musical made about it.'

'What about *Jesus Christ Superstar*?' he said. 'Come on, let's go and find something to eat.'

'This is very sweet of you, Alistair,' she said, as they sat in a candlelit bistro. She had hardly expected her aggrieved account of her conversation with Frank to result in this. Alistair had queued for hours to get the tickets, and had ended up having to buy them from a tout.

'Happy birthday,' he said, producing a parcel wrapped in pink tissue paper with a silver ribbon.

She gave a little exclamation of delight. 'How did you know it was my birthday?'

'It was on your CV.'

'They're a perfect fit! My glove size wasn't on my CV.'

'I looked at your hands and guessed. Perhaps CVs should include things like that, in case the person gets the job and someone wants to give them a present.'

'You guessed right,' said Daphne, putting the gloves away. 'They're funny things, birthdays, aren't they? I mean, what, really, is one celebrating? Another year of not achieving – '

'*Not* achieving?'

'Not achieving what one wants. If one had achieved it, what would one do with the rest of one's life?'

'Birthdays are for friends,' said Alistair. 'They're a chance to express things that . . . well, might be difficult otherwise.' She waited while he looked embarrassed. He changed the subject with relief. 'What *do* you want to achieve? I mean, you obviously love your work, but is it enough?' The waiter arrived. Daphne told Alistair what she wanted to eat, and Alistair told the waiter. Alistair asked if she had seen anything she liked on the wine list, and she replied, 'You choose.'

'How do you see yourself in ten years' time?' Alistair persisted.

'Goodness, I don't know,' Daphne laughed, turning her head slightly to listen to the music, taped Simon and Garfunkel. 'What's all this in aid of?'

'I'm leaving START,' he said.

'You can't.'

'I can.'

'To do what?'

'There's a scheme for what are politely known as pre-retirement executives to be seconded to community projects in high unemployment areas. Frank drew it rather pointedly to my attention the other day.'

'But that doesn't mean you have to,' said Daphne in alarm.

'I think I'd quite like to. Come on, Daphne, admit it. I'm a has-been who's never been. I'd like to do something worthwhile while I've still got some juice in me. Otherwise I'll have passed through this world without anyone even noticing.'

Daphne was perplexed. On joining START Selling, she had seen Alistair as an older version of the other men – hard but affable, energetic, busy and therefore exciting. In time, as the others revealed themselves as spiteful bullies, he had appeared kinder. She had supposed that something in her own character drew forth this response from him. It had not occurred to her – as it had obviously occurred to Frank, and as indeed it now appeared – that he was suffering from burnout. 'If you pass through START Selling, I shall notice,' she said. 'I shall notice the Alistair-shaped gap you leave behind. You are my only friend there.'

'Apart from Lindbergh Stanley, who takes a warm personal interest in the welfare and progress of – '

'Of all his staff, don't be silly, Alistair.' She was still needled by Lindbergh Stanley's failure to keep his appointment with her, and the absence of any explanation.

'He's never taken an interest in me, warm, personal or otherwise.'

'And he's never set eyes on me.'

'Don't you believe it,' said Alistair. 'He's probably watching us now, by satellite. Look. All I want to say . . . I'm making a mess of this. I'm not asking you to make my decision for me, I've made it.

I'll be in Cardiff. That's not very far away. Well, it's far enough away that we wouldn't see each other again unless we made a point of it.'

'Yes, that's true,' said Daphne, as her avocado vinaigrette arrived. 'This is delicious,' she said, playing for time.

'So . . . can we?'

'Can we what?'

'See each other?'

'Of course we can!' The enthusiasm she heard in her own voice made her panic. She had been manoeuvred into this. *I've made my decision*, he had said, and she was being required to fit in with his decision. 'If you have time,' she said sweetly.

'Now, Daphne, don't be like that.'

'I'm not being like anything. I'm sure this – *secondment* – will be very absorbing. And you'll meet lots of interesting people. New friends, very different from the ones you have here . . .'

'All right, Daphne.' *He's angry*, she thought. But his hand, when he reached across the table and took hers, was very gentle. *He's angry, but only with himself*. 'I've blown it anyway, I might as well make it worse. I can't bear to go on working with you, *just* working with you. I can't bear seeing you and knowing that I'm only seeing you because we happen to work for the same company. I want us to choose to see each other, or not see each other at all. And if I'm not putting it any more strongly than that – if I'm not asking you to marry me and come to Cardiff with me – it's only because it wouldn't be fair to you.'

'Why not?' she said in a light tone, looking him straight in the eyes. 'Do you snore?'

'I've no idea,' he said. 'Want to find out?'

Daphne was speechless and embarrassed. Her limited experience of sex had been such as to lead her to the conclusion that she could take it or leave it alone, and was best advised to leave it alone, its compensations being far fewer than the toll it took on her peace of mind and ability to concentrate. But Alistair had worked himself up into quite a state about this, and she must go carefully lest she frighten him off before she had decided what to do. Her mind refused to accommodate the possibility of life at START without him.

She looked down as if to hide a blush. Music filled the silence between them. He said, 'I'm sorry if I offended you.'

'Why is it always Simon and Garfunkel in bistros?' she enquired.

'They have their bistro licence taken away if they play anything else.'

'Feelin' groovy,' Daphne hummed.
'Still crazy after all these years,' Alistair sighed.

24

'You'd be working with bitumen,' said Alan Morant, the personnel consultant, when Gina met him in a cocktail bar for a preliminary chat. ('Neutral ground, Miss Heriot. Nothing either of us says is binding one way or the other at this stage.') 'And bitumen products. Do you have any experience in that area?'

Her present employers, Franson & Franson, were doing rather well at the moment with a roofing material which they advertised as 'the plastics industry's answer to bitumen felt,' but she did not mention this as her reason for knowing a bit; nor did she say that she had been doing her homework, Oliver having tipped her off as to what the job was. She was not even supposed to know the name of the company on whose behalf Alan Morant was interviewing her. She thought this slightly silly. If the powers that be at Stalton Industries had one ounce of imagination, they must know that she knew. Whatever level of dullness their own marriages had sunk to, they must surely remember being engaged, the happiness, the confidences, the planning . . . how could she and Oliver be planning anything with this unspoken between them? Still, now was no time for going against the proprieties.

'I know a little.'

'You'd be given full product training, of course. Our client – we'll call them Company X for now – is a major supplier to the road construction industry, and they're the kind of people you'd be looking after. Don't mind getting yourself dirty, eh?'

Gina confirmed that she did not mind. 'Can you tell me about career structures at Company X?'

'I think I'd like to find out a bit more about you first,' he replied, his heartiness masking a rebuke.

Gina wondered whether this was because he thought it more proper for a person to get a job before they started wondering about being promoted out of it, or because he was working to a script. 'Of course,' she said.

'I think you can safely assume that you would advance on merit, in the light of your own circumstances.'

Open mouth, extract foot, she thought.

'You've just had the one job since university?' he said, reading from her CV.

'Yes. I wanted to start in a small company. You get a little bit of everything. But I'm ready to specialize now.'

'May I ask what you're earning?'

She considered a little joke – *about twice what I'm getting* – and abandoned it. She explained the arrangement she had with the Franson brothers: a small basic salary and a generous commission. She did not say that the Franson brothers looked for ways to pay some of her commission in cash.

'Company X doesn't pay commission. They take it for granted that their representatives don't have to be starved into doing their best.'

'Of course. . . .'

'But I think you'll find that you're significantly better off. And the company benefits are good: six weeks' holiday, pension, of course, various discount schemes, travel club, sports club – excellent sports club, I'm an associate member – car – '

'I've got my own car.'

'Company X prefer their representatives to use the company fleet.'

'Of course,' said Gina again, wondering if it was just her imagination that told her she kept saying the wrong thing. She was fond of her own car, but it would not be a serious loss to sell it; the money would come in handy, she and Oliver faced an expensive few months. 'What about maternity leave?' she said. She could not believe she had said it. It had slipped out. She must be mad. She had actually taken the trouble to remove her engagement ring, not with a view to lying about her circumstances but with a view to not drawing attention to them.

Oliver had thought this unnecessary. 'It's not going to damage your chances, to be engaged to someone who's already with the firm. It's a plus, they can feel secure about you. If you're married to me, you're not going to rush off to the other end of the country to marry someone else, are you?'

'Not immediately,' Gina had agreed, but she had left her ring off anyway.

'Maternity leave,' said Alan Morant, leafing curiously through his folder.

'It's academic, I mean I'm not even married, er, yet, but – '

Alan Morant closed his folder. 'I think you can safely assume that Company X doesn't lag behind on anything. I can't tell you where you'd be based,' he added, as if relieved to return to matters with which he was familiar, 'because that would involve identifying the company, but may I take it that you're free to move anywhere in the UK?'

She nodded. She and Oliver already had their eye on a house, conveniently placed for both of them.

'And your present job involves you being away from home over-night during the week, so that wouldn't be a problem?'

'Well, I've got half a dog,' said Gina, realizing for the first time that she would have to give Pimple to Julia, her neighbour. A small sacrifice, she decided. She would find out about maternity leave at the interview proper, but only if they brought it up. If they did not mention it, she would not either. She and Oliver did not plan to have children for many a long day, they had only discussed it in a vague and joky manner. The law, she knew, gave her certain rights. 'I think you can assume that Stalton's have heard of the pill,' Oliver had said. 'We do make it.' She wondered in safe, pleasurable horror how she would have fared if she had come to maturity in the days when she would have had to make a choice between her love and her work. It would be like choosing whether to have a leg amputated or both eyes removed.

'One last question,' said Alan Morant when they had been together for an hour. 'Are there any companies by whom you would definitely not want to be considered?'

'I'd work for anybody,' she said warmly. 'Anybody as good as your Company X sounds.'

'I'm so jealous,' said Oliver, 'that I want to spit.'

'Why?'

'Going back to school and socking it to them.'

'I'm not going to sock anything to anybody. I'm just going to tell them that industry is fun and their country needs them. Never mind darling – ' she had started calling him darling. 'Your day will come.'

'Me? My school hated me. My face didn't fit. It was a tradition that everyone in the sixth form was made a prefect. It didn't mean much but it looked good on the UCCA forms. My year they made an exception. "This particular poacher cannot be trusted to turn gamekeeper." They actually said that.'

'Why is it,' Gina wondered aloud, 'that men always boast about how bad they were at school?'

'And women always boast about how good they were? Different schools, in our case. Very different.'

'All right, so I went to a good school. Doesn't mean I liked it.'

'Don't give me that. I bet your name's up there in gold.'

It would be. It would be fun to see it.

She spent a long time deciding what to wear for the careers evening. The girls would be watchful and critical. She had a dim memory of hats and gloves . . . but that must have been speech day, surely . . . for a careers evening a speaker must look businesslike. She decided to splash out, buy the outfit that she would eventually wear for her interview at Stalton's, and break it in at the careers evening. She bought a smart purple-and-black patterned skirt with a co-ordinated jacket and a silky blouse with a tie neck. In for a penny, she finished herself off with a printed leather bag and new shoes.

'Now you're not to say anything awful,' she warned Oliver.

'Any suggestions?'

What she meant was that she did not want him to say anything that would lead the nuns to realize that she was having sex before marriage. She wondered if they knew that their old girls did.

'You look wonderful,' he said. 'They'll all get crushes on you, like me, and besiege the labs. Hey, you're nervous. Why are you nervous?'

'I want to be – ' she hunted for the word ' – dignified.'

'You will be dignified. You're the most dignified person I know.'

'I just think – when I get there – I won't be grown-up any more.'

They reached the school half an hour early and were shown, by an unknown and deferential nun, into a reception parlour which Gina had never seen before. The carpet was thick and soft, and on the wall there was an Old Master with a religious theme. Gina could hear nuns moving around outside the room, the soft, familiar swish of their robes and the rattling of beads.

Oliver was eyeing the furniture. 'This must be worth a few quid. I thought they took a vow of poverty.'

Gina said irritably, 'People say such obvious things about nuns.'

'No one asked them to be nuns. But what's the point in being a nun if you're going to live in the lap of luxury?'

'You'll be saying next, what's the point in sending people to prison if you let them have tobacco and televisions? You sound like a Tory lady –'

'You would know,' said Oliver.

'They can't leave,' said Gina. 'Well, not without a great fuss.'

'What's stopping them?'

'Something in themselves. They've made a promise. It's nothing to laugh at. Listen, that's Sister Brede.'

'I can't hear anyone.'

Sister Brede's approach had a unique sound, for she always carried the keys to the science labs, bashing against her crucifix as she walked. She looked just the same, she had not aged. She embraced Gina and kissed both her cheeks, which Gina found very moving. She shook Oliver by the hand.

'Your fiancé, Gina! I didn't know.'

'I only asked her recently, Sister,' said Oliver. Gina wanted to hug him. She had instructed him in etiquette. Always say *Sister* at the end of sentences, and if you say *Jesus* bow your head. *Why should I say Jesus?* he had replied. 'I've just been admiring your furniture, Sister.'

'Thank you. This cabinet is particularly beautiful, isn't it?'

Quite right, thought Gina. *Don't justify it by saying it was a bequest, or it's just for visitors.* Sister Brede must be magnificent in confession. *Here I am, Father*, she would say: *and here is what I've done.*

A tray was brought in with a decanter and seven glasses. The other two speakers – a local government official whom Gina recognized but hardly knew, being three years her junior, and a publisher friend of the school – arrived with their partners and they all stood about drinking sherry. *Sociologists*, thought Gina mischievously.

The publisher's wife lit a cigarette, and Sister Brede fetched an ashtray without comment, so Gina and Oliver lit up too. Sister Brede explained between sips at her sherry that each speaker would have ten minutes and then there would be time for questions from the audience of fifth and sixth formers and their parents. When the little party left the parlour, Gina felt completely grown-up.

She was not ready, though, for what met her eyes when she entered the school hall: the impossibility of telling which of the women in front of her were really girls and which their mothers. The mothers looked so young, but they must have been at least ten years older than Gina to have daughters of this maturity. Gina wished the daughters had been told to wear their uniforms.

The mood of the evening was subdued, even depressed. The two speakers who went before Gina had little for the comfort of their audience. What they said was, in essence, the same. If anyone had an ambition to go into local government or publishing, she could shorten the odds against herself by starting to prepare now (taking an interest in politics; reading widely outside her exam subjects) but her best plan was to consider alternatives, because she would probably not get in, all vacancies being, in the experience of the speakers, heavily oversubscribed.

Understanding now why Sister Brede had kept her for last, Gina rose to her feet. 'Industry is crying out,' she said, 'for scientifically qualified people. With a degree in science, computer studies, technology or engineering – or even with A levels – you will find a wide range of jobs open to you. You may find that you don't have to apply for them. They will apply for you!'

She saw Oliver smiling encouragement from the front row. No one else was smiling, though, and her heart failed her: had that remark been too boastful? She moved on hastily to talk about road surfacing, a subject upon which she had been working to make herself an authority. 'However we came here this evening – by car, by public transport or on foot – we took it for granted, didn't we, that the road we used would bear our weight and the weight of our vehicle. And so we should – and so it did – but it didn't happen by chance. The purpose of scientific advance is to make life easier for all of us, including those who think they aren't interested in science.

'I'm here to offer you the challenge of getting interested; the challenge of contributing to the industries that give you your cars, your clothes, your cold-cures . . . and the skid-resistant surfaces on your roads.'

As Gina spoke, she wished she had three eyes: one for her notes, one for her watch (the other speakers had not overrun, so she must not either) and one for her audience. She had read somewhere that the secret of public speaking was to forget about speaking to a roomful of people, to single out one person and speak to them. Gina was looking for two people. She was looking for a girl who, like her younger self, was already awed and fascinated by her growing knowledge of what could be done with the earth's gifts, oil and gas and minerals; and another who, until this moment, had been a sociologist, but who, fired by Gina's enthusiasm, would go tomorrow to Sister Brede and ask to change subjects.

Time was getting on and she did not want to be remembered solely as the person who had told her audience everything they ever wanted to know about bitumen binders, so she moved her eyes to her next key word which, underlined in fluorescent yellow, was 'UNFEMININE?' If girls had anxieties on that score, there was no point in ignoring or despising them; far better to meet them head on, to instance herself and the happy state of both her personal life and her professional life as proof that girls today could have everything they wanted, if they just wanted it enough. But something made her hesitate. To have her speak so personally might embarrass Oliver. It might embarrass everybody, herself included. The local government officer had explained briefly about working part-time for a while to accommodate the needs of her children; the publisher had not mentioned personal or domestic matters at all. Gina decided to follow his example.

'Modern industry employs the best man or woman for the job. It cannot afford to do otherwise.' Let these girls form their own conclusions from her appearance and manner, the diamond on her finger, the glow in her eyes.

There were no questions. Sister Brede, from the chair, seemed embarrassed about this and Gina guessed that the girls would be in for a contemptuous scolding in the morning, for their spinelessness. But when Gina and Oliver were getting ready to leave a rather truculent man came over. 'I've got a question.'

A girl called from the door. 'Come on, Dad. We're going.'

'That's Felicity, my eldest. We've got twins at home. Sylvia and Stanley, they're seven. We've always treated them exactly the same, my wife's like you, she's very hot on that. Whatever one's had, the other's had. They're seven now – '

Annoyed by the man's aggressive attitude, Oliver said, 'You mentioned that.'

'Seven, they are, and Sylvia's interested in dolls and helping her mother and Stan likes machines. If an aeroplane goes over, he looks up and wants to know all about it, she couldn't care less. What does that say to you?'

Gina said, 'I don't know.'

'Don't think about it, do you? None of you do.' He stumped off triumphantly.

Gina was bewildered. 'What was all that about? I'm not interested in making girls do science if they don't want to.'

'If we have children,' said Oliver, 'they'll do exactly what they want.'

'Right. What do you mean, if? Don't you want to have children?'

'Not yet.'

'Of course not yet,' she said. 'But – '

'In about five years,' he said.

'You've got it all worked out, then?'

'You'll be thirty. Lots of women have their first pregnancy when they're thirty.' Sister Brede was coming over to say goodbye and thank you. Gina trod on Oliver's toe. 'Change the subject,' she whispered.

25

Roy and Alex Franson left their representatives free to organize their own time. As long as Gina and her colleagues brought home the bacon, stayed in touch by phone and made the mandatory once-weekly visit to the office, Roy and Alex did not concern themselves unduly with what they were doing the rest of the time.

It was just her luck, then, that they should happen to choose the wrong day for a meeting at which they wanted everybody present.

She supposed she could invent an unmissable call, but she did not like the idea of lying to them. She told them that she had been planning to take a day of her holiday entitlement.

'What for?' said Alex. 'Getting measured for your wedding dress?'

'Something like that.' Actually she and Oliver had decided to postpone their wedding until she was settled in her new job, so that they might have a reasonable honeymoon, but Alex seemed to assume that there was something gynaecological about her coyness and contented himself with grumbling that *he* could not take days off whenever he felt like it.

'That's show business,' said Gina.

The interview at Stalton Industries lasted all day. She talked to people from Personnel, Marketing Management and Sales. She was asked how much she knew about the company and she let it be known that, through Oliver, she knew a great deal and liked all of it. No mention was made of other candidates, and the cautious conditional verbs favoured by the head-hunter (*they would want you to start as soon as possible . . . you would be one of a team of ten representatives, each with your own region*) were replaced by clear statements: 'You will spend ten days at head office on company orientation and product training, and then someone will come out on the road with you . . . you'll work closely with Hilary Foreman, your sales assistant, who looks after the bitumen boys. We'll have to stop calling them that now, I suppose . . . You'll have some leeway for discounting, but stay in touch with Hilary on that, because you've got to keep within the overall pricing strategy, which changes . . .' She was given a brief tour of the offices, and promised a more detailed visit to the various production sites as part of her company orientation. She was introduced to the manager of the Sports & Social Club. She ate lunch in the Directors' Dining Room with Paul Young, the Bitumen Products sales manager who would be her immediate boss. He told her to call him Paul and asked if she had had a chance to meet old Hils yet.

'Who? Oh, you mean my assistant.'

'Partner,' he corrected. 'Well, all right, technically she's one grade down from you, and she's my assistant, but we do try to think in terms of partnerships rather than hierarchies, particularly where old Hils is concerned. She's rather special. *Very* special, is old Hils.' He smiled ruminatively.

'In what way?'

'She's the only woman in our division. So far. She used to have your job.'

'Oh . . .'

'Then she went off on maternity leave. She had a try at going back on the road, but it didn't work out, so – '

'She was demoted?'

'You won't use that word when you've met her,' said Paul. He explained that Hilary Foreman had gone down a grade at her own request. She had been a sales assistant before she was a representative, and this experience had enabled her, with the help of her husband who was in Personnel, to put together a convincing proposal to the effect that, with minor adjustments to company thinking, the job of sales assistant could be done from home . . . home being, Gina gathered, fairly close at hand.

'And how's it working out?'

'It's a bit early to say. We're one body short until you join . . . or whoever we appoint . . . and we've got someone filling in at the moment, so it's not fair to judge. There's no reason why it shouldn't work, though, most of us think it's a great idea, particularly if the alternative was to lose Hils. That's what most of us feel, so if you hear anything different, ignore it.'

'That sounds ominous.'

'I'll put it no higher than this,' said Paul. 'If it should turn out not to work for any reason, there are people in the company who would be neither surprised nor disappointed. But it will work, she's a remarkable woman, not everybody could do it. . . .'

A meeting with Hilary had been fixed for the afternoon. From conversations politely veiled but clearly overheard, Gina gathered that, because of some unforeseen occurrence, no one was free to escort her without inconvenience. Wanting to establish herself as a person of flexibility and initiative, and preferring, for some reason, to be alone when she first met the highly thought of woman whose job she was to take, she said that she would find her own way, and this appeared to be appreciated.

She knocked at the front door of a recently refurbished semi in a street so close to the Stalton's complex that it was almost literally in its shadow. There was a short delay and then, through blurred glass, Gina saw a figure approach, pausing for a second to do something to her hair.

Hilary was a tall, big-boned woman of about thirty, with a pleasant, open face and the soft looseness to her body which Gina had often noticed about new mothers and could not help finding deeply unattractive. She understood the physiological reasons for it and knew that it did not happen to everybody, nor was it necessarily permanent if it did . . . but the phrase *gone to seed* was unavoidable.

'Paul not with you?' said Hilary, after they had introduced themselves. The baby was wailing in the background.

'He said he'd try to look in later.'

Hilary laughed. 'I bet he did. He knows my feeding schedule better than I do. When I get the old tit out, he doesn't know where to put himself. God, I shouldn't say that, should I? I'm supposed to be impressing you.'

'I thought I was supposed to be impressing *you*.'

The doors leading off the neat hall were all closed. Hilary led Gina through one of them into a clean, well-ordered office. The phone, the computer casings and the filing cabinets were all colour co-ordinated with the carpet, just as Gina had seen them at Stalton's head office. Maps on the wall were divided into territories, with pins and tapes showing the locations of customers and their projects, road surfacing, canals and sea-defence works at different stages of completion. There was a huge photograph of a sea wall with waves beating against it, and a number of vertical-section diagrams. One of the VDUs showed currency fluctuations in world financial centres; another reported on the present location of the division's road and rail tankers. A desk tidy shaped like a giant molecule had paperclips, drawing pins and erasing materials conveniently to hand. 'When do you start?' said Hilary, apparently finding it easier than Gina did to ignore the crying baby.

'I don't think they've made their decision yet.'

'Go on with you. You're the first one they've sent to see me. And it's so convenient, isn't it, with you marrying Oliver. I'm really pleased about that, congratulations. I love Oliver.'

'So do I.'

'Now, now, don't be touchy.'

Gina did not think she had been. She wondered if she ought to say that she did not mind if Hilary wanted to finish feeding the baby.

'Have they told you what car they're going to give you? You'll probably have my Sierra. You can see it there.' Hilary pointed out a dot near the sea wall in the photograph. That was mine,' she said nostalgically. 'All that water going whoomph, whoomph . . . I loved going there. Maybe I'll be able to fix it to come with you when you go, it's not quite finished yet.' Gina could not make Hilary out, could not get the measure of her. There was nothing wrong with her. She was friendly and informal, but when the phone rang, as it did repeatedly, she appeared businesslike and in control. Maybe it was the incongruous sound of the baby that was arousing Gina's unease. 'I'd better shut that sprog up,' Hilary said at last. 'Don't mind if I do it down here, do you?'

Gina did not. The baby was pretty and intelligent-looking, and a sequence of thoughts passed through its eyes (Gina had not taken in whether it was a boy or a girl) as clearly as if they had been spoken aloud. *Who the hell are you?* was followed by, *All right, you can stay if you insist* and then, *THAT's what I was waiting for!* as Hilary proffered a huge white breast, wincing theatrically as the baby fastened on the nipple. Gina's own nipples itched and hardened against the insides of her clothes. 'What's . . . the name?'

'Jeremy,' said Hilary. '*Not* Jerry. Now, I'm liaison between you, Joe Customer, Deliveries and head office. You phone orders in to me and I process them. You also phone me if you don't get the order. I have to know where you are.' The phone rang on her words and Hilary launched into a matey conversation with someone called Simon. Still feeding the baby with great deftness, she took dictation from Simon, entering numbers into the computer. Gina gestured that she would take the baby if Hilary wanted, but Hilary seemed keen to demonstrate how easy it was. In spite of the personal unease that Hilary aroused – and Gina still could not, in fairness, find any reason for it – she was impressed. Clearly the company valued Hilary enough to adapt to her needs; and there was no reason why, if Gina could make herself similarly indispensable, they should not adapt to hers too, if and when the time came, albeit she did not have the advantage of a husband in Personnel. 'Trevor's really sorry to have missed you,' said Hilary, as if reading this thought as she put the phone down, 'but he reckons I'm as good a judge as he is.'

And what is your judgement? thought Gina, but she did not say it.

'This one always says "BP offered a discount" so that's what we call him.' Hilary was, between phone calls, talking Gina round her territory, characterizing individual buyers at the wholesalers and construction companies with which she would be dealing. The baby was still at Hilary's breast, seemingly unaware of the activities of the person at the other end of it, as, indeed, Hilary seemed to be unaware of him. 'It's a sort of ritual, don't take too much notice, but never offer anyone a better deal than you give him, otherwise you'll never hear the end of it. Now, *this* one never makes appointments. You're expected to turn up and wait. His secretary's one of us, though, so make friends with her and she'll see you right. Make sure you happen to be passing when he happens to be free. This one hates women, this one eats garlic, this one hates everybody . . .' The front door bell rang. 'Shit. That's either a typist or Paul. Could you go? If it's Paul, could you say "Hello, Paul" very loudly?'

Gina opened the front door. 'Hello, Paul.' Paul followed her into the office where Hilary sat dandling the baby, her breast buttoned safely out of sight. 'Hi, Paul. I've just been introducing Gina to the real boss. Want him back, Gina?' Hilary put Jeremy into Gina's arms, and passed to Paul the pile of papers that had been generated by the various phone calls.

Jeremy was grizzling indignantly, and Gina did not blame him. He was hunting for her breast and she was sorry not to be able to be of service. But she was pleased to find that when she held him upright against her shoulder and patted his back in the way she had seen mothers do, he quietened down. She took this as proof of her instinctive maternal skills until wetness round her neck told her that Jeremy Foreman had only been drawing breath preparatory to vomiting.

26

'That's done it, eh, Hils?' said Paul, laughing it off with genial embarrassment.

'It's nothing,' said Hilary, dabbing at Gina's neck with tissues. Gina was not sure, but she thought Hilary had been about to spit on one of the tissues before recollecting herself.

'I don't suppose Gina realized that being puked over was part of the job, did you, Gina?' Paul went on. 'Still, better that than the other end . . . I remember once with my youngest . . .'

'Couldn't be helped,' said Gina, who supposed she could join Hilary and Paul in seeing the funny side if she tried hard enough. 'I think I'll go and have a wash.'

'There's no need,' said Hilary. 'I've got it all out.' Hilary did not offer to show Gina to the bathroom, but Gina found it without difficulty by climbing the stairs and following the smell. The bath and the wash-basin were full of reeking nappies. Hilary had obviously had a try at tipping some of their contents down the lavatory and, in a few cases, missed. Gina held a handkerchief under a tap and dabbed angrily at her collar, breathing through her mouth. She heard Hilary plod up the stairs and call to her: 'Not in there. We don't use that bathroom.'

'Thanks for telling me.'

'Oh, don't be angry. . . .' The tone was so uncharacteristically forlorn that Gina suspected the incident was still being seen as a joke, but the Hilary who stood there with the baby when she came out was barely recognizable as the brash, confident juggler of a thousand tasks whom Gina had seen downstairs in the office. The baby was in tears and Hilary seemed on the verge of following his example. 'I'm sorry,' she said. 'I'm really sorry.'

'That's all right.'

'Please tell Paul that you asked to hold him. Please. It would be a perfectly natural thing for you to do.'

Gina supposed it would, but – 'Why?'

'Because this is what they think I'm going to do, you see. They think I'm going to do it to customers, turn the place into a nursery. Look, if you decide not to take the job, fine, that's up to you, but please say it's for another reason, otherwise they'll say it's my fault for making a bad impression – ' Hilary's eyes filled with tears, which embarrassed her and touched Gina. Of course she was going to take the job if it were offered to her. It had already been established that most of her contact with Hilary would be via the telephone, and if the rest of Stalton Industries was prepared to adapt to Hilary and Jeremy, tolerating the teething troubles (and the digestive ones) of an arrangement whose success could only be in the interests of Gina and others like her, then she could too. Hilary took Jeremy into one of the bedrooms. Gina went downstairs to rejoin Paul. Her future boss he might be, but she was determined to deal briskly with any reference to the incident. His collar had not been puked upon, so it was not his place to feel indignant on Gina's behalf, or, indeed, apologetic on Hilary's. What had happened had been between Gina and Hilary. Hilary had apologized, so there was an end to it.

'I'll take you back now,' said Paul. 'I've got a few other people who want to meet you.'

The summons arrived for Gina to give evidence against the Stalton's driver who had nearly collided with her in January. She was horrified. She had almost succeeded in forgetting about it.

'I think I'll plead guilty,' she said to Oliver.

'What are you talking about? You're a witness.'

'Joke. They're really going to love me, aren't they, if I get one of their drivers disqualified.'

The trial was several weeks ahead; Stalton's would have made their decision by then. They would have made it by now if Hilary's and Oliver's optimism, and Gina's own, had been justified. Oliver brought home rumours of other candidates being looked at, and directors having second thoughts about the whole arrangement. Gina's tension was made worse by the behaviour of the Franson brothers. They had always treated her well, but now they reminded her of a wife who has just started to suspect that her husband is having an affair and wants to win him back. They praised her. They made solicitous enquiries about her schedule, was it too heavy? They hinted at a bonus in the offing. When they announced that it had been decided that she needed a secretary, she realized that she would have to tell them.

'You're a dark horse, aren't you, Gina! You didn't say you were thinking of leaving when we sent you on that expensive course!'

'I didn't know then,' she told Alex Franson miserably. He was the more volatile of the two brothers, and she had decided to tell him first, on his own, so that Roy could be brought in to calm him down.

'Tell that to the marines.'

'Are you accusing me of lying? I didn't ask to go on any course. Frankly, I didn't think I needed it, it didn't tell me anything I didn't know. It was while I was there that they got in touch.'

'Very clever of them.'

'Oh Alex, come on. They didn't say, "Look, Gina Heriot's gone on a START Selling course at her company's expense, let's snap her up afterwards." '

'How do you know they didn't? Roy. Come in and listen to this.' Roy stood with his shoulders hunched as Alex told him that Gina was leaving. He looked like an eagle, the bald-headed eagle of the American emblem. Alex was slightly birdlike too: a rather fussy sparrow. 'Nothing's definite,' she said. 'They asked for me, I was interviewed and it seemed to go well. I just thought you ought to know it was a possibility. When it's definite – if it's definite – I'll tell them that I've got to give you proper notice. I'll help you choose my successor, show them around – '

Roy spoke quietly. 'Do you think,' he said, 'that we are stupid?'

'No.'

He took a bunch of keys from his pocket and went to the cabinet where Gina kept those of her papers that she did not have at home. He locked it with a flourish and stood in front of it as if defending it from attack. His eyes gleamed. He looked slightly mad. 'I'll follow you.'

'What do you mean? Where?'

'To your house. Presumably you have no objection to my removing papers that belong to us.'

'What are you talking about? You can't fire me for – '

'I repeat my question. Do you think we're stupid? You are now an employee of Stalton Industries.'

'But I'm not! I may not be.'

'And it hadn't entered your pretty little head that you might improve your chances by taking all our customers there?'

'Roy!'

'I'll follow you home.'

'If you're firing me without notice,' said Gina quietly, 'you owe me a month's salary.'

'So sue us,' said Alex.

'Yeah,' said Roy. 'See you in court.'

'They're not serious,' Oliver consoled. 'Just go out and make your calls as usual and make sure that they know ... find some reason to phone them and talk as if nothing's happened. If they were serious, they'd have given you a cheque, they know they can't get away with that.'

Gina was not so sure. In deciding to tell the Franson brothers of her plans, she had thought only of their convenience; she had not taken account of their feelings. They were an odd pair of men: obsessive, temperamental and – this was the worst of it – proud. Suppose she was not taken on by Stalton's. How low would she have to grovel to get her old job back? She could probably demand it and have a case – but working on that basis at Franson & Franson was unthinkable. They would never let her forget that she had once tried to get away, and failed. She decided to follow Oliver's suggestion, to go to work as usual, but she met the postman on the path and he gave her an envelope containing a cheque and Form P45.

27

Our Ways House was a modern seven-storey office block between the Strand and Covent Garden. Teresa had been to it before, when she used to meet Greg Sargent for their annual lunches. Then she would be invited to take a seat in the hushed lobby to wait until his secretary was sent to usher her into his presence. Today she simply announced who she was and was waved through to the lifts. She was asked if she knew where to go and she said that she did.

The lift rose through Our Ways Fashions, Our Ways Motorcycles, Our Ways Foods, Our Ways Promotions, Our Ways Finance. It was lined with mirrors. Teresa never used to dress up to have lunch with Greg; she used to make a point of looking like an impoverished radical, to remind him who she was and who he used to be when he had loved her. But today she was wearing a new dress, and tights, and shoes with little heels.

She did not necessarily intend to continue in this way, but on your first day you could not be too careful.

The lift stopped. She turned right and walked along the thickly carpeted corridor towards the door that announced: 'NEW ATALANTA. THE MAGAZINE FOR THE WOMAN WHO KNOWS THAT THE BATTLE IS OVER AND SHE HAS WON.'

She went straight to the editor's office to announce her arrival. ''Morning,' she said.

'Good morning, Teresa,' said Brenda Sargent, smiling back at her.

Teresa had not allowed herself to feel personally slighted when, twelve years previously, Greg had announced his engagement to

Brenda. There had never been any question of Teresa and Greg getting married. Teresa had thought marriage an irredeemably corrupt institution, and so had he. They had both been going out with other people, and it had been ages since Teresa had let Greg know that none of her other partners was as important to her as he was. There had been no place for such declarations in the matey rivalry into which the outward expression of their feelings for one another had declined. They had, since their university days, got themselves into a silly game of busier-than-thou. Whenever his work kept him from seeing her, she had felt a need to retaliate at some later date by putting *Atalanta* business before him, whether or not this was strictly necessary. Over and over again this had happened, and, fools that they had been, they had never talked it out.

'Hello there,' they used to say, hugging each other like brother and sister. 'What was your name again?'

Or, 'Hello, stranger.'

'Hello, Teresa. Look, I'd better tell you, I'm getting married.'

'That's wonderful, Greg. Who to, have you decided?'

In describing Brenda, he had been at pains to let Teresa know that he was not running from the challenge of loving a busy feminist to seek solace with a simpler soul. Brenda was, on the contrary, a clever and assertive woman, not unlike Teresa herself. Brenda was a sub-editor on *Woman's Nest*, a job she disliked because of the magazine's obsession with knitting. Brenda had nothing against knitting, but she did not want to read about it. For reading she preferred *Atalanta*, which she admired, as she admired Teresa, about whom Greg had told her a great deal and whom she was looking forward to meeting. She had a degree in English and a diploma in journalism. She had many ambitions, one of which was to have three children. She believed that children needed their mothers at home during the pre-school years.

'You think that too, don't you, Greg? I'd sign her up at once if I were you.'

Greg had done this. Brenda had abandoned *Woman's Nest* to set up a nest of her own. The three little Sargents were gifted and rewarding. And now that the youngest was at school, Brenda was ready to return to paid employment.

'This is Jessica, my secretary,' said Brenda. 'Jessica knows everything.' Jessica looked as if this was true but she preferred not to brag about it. 'After we've had our little chat,' said Brenda, 'Jessica will show you around and introduce you to everybody.'

'Hello, Jessica,' said Teresa.

'Hello, Teresa. Would you like a cup of coffee?'

'If you're making one.'

'And shall I take your jacket? I'll show you the cloakroom later.'

Brenda said, 'There's nothing much happening this morning, so just settle in and orientate yourself. You'll find great piles of bumpf on your desk already I'm afraid, so you can have a look through that. Greg might want a word, he'll phone down if he has time. We've got a meeting this afternoon to talk about the relaunch. Let Jessica know if you need anything.'

Jessica took Teresa round the large open-plan office, introducing her to Nadia, the assistant editor, who had been poached from another magazine; Pam, the production manager, who, like Brenda, was returning to paid work after a break to do the other kind; and Lucy, the features editor, who used to be a freelance. Teresa also met Laura and Tess, a typist and a word processor operator upon whose services she must feel free to call. 'We'll call you Teresa, and Tess, Tess,' said Jessica. 'And then we won't get confused.' Teresa agreed that this seemed a good arrangement, and so did Tess, and so did everyone, smiling at each other with the awkward good will of newcomers shortly to be thrown into the thick of working together. 'Now, this is you,' said Jessica, when she had finished introducing Teresa to everyone who was in, leading her to a wide, light area whose perimeters were marked by filing cabinets and shoulder-high partitions. There were two new desks, an assortment of chairs and plenty of shelf-space, some of it already filled with the latest editions of various media reference books and directories. A vase of fresh flowers stood on the windowsill, and there were two telephones.

'There's stationery in the drawer, but I didn't know what you'd need. If you want anything else you can either fill in a requisition form or do what everyone used to do in my old job, which was steal mine.'

'Do I get a typewriter?'

'If you want one. I'll leave you to it now, shall I?'

'Yes, I'll be all right. Thank you, Jessica.' Gingerly, Teresa lowered herself into the peculiar-shaped desk chair, finding it surprisingly comfortable. On top of the pile in front of her was a folder marked 'Welcome to Our Ways.' This contained routine information for new staff, including a personal letter of welcome from Greg which, making no reference to the fact that they had met before, struck her as rather impersonal. There was a diagram of the company's structure with him at the top of it, promotional literature from the various subsidiaries, a copy of her contract of employment, and luncheon vouchers.

Well, well, well, she thought. *This is all very grown-up, isn't it?*

She had not sold *Atalanta* to the Sargents without examining all the alternatives. She had not given in without a fight.

On discovering that all her worst fears were to be fulfilled – that *Atalanta*'s printers and creditors, Big S, had the receivers in and *Atalanta* would be next if it could not pay its bill – she had gone first to her sister Marion. They had met in the staff canteen of the TV company where Marion worked, and Teresa had asked Marion to give *Atalanta* a thousand pounds, and to persuade nine of her friends to do the same. 'I know it's a lot to ask, I know it's not small change, heavens, but you can afford it, can't you? I mean, you'd spend that on a holiday, wouldn't you? *Atalanta* needs it,' Teresa had pleaded, and then, remembering Daphne, she had added, 'and you need *Atalanta.*'

She had not been expecting Marion to write a cheque there and then. Marion had her differences with Teresa, and indeed with *Atalanta*, though these had not stopped her being generous to it in the past. Teresa had expected Marion to do a lot of grumbling before agreeing. The hostility of Marion's response had been a shock.

'Who needs it? I don't, and neither do any of my women friends. We're cleaner-fish, remember?'

This was a reference to a recent *Atalanta* feature, jokily signed 'by our marine biology correspondent' and written in the style of a learned paper. It had concerned a curious breed of fish that lived in the South Seas. Cleaner-fish were all born female, but at some point in the life cycle of the shoal, under the influence of stimuli not yet fully understood by science, one of the females would sprout male genitalia, grow in size and start lording it over the others, bullying them and taking all the food.

'That was supposed to be a joke about Thatcher,' Teresa had said.

'Oh yeah?' Marion had retorted.

'Look, I promise you, this is positively our last appeal. We won't ask for another penny from anybody, except what you'll willingly pay for a first-class product.'

Marion had replied, with the careful enunciation of someone who had been saving something up: 'If I had a thousand pounds to spare, I wouldn't give it to you. I'd give it to Mum and Dad towards the pension money that you took off them.'

Before becoming a newsreader, Marion had worked on the kind of consumer programme that sent reporters to confront confidence tricksters with their misdeeds, live on camera. While loyally cheering Marion on, and holding no brief for the villainous victims trembling before her well-researched accusations, Teresa used sometimes to feel slightly sorry for them. She had felt even sorrier, that day in the staff canteen of the TV company. She had almost expected cameras to appear, trained on her face.

'I feel awful about that. That's why I'm going to make sure they get it back.'

'You are, yes. You're going to get it back from Greg.'

'Never.'

Teresa's *never* had put Marion into a rage the like of which Teresa had not seen since childhood. Marion had seemed for a moment to forget where, and who, she was. 'My God, it must be lovely to be so principled at someone else's expense. Not content with living off them – yes, I know, you pay rent, but not what they could get if you were a proper tenant – *grow up, Teresa!*' Marion had hissed through the monogrammed coffee cups. 'Join the grown-ups! This isn't some student rag week you're in! You know what? I always thought it was a bit unhealthy, you living there. And then I thought, oh well, Mum and Dad aren't the types to exploit her. But it's you, isn't it? You don't want to leave home, do you? You don't want to grow up. You'd rather keep *Atalanta* as your little hobby, paid for by Mummy and Daddy and kid sister. If you go to work for Greg he'll pay you a real grown-up person's salary and then you'll have no excuse for not doing real grown-up things like moving out and smartening up and realizing the world isn't perfect and deciding which particular form of imperfection you're going to have to settle for. . . .'

Sitting at her desk now in Our Ways House, feeling extremely grown-up on her first day as *New Atalanta*'s business manager, Teresa remembered this conversation and searched her scanty knowledge of anthropology to see if there were, or ever had been, societies in which, in the interests of tribal harmony, brothers and sisters broke off contact with each other when they reached adulthood. It would make sense, because the intimate knowledge of a person's failings that came from having shared their childhood could put vicious weapons into the hands of adults.

Teresa smiled ruefully at the remembrance of her response to Marion's outburst. It had hurt so much that it had almost taken her breath away, and this was before she had given any thought to the possibility that there might be some truth in it. Rather than ponder this, she had searched for some similar, below-the-belt insult to heave back at Marion ... something she knew about Marion that she could wound her with ... glamorous Marion, beloved of millions ... little Marion who must always have an audience, first with the party pieces, youngest winner ever of the Rotary Club Schools Debating Competition ... '*Shut up, big mouth!*' Teresa had snapped, there among the media stars. Following this indignity she had gone straight to a meeting of the *Atalanta* collective – brief, acrimonious and utterly predictable – and then she had gone to see Greg.

28

Besides their ability to change sex, cleaner-fish had another interesting characteristic. They got their food by eating algae and sediment from the teeth of sharks, hence their name. The sharks, of course, allowed the cleaner-fish safe conduct into and out of their mouths to perform this service. The *Atalanta* collective thought that 'women who know that the battle is over and they have won' – those for whom *New Atalanta* was intended – sounded like women who had an equivalent arrangement with their male bosses. They would not hear of their magazine being turned into a news sheet for such traitors.

Legally it did not matter whether they would hear of it or not hear of it, but Teresa had refrained from pointing this out, striving to gain their approval – or at least their grudging good wishes – for what she had already decided to do. When someone made a remark to the effect that Teresa's parents should not worry too much about losing five thousand pounds, since most people's parents did not have five thousand pounds to lose in the first place, she had realized that the approval of the collective was something she would have to do without. A gossip magazine had helped too, by publishing what purported to be an insider's view on why Teresa had been appointed to the job of business manager of *New Atalanta*, 'despite her proven unsuitability for the task'. It had suggested that she and Greg were still sexually involved, and that the all-female staff of *New Atalanta* had been selected with a view to their being a harem for him, an arrangement that Brenda was going to have to put up with as the price of being given 'something with which to amuse herself now that the children are at school'.

Cleaner-fish, eh? Teresa thought now. *Proven unsuitability for the task, eh? We'll see about that.*

Among the many folders on her desk was one containing copies of memos from Greg to the marketing managers of his various subsidiaries, mentioning that she had been appointed to sell advertising in the magazine and urging that she be given every assistance. Their obedient replies, ordering a page of full colour here, a half-page there, showed that they had got the message.

She felt patronized, as if Greg thought that she thought that Our Ways could make money by selling to itself. She consulted the Our Ways House Internal Directory and picked up the phone.

'Fashions Marketing. This is Carl Foxon, can I help you?'

'This is Teresa Beal from *New Atalanta*.'

'Hi, Teresa, welcome aboard. Your first day? What can I do for you?'

'I see you're going to advertise your jeans with us.'

'Greg said we had to, but we were going to anyway.'

'Thank you. When can I see the artwork?'

'When do you want it? Actually, you can see it in – ' he reeled off the names of the women's magazines already running the ad that would appear in the first issue of *New Atalanta*.

She would need to receive these magazines on a regular basis. Getting subscriptions organized seemed like a useful way to spend her time. She went to ask Jessica what the procedure was. Jessica was taking dictation from Brenda who, far from appearing to mind being interrupted, looked delighted, as if Teresa had just shown a remarkable piece of initiative. 'Actually that is all in hand, Teresa, but thanks for thinking of it. The magazines are around somewhere – '

'I'll find them, then.'

'Go and find them for her, Jessica.'

'There's no need,' Teresa said, but suddenly she was back at her desk with the magazines in front of her, crisp and new and unmarked.

Having acquainted herself with what the proposed Our Ways jeans spread would look like, she took a new pad of paper from the drawer and started to list those companies which were advertising in the other monthlies and which might therefore be persuaded to buy space from her as well. She had always wanted to do this at *Atalanta* but had never been allowed to until it was too late.

Another thing she had always wanted to do was to take account executives from advertising agencies out to lunch and lay it on the line to them that it was ridiculous to run campaigns aimed at women if they did not include feminists. It seemed that Greg had arranged this for her too. The desk diary revealed that she had a lunch date every day this week, today excluded, she noted with relief. Among the products that her guests were responsible for advertising were lingerie, credit cards, sanitary wear, cars, wines, books and 'baby-care'.

'Babycare' with a small 'b'. Teresa made a note to watch out for this one. If it meant babycare products, then of course there was no problem. But there was an anti-abortion campaign which specialized in putting images of chopped up fetuses in women's magazines as a way of getting their point across. 'Call this babycare?' they said. 'Don't *you* care?' Teresa did not propose to allow anything like that.

'Are you going out for lunch, Teresa, or shall Jessica bring you some sandwiches?'

'I'll go out, I think.' Everyone else was staying in and she supposed it would be sociable to join them, but she had been looking forward to having a lunch hour . . . so different from the days in the *Atalanta* sweatshop when she and the others would work on and on, putting the magazine together or having meetings, until the rumbling of somebody's stomach or an explosion of temper would draw attention to the fact that lunch time had come and gone.

She was not hungry so she just wandered about, enjoying the knowledge that should anything arise in her absence, it would be efficiently dealt with. She felt neither anxious nor guilty. It said in her contract of employment that she should have an hour for lunch and that was what she was having.

She looked in the windows of the fashion shops. Was it her mood that made this year's clothes look so attractive, was it her imagination that they would suit her? Had her indifference to clothes all these years really been a matter of principle, or had it been part of what Marion had so cruelly referred to as her refusal to grow up? Perhaps it had been neither of these things. A case of sour grapes was a more likely explanation: being unable to afford to be fashionable, she had dismissed the notion as silly. Which it was, of course, but people did not drop dead from being silly. She tried on a trouser suit for the hell of it and, also for the hell of it, bought it, paying for it with her new credit card as if to check that the card meant what it said. The shop assistant seemed to assume that it did.

Teresa had been helped in making her decision to take this job by an anonymous satirist's announcement that she could not do it. She wondered whether Brenda had been similarly wounded or challenged by the sneers. She had not said anything about them, though she had assured Teresa that she did not believe that she and Greg were having an affair. 'I knew you and he used to have lunch together every year. Sometimes, if he forgot to arrange it, I'd be the one to remind him.' Teresa did not know whether this remark had been deliberately cruel, or just honest. In fact, as the new staff of *New Atalanta* gathered for their afternoon meeting in the Our Ways board-room, she realized that she knew very little about the woman who was now her boss. Teresa had not been a frequent visitor to the Sargent home over the years, though often invited to things like christenings and parties to celebrate the New Year.

Brenda was of medium height, fleshy and gangly, with hair that always looked as if she had just run her hands through it, though whether in exasperation or bliss was not obvious from her calm, bland features. She wore a black suit with a black and white floral blouse as if she, like Teresa, were wanting to make a businesslike impression on her first day. She took her seat at the head of the table. Greg sat at the far end with the air of one who does not intend to intervene but just wants to keep an eye on things, and be available in case of emergencies.

Brenda welcomed everyone and outlined her plans for the maga-zine, characterizing the readers, to whom she referred in the singular as 'New Atalanta Woman'. She spoke with quiet and friendly firm-ness which Teresa, trying to be fair and supportive, struggled not to see as the way Brenda probably addressed the little Sargents when getting them organized for an outing. A pink rash round Brenda's neck suggested nerves, as did her habit of going back repeatedly over sentences and clauses, as if not quite happy with their phrasing and wanting to have another stab at it. But that, perhaps, was the hallmark of a natural-born editor. 'The idealism of the former magazine is not going to be abandoned. I think we can rely on Teresa to keep us up to the mark as far as that's concerned. Well, I don't mean just her, of course. But we're very glad to have her as our link with the past. What I mean is – ' Brenda decided to scrap this paragraph and start again ' – what I mean is, we were all loyal readers of *Atalanta*. We were loyal to it, in spite of the fact that it didn't always – ' Brenda gave Teresa a nervous little glance to see how she was taking this. *She's frightened of me*, Teresa thought with compassion, astonishment and some satisfaction. *What on earth does she think I can do?* She remembered something Greg had once said about Brenda's reaction to *Atalanta*: *She doesn't read it. She just puts it on the pile and says, 'This thing's boring now.'* But Brenda was struggling and Teresa gave her an encouraging smile. *We've got plenty of reasons to be enemies*, she thought. *So let's be friends.*

' – we didn't always understand it, because it seemed sometimes to be the private property of some exclusive little circle which we weren't members of and didn't speak its language, if you like – ' along with *if you like* went a tentative wiggle of the first two fingers of each of Brenda's hands, held up level with her mouth to signify inverted commas, to signify that she did not want what she had just said to be held against her if there were objections to it. So far Teresa had no serious objections: if Brenda had doubts about her position, so much the better, so much the easier for Teresa to use her influence to curb any excesses that might appear. 'New Atalanta Woman,' Brenda continued, 'is feminist-stroke-feminine. How did it ever come about that those two words mean different things? She knows the battle's over and she has won, but she also knows that she can't afford to be complacent. She enjoys her victories and lives life to the full but she's not about to become – '

A cleaner-fish? thought Teresa, glancing at Greg to see whether his mouth was open. To her intense delight it was, just slightly, in an expression of exemplary attentiveness to his wife's words. The tips of his teeth showed. They appeared very clean.

The reason he had his mouth open was that he was getting ready to speak. As soon as Brenda reached the end of her introductory stream of clichés, he took the floor with budgets and balance sheets and flow charts. He outlined his financial forecast, the limits within which production costs and overheads must be kept, the income he expected from advertising and sales. Teresa felt irritated. She ought to be doing this; or she ought, at least, to have seen the figures in advance. What was she to be, his assistant, his mouthpiece? 'I'll be handing all this over to Teresa, of course,' he said casually, and went on to explain that although he was prepared to run *New Atalanta* at a loss for eighteen months, should this turn out not to be necessary his appreciation would be reflected in everyone's salary.

They moved on to discuss features. Brenda had already commissioned her cover story. 'WHAT BATTLE?' it was to be called, 'AND WHO HAS WON?' There was only one possible answer to this question, Teresa supposed, given *New Atalanta*'s promotional slogan, but when Brenda announced who was to write the piece – an utterly reliable alumna of *Atalanta* – she realized cheerfully that even if the article were required to conclude that women had won, it certainly would not conclude that they had won everything.

The next feature sounded good too. It was to be about women

drivers. It was to take on the recently published findings of a certain male psychologist, to the effect that women's brains were inherently unsuited to the negotiation of complex road junctions. It was to refute these findings. And to anyone who did not accept the refutation, it was to put this question: if junctions have been built so that men can handle them and women cannot, why is this?

There was to be an article about women's lives in Libya, the first of a series of international reports written by locally based stringers. There were to be features about women setting up their own businesses, with helpful comments by a business consultant (Greg) on how they might increase their chances of success. There was to be fashion, of course, but the emphasis would be on practicality and economy, subjects in which New Atalanta Woman was more interested than she was in always being up to some industry-defined minute. Beauty would be related to fun and health. Cookery would emphasize the fact that whereas sometimes New Atalanta Woman liked to push the boat out, there were other times when the shortest time spent in the kitchen was not short enough.

'And what about New Atalanta Man?'

Everyone turned to look at Greg, who had said this. 'What about him?'

'Doesn't he spend any time in the kitchen?'

'He'd bloody well better,' said Brenda cheerfully, as if this were the continuation of some private but not-too-serious marital controversy. And it was agreed as a matter of policy that feature photographs showing domestic activities taking place should always include a male participant.

' . . . where appropriate,' said Greg to Jessica, who was taking minutes.

Teresa said, 'Can we say the same of the ads?'

'That's more difficult,' said Greg. 'We can't expect to have special campaigns designed for us.'

'No, fair enough. But what about your own companies? What about this, for instance?' Teresa passed around the advertisement for Our Ways jeans.

'I don't see anything wrong with it,' said Greg. 'They're not particularly tight, or anything.'

Teresa was just about to explain what she thought was wrong with the advertisement – as much to gain some impression of where her new colleagues stood on such matters as out of any hope of winning her point – when Nadia stepped in. 'I think there's more to New Atalanta Woman than her backside and her crotch, don't you, Greg?'

After Greg and Brenda, Nadia was the most senior person in the hierarchy. She was Brenda's assistant and deputy. She was also a friend of the Sargent family. She had been head-hunted from a rival company, and might be head-hunted again. Teresa watched Greg writhe. 'Nobody's ever complained,' he said.

'New Atalanta Woman will,' said Nadia. 'We're hoping Teresa's former readers will come to us. They've been educated – by Teresa and her friends – to complain about things like this. And not to buy the product.'

'I have been thinking of a more active image for our jeans,' said Greg. 'Women riding bikes, something like that? Or horses?'

'Could some of the women have faces?' said Nadia.

'And could some of the faces be black?' said Teresa.

'Shall we leave that with Greg?' said Brenda. 'We've got quite a lot to get through.' She looked as if she were refereeing a family quarrel. She could see both sides, and she did not want there to be any unpleasantness.

29

'I liked it,' she told Sam, her lover. 'I think I'm going to like it.'

'Well, wait till the end of the week,' he advised, but when the end of the first week came and she had had lunch with four advertising executives, two of them slightly obnoxious, two of them totally so, she still liked it. Of the slightly obnoxious executives, one, a woman, had expressed condescending pleasure at the fact that *Atalanta* had 'come in from the cold at last', and the other, a man, had wanted to know whether she seriously expected him to advise his lingerie clients to advertise in *New Atalanta* since the women it was aimed at had all burned their bras. Of the totally obnoxious executives, both men, one had insisted in the nastiest possible way on choosing the wine and paying the bill, and another had indulged in a bout of name-dropping: well-known feminists with whom (it had been implied) he had had sexual intercourse. In at least one case Teresa knew that this was very unlikely indeed, but she had dealt with this man, as she had dealt with all the executives, in a way of which Daphne Barclay would be proud, were she a different person. She might even be proud of it if she were the same person: selling was just selling, after all. The ruder these people had been to Teresa, the harder she had sold to them. She had badgered them with their need to communicate with New Atalanta Woman: what would their clients think of them if they let this important new constituency get away? She had answered their questions with further questions – 'How long before *New Atalanta* folds?' 'Does Greg Sargent strike you as the kind of man who'd throw good money after bad?' – turned objections into benefits – 'Your readers don't drink wine, they drink pints.' 'Tell them how nice your wines are, then, and they'll change' – and, in three cases out of four, closed a sale.

The amounts of space booked were not large – tokens, she reckoned, so that if the magazine did take off as she kept promising it would, the agencies would not appear, in the eyes of their clients, to have missed the bus containing New Atalanta Woman with her modern outlook, her eagerness to try new products, her flexibly radical opinions and her jingling purse.

At times during the lunches, Teresa had found herself saying things of which she could not quite approve. In response to questions from the man who claimed to sleep with famous feminists, she had said that no, she was not a lesbian. She ought, of course, to have told him to mind his own damn business. But she had programmed herself to be polite no matter what. She had wondered whether an invitation to bed was to follow. What had followed was in many ways worse: a space booking, like a reward for good conduct. Her discomfiture had amused him. *This is what they're like*, she had told herself. *For years I've avoided meeting men like this because of the way I've lived. But this is what they're like, and this is what New Atalanta Woman has to put up with every day of her life. And that's why she needs me to hang in here and make sure that this time her magazine survives.*

Another thing that Teresa was pleased to have done in her first week was to re-establish contact with the women's movement. Not the most radical parts of it, certainly not the *Atalanta* collective, but the businesses, those that used to buy space in *Atalanta*, those that had always had to break even, those that knew the score: the shops, the cafés, the publishers and Women's Wheels, a feminist garage.

It had not started well.

'Sorry, Teresa, we can't,' said Penny from Women's Wheels.

The correct response to that would have been, *May I ask why you think you can't?* In fact, Teresa had said, 'Ah, come on, Penny, give me a break. You always used to.'

'That was . . . good will. I don't think we ever got anything out of those ads. And I can't believe the rates you're charging now.'

Tell me. What would you have expected to pay, for so many extra readers?

'How about a spot of good will now?' Teresa had lowered her voice. 'I'm telling you, this place is teeming with feminists.' She had returned to her normal pitch. 'Has it ever occurred to you that roundabouts are the wrong shape?'

'No.'

'Well they are, it's all a male plot to keep women from driving. What an environment to sell the services of a feminist garage. All right, you don't feel any good will. What about ill will? You could say: "Women's Wheels Welcomes *New Atalanta* and Looks Forward to Its Immediate Bankruptcy – " '

'Of course we don't – '

' "May all your typos be libels. May all your pages drop out." '

'You are in a state, aren't you?' Penny had said with some concern. 'How about a quarter of a page at the old price?'

'No, no. I don't want it out of pity. I want you to advertise with us because it makes good commercial sense or not at all.'

'It doesn't.'

'You can have one out of pity if you want.' Teresa had suddenly felt homesick for all her old friends. 'How are you all, anyway?'

'How are *you*?' said Penny. 'Are you calling from your office? Can you talk? We're all dying to know what it's going to be like.'

Teresa had cleared her throat. '*New Atalanta* is the magazine for the woman who knows that the battle is over and she has won.'

Penny had let out a long, rich snort . . . and booked a quarter-page. And that was how it was going. People ground whatever axes they had to grind . . . and booked space. They laughed or sneered or patronized, but as long as Teresa sat tight and asked for the order, they booked space. One of these days someone might actually be nice and respectful and serious and courteous as they booked space, but the important thing in the meantime was that she was successfully persuading them to book space in a radically minded magazine upon which they had not yet set eyes. She was persuading them that something important was about to happen, and it was in their interests to be part of it. She wondered how much of this she ought to thank Daphne Barclay for, and how much of it had been in her all along.

'I've been thinking I ought to take up some hobbies,' she told Sam.

'Some what?'

'For the first time in my life, I know when I've finished work. I come home in the evenings and I'm home. I don't go to meetings and no one rings me up. They ring Greg and Brenda, they have the nightmares. And weekends – two whole days all to myself. The luxury of it. And money I don't keep feeling I ought to plough back into the magazine and live on less – '

'It's all right for you,' he grumbled. His freelance work was going well, but its demands on his time were enormous and erratic.

'When you're as old as me,' she told him, 'you can have evenings and weekends as well.'

She did not catch what he said next. She had to ask him to repeat it. 'If you've got all this money, we could buy a house.'

'A what?'

'I want to live with you, Teresa.' He showed her an advertisement in the evening paper. It was a table in which hopeful house purchasers could compare the amounts they were currently paying in rent with the value of a property they could buy if the rent were translated into mortgage repayments. It seemed that she and Sam could afford something called a 'Starter Home' near Epping Forest, five minutes from the Central Line.

'What in God's name is a Starter Home?'

'It's for young couples. It's a way of getting your toe into the mortgage market. You buy one of these little boxes, live in it for a couple of years, do it up, sell it and get something better.'

She told herself that the pounding in her heart arose from pleasure at what he had just confessed: that he wanted to live with her. That he saw their relationship as permanent. That he liked being with her. That her resigned waiting for the news that a younger woman was about to take him away from her was foolish, that her fears were unfounded. But she was too honest not to recognize terror when she felt it. By living in her parents' granny flat, she had thought that she had escaped house-purchase, with its responsibilities, its fabulous debts. *Do it up*, he had said casually. Knock down walls in your spare time. Put in a bow window, a sun-roof. She lacked the skills. She lacked the nerve. She told him this. He shrugged. 'Go to an evening class in home maintenance. You just said you wanted a hobby. Of course, if you don't want to . . .'

She did not know whether she wanted to or not. It was astonishing enough to know that he wanted to. Presumably he had taken account of the possibility that he would discover things about her, if he lived with her, that were less than lovable. He might find out that she was crabby and had disgusting habits. Actually, she did not think that her habits were all that disgusting, but how would she know? She was used to them. There might be things that she had never thought of as disgusting, but which would revolt him. *Of course, if you don't want to* – She did not know whether she wanted to or not. She could not imagine it.

She enrolled for a course in basic plumbing, and another in carpentry. On other evenings, if she was not with Sam, she went out with her new friends at *New Atalanta*, went to their homes or had them to hers. Or she stayed at home alone, adding to her discovery that a great many books had been written and published over the last few years that were not about feminism, both fiction and non-fiction. Some of them were excellent.

Her carpentry tutor was a man, but very nice: she told him that she was hopeless, knew nothing, and he said, 'That's what I'm here for.' He said that he would have her putting up shelves in no time. It occurred to her that, should this turn out to be true, she must not put up the shelves in her own flat, for that would imply that she did not intend to move out and she had not decided this. She asked her mother casually one day whether she needed any extra shelves, and her mother replied that you could not have too many shelves in your kitchen.

She could not imagine buying a house with Sam. She could imagine it all too well. As things stood between them, if he decided to end their relationship, it could be done with the minimum of fuss. But if they shared a house, there would be endless wrangling. There would be comic-grotesque arguments about whose record and whose dinner plates . . . or perhaps they would build a partition down the middle of the house, behind which he would entertain his new lover. He did not mention the matter again and neither did she but she hoped that he would take it, from the enthusiasm with which she was pursuing her studies, that she was giving it serious consideration. She hoped he understood that her life was changing with breathtaking speed at the moment, and another big decision was quite beyond her.

She had tried to hold out, when negotiating the sale of *Atalanta* to Greg, for generous compensation for the outgoing collective. But his solicitor had pointed out that he had no obligations in that department: none of the collective members had been an employee of *Atalanta* in the legal sense, they had no contracts of employment, and had been paid in cash while claiming social security. This being so, it was probably not in their interests to be mentioned in the agreement. 'I think you can rely on me to do the decent thing, Teresa.' Greg's idea of the decent thing had turned out to be a derisory few hundred pounds between them, with heavy hints to the effect that they would have got more if they had not made such a fuss. Still making the fuss, they had taken the money and retreated to Collindeane Tower.

Collindeane Tower was the half-derelict block of flats in South London where *Atalanta* used to have its base and where other impoverished feminist projects still squatted: the Survivor Centre for victims of rape and battering, a second-hand clothes exchange called Goddess Garments, and the Collindeane Newsletter. Teresa was surprised to find the Newsletter still arriving at her home. She had assumed that she would be struck off, though her subscription still had several months to run. She opened her copy with caution, expecting to read hard words against herself. She knew she was hated, though the Newsletter gave no evidence of this: she was not mentioned, she felt forgotten, written off, which was somehow worse. She could remember times when the Collindeane Newsletter used to drip with abuse for named and unnamed individuals suspected of doing the movement down. Now it seemed to contain nothing but appeals, and these appeals went as directly to Teresa's heart and conscience as if she were the person responsible for their necessity.

'Goddess Garments needs women to wash and mend clothes at home.' 'The Peace Camps are STILL THERE, please go and stay.' 'The phone rota at the Survivor Centre needs volunteers, and money to pay the bill . . .' 'Sisters, I am dying.' Teresa's blood seemed to pause. She ran her eye to the bottom of the letter to see whether it came from somebody she knew. The signature was just 'Molly'. Teresa did not remember anyone called Molly. 'There is no further treatment that can help me and I am ready to die but I need your support, your strength and love . . .' The address was in Suffolk. Teresa bought fifty-two postcards from an art gallery, images of female deities, and fifty-two stamps. She put the stamped cards in a pile near the tin where she kept the milk money so that she would remember to send one each week. (Teresa sent most of her private letters from the office these days, but this was different.) 'Dear Molly, I am thinking of you. I don't know how to send strength, but please take all you can from me. I'm looking forward to writing to you once a week for a long time. Love and sisterhood, Teresa.' She did not put her full name in case Molly belonged to a school of thought that would make strength, love and sisterhood unacceptable from such a source.

30

The Collindeane women were not, of course, invited to the *New Atalanta* launch party, but she wondered if they might turn up anyway: picketing outside with their begging bowls, or marching in past the photo-montage of women for whom the battle was over, they having won their court cases, been appointed or elected to the positions they sought, had their courses approved or their books published.

If the Collindeane women restricted themselves to picketing, Greg and Brenda would know exactly what to do: far from causing an unpleasant scene by summoning the police, they would send a waiter out with a bottle of wine and a tray of canapés.

Greg had his jacket off and his sleeves rolled up, having popped down from his office to make sure that everything was all right with the construction of the display. (Brenda was looking after the caterers.) There were blown-up pictures of equal pay strikers, torch-light processions for the Sex Discrimination Act, campaigns to protect abortion rights. Teresa looked at them fondly and with nostalgia. *Weren't we beautiful?* she thought.

'Are you there?' Greg murmured over her shoulder.

'I'm there but you can't see me. I'm the one behind the banner.'

She could not help but be proud of all the feminists portrayed in this hall of fame: politicians, writers, entertainers, entrepreneurs, bus drivers, trade union leaders, artisans and academics. Interspersed with those to whom clear statements of commitment to the women's cause could be attributed, were others to whom they could not, but who had nevertheless blazed important trails: on to an oil rig in one case, or into boardrooms, archaeological digs, the cockpits of aeroplanes and, of course, Number 10 Downing Street. '*She*'s not coming, is she?'

'We sent her an invite but she hasn't replied,' said Greg.

Teresa stared at him. She had been joking.

'Do you think that means she is coming?' he said, 'or she isn't?'

'You'll be drummed out of the SDP.'

'We've invited all of them.' He waved at the photographs. 'Wouldn't you like to meet her? Aren't there things you'd like to say to her? Or would you chicken out?'

The Collindeane women did not appear. They probably had more important things to do. Teresa drifted about, smiling hospitably as if the party were her party, urging guests to drink up as if the drink were her drink. There was a great variety of things to drink. Teresa intended to make the most of this, particularly the malt whisky for which she had a passion, not often indulged. She knew her own capacity well and would not get drunk. 'Congratulations,' people said. 'Congratulations on the magazine, it looks wonderful.' They were not, of course, referring to the fact that Teresa had exceeded by ten per cent the advertising target that had been set for her, not counting the space that had been compulsorily purchased by Our Ways subsidiaries. No one noticed advertisements in that way. Daphne Barclay had been right when she said that people who thought themselves superior to salespeople were only free to do so because of the efforts of the very salespeople they despised. (Why was Daphne Barclay not here? Greg and Brenda would surely have invited her, had Teresa thought to suggest it. She would not be out of place.) Teresa spotted the journalist who had written the cover story, 'WHAT BATTLE AND WHO HAS WON?' 'Magnificent,' Teresa told her. 'Beautiful piece of sneaky, two-edged feminist writing. Anyone would think that you believed some of the things you said more than others. Congratulations.'

'I do my best,' said the journalist modestly. 'And congratulations to you.' Teresa drifted off, looking for Sam who had said that he would come if he could but she was not to worry if he did not make it. She received congratulations and handed them out. She did not always know what she was congratulating people for, but there must be something or they would not be here. She had another malt.

'Aren't you the girl who reads the news?'

At this very moment, Marion would be applying her make-up preparatory to doing just this. She was enormously disappointed to have missed the party. Teresa stared balefully into the pouchy eyes of the middle-aged man in the green suit who had put the question, and said, 'You're very sharp-eyed.'

'Slipped up the other night, didn't you? When you tried to get that fellow in Beirut and he wasn't there.'

'Congratulations on – '

'Got a bit flustered, didn't you? Don't they train you for that kind of thing?'

'What do you think of the magazine?' *And who the hell are you, anyway?*

'My wife'll want to meet you,' he said.

The wife stood, lonely and furious by the photograph display, reading *New Atalanta*. The man presented Teresa – 'Reads the news' – and departed.

'I've never seen you read the news.'

'That's because I don't. I'm Teresa Beal, business manager. What do you think of the magazine?'

'Better than it used to be.'

'Oh.' Teresa took a sip at her drink. 'Um . . . are you in publishing yourself?'

'I'm not, no.'

'Have you had a nice day?'

'Not particularly. Go on, say it, you're dying to. *What do you do?* Nothing at all, I'm a housewife, any more questions?'

'Do you, er, like being a housewife?'

'Trick question!' the woman crowed. 'If I say yes, you'll despise me for liking it and if I say no you'll despise me for doing it. I don't see anything in *this* – ' she flapped the pages of *New Atalanta*, making them sound like an angry bird trying to take off ' – about the Inland Revenue telling him about my building society interest when I don't even know what he earns.'

Teresa was starting to feel that she had had enough. Unless this woman was a newlywed, which seemed unlikely, she must know that it was her husband's practice to abandon her at parties, so why had she not stayed at home with a good book? This was not the first time that Teresa had been accosted by a housewife who seemed to want to blame her for the disappointments of the occupation. If Teresa were to speak freely, she might say that it was the other way round: it was the continued and inexplicable willingness of women to become housewives that was responsible for many of the disappointments of women like Teresa who were not so willing. 'There are a number of campaigns running for separate taxation,' she said. 'But I expect you know that. I expect you're involved, feeling as strongly as you do. Brenda! Come and meet . . . sorry, I didn't catch your name. She's got an idea for an article she wants to write.'

Brenda obviously knew the woman. 'Lovely to see you, Olivia. How are the children?'

Teresa went to talk to Penny and the others from Women's Wheels. They wore bow ties and clean overalls and the Our Ways photographer kept taking pictures of them.

'Seen your ad?'

'Yes.'

'Happy with it?'

'It looks all right.'

'Want another?'

'I wouldn't mind another of these gins,' said Penny. 'Lovely party, Teresa.'

'I'm glad you could come,' Teresa murmured, as if the party were hers. She could see the man in the green suit being dragged over by his wife. He was doing a pantomime of reluctance and fear and being fetched by the scruff of his neck. 'You know what this is going to be, don't you?' Teresa whispered. ' "You're a feminist, tell my husband to stop being a pig." '

The Women's Wheels women gathered protectively round, but the man in the green suit barged through. 'My wife tells me you're an impostor. You don't read the news at all.'

'How *is* Marion?' said Penny. 'She handled that Beirut cockup beautifully.'

Olivia told her husband loudly, 'Teresa thinks you should put your pay slips on the kitchen table.'

Teresa turned towards the entrance of the room as if mesmerized with awe and delight. Her voice trembled slightly as she said, 'Good for her. I never thought she would come. She said she was working on Cabinet papers this evening.'

The Women's Wheels women caught on at once. 'What an honour!'

'She doesn't often go to parties.'

'That's because she's shy.'

'But being as she's a personal friend of Teresa's –'

'Please.' Teresa raised a hand. 'I don't like to talk about it.'

'I can't see anyone,' said the man in the green suit, standing on tiptoe.

'That's because she's surrounded by detectives.'

The couple rushed off to look. Teresa filled up everybody's glass, including her own.

Greg was working his way methodically among the women guests, issuing them with seigneurial kisses. But his eyes hooded over when he saw Teresa. 'I've been looking for you,' he said. 'Look. You've got a sense of humour. I've got a sense of humour. But not everybody . . . you've upset Olivia.'

'Oh no!'

'Will you come and meet them properly? They don't know who you are, and they think you're a bit peculiar.'

'They got that right. . . .'

'She's married to Dirk Lanscombe, for heaven's sake.'

Whoever he was. Greg probably owed him money.

'Is that my fault?'

'Teresa, I think I'm going to send you home.'

She might have found this funny, but for the fact that the Women's Wheels women were giving her warning looks, and a number of other people were staring, and on the floor was a little pool of malt whisky which could only have come from her waving glass. 'Fine, Greg. Get me a taxi. Thanks for a wonderful party. So sweet of you to invite me.'

The taxi fare was expensive. Fortunately the driver took credit cards.

She let herself into her parents' house by means of her own front door, and climbed the stairs to her flat. She had no idea what the time was. The party had still been in full swing when she left. She wished she had given someone a message to give to Sam if he turned up. She wished a great many things. She wished that Greg had not slipped an additive into her malt whisky, which, in its pure state, could be drunk in large quantities with relative impunity. The additive was now making her feel hungover and sick and hungry and pissed all at once. She wished that the alternatives offered to her by her little fridge were not so stark. She could fry something frozen, which would be quick and convenient and disgusting; or she could make something sensible, a cheese and walnut salad, only she knew exactly what would happen: she would eat all the cheese and all the walnuts while she was making it, and would end up with something green and disappointing.

Molly was almost due for another of Teresa's weekly postcards. Teresa took one down from the kitchen shelf and wondered what to write. Did Molly want to hear about parties? Did helping someone die mean reassuring them that life went on, or reassuring them that life was not all that wonderful? The story of the party might amuse Molly, or it might fill her with grief. *You had a job. You had a job, you were starting to make something of it, and you threw it away. What have I got? Cancer.* (Teresa assumed that Molly had cancer. It was usually cancer when the person was young and knew that they were dying and said things like, *There is no further treatment that can do me any good.* Teresa assumed that Molly was young.) If Molly were irritated by Teresa's postcard, by any of her postcards, Teresa herself would never know. Teresa would not necessarily know about it when Molly died. Molly might be dead already. Teresa did not put her full name or address on the cards, so there was no way that Molly's friends could write and inform her. They might put a notice in the Collindeane Newsletter, of course, but in their grief they might forget. 'Dear Molly, the weather here is so-so. I hope it's better with you.' Teresa was running out of things to say to Molly. It was difficult, knowing nothing about her, not even knowing that she was alive. Might Teresa have to go on sending these cards until the end of her own life? It was a small enough responsibility to have, and it had been freely entered into, but she found it alarming. *Dear Molly, I think I may have lost my job.*

Poor you, replied Molly, ironic and brave.

Molly's bravery entitled her to be ironic. Teresa would not let her down.

Teresa did not lose her job. Greg let it be known that he would not expect there to be any repetition, on Our Ways premises, of her behaviour. She did a mental search for times in the past when he had drunk too much and been rude to her friends, or, indeed, had been rude to them without the excuse of having drunk too much. Unable to remember any such occasion recent enough to be meaningful, she abandoned the ploy and took pleasure instead in the realization that Greg was her boss, nothing more, and she was at liberty to dislike him in the way all bosses must expect to be disliked.

Partly to ensure that he knew this, and partly because it was important to her to be on good terms with Brenda, she said sincerely to her: 'Sorry I got drunk at your launch.'

And Brenda said, 'Nonsense, I thought you were very funny. And anyway, it was *our* launch.'

Our launch, our magazine. Not MINE any more – was it ever? – but OURS. Mine and Jessica's and Nadia's and Brenda's . . . we do what we want, we have New Atalanta Man on the run.

In office parlance, the term 'New Atalanta Man' was generally taken to mean Greg. 'New Atalanta Man's got a furrowed brow this morning.' 'New Atalanta Man wants to see you in his office.' When

Greg himself used the expression, he applied it more widely, referring to his suspicion (shortly, he hoped, to be confirmed by a readership survey) that the magazine had a keen male following. (Teresa was to organize the survey, but Greg would phrase the relevant questions.) According to Greg, New Atalanta Man was supportive of the magazine's aims and loved to read his wife's or his women friends' copies, though he rarely put his hand in his pocket and bought a copy for himself.

Sometimes Greg wanted feature articles modified to make them more meaningful and relevant to New Atalanta Man. For example, he thought the occasional male fashion feature would be nice, and a source of advertising revenue. And he did not see why, as long as all the fiction was *about* women, it also had to be *by* women. Teresa and the others explained to him, and he gave way. The friendship and solidarity that was growing up amongst them was a source of great delight to her. She remembered the allegation that Greg would look upon the *New Atalanta* staff as his harem. In fact he treated all of them with unfailing propriety, whereas they reserved the right to ridicule him behind his back when he deserved it, and to scheme against him as women had always schemed against men, never forgetting his ultimate power but searching for ways to circumvent it. Teresa's enjoyment of this process was marred only by consideration of the role of Brenda, who tried to be all things to all people. It was acceptable to refer to Greg as New Atalanta Man in her presence, but only with the broadest and most affectionate of smiles upon one's face. Serious indignation and plotting must be kept for times when Brenda was not there. One example of this concerned the anti-abortion advertisement: Nadia obtained, from friends on magazines that had run the ad, confirmation that they had lived to regret doing so, under a deluge of protest letters and subscription withdrawals. 'We don't want to be out of step with New Atalanta Woman, do we, Greg?' Recognizing a brick wall when he ran up against one, Greg had yielded and thanked Nadia for saving *New Atalanta* from embarrassment.

Clearly realizing that there were limitations to her all-girls-together style of management, Brenda was sometimes quite authoritarian and snappy, and never more so than when she sided with Greg. She did not always side with him, but when she did the pair of them were irresistible and everybody knew it. This made the other women cunning. Teresa thought it sad that Greg was thus succeeding in making Brenda an outsider among her own staff, but then nobody had forced her to marry him.

Our magazine. The heart-warming letters that poured in from readers were addressed to the editor, but Teresa allowed her heart to be warmed by them also. *I pay for all this, you know,* she thought. *I make it all possible. You don't know my name (it's there on the masthead if you care to look) but I'm here. I'm the breadwinner.*

One day a reader's letter did arrive for her. It came from Ann Mitchison in Sunderland. Its tone started out as appreciative, but, having got that out of the way, it turned challenging. Teresa did not remember Ann Mitchison as a challenging person; it appeared that Teresa was not the only person upon whom START Selling – Women! had wrought its magic.

31

Ann Mitchison went into the public library and asked for the local newspapers from ten years back. She sat down with the birth announcements. She filled in columns in an exercise book marked PROSPECTS. The columns were headed NAME OF CHILD, DATE OF BIRTH, ADDRESS.

Some of them would have moved house, but you could not have everything. 'Dear Mr and Mrs so-and-so,' she would write. 'I see it is your son/daughter's birthday in a few weeks. Have you thought of giving him/her something different this year?'

She looked up play groups and nursery schools in the Yellow Pages. 'Would you agree that the pre-school child needs toys that are safe, entertaining and educational? Toys that demonstrate mechanical principles in a clearly understandable – '

She visited toy shops and craft shops. 'May I have a few moments of your time to show you this? It's hand-made by a local craftsman and it's based on an original by A. J. Ribson – '

'Who?' said the buyer.

'A. J. Ribson, the, er, Victorian engineer. What you do, you fill this up with water and it, well, it moves.'

'I see.'

'I'll be happy to demonstrate it to you if you've got some water handy.'

'It's certainly very unusual,' said the buyer, when she had got the model moving, the peacock opening and closing its tail. 'I'll take three and see how they go.'

'Three?' said Ann.

'I can't take more, I'm afraid.'

'I've only got one,' she said.

'Tom, we've got to get a bit of a system going here.'
'Right, Mam. You're the boss.'
'I could have sold three peacock fountains today.'
'You've been on at me to make windmills.'
'That was last week.'
'How long do you think these things take?'
'Too long,' she said. 'You've got to speed up.'
'Mam, you're selling my models as an alternative to shoddy mass-produced toys, right? Now you're telling me to skimp.'
'I'm not, but –'
'There aren't any more hours in the day than I put in.'
'I know, pet. What you need's an assistant.'
'Make that four,' he said.

The figure they had to keep their eye on was forty pounds a week. Forty pounds a week clear profit. Forty pounds a week was what Tom was getting as his Enterprise Allowance. Forty pounds a week was what they would lose when his Enterprise Allowance ran out, four months and two weeks from now. Forty pounds a week was what they had to replace. Until they achieved this, there was no point in thinking about spending money on anything else.

People talked about businesses 'taking off'. She liked the expression, it made her think of geese running and running and then, just when you thought they would never make it, rising gracefully into the air.

Geese, or aeroplanes. Ann had never flown but she could imagine being wafted upwards by a great rush of energy. She had seen it in films. Another thing she had seen on film was a plane not all of whose engines had been operating on full power at the moment of take-off. It had skidded off the runway and burst into flames.

She had a horror of debt. Her accountant said that this was an understandable and in some respects praiseworthy attitude. It was also one with which a person would not last long in business.

'Banks like lending money to businesses, Mrs Mitchison. They enjoy it. It's what they're there for.'
'But we already owe a thousand pounds to my sister.'
'Is she pressing you for payment? No? Hang on to it, then. But you're right not to take on further commitments at the moment. Let's look at making better use of the resources you've got.'

By *the resources you've got*, Miss Hutton meant Tom.

'Tom, those milkmaid dolls – '

'Those bits of wood that you and Shelly put frilly dresses on, you mean.'

'They sold.'

'Right. I'll knock off a dozen. Now is that before or after two peacock fountains for the craft shop? Is it before or after six windmills for bairns with birthdays coming up?' He was tired and frustrated and angry. 'Just tell me, and then I'll know.'

'*I* don't know,' she said. 'I don't know what to do.'

What they needed was a few more people like Gina Heriot: people interested in executive toys and prepared to pay for them. They could be a gold mine. Ann had been nervous about invoicing Gina for another £19 over and above the £10 deposit she had paid for the oil derrick. She had expected an indignant reply and a refusal to pay, but the cheque had arrived, along with a note appreciative of 'this beautiful piece of work'. It had been a beautiful piece of work. It had been Tom's first commission from a stranger and he had gone to town on it. He had gone to town to the public library and found out a great many things about drilling technology . . . things which, in Ann's opinion, he did not need to know, things which she certainly did not want to hear about.

'That's the rotary table, Mam. That's the kelly – '

'She's not going to go out drilling with it. All it's got to do is sit on somebody's desk and look nice.'

'Mitchison's *Working* Models. If it doesn't work, they'll have us under the Trades Descriptions Act. You ask our accountant.'

She aimed a cuff at him. 'The time you're spending on this, we'll need to ask Gina for close on £100 – '

'Go on, then,' said Tom. 'She sounds as if she can afford it.'

When he was not off educating himself in the ways of oil rigs, he was at his precious museum. He was in love with the past. She supposed this was because he saw the past as a time when craftsmen were respected. Ann herself had no time for the museum. It gave her the creeps. This was not only because all the old shipyard machinery brought back sad memories of her marriage, but also because Tom's friends there were weird and peculiar: funny old men obsessed with trams, robots and perpetual-motion machines. Tom fancied himself as a latter-day A. J. Ribson. She wondered if Ribson himself had had a mother whom he used to drive crazy.

Making a virtue of necessity, she approached the museum's souvenir shop, asking if they would stock models of exhibits. They agreed. And, to give Tom his due, models sold from the museum shop as fast as Ann could put them there. But this was not fast enough.

It was too easy, anyway, the museum shop. People did not go to the museum in the first place if they did not have an interest in historical objects. In the museum shop, Mitchison's Working Models sold themselves. But if they sold themselves, what was Ann's role? She was a diploma-holding saleswoman. She wanted to start selling.

She saw a sign outside a church promising a craft fair.

'SOFT TOYS, POLISHED STONES, PATCHWORK, LACE, KNITTED GOODS, WEAVING, WOODWORK, HAND-PAINTED CHINA.'

The man on the door who took her 30p admission wore a T-shirt: 'CRAFT WORKERS DO IT BY HAND.'

'LEATHERWORK, ENAMELLED JEWELLERY, CAKES, CARDS, MUSICAL INSTRUMENTS, DRIED FLOWERS, FLORAL PICTURES . . .'

It seemed strange to do business in a church. It was to help the unemployed, she supposed. The altar had been cleared and covered over, and fenced off with stacked-together pews. The stalls – tables with white cloths – were all at a safe distance from it. She approached a table marked 'DOGGY'. The goods it had for sale all had something to do with dogs: stuffed dogs, wooden dogs, drinking cups and shaving mugs with dogs painted on the side, dog-shaped pincushions. She asked the stall-holder: 'Is it your own business?'

'Well, it's just a hobby really,' the woman replied. 'I love dogs but I can't have them because of my asthma, so this is the next best thing.'

Walking from table to table, Ann guessed that for a great many of these people their craftwork was no more than a hobby. Even if the quality of much of their work were not so indifferent (toilet-roll holders made of baked beans tins covered in felt; shells decorated with sealing wax trying to be ash trays; knitted cactuses) the quantities they had for sale did not suggest any possibility of making a living. And their prices were very low. She sighed. They could afford to keep their prices low if they were only doing it as a hobby.

But she gathered from a conversation with a printer of greetings cards that many people did make a living from it. Craft fairs were held all over the country, with work of a much more professional quality than this. Buyers from big department stores and mail-order houses sometimes attended.

'Do you go to these fairs yourself?'

'It's hardly worth my while. It's just – '

' – a hobby?'

'Well, a little bit more than that,' the printer conceded, handing Ann a leaflet.

'If there was – like, an agent – ' Ann began. 'If there was someone who'd take your lovely cards round the fairs and sell them for you on commission, would you be interested?'

'I might be.'

She moved from stall to stall, putting her question, collecting leaflets.

She descended the steps into the crypt. It was dark and the air was full of flute music, breathy and tuneless. It came from a tall man, thin as a skeleton. He played with a haughty, faraway expression on his face, as if it was all right with him if anyone wanted to buy one of the flutes in the basket at his side, but he was not too bothered one way or the other. The only people who looked in any way serious about their work were a young couple blowing glass into the shapes of birds and flowers and animals, their black-goggled faces lit up like the faces of devils, Mr and Mrs. The wife was heavily pregnant, her belly came between her and her work and she kept putting her hand on it as if she wanted to shift it out of the way. Behind her in a carrycot slept a new baby.

You're going to have your hands full, Ann thought, and she approached the couple with her idea of selling their work on their behalf. They looked as if they might be interested, but of course part of their work involved demonstrating their craft and Ann would not be able to do that for them.

She could not think of an answer to this objection, so she agreed with it.

'And anyway, it's the only social life we get,' said the man. 'We're stuck in the workshop all week, and we like going to craft fairs.'

'We're not going to be able to get around as much as we have been though, are we?' said his wife.

'No, but I'd miss the social side,' said the man. Ann took their card and went to talk to the man with the flutes. 'Have a blow,' he invited, waving at the basket and carrying on playing.

'I don't think I will. I'm tone-deaf.'

'Everyone can make music,' he told her, but when she tried to broach the subject of being his agent he just went on playing.

She talked to a few more people, both in the crypt and back upstairs. There was some interest, but not enough. What the glass-blower had referred to as 'the social side' was obviously important to a lot of them as the reason for not wanting to give up going to craft fairs. She wondered what Miss Barclay would say to that. *In the time you'll save by not going to craft fairs, you can build up your social life nearer home.*

It was only an idea. She could not even drive.

'I've heard you need a lesson for every year of your life,' she told Pat, her sister. Having had the idea she was alarmed by it and was trying to talk herself out of it.

'I'll teach you,' said Pat.

'You should never be taught to drive by your own flesh and blood.'

'Who says that? The driving schools.'

'I'll think about it.'

'You'll do it. Who ever heard of a saleswoman with a diploma and no driving licence?'

'THE TRUTH ABOUT WOMEN DRIVERS!' said the cover of a magazine in Smith's. She recognized the name of the magazine as the one Teresa Beal had brought to the selling course, though she would not have recognized it otherwise. Teresa had certainly cheered it up.

She felt a bit persecuted. Now that she had had the idea of learning to drive, everyone was conspiring to make her do it.

Everyone was conspiring to make her not do it, according to the article. Driving schools were sexist, and so was the car industry. Once women got over this, they made the best drivers.

Ann turned with relief to an article about women setting up their own businesses, one of a series, the magazine promised. This month's interview was with a vegetarian caterer. It ran for three pages and included a photograph of the caterer standing, with her staff of four, beside a huge buffet which, according to the caption, contained no animal products whatever. 'For some people it's a matter of principle,' said the caterer. 'But you'd be surprised how many people don't know that vegetarian food is, quite simply, nicer.' A contact address and telephone number were given, and there was a list of suggestions from a business consultant, such as that the caterer should build up the company banquet side of her work and make more use of vegetarian convenience foods from supermarket chains, Our Ways, for example. Next month's feature was to be about a woman who did luxury re-upholstering of the insides of cars.

You don't know the half of it, thought Ann bitterly. *If you think the battle's over and you've won, why don't you come up here and see what it's like at the sharp end?*

32

He still read the Situations Vacant. And this morning, here it was: 'WAYLANDS MUSEUM. LIVE-IN CARETAKER'.

It was perfect. He had only to ask for it and it would be his. They knew him there. They knew he was a good worker, and he knew them. He knew the museum inside out and loved every inch of it. Who better to take care of it? They had said that they were sorry to see him go. They had said that they would always be glad to see him back. He was only surprised that they had not contacted him direct, instead of advertising. But perhaps there was a rule that said they had to advertise.

His mother might be disappointed at him giving up the business, but it was doomed to collapse anyway once the Enterprise Allowance ran out. She had not told him this in so many words and he had no head for business, but he could add up.

Why should she be disappointed? She had set the business up for him, so she would be pleased when he no longer needed it. He could still make models in his spare time when he lived at the museum. What better place? And his mother could still sell them for him, if she wanted to, as a hobby. She was entitled to a rest after her hard life.

Or she could find herself a little job. She was not getting anything out of Mitchison's Working Models. She lived on her widow's pension, as she always had.

Do you want to go on drawing the dole for the rest of your life? The signs in the Job Centre goaded people to stop waiting for someone to employ them and go out and employ themselves.

Because that's what you can look forward to, they might have added, *if you don't make a go of this. Drawing the dole for the rest of your life or until we abolish it, whichever comes first.*

But if he got a job, he could save them the bother of telling him to come in, his time was up.

It would be their time that was up. In his case at least they could forget their fancy tricks for taking people off the unemployment register by calling it something else. Who needed that? Not Tom, if he got this job.

It was the perfect solution, it was the perfect job.

It was not quite perfect.

He forced himself to look again at the advertisement, to take in what he had seen but had not acknowledged.

'LIVE-IN CARETAKER AND WIFE.'

Well, why not? Why not? Sooner or later he would marry someone, so why not Shelly, why not now?

He fought off a twinge of disappointment, a sense of being deprived of something. It was like being a child on Boxing Day, knowing that Christmas had not been quite as good as you had expected, knowing that you had a whole year to wait before you would get another one.

Marriage was for life, or so you were expected to say when you signed on for it. You did not get a second chance after a year, a second choice.

This seemed rather cold and businesslike. It lacked romance. But maybe all the romance was a myth: stories, propaganda. People got married for dozens of reasons. They got married because they had to. They got married for money. In some parts of the world they got married because their parents told them to, to partners their parents had chosen for them. It worked out. In fact there was a lot less divorce in those societies than in the West, or so he had heard.

So why not get married to get a job and a home? Two jobs. Shelly would have a job too. Caretaker and Wife.

He discussed it with Chris, wanting to talk himself into it. Chris was no help.

'You're taking a chance if you ask me, Tom. I mean, they might want you to bring her to the interview.'

'Of course they'll want her at the bloody interview! The job's for two.' He was disgusted at his friend's cynical attitude. 'I'll take her along as my fiancée.'

'Aye, that's what I mean. You might not get the job, but you'll still have the fiancée.'

He knew this. He did not thank Chris for pointing it out. 'We can't get married if I don't get the job. That's obvious.'

Chris put a brotherly arm around his shoulder. 'It's obvious to you, man. It's obvious to me. But I doubt it'll be so obvious to Shelly.'

It would be obvious to Shelly if he told her in advance. And that was what he would do. He would play fair. He would put his cards on the table and she could say yes or no.

If she said no, fair enough.

It was a Saturday morning when he went to ask her. His mother had gone to a craft fair, part of a Summer Festival being organized by local businesses and community groups. Other events of the Festival included a circus, sports, an Old Tyme Music Hall and a procession of floats through the centre of town and out along the seafront. 'Let's go and watch it.'

'I want to go shopping,' said Shelly.

'What with?'

'We can look, can't we?'

'We can go shopping afterwards,' he said.

'After what?'

'After the procession.'

It was not difficult to find a quiet place on the seafront from which to watch. There seemed to be more people on the floats than cheering them on in the way they wanted. This was either funny or sad. He was not sure which, and he was too tensed up to decide.

A military band marched by, but there was none of the recruitment literature that used to be handed out in former years. Building societies, trade unions and the Blood Transfusion Service all had floats on the backs of lorries, crawling along the seafront in the bright, chilly sunshine. Miss Sunderland threw petals, helped by the one who had come second.

'Aren't they sweet?' said Shelly, looking at an Old Woman Who Lived in a Shoe float, got together by a local play group.

He saw his chance and opened his mouth. 'Think you'll make a good mother, Shell?' Something seemed to have happened to his voice.

'One day,' she said. 'Perhaps.'

He recognized her tone. He recognized it from times when Chris had needled her about wanting to get married. It was the tone in which she always retorted that she did not want to, particularly. The tone implied that nothing was further from her thoughts.

He remembered his own conversation with Chris. It had annoyed him because it had made him feel guilty. It had made him feel that he was somehow short-changing Shelly, short-changing himself, by being so unromantic. But he had to be honest with her. And it *was* romantic. He had set out this morning with butterflies in his stomach, as terrified that she might say yes as that she might say no or be angry. But seeing her now in her lemon-coloured summer dress, shivering slightly with her bare arms but refusing to put her cardigan on, he thought he could imagine nothing more romantic than to be her husband, living with her in the little caretaker's cottage. During the day they would have their work. In the evening, when the visitors had gone home, the whole world of the museum would be theirs.

' "Do you want to go on drawing the dole for the rest of your life?" ' he quoted.

'Not particularly.'

'Because you see – ' he rushed it. 'There's a job going at Waylands for a man and wife.'

'And?'

And she was going to make him work for it. He waited while Women Against Pit Closures passed, collecting money.

'I thought perhaps if you and I – '

'We're not man and wife.'

'We could be.'

She stared at him. Was she going to turn him down? He did not think that he could bear it. 'I want to,' he said. He did want to. For the moment the job at the museum was secondary. He had asked her and he wanted her to say yes.

'How long for?' she said. 'How long have you wanted to?'

'I've been thinking about it. And the more I think about it, the more I want to.' One part of him rebelled against the way she was making him say it again and again. Another part of him could have gone on saying it for ever. 'I want us to get married, Shell. Don't you?'

'I've wanted to ever since I met you.'

Oh, you have, have you? So what was all this 'nothing could be further from my thoughts' routine? Playing hard to get, were you?

He had done it now.

He paused to take stock, to consider his feelings. To consider her feelings. He had not yet made the position entirely clear. What should he do next? Kiss her, or –

'Tom! Hide!'

'Eh?'

'It's them.'

It was the Rideemus barge, reconstructed out of paper on the back of a lorry. 'RIDEEMUS! PUTTING A SMILE BACK ON THE FACE OF THE NORTH-EAST!' Tom's and Shelly's visit to the barge back in January had certainly aroused a smile or two, both at the time and since, but not for the reasons Rideemus had in mind.

They had laughed about it, but they had become annoyed and uneasy too. The pestering had gone on and on. First there had been the invitation to a meeting on 'How Young People Can Brighten Up a Depressed Area.' This had been followed by 'Unemployment: Its Meaning and Purpose.' They had missed both of these, only to receive letters from Judith regretting their absence. 'I expect that, being a company director, you were *much* too busy!' Tom's had said. 'We know your time is precious, but may we prevail upon the good will you showed once in visiting us, to ask for a few hours? We share local residents' concern about litter in Sunderland's streets, and we are looking for volunteers to join us in a Grand Clean Up! If every person receiving this letter would pledge to fill just one Rideemus Refuse Sack, think what a difference it would make! If you think we're just a load of old rubbish, now's your chance to prove it! If you don't come we'll take the hint and stop pestering you, but thanks for reading this and Laugh with the Lord . . .' Tom had been so pleased about this final promise that he had almost gone out and filled a rubbish bag out of gratitude, but two weeks later a printed invitation had come for a Grand Beach Barbecue. 'Hope you can make it, Laugh with the Lord, Judith.' And now Judith stood before him, dressed as a clown. 'Tom! Michelle! Where have you *been*? Didn't you get my letters?'

'Oh, hello, Judith,' said Shelly politely.

Goodbye, Judith, he thought.

'Coming for a ride on our float?'

'I don't think so.'

'You can't say you're too busy! Not today.'

'We were just – ' Shelly looked as if she wanted to tell Judith what they had been doing, what they had been discussing. She looked as if she wanted congratulating on her engagement.

' – on our way,' he said.

'All those people you can see on the float,' said Judith, 'they're just ordinary local people who've agreed to come a little way with us and tell us a joke. That's all we'd be asking you to do, tell us the first joke that comes into your head.'

'What for?'

'Officially,' said Judith, 'it's for "academic research".' She made a face. 'We're collecting examples of regional humour. But it's a lot of fun too. Come on. What have you got to lose?'

'We could go a little way, Tom.'

He glared at Shelly. He changed the glare to a wink that said, *Can't you see they're barmy?* He could not have her making public announcements until everything was sorted out.

'Oh well,' said Judith.

'Nice to see you again, Judith.'

'Take one of these anyway,' said Judith. It was a leaflet inviting young people to join a Rideemus Community Volunteer Project. 'Any chance of you helping out, Michelle?' She had not given up on Shelly. Shelly herself made a show of interest . . . as a way of defying him, Tom supposed. 'What sort of thing is it?'

'Anything the local community needs doing, we'll do it. Within reason! So if you've got time on your hands . . .'

'I may not have, much longer,' said Shelly, inviting Judith to ask, *Why not?*

'Come on, Shell,' he said, leading her away. Judith trotted off in her clown costume, to rejoin her float.

As the procession moved along the coast, he took her across the beach and up on to the pier. As they walked towards the lighthouse at the end, he quietly and reasonably explained the situation to her. He was not telling her anything she did not know already, and she did not argue with him, but it seemed to him that the more reasonable he tried to be, the worse he sounded. 'I'd've said all this before,' he said. 'If I hadn't been so rudely interrupted. So, you see how it is, Shell? Shelly? Mee – chelle? Say something.'

'You only want to marry me to get the job.'

'Did I say that?'

'Sounded like it.'

'You weren't listening then. I just don't want there to be any misunderstandings. We'll get the job. No problem. Only if we don't, we wouldn't have anywhere to live. I mean, it's no way to start married life, is it? With my mam or your parents.' He was hoping to get credit for honesty at least, but he might as well have lied. She could not look more upset. He could not feel more guilty. 'That's all I'm saying. We'll just have to wait a bit longer if we don't get the job. Till we come up on the housing list.'

'So you're not saying you'll only marry me if we get the job?'

'Shelly. Give me some credit.'

'Oh, Tom. I love you, I really love you.'

'References,' he said, getting down to business. 'We'll need references.'

'I could put one of my teachers from school. Who've you got?'

'I can take my pick from the top brass of the museum itself.'

'You don't think we're too young?'

'Didn't say anything in the advert about an age limit.'

'Can we tell people?' she said.

'Well . . . maybe we'd better wait till it's definite.'

'I mean, that we're engaged?'

'What?' he said. He took one look at her face and said, 'Oh aye. We can tell people.'

'What did I say?' Chris crowed.

'I changed my mind. Job or no job, I want to marry her anyway.'

'You had it changed for you.'

'Piss off.'

'What's this, Community Volunteer Project?' Chris looked at Judith's leaflet. 'I'd join this if I were you, Tom. You might be able to get a transfer to the Foreign Legion.'

33

What is this job anyway? she thought. *This 'arrangement'? By whom has it been arranged, and for whom? Not me, that's for sure. I'm being taken for granted. Never mind what it says on my job description, I'm the nursemaid.*

It was the Stalton Industries Bitumen Products sales conference: Gina's first opportunity to fit names to faces and meet the Beach Boys en masse. 'Beach Boys' was what Hilary called Gina's colleagues in the sales team. She tended to swallow her words, to pronounce bitumen 'bitchmen'. They had not appreciated being called that, apparently, but 'Beach Boys' was fine. 'Wish they all could be California girls . . .' they sang, greeting Hilary with hugs and kisses and enquiries after the baby. Gina was not a Beach Boy. Gina was just Gina. 'The Beach Boys and Gina.' That was the sales team.

It was not this that worried her. One must expect to feel an outsider for a while in a new job, and Hilary and the Beach Boys were old colleagues. Hilary had gone down a grade to look after her baby, and they were letting her know that they still regarded her as one of them. *But aren't I one of them?* thought Gina now, sitting alone in the lunch hour with Jeremy, Hilary's baby, screaming on her lap.

Normally based at home, Hilary had had to come into head office that day for the sales conference. She had been let down by her babysitter so she had brought Jeremy with her. Trevor, her husband, who worked in Personnel, had arranged for a secretary to look after Jeremy during the morning's business, but now the secretary had gone to lunch. 'Just hold him for a moment, would you, Gina?' Hilary had said, and she had not been seen since.

She had things to do, of course. Technically a desk-based assistant to the sales team and Paul, its manager, she seemed determined to let it be known that in reality she was no such thing. Paul, half seriously, half humorously, went along with this. This morning, when announcing plans to reward the sales team for its magnificent performance over the half-year by raising everybody's targets, he had referred to Hilary's role in the formulation of the figures. 'Hils and I are sure you can do it.' And amid the boos and hisses that had followed, Hilary had sat looking innocent and smug. Now, in the lunch hour, she had the technical staff to supervise as they set up videos for the afternoon's presentation concerning various motorway repair projects from which Stalton's hoped to win orders. But she must be nearly finished. They did not need supervising. Hilary just had a supervisory nature.

'Could you shut up, please, Jeremy?' said Gina, in the little room to which she had taken him to avoid disturbing people. 'No? All right, then, we'll just have to bloody well disturb them.'

Hilary was back in the dining room, relaxing over coffee with the Beach Boys. '*There* you are!' she cried. 'I thought you'd kidnapped him.' Gina returned Jeremy to his mother. He stopped crying. The Beach Boys were full of admiration. 'He knows better than to play Hils up.'

'Don't we all?'

'It's his teeth,' said Hilary. 'He's as good as gold with Gina normally.'

At home that evening, Gina described the incident to her fiancé Oliver with some indignation. 'Which one of us is the assistant? This is what I ask myself.'

'Well, I suppose you have to be a bit adaptable,' he said.

She let this pass but she kept it in mind. He might wish he had not said it, come the weekend. He was going to have to do some adapting himself. She was taking him to meet the family.

She took the corner slowly on the familiar Dorset road and accelerated up to sixty in the openness beyond. She started to sing: 'I can see the sea! I can see the sea – '

Oliver joined in. 'Eee – i – addio, I can see the sea.'

'No,' said Gina. 'It's "hey ho falerio, I can see the sea." It's an old folk song, been in the Heriot family for generations. Don't go messing it up with your football chants.'

'Sorry, I forgot your family were all rugger buggers.'

'You'll soon remember if you start saying things like "eee – i – addio" when we get there.'

'What else mustn't I do?'

'That was a joke,' she sighed. 'Please don't start doing your inverted snob bit.' Typical of Oliver to join in with a joke and then make a unilateral decision that it was not funny and become prickly. He was nervous, she supposed. Himself the only child of two only children, he had (incredibly to Gina, when he first told her) no relatives apart from his parents. Gina, on the other hand, had three sisters, seven aunts and uncles, all of them married, twenty cousins and five little cousins once removed. She also had one surviving grandmother, and it was to her house that they were going.

Oliver took one look at the house and said, ' "Last night I dreamed I went back to Manderley." '

'It's lovely, isn't it? My great-grandfather built it.' She eyed the cars in the drive, recognizing most of them but wondering who had acquired a new Rover 800. There was no movement behind the windows: the family were probably out on the lawn at the back. She repaired her lipstick, ran a comb through her hair and handed the comb to Oliver. He returned it unused but she did not comment. 'Now listen, darling, I love them all but they can be a bit much. So you give as good as you get, talk about football or anything you like. I'm not going to chaperone you, but if you get miserable just say the word and we'll go. *After* lunch. Mrs Tabia's chocolate mousse has to be eaten to be believed.'

'Who's Mrs Tabia?'

'Oh, she's – ' Had she not told him about the Tabias?

'A servant? Your grandmother has servants?'

'Of course they're not servants, they're friends. They live in and help ... Mrs Tabia, how lovely to see you!' She bent to kiss the little overalled woman who opened the front door. 'This is Oliver, my fiancé.' Oliver would not have missed the overalls.

They walked through the quiet house towards where the French windows opened on to the crowded lawn. Nobody had noticed them yet. Gina squeezed Oliver's hand. 'All right, darling?'

'Of course I'm all right.'

'Granny, this is Oliver.'

'How lovely!' The elegant old lady made no attempt to rise from her folding chair in the shady corner of the verandah. 'Don't tell anyone I said this, Oliver, but – ' she raised a ringed and blotchy hand to her mouth and whispered ' – you've got the pick of the bunch.'

'Granny says that to all the fiancés.'

'How many fiancés has she had, Mrs Heriot?'

'It was just the half-dozen, wasn't it, Gina? Always in demand, the Heriots. Your mother's been telling me about your new job. Is it true they asked for you?'

'Yes, they thought I'd be the perfect person to look after my assistant's baby, and sell bitumen in my spare time.'

Not understanding this, Gina's grandmother murmured, 'The *opportunities* you young people have!' in tones of doubtful admiration. Gina was surprised by the bitterness she had heard in her own voice. Hilary was not that bad. She did ask Gina to babysit rather often, but Gina could always say no. She hoped that her grandmother did not feel that her question had been snubbed. She described her job. 'Bitumen's that black sticky stuff that holds the stones together in roads. I sell it.'

'Yes, dear, I know you do, but how?'

Gina's mother appeared, waved a temporary greeting and bore Oliver off to get him a drink and introduce him to people.

'Sometimes I go to wholesalers who already buy from us,' Gina explained. 'I don't have to sell to them exactly, but I have to make sure our prices stay competitive, try and get them to up their orders and generally keep them happy. Sometimes we get involved at the tendering stage of a project, and then it's up to me to advise the contractors on the types of materials they're going to need, and make sure they buy them from us.'

'But how can you advise them? How do you *know*?'

Gina enjoyed basking in the awed admiration of her grandmother, but did not want it to go too far. 'I just look it up in company manuals. Anybody could do it.'

'I'm sure I shouldn't be able to,' said her grandmother. 'I don't know a *thing* about science . . . oh, hello, dear!' Another branch of the family had arrived. Gina wandered off to join Oliver. A large Scotch in his hand, he was being introduced to three of the male cousins who were asking him what car he drove and how long it took him to get up to ninety.

'I haven't driven it abroad yet,' he said, and they looked at him as if he were letting the side down.

Mrs Tabia beamed in the doorway and rang the little silver bell that signified lunch. This was greeted with a chorus of abuse from Gina and others of her generation.

'I wanted to ring it!'

'You rang it last time!'

'Mrs Tabia, you're a spoilsport!'

Each of them rang the bell in turn while the children looked superior and embarrassed. The family trooped through into the long dining room into which two tables had been crammed, one for adults, one for children. The eldest child claimed the right to sit with the adults. After some discussion this was granted, whereupon the second eldest took up the claim. 'I was just the same,' said Gina. 'How are you doing?'

'How am I doing what?'

'Are you enjoying yourself?'

He was uneasy, and she held out stoutly against the senior aunt's edict that husbands and wives must not sit together. 'We're not husband and wife yet,' she said, keeping Oliver with her. 'Where's Granny?'

'Got locked in the lavatory, I expect,' was the consensus, but Oliver got up at once and Gina followed and they found her still on the verandah, having difficulty rising from her seat. One of her sticks had fallen out of reach. Oliver said, 'I'm terribly sorry, Mrs Heriot. How rude of us just to leave you to fend for yourself.'

'I'm used to it, dear. When my family are all together, I look round and I think, these are all *mine*. But for me, most of these marvellous people wouldn't even exist – '

'All your fault,' said Gina.

'Exactly. So when they behave like oafs, I have to share the blame. And Oliver dear, please call me Granny. You're family now.' Gina wondered how he felt about this. *I expect I'll be told*, she thought.

Everyone sat down for the meal. Dishes and plates were passed back and forth until one of the children said, 'What about grace?'

'What *about* Grace?'

'Grace!'

'Where's Grace?'

'Grace who?'

'If the children want to say grace,' said Gina's grandmother, 'then I think grace should be said.' She rose laboriously to her feet and everyone was shamed into following her example. Amid groans and laughter they discussed which grace should be said and who should say it. Someone said: 'Good food, good meat, thank God, let's eat.' The grace collapsed in disarray. Oliver was the first to sit down and start helping himself to food. He looked annoyed.

Gina whispered, 'Jeannie and Fiona have just started at convents. That's where it comes from.'

'For heaven's sake, why do you all go to convents? You're not Catholics.'

Gina's cousin, Fiona's mother, heard the question and explained:

'I think nuns still have the edge on the others when it comes to education. I'm sorry if you think we're irreverent. Are you a Catholic yourself?' Her tone implied that, if he had been, the family should have been warned.

'No,' said Oliver. 'I'm not anything, but I couldn't tell whether you were serious about saying grace, or if it was a family joke.'

Anecdotes, teasing and general abuse poured back and forth across the table. At Gina's side, Oliver ate in stolid silence, shrinking into himself, his neck pink. She wished everybody would be a bit quieter, a bit more sensible. They always did this to newcomers. They called it 'seeing what they're made of'.

'Are we overwhelming you, Oliver?' asked Gina's uncle.

'Oliver isn't blessed with a mob like you,' said Gina. 'He's an only child.'

'Good God.'

'The poor thing.'

'Why is he an only child?'

Gina froze in the expectant silence that followed this intolerable question. Oliver smiled. 'My parents took one look at me,' he said, 'and asked themselves, "Why repeat perfection?"'

He was cheered to the echo.

Everyone wanted to know what the plans were for the wedding. Gina explained that they had postponed it until late in the year so that she could get settled in her new job and build up some holiday entitlement. Her grandmother said, 'I don't think I'll be able to come, dear. I'm sorry, but parties and travelling are getting to be a bit much for me.'

'It's not fair. You came to everybody else's weddings.' She was only joking. She assumed a comically sulky expression to prove it. But Oliver said, 'Don't be silly, Gina. Of course we understand, Granny. We'll have a video made and send it to you.'

This suggestion brought out stories of other weddings at which attempts had been made to film the ceremony, and the choir had demanded performance fees, as had, in one case, the vicar.

'Why don't you get married from here?' said an uncle. Gina thought this a lovely idea and she turned to look towards her grandmother, but her seat was empty. 'I think she's gone for a rest,' said Oliver.

'Let's go and see if she's all right.'

The old lady was sitting on her bed, unfastening her shoes. 'I just wanted to slip away. I don't want any fuss.'

'Any fuss!' said Oliver. 'It's your house.'

'Should Oliver go out, do you want to get undressed?'

'No, no, I'll just have a little lie-down.'

'And here's something for you to think about,' said Gina. 'It's entirely up to you, of course, but it's been suggested that we might have the wedding – '

' – on video,' said Oliver. 'Have you got a video recorder? If you haven't, we can arrange for you to hire one.' Gina gave him a questioning look but he did not meet it. Her grandmother did not respond to what had been said. They left her to sleep. As they were returning downstairs, Gina said, 'Sorry. I should have asked you before I asked her. It's your wedding too.'

He patted her bottom.

'Don't be silly, this would be a lovely place for a reception, but I don't think your grandmother would like it. It would be a bigger party than this, wouldn't it, and she's out for the count.'

'She'd say if she felt like that.'

'Go on with you. I don't know anything about grandmothers, but I would guess that whatever little Gina asks for, little Gina gets.'

She admitted this and felt glad that she was marrying a sensitive man who would put a brake on her selfishness. She grabbed him by the sides of his collar and gave him a quick, biting kiss. 'God, Oliver. I love you *so much*.'

Everyone sat out on the lawn, in deck chairs and on cushions. Someone suggested cricket and divided the family into two teams. They raced off to the shed to uncover bats and stumps. 'I wonder if that old tennis net is there,' said Gina to her sister. She explained to Oliver: 'When Susan and I used to come here for the summer, Granny got Mr Tabia to mark out a tennis court on the lawn. It must have been an incredible nuisance for her, looking back.' Oliver said that if the only way he could persuade Gina and Susan to frolic about on his lawn in short skirts was by turning it into a tennis court, then turn it into a tennis court he would.

Oliver was not a cricketing man, but his experience with squash gave him speed and a good eye for the ball. She watched with pride as he knocked the Heriot family's top bowlers all over the lawn. At four thirty, her grandmother reappeared with Mrs Tabia and a tea trolley. She looked completely restored. When people started to leave, she sat in her chair beaming happily as they queued up for kisses. She pressed pound coins into the hands of the great-grandchildren. 'And you shall have one too, Oliver, because you're new.'

'Thank you, Granny,' said Oliver solemnly.

'That's not fair,' said Gina's sister.

'Yes it is,' said Oliver. 'I never had a granny to give me things.'

Gina was pleased that, after an uneasy start, he had entered into the spirit of the occasion. 'You certainly made a hit with Granny,' she said, as they drove away.

'She's a lovely lady.'

'And the others? You hated them.'

'No . . .' he smiled and pondered. 'No, given that I had to spend the day with a bunch of people who never stop talking and think everything about themselves is wonderful, I can't think of a nicer . . .'

'I suppose they are a bit like that. We are. But we make each other worse. We're all right on our own, but when we get together –'

'It's nice that you *do* get together. There's a sort of – spirit. I mean, you probably have your differences, but you enjoy being together. You'd help each other through thick and thin – you're a *family*.'

Gina thought this was putting it a bit strongly. Not every member of the Heriot family was invited to these gatherings. Some were excluded by general consent as being too boring. Still . . . why spoil his romantic vision?

'I'm looking forward to having a family,' he said.

'Good, because you've got one.'

'And our own. In about five years.'

'Oliver . . .' she squeezed his hand. 'Thanks for today.'

'What? I enjoyed it.'

'I mean, thanks for enjoying it.'

34

Having cracked all the usual jokes about one's wedding day being the happiest day of one's life (*you mean it's all downhill after that?*), Gina was surprised at how moving she found the ceremony. She considered the gathering to be primarily a social one as she and Oliver were already living together; but she felt somehow different after the music, the prayers, the grand, timeless words of human and divine love – happier, more committed, older.

Oliver's parents were at the wedding, as were ninety-seven per cent (he calculated) of all Gina's known relatives, including her grandmother. Friends and colleagues came from Stalton's, including Hilary's husband Trevor, but not Hilary herself, who had an upset stomach. Sister Brede came, paying polite attention to the Anglican service, and, best of all, Roy and Alex Franson came, Gina's former employers. She had invited them without much hope, and had been delighted to receive their acceptance. The quarrel with them had left a nasty taste in her mouth – they had, after all, given her her start at a time when larger, more prestigious employers had not wanted to know her. They brought a clock of carved onyx as a wedding present. 'And I've got a present for *you*,' she said, giving them the model derrick that Ann Mitchison's son had made, and which, when it arrived, had filled her with the sadness of not knowing what to do with it.

Roy and Alex gazed at it in silence. Had she offended them again? 'Where did you get it?'

'I had it made.'

'I think she's extracting the michael, Roy.'

'I think she is.' They laughed, they were pleased. 'You'd better tell us who the suppliers are, Gina. We can give them away as Christmas presents, show our clients we're thinking big.' They kissed her and shook Oliver by the hand. 'Lots of luck, Gina. Lots of luck to both of you.'

The reception was being held at her parents' house. While she was getting ready to go away, Hilary rang up. Gina's immediate reaction was one of irritation, as she assumed that Hilary had some business matter to discuss. Hilary did tend rather to assume that since the demands of her baby required her to work odd hours, Gina too was permanently available. But Hilary just said, 'Have a wonderful time and don't do anything you wouldn't do normally.'

'Thanks, Hilary. Are you all right?'

'I'm fine as long as I stay within ten yards of the lav.'

'You ought to see the doctor.'

'It's only the usual.'

'You're not pregnant again?'

'Not sure yet, but we have been trying.'

Gina said nothing.

'Might as well get it over in one fell swoop,' said Hilary cheerfully. 'Two'll be no more bother than one. Have I got the number of where you're going to be?'

'I sincerely hope not,' said Gina. The possibility that Hilary might interrupt Gina and Oliver at a moment of nuptial tenderness with a query about an order for bitumen emulsion had been a running joke between them for several weeks.

The honeymoon was to be spent in Scotland. They would take the car up on the overnight train and tour around. They only had a week, so it had not seemed worth going abroad.

'What did you think of the Timpsons?' Gina asked Oliver as they drove off. She had explained in advance that the Timpsons were a boring branch of the family and were consequently only invited to the largest gatherings. He had said that he looked forward to meeting them.

'No worse than . . .'

'Careful. I can insult them, you can't.'

'Lovely people,' said Oliver. 'They wanted to know where we got the table linen from, so I referred them to your mother. I don't know what it is about your family, Gina . . . they talk about nothing but objects.' He said this innocently, wonderingly, but Gina felt stung.

'I thought you liked them.'

'I do, most of them, but you have to admit it's true. Every knife

206

and fork had to be picked up and admired and who did the flowers and doesn't Gina look lovely, where did she get her dress?' He was warming to his theme. 'It was the same that day we went to your grandmother's. Who's got the fastest car? Who's got – ?'

'It must be awful for you,' said Gina, 'after all the fascinating conversations you're used to with your parents, about world politics and the meaning of life.'

'I'm not getting at you,' he said. 'I'm trying to make a serious point, and it's a compliment if you let me get to it.'

Gina decided that it was too corny for words for them to start a quarrel in these circumstances. She suggested that they stop the car and remove the boots, L-plates and chamber pots that had been affixed to the rear mudguard in a flash of originality by one of the younger Timpsons.

'Now,' she said, when they were on the move again. 'Can you get to the compliment quickly?'

'Well, I grew up in a council flat, as you know – '

'Council flat? Council flat? You were lucky. I grew up in a card-board box.'

'Yeah, some cardboard box. You grew up in that amazing house of your parents, where everything matches and fits and shines. And when you weren't there, you were at your school, or your grand-mother's place, or Oxford . . . there was no *ugliness* in your life. And that's where you get it from.'

'My ugliness?'

'No, you twit. Your confident beauty. Your clear-eyed, straight-necked, I-belong-here look.'

Gina supposed that this was the compliment. It pleased her, of course, that Oliver thought her beautiful, as had others before him . . . but it had never occurred to her before to put her looks down to anything more than good fortune, good health and good care. Now she supposed there was some truth in what he had said. A great deal of her growing up had indeed been done in beautiful places where, as he put it, everything fitted and matched and shone. The discovery that the whole world was not the same had been a relatively recent one. 'Your parents' flat's very nice,' she said. 'But I know what you mean, they're not all like that, are they? I went to a real dump once – '

'That was very broad-minded of you.'

'Actually I was doing good works. Student Voluntary Service. We were painting one-parent families. Their flats. And there was this one place where they had plastic sinks and they'd melted.'

'I expect they'd been putting their chip pans down in them.'

'That's exactly what they'd been doing. They were furious, but I don't know what they thought we were going to do about it.' Gina remembered the indignation of the tenants, and the answering indignation of herself and her friends at the way these people, whom they had only been trying to help, had equated them with the authorities, 'the council' who could wave a magic wand and produce stainless-steel sinks. She remembered too her awe at their prodigious smoking, their choice of the most expensive brands while she and her fellow students contented themselves with roll-ups. *You shouldn't*, she remembered thinking. *Not if you want to be taken seriously as poor, not if you want sympathy.*

They had not wanted sympathy, they had wanted new sinks. Gina doubted that they had got them, and, musing now on Oliver's words, she thought it probably would damage one's self-esteem to go about one's daily business surrounded by such uglinesses and inconveniences as melted sinks, sinks that were still functional but which had turned brown like stained lavatory bowls and into which one must not put hot saucepans. She remembered her own personal tennis court on her grandmother's lawn – hers, and her sister Susan's. It had in many ways been inferior to the public courts on the seafront. It had not been fenced in – balls were always falling into the goldfish pond and having to be fished out. The net had been too high, and difficult to adjust. But they had preferred it. It had freed them from the ordeal of playing tennis under the scornful eyes of local yobbos. It had been theirs.

'You never lose your nerve,' Oliver insisted now. 'Do you?'

'I do when you creep up on me.'

'That's just fooling around. I mean really lose it. At work, say.'

'Do you lose yours?'

'You mean you haven't noticed? Some mornings – '

'Oh, *mornings*. You're just not a mornings person.'

'Some mornings,' he repeated, 'I drive to the end of the road and think, instead of turning right, what if I turned left?'

'And went where?'

'Anywhere. Away. I think to myself, Stalton's must be mad, putting me in charge of a group of blokes selling pharmaceuticals. It's real life-and-death stuff. They must know I can't handle it.'

'If you couldn't handle it, you'd be out.'

'I may be,' he said.

She looked at him in alarm, hoping that he was joking. He did not smile as he told her what the problem was. He spoke in the stressed tones of someone who would have preferred not to give substance to an anxiety by putting it into words. He had been working all week on a product report which was supposed now to be in the hands of his secretary Janice for typing and distribution. But he had no memory of having given it to her. The more he thought about it, the more clearly he could see it on his desk at home.

Gina reminded him that their neighbours had keys to their house. If he was still worried by Monday, he could phone Janice and she could go round and collect the report. And even if such a remedy were not so easily available, it was hardly a matter so serious as to merit dismissal.

'It terrifies me, though,' he said, 'when I do things like that.'

They had reached the Motorail terminal. 'Life's tennis balls may fall into life's goldfish ponds,' she said, getting out of the car. 'But they can always be fished out.'

'Blimey. What's that?'

'It's an old proverb,' she said. 'It's been in the Heriot family for generations.'

You Can Have It

35

Having taken the car up to Scotland on the train, they drove home along the east coast at a leisurely pace, stopping to explore anywhere that took their fancy. They had had – were still having – a lovely honeymoon, they agreed, frequently. It was wonderful to be away from work, a subject that they had agreed not to discuss.

They particularly admired the scenery of Tyne and Wear – a startling mixture of natural and industrial grandeur, chimneys and cliffs and the stark outlines of collieries – and they stopped to walk on a beach, leaving the car in a municipal car park.

Apart from hopeful attempts at tourism – worn signs in seafront hotels urged passers-by to participate in National Eating Out Week – the little town did not appear to have much going for it. The Odeon-turned-bingo-hall was up for sale. Horse-hair leaked from a sofa in the sooty window of an upholsterer's shop and notices announced that the shop would cease trading on a date some eighteen months previously. A telephone number was given for enquiries.

'Bloody hell,' Oliver muttered, staring at a poster in the window of a building society which, alone in the row of shops, appeared to be thriving. 'EVERY CLOUD HAS A SILVER LINING,' it read, above the grey face of a helmeted miner. 'IF YOU ARE LEAVING THE COAL INDUSTRY FOR ANY REASON, WE CAN GIVE YOU GOOD ADVICE ON HOW TO MAKE USE OF ANY LUMP SUM YOU MAY HAVE TO INVEST . . .'

'That's so sick,' said Oliver. ' "For any reason" indeed.'

Gina agreed that it was very sad, and they made their way to the beach. They walked under brown loamy cliffs which had been eaten away by sea and wind into intriguing caves. They discussed whether these would be safe to explore, and decided against it. They strolled arm in arm, stopping for long kisses. They remarked on the bravery of a lone man defying the autumn air to take a swim. They reminisced about Pimple, Gina's former dog, and said how much he would be enjoying himself if he were here, hoped he was enjoying himself anyway with his new owners. They found some pale-shelled winkles that looked as if they had jaundice and wondered whether or not it was possible for a winkle to contract jaundice, and, if so, whether Stalton's Veterinary Pharmaceuticals had a remedy. 'We're not going to talk about work.' From a distance they spotted what looked like a tiger lurking in tall, coarse grass, and stalked it until they were sure that it was only a piece of rust-coloured carpet. Water trickled from a broken pipe in the cliff: it did not look or smell like sewage, but it could hardly be anything else, they agreed, with the seagulls gathering like that. 'Who'd be a seagull?'

It was at this point that Gina remembered that Ann Mitchison and her son lived around here somewhere. 'Let's go and see them.'

'Why? Are you bored?'

'Of course not, but we could thank them for the model and tell them that Roy and Alex want some more. They'll be pleased. Anyway, I want to show you off. Northern people are very hospitable, aren't they?'

'Oh yes,' said Oliver. 'And musical too. Or is that the Welsh?'

'Now what have I said?'

'I think it's a bit of an imposition, to turn up on her doorstep.'

'We won't. I'll phone her up and say we're here and thought we'd drop by and say hello. If she's busy, she can tell us to get lost.'

'She won't.'

'Why not? I would.'

'*You* would. She won't. She'll probably rush around and make a meal for us . . . go on, then.' He smiled tolerantly. 'But tell her we won't be staying long.'

'It's taken off,' said Ann. 'It's fantastic. I can't believe it.' Far from doing what Oliver had feared and offering them a meal, she seemed, though politely pleased to see them, much too busy to stop. Once they were in the flat, she seemed hardly able to distinguish them from her staff. Staff she appeared to have in great numbers: the table in the kitchen to which she took them was covered with oilcloth and sitting round it were a group of young people painting the faces on dolls and sewing tiny garments. A girl of about seventeen crouched in the corner of the kitchen (there being no room for her at the table) sticking photographs and Letraset on to what appeared to be layout sheets for a publicity hand-out. Ann introduced her as 'Michelle, my son's fiancée. Listen to me. I've not even congratulated you on your marriage. Were you engaged when you came on the course, Gina? I don't remember you saying.'

'No, but I went home and was deluged with offers. Marriage, new jobs . . . How about you?'

'Well, I've not had many offers of marriage lately. But Teresa's certainly come up trumps.' Apparently Teresa Beal had arranged for her magazine to feature Mitchison's Working Models, and a flood of orders had resulted. 'Non-sexist toys,' Ann explained.

'I see,' said Oliver solemnly, looking as if he were about to say something flippant. Gina glared at him.

'Shall I make some tea?' said Michelle.

'If you would, pet.'

Gina examined some of the dolls. There was a bricklayer, a mechanic of some kind, a doctor, and an executive in a suit, all of them female. 'Mitchison's Working Women,' said Ann.

'Got any reps?' said Oliver.

'No, I'm in charge of the selling side and these are some friends of Tom and Michelle's who've come in to help with production.'

'No, I meant have you got any rep dolls?'

Ann picked up a doll with a briefcase and a big smile. '£9.90, that one is.'

Calmly, Oliver paid.

'I'll go and fetch Tom,' said Michelle.

'Take Gina and Oliver with you. They might like to see the workshop.'

The workshop was a garage, crowded, like the kitchen, with youngsters. Tom Mitchison was a skinny young man, sharp-featured and earthily good-looking. He was acting in a supervisory capacity, a role with which he did not appear to be entirely comfortable. He seemed at once happy to be called away and anxious about leaving his charges, though they looked industrious enough, fitting together parts taken from boxes marked with the name of a wholesale supplier. 'All know what you're doing, do you?'

'Yes, that's all right, Tom,' they replied cheerfully. 'You go and have your tea.' There was no resentment in their tone. Michelle said to them, 'I'll bring your tea down to you.'

Tom Mitchison paid little attention to his fiancée. He walked ahead with Oliver, leaving Gina to walk with Michelle.

'When will you and Tom be getting married?'

'Oh, I don't know,' said Michelle. 'As soon as the dust settles.'

'It's wonderful, isn't it?'

Michelle sighed and did not reply. 'Did you have a big wedding, Gina?' she asked wistfully.

The workers in the kitchen offered to take tea down to their fellows in the garage. 'We don't want to interrupt you when you've got company, Mrs Mitchison.'

'Interrupt! You're helping me.' Ann looked as if she would prefer them to go on with what they were doing, but they trooped off with a tray. They seemed very obliging and friendly. 'Come and say goodbye to us before you go, Gina and Oliver.'

Oliver was telling Tom how pleased the Franson brothers had been with their model, and how they had said that they might order more.

'Let's have their name and address, then,' said Ann, picking up a pen.

'Keep quiet, for heaven's sake,' said Tom affably to Oliver. 'I've got more orders than I can fill as it is, after this – ' he pointed to the pile of *New Atalanta*s. Ann said that Gina should take one. ' "The magazine for the woman who knows the battle is over and she has won," ' Gina read.

'It's true, isn't it, Tom?' sighed Oliver. 'It's been a rout. Still, you're better off with too many customers than too few, aren't you? Make them appreciate you. Say it's a limited edition and they'll have to wait their turn.'

Ann said, 'They'd not say that if Miss Barclay were here, would they, Gina?'

'Not more than once.'

'Miss Barclay this, Miss Barclay that,' said Tom. 'I'm glad you've come, Gina, because we can get this sorted out once and for all. Did Miss Barclay walk on water or not?'

'The swimming pool was closed, otherwise I'm sure she would have.'

The door opened and an older, larger version of Ann appeared, waving a set of car keys. 'It's only me. Oh, I didn't know you had company.'

'Come in, Pat. This is my sister Pat. This is Gina, who was on the course with me, and this is Oliver. They're on their honeymoon.'

Pat congratulated them and said, 'I've heard so much about that course, I feel as if I was there myself. Let me see if I can place you. Were you the women's libber?'

Oliver sniggered quietly and Gina kicked him. 'No,' she said, welcoming the first opportunity she had been given to say something about herself. 'I work for Stalton Industries – '

'And so do I,' said Oliver.

'Oh, that's nice,' said Pat. 'Man and wife working together. Tom and Michelle nearly got a job like that, didn't you?'

'Nearly,' said Michelle, with a touch of bitterness.

'Never mind,' said Ann, in smoothing-over tones, 'it's turned out for the best.'

Pat had come round to take Ann out for a driving lesson. The two of them went through the motions of saying that it could wait till later, but it was clear to Gina that she and Oliver were *de trop*, so she said that they must be on their way. The five of them left the flat together, Pat and Ann to go for the driving lesson and Tom to return to his workshop. Michelle stayed behind to wash up the tea things and get on with her layouts, using photographs from *New Atalanta*, prints of which had been supplied free.

Ann asked Gina and Oliver to drive off first. 'I can't bear to be watched.'

'And I can't bear to watch,' said Tom. 'I'm going back to work.'

'We'll come and say goodbye to your friends,' said Gina. ''Bye, Ann, good luck. I'm so glad everything's working out. Goodbye, Pat, it was nice to meet you.' They waited in the crowded and stuffy workshop until Ann had had plenty of time to make her departure. 'I don't envy her,' said Gina. 'I thought I'd never get the hang of it.'

'Long journey ahead?' asked one of the workers. 'Take this in case you get bored.' She handed over a large envelope.

One of the others said, 'Of course they won't get bored. They're on their honeymoon.'

36

'We wuz robbed, if you ask me,' said Gina. Oliver was driving and she was examining the saleswoman doll. Apart from its clothes, which were nicely made, it showed none of the workmanship of the oil derrick. Its arms moved up and down – so that it could shake hands, presumably – but apart from that it was immobile, roughly put together from ill-fitting parts. 'You couldn't give this to a young child. The wood's all splintery.' An arm came off, revealing a mean-looking spike. Gina let out a manic laugh. 'On the other hand, we could give it to little Jerry.' Hilary and Trevor Foreman were emphatic about their son's name being Jeremy, so Gina and Oliver called him Jerry behind their backs, on principle.

'Now, now. We agreed not to talk about work. What's in the envelope?'

Gina opened it and read, ' "The Rideemus Institute for the Study of Psychotheolistics. Thank you for agreeing to take part in our survey on the Human Laughter Response. Please study the following jokes – " '

'Do what to them?'

'Study them, and "note your response on a scale from one to five." One equals extremely funny. Five equals not funny at all. What is this?'

'Try me on the jokes.'

'All right. "Man to doctor: Doctor, I've lost my memory. Doctor: When did you first notice this? Man: When did I first notice what?" '

' " – did I first notice what?" Yes, I've heard it before.'

'Give it a number.'

'Three. Ask me another.'

' "Man to doctor: Doctor, everyone keeps ignoring me. Doctor: Next please." '

Oliver roared with laughter. Gina said, 'Shall I put you down for a one?'

'No, it was too near the bone. Not funny at all. Are they all about men and doctors?'

Gina flicked through the pages. 'No, some of them are about women and doctors and some of them are about meeting St Peter at the pearly gates and some of them are about couples on their honeymoon – '

'Let's have some of those.'

'And some of them are about – yuk. "What do you call a starving Ethiopian with boils?" There isn't a code number for "sick".'

'He would be, wouldn't he?' said Oliver. 'A starving Ethiopian with boils would be pretty sick.'

'You're sick,' said Gina. 'Those people are sick, this whole thing is sick. And when you've filled it in, you add a few simple facts about yourself and wait breathlessly to hear whether you've been invited to take part in a free Psychotheolistics Seminar costing £400.'

'Interesting people.'

'The Mitchisons, you mean?'

Oliver laughed. 'Your friend Ann seems to have everyone pretty well organized. It's families again, isn't it – ?' He shook his head as if at some novel phenomenon which filled him with wistfulness. 'They haven't got any money so they go outside the money economy and do it all themselves. Their friends help with the model-making, the girlfriend does the art work, Ann's sister teaches her to drive . . . It's nice. Unalienating. What will our kids do for us, do you think? How long before they can write memos?'

'They'll write my memos before they write yours.'

They drove on peacefully, their earlier tension gone. Gina thought how odd human beings were, needing the constant reassurance of conversation even when they were in love with each other and had everything in common. They told jokes, chatted, swapped the driving around and stopped for dinner. It was after midnight and very dark when they reached home. Gina opened the front door and waited. 'You're supposed to carry me.'

'The battle's over and you've won,' he retorted. 'You can carry me.'

They fooled around and carried each other. In his way of abandoning jokes when he had had enough of them, Oliver suddenly became tense and strode into the house. Gina went back to the car for the luggage. 'Oi,' she called. 'I'm not the beast of burden around here.'

He was at his desk, checking that his secretary had come in as requested to collect the missing report. 'It doesn't seem to be here.'

'Good.'

'That might mean she couldn't find it. I should have phoned back to check – '

'You've been worrying again, haven't you? You'll get ulcers on your ulcers. *Look*, Oliver.' She pointed to a note: 'Report collected, all present and correct, welcome back, see you Monday, J.' This ought to have consoled him, but it made him worse: 'So I *did* leave it here. I was hoping it might have turned up at the office. God, Gina,' he said sheepishly, taking her in his arms. 'Did you know you were marrying a nervous wreck?'

'Gina, could you call me back immediately you get home, this won't keep till Monday,' barked Hilary's voice on the answering machine.

'Sod that for a game of soldiers, I'm tired,' said Gina, playing the rest of the tape.

'Gina, I don't care what time it is, I've got to talk to you!' Hilary's message was repeated four times, in tones of mounting hysteria.

'Maybe you'd better call her,' said Oliver.

'What?'

'Something's worrying her, and it's awful when you get something on your mind – '

'She should get it off her mind, I don't know what's the matter with you people – ' It might, on the other hand, be amusing to take Hilary at her word and phone her now. She could not believe that Hilary would be awake, and Jeremy certainly would not be. To wake the two of them would be a fitting revenge for the many times when Gina herself had been woken.

But Hilary snatched up the phone as if she had been waiting for it to ring. 'Can you come round? Now?'

Did you have a nice honeymoon? thought Gina. *Welcome back. Sorry to land this on you, at half past midnight.* 'What's wrong, Hilary?'

'I'd have to *show* you.'

The anger and alarm in Hilary's voice made Gina uneasy. Something really terrible must have happened. Something fairly terrible had happened: when Gina reached Hilary's house, Hilary led her into the office and, without preliminary, started shouting at her. She shouted quietly – whether out of fatigue or respect for her baby was not clear – but she shouted. 'It's been bedlam this week. Your customers have been going crazy. They've been getting the wrong orders. Wrong quantities, wrong grades – '

Gina listened wearily as Hilary ran through the specifics. It certainly sounded as if there had been one almighty cockup – several – but Gina's job was to get the orders, not to process them. She tried to feel sorry for Hilary, who was deathly pale and shaking. She tried to understand that, besides having been ill and possibly being pregnant, Hilary had had an anxious week of trying to sort out problems. She tried to sympathize but she could not, because Hilary was not looking for help in sorting out what had happened; she was looking for someone to blame it on.

'I've never seen such a dog's breakfast as the order forms you sent in before you went away!'

'What?'

'I took them out of the envelope and they were all over the floor!'

'What?'

'You've been using the wrong paperclips! That's right, Gina, laugh. If you had my job, you'd know what a pain in the arse it is when reps have their own ways of doing things – did you have a nice honeymoon?' The transformation was complete. Hilary was all charm. Gina might have dreamed what had gone before. She might be dreaming now. It was eerie, sitting in this little outpost of Stalton Industries, this silent suburban house, with a woman driven distracted by overwork while her husband and baby slept upstairs and the black night pressed against the window.

'Yes, thank you,' Gina murmured. 'Will this really not keep? You look absolutely knackered.'

'I'm all right.'

The baby cried. Hilary got up.

'Can't Trevor – ?'

'Won't be a minute.'

Jeremy fell silent, and Hilary came back.

'What did you give him, laudanum?'

'It worked,' said Hilary. 'Listen, Gina, now you're here, there's something I've been meaning to discuss with you in private.'

Now I'm here? You summoned me here.

'You were fortunate to join Stalton's the way you did, Gina. It's very rare indeed for someone to go straight into the sales force without doing time as an assistant in the office first.'

Hilary made it sound like a prison sentence. Perhaps that was how she saw it. But she had chosen to go back to it.

'It was a special arrangement, of course, for Oliver. And for you.

Stalton's Personnel take a very realistic view of the couples problem. They know they can't rely on men like Trevor and Oliver to marry little mice who'll up sticks and follow the lord and master. They know they've got to accommodate the wives' careers as well. If they'd offered you a job as an assistant, you'd have turned it down, wouldn't you? Because you were already a rep with the Brothers Grimm.'

'Franson & Franson.'

'Franson & Franson.' Hilary did not miss a beat. 'I think you may have lost out. Forget what I said before about last week's little shenanigan. I'm not criticizing you. Considering how little you knew when they first sent you out on your own, you've been doing amazingly well, and made very few mistakes.'

Gina was not aware of having made any mistakes. If she had made any, she would have expected to be told about them in a normal way, at a normal time and place.

'The point is, Gina, if you want to rise in the company, and I take it that you do, you're going to be at a disadvantage if you don't know the mysteries of administration, down to the requisitioning of the last paperclip. It's interesting that you laugh at that,' said Hilary, though this time Gina had not laughed, 'because it rather proves my point. You'd have thought a person was barmy, wouldn't you, if they'd sat down with you during your company orientation and read you a little lecture about what size paperclip to use.'

'Hilary, if my use of the wrong paperclip contributed to you getting my orders muddled up, then I'm very sorry. I will try to improve.'

'How can you improve when you don't know? Last week it was paperclips. Next week it'll be something else.'

Gina yawned. 'What are you driving at?'

What Hilary was driving at was that Gina should spend some time at Hilary's elbow, learning her job and, later, doing it.

Gina was wide awake again. 'My own time, you mean? Oh yes. I can't think of anything I'd rather do.'

'Company time.'

'And what about my calls?'

'Who does your call schedules?'

'You do.'

'There you are then. Leave it to Mizz Fixer.'

The conversation was getting out of control. Hilary seemed to think that something had been agreed. Gina said, 'There's no way that I can spend working hours here *and* get round to all my customers. *What* did you say?'

'I said if you learned my job, we could swap over. I could do some of your calls for you.' For a moment Hilary seemed abashed by the outrageousness of this suggestion, but the moment did not last. Hilary's voice and breathing sped up. Her eyes danced. 'I know most of your customers already, I've worked with them. It would be a way of keeping my hand in. Oh go on, Gina, just once or twice, before I'm too enormous to get into the car. Once little whatsit's here, I'm going to be really hemmed in. Be a sport.'

'And would you like a cut of my salary too?'

'Oh no, that's all right. Trevor and I are doing OK.'

'Doing OK at what?' said Trevor in the doorway, wearing his dressing gown, holding the grizzling baby. 'Hullo, Gina, nice honeymoon?' He did not seem in the least bit surprised to see her.

'Did he cry?' said Hilary, taking Jeremy. 'I didn't hear him, I thought I'd shut him up.'

'Don't stay up too late, you girls,' said Trevor, wagging a roguish finger, and he shuffled off, yawning.

Gina said, 'I'm going.'

'But you'll think about it.'

'No. It's out of the question.'

'But you said –'

'I'll do the job I was employed to do, thanks, Hilary, until such time as I'm officially told otherwise.' As she drove home through the dark, empty streets, Hilary's hostility was like a presence at her side. She was nervous. She found herself reliving the accident she had had when a Stalton Industries lorry had nearly run her off the road. *But you said* – What had she said? Surely Hilary had heard the sarcasm in Gina's voice when she made her remark about sharing salaries? She did not want to go on working with Hilary in this mood, being dependent on her. She had felt this unease before, this sense of being in a state of total noncommunication with someone she thought she knew. She had felt this way about her grandmother, her dead grandmother, in the last days of her senility; she had felt this way about a friend at Oxford who had been undergoing a nervous breakdown.

37

In her interview with the *New Atalanta* journalist, Ann Mitchison had been enthusiastic about START Selling – Women! 'It made me more assertive,' she had said. 'More positive, more businesslike.' Reading this in proof, Teresa had phoned START Selling in the hope that they would buy an advertisement, something along the lines of: 'We did it for Ann Mitchison, we can do it for you!'

She had asked for Daphne, not because she imagined that Daphne was responsible for the company's advertising, but because it was one of Daphne's own maxims that, wherever possible, you should start with someone you knew, someone who would direct you to the Specific Person with Authority to Spend Money, the SPASM.

But the START Selling switchboard had admitted to no knowledge of Daphne. 'We don't have a Daphne Barclay here,' they had said, as if 'a Daphne Barclay' were something disreputable. Teresa had tried again with another name familiar to her from the course literature, Alistair Brunt, but they had said that they did not have one of those either.

'It's as if she never existed,' Teresa had said in puzzlement to her colleague Nadia.

'She's probably been lowered into the Thames in a concrete overcoat.'

'Oh dear. Like that, are they?'

'They're a very shady outfit. They have branches in the Third World for turning human beings into capitalists. Or so I've heard. I don't know that much about it.'

Teresa had turned to someone who would know: Beverley, one of her erstwhile friends on the *Atalanta* collective. Beverley's rage and sorrow over Teresa's sale of the magazine had been both predictable and appalling. But their friendship went back a long way – they had first met when Beverley was still at school and Teresa had come along to talk about the magazine as part of a Girls' Project – and, hoping for some sign that she had been forgiven, or might one day be forgiven, Teresa had phoned her to ask whether, through her Third World contacts, she had any knowledge of START Selling International. 'I'm wondering if they're the sort of people we should have advertising with us.'

'Sure,' said Beverley. 'If they're who I think they are, they teach people to go round the villages with cigarettes and baby milk. Just up your street.'

'Oh Bev – ' Teresa paused, and added the rest of her name. 'Beverley, we're not that bad. Do you read it?'

'The stuff on Libya was all right.'

'I'll turn down the START Selling ad.'

'Was there anything else?'

'Yes. I miss seeing you. All of you. What are you doing these days?'

'There's nothing to do. The battle's over and we've won.'

'Beverley – '

'Yeah, all right. I miss you too. Want to do some work for Goddess Garments?' The washing machine at Collindeane Tower had finally given up the ghost, and the money that used to pay women to mend and generally refurbish the clothes had run out. Volunteers were needed. Teresa offered at once, but in seeing this offer as her passport back into favour she had been overly optimistic. 'I'll bring the stuff round to you,' Beverley had said, from which Teresa had concluded that she herself would not be welcome at Collindeane Tower. ALL WOMEN WELCOME, TERESA BEAL EXCLUDED.

Beverley had not come. But Teresa knew that it was one of the paradoxes of working in voluntary organizations, that you were sometimes too busy to organize people to help you. She allowed herself to hope. She was glad to have re-established contact and felt grateful to START Selling (from whom she made no further attempt to solicit advertising) and Daphne Barclay for having brought this about. She wondered what had happened to Daphne. Was it too much to hope that she had left START in disgust on some point of principle? It probably was. But since working for *New Atalanta*, Teresa had encountered a great many businesswomen who were not feminists, and had discovered that this was not necessarily a bar to friendship with them. Daphne was probably working for another sales training company. She was probably in mid-harangue this very minute. Teresa wondered who the delegates were, what they were like. Daphne would be less than human if she did not enjoy working with some groups more than others, but then Daphne quite possibly was less than human. Or more. Teresa imagined her, flanked by her flip-charts, her frail little body, her far-from-frail personality, her stocky legs, her unanswerable voice, firm but with its appealing edge of music and playfulness . . . *Your being here proves that you have already closed the most important sale of your career, you have sold your-selves, let's give ourselves a round of applause for being here!*

'Shame, shame!'
   'No!'
   'Oh! Resign!'
   'Order!'
Tonight's news featured a major altercation during Prime Minister's Question Time. The Leader of the Opposition was suggesting that she had, in a recent statement, fallen somewhere short of frankness.

The Prime Minister was furious. 'I ask the Right Honourable Gentleman to withdraw!' she shouted.

Teresa was making love with Sam on her sitting room carpet. They had started with a cuddle and got carried away. Or rather, he had got carried away. Teresa would have been content to stay with the cuddles which, as administered by Sam, were something of an art form. 'I ask the Right Honourable Gentleman to withdraw,' she murmured.

'I hadn't forgotten. Trust me.'

He was too enthusiastic to be trusted in such matters, unfortunately. She eased herself away from him and offered her hand as an alternative. It was lovely to arouse and be on the receiving end of so much youthful passion, but she had not got her cap in.

'What did you do that for?' he said after a while.

'What?'

'You moved your head.'

'It's my head. Aren't I allowed to move it?'

'Not to watch television, no.' He crawled towards the set, shirt unbuttoned, erection hard, balls swinging, trousers and underpants at half-mast, a marvellous sight.

'Don't turn it off,' she said. 'I'll deal with you later.'

'Well, as long as it's not *Cagney and Lacey* after this,' he grumbled.

'The Right Honourable Gentleman has no basis for his disgraceful allegation,' said the Prime Minister.

Sam did his Thatcher impersonation. ' "Take that back, you cad. Come outside and say that." She sounds like a schoolboy.'

'She sounds as if she wants to cry,' said Teresa.

'Are you kidding? What with?'

'She does. Her voice is full of tears. Can't you hear them? You probably don't know . . . it hurts to go on shouting like that when you want to cry. Well, how would you like it? Being called a liar in front of millions of people.'

Sam was amazed. 'Are you saying she's not lying?'

'I think . . . I think telling lies is the one thing she doesn't do, actually. That's the hell of it. She's like Hitler in that way. She says what she's going to do and everyone thinks she can't mean it. They vote her in, she does what she said she'd do and everyone's so embarrassed they say she lied.'

'She's a man,' said Sam. He seemed to think this a supportive statement – one that would end the discussion and get them back to what they had been doing – but Teresa was having none of it. 'Oh no she's not. Thanks for the thought, but we can't get out of it that way. She's a woman all right . . . Oh, that lovely man,' she sighed later as the titles rolled for *Cagney and Lacey*, and Detective Lacey kissed her husband full on the mouth. 'He's just like you.'

'He's fat.'

'Hey, put it away, there's someone at the door.'

'Beverley. How lovely to see you.' *Great that you chose this evening, Bev, when Sam's here and the air of the flat is rich with the smells of heterosexual activity and Sam's bound to let some remark slip about the bijou little Starter Home that we're hoping to buy and do up and sell at a profit* . . . Beverley held a fat plastic sack in front of her like a barrier. Teresa took it and put it on the floor. She put one hand on each of Beverley's thin shoulders, slowly, as a cautious lover might, leaving space for Beverley to withdraw, quite prepared to accept a rebuff as no more than she deserved for her temerity. Beverley did not move, so Teresa leaned forward and gave her a single light kiss on the cheek. One of Beverley's hands brushed her shoulder as a token of a return embrace.

'Will you come in?' said Teresa. 'Sam's here,' she added. There were women at Collindeane Tower whose aversion to men was such that they would regard it as an intolerable piece of deception to be brought into the presence of one without prior warning. But Beverley

227

was not one of these, as Teresa knew perfectly well, and she wondered why she was being so defensive. Beverley and Sam knew each other already, from the brief days of Beverley's flirtation with the Labour Party Young Socialists. Beverley greeted Sam with a lot more warmth than she had shown Teresa, perhaps because their camaraderie was fixed and unimportant and Beverley was not thereby giving anything away. She started chaffing him about watching *Cagney and Lacey*, a programme for white liberals. 'Has Cagney had the row with the loo-tenant yet?'

'Not yet,' said Sam.

'And is Lacey still worried about her son? I don't know why you bother, it's the same every week.'

'It's not me,' said Sam, jerking his thumb in Teresa's direction. 'It's her. Glued to the set.'

Teresa supposed that this was his idea of being helpful. As long as everyone was teasing everyone about a TV programme, they were not having to talk about anything else. She decided to join in. 'You both seem to know a lot about it, considering how contemptible it is.'

'Actually, Bev, she wasn't watching *Cagney and Lacey*. She'd just started to explain to me why she'll be voting for Thatcher next time.'

'So soon . . .' Beverley murmured.

Teresa was furious. As soon as she and Sam were alone she would hit him. She felt she could actually hit him, to hurt. *Fair enough, keep the conversation light until you can find a reason to leave us alone together. But you don't have to say bloody stupid things like that. It was a joke. I'm damned if I'll leave it as a joke.* 'All I said was that people who say Thatcher's a man – I name no names – are copping out of the fact that she's one of us.' Beverley's face showed that, far from saving the situation, this had made it worse. 'Physically, I mean,' she added lamely.

'She's not one of me,' said Beverley. 'Physically or any other way.'

'Me neither,' said Sam.

'A male invention I'll grant you,' said Beverley. 'She's a robot. I mean, she saves you a lot of arguments, doesn't she, Sam? When women say we don't have access to power because men have got it all, you don't really have to say anything, do you?'

'I wasn't trying to say anything, I was trying to watch *Cagney and Lacey*.' It dawned on him that his presence was surplus to requirements. 'Are those the Goddess Garments?'

'They will be, when Teresa's done a bit of work on them.'

'I'll do a bit of work on them, I'm sure you two have lots to talk about.' He picked up the sack and headed off in the direction of Teresa's parents' garage which was where the washing machine was kept.

Teresa decided to let Beverley speak first. For now she was either absorbed in the TV programme or pretending to be, to cover the awkwardness. Teresa herself had lost the thread of the story. She was more interested in imagining how it felt to be as young as Beverley and Sam, to have no memory of being politically conscious at a date BT, Before Thatcher. To have no memory of feeling positively wistful about the idea that there might, one day, if the women's movement continued to make strides, be a woman prime minister.

She's a male invention, a robot. Teresa had her own ideas about what men – men of her generation and peer group – had been doing when, spotting the first choppy waves of women's rebellion on their horizon, they had resolved simply to batten down the hatches and wait for it to pass. They had not been building a robot, they had been thinking about domestic back-up arrangements for their careers. The solution they had come up with had not been difficult to find. If the women's liberationists did not come to their senses in time, the men had realized, they need only wait for the next generation, getting what they could in the meantime. The next generation, seeing their older sisters set aside and disappointed, would be much more amenable. The problem of whom to marry would have appeared far more urgent to these young men than any need to invent a prime ministerial robot to call the women's movement's bluff.

Beverley, though, would have to think Margaret Thatcher a robot, working as she did from a place that proclaimed *All Women Welcome*. Were Margaret Thatcher to turn up one day at Collindeane Tower, expecting her welcome, she could be turned away with impunity. *Robots Not Included.*

Cagney and Lacey caught their criminal. Beverley looked as if she were about to leave. Had she, like Teresa, lost her nerve for talking, or had she never meant for them to have a talk? In Beverley's eyes Teresa had done a terrible thing in handing *Atalanta* over to the Sargents. Beverley would never admit that it had turned out not to be so terrible after all. Teresa would bide her time and earn her passage. When she had done her work on the Goddess Garments, she would return them to Collindeane Tower herself. Someone would have to look her in the eye and say, 'Thank you.'

'Do they need much doing to them?' It was conversation only; but it sounded like an appeal to be let off lightly.

'Some of them are rubbish,' said Beverley bitterly. 'They think anything's good enough for working-class women and kids.'

Teresa noted *they* with cautious pleasure. *They*: people who contemptuously toss old clothes in the direction of the poor without bothering to wash them or replace buttons. Teresa was not for the moment included among *they*. Beverley went on to say that she knew claimant families who would go without food rather than buy second-hand clothes, they felt so degraded by them. Goddess Garments hoped to start stocking inexpensive new clothes, if they got their grant. Goddess Garments were hopeful of getting some money from the European Community. A sub-committee of a sub-commission had been embarrassed to discover money in a bank account, left over from the Women's Decade. They were looking for groups to give it to.

'Why are you looking like that?'

'I'm not looking like anything,' said Teresa. She guessed that she was expected to offer some of her ill-gotten gains from *New Atalanta* towards the cost of changing the image of Goddess Garments, but she and Sam were going to need every penny they had for their new home, unfortunately.

Walking Beverley to the gate, Teresa said, 'Do you have any idea of how Molly is? Or who she is, for that matter?'

'Who?'

'She's this woman who's dying – '

'Who?' said Beverley sharply. 'Who's dying?'

'I don't know who she is. Do you know someone called Molly who it might be?' Teresa explained about the weekly postcards.

Beverley said, 'No. No, I don't know anyone called Molly. Shit. She's dying and she knows it and she asks people to . . . you write to her every week? That's nice.' There was no irony. Teresa thought sending postcards a small enough thing to be doing, compared with Beverley's many commitments, but Beverley was impressed and touched, and the goodbye she gave Teresa was the warmest thing that had passed between them all evening.

Teresa had only brought up the subject of Molly to fill a silence. She had not been seeking kudos. But it occurred to her now that if Beverley had not seen Molly's note it would not be because she did not read her newsletter. It was far more likely that Beverley had chosen subconsciously to blank out on the tragedy. Age might have blunted the edge of Teresa's idealism, but it had enabled her to respond to Molly's poignant appeal with compassion and without the sort of panicky horror which, fifteen years ago, might have led her, too, to turn the page. 'Dear Molly,' she wrote later. 'You've helped me to patch up a quarrel with a friend.' *You and Daphne have,* she thought, for without that original idea to sell space to START she would have had no excuse to contact Beverley. 'I won't bore you with the details, but thank you.' *Thank you for what? Thank you for being ill? Thank you for being THERE. If you are there.* 'Love and sisterhood, Teresa.'

38

Teresa had accumulated a great deal of experience, over the years, of raising funds for feminist projects. 'You're good at talking to middle-class people,' was how it had been explained on more than one occasion, and Teresa had borne this with fortitude.

Part of her experience was that whenever two or three women were gathered together in the name of getting some money, someone was always bound to say, 'What about Europe?' Someone always knew of a women's group to whom Brussels or Strasbourg had given sufficient funds to pay four workers or buy a building. But the name of the group thus endowed was never known. It was always someone's cousin's lover's friend who had the details. The precise name of the funding agency was never known either, and Teresa had come to the conclusion that it was an urban myth, a Holy Grail that did not exist. But she hoped now for Beverley's sake that it did exist, and that Goddess Garments would be successful in their application.

She hoped too that the application would be written with success in mind. This was probably Goddess Garments' last chance of getting real money from anywhere. She hoped that the collective would give a lot of thought to what grant-givers wanted to hear, and say it back to them: not: 'We're poor, we're good, and everyone is being horrible to us' but: 'If you give us money now, here's how we're going to use it to ensure that we'll never have to ask you again.' That was what donors and benefactors wanted to hear: that they would never be asked again. It was easier to be generous in such circumstances than if you thought you were tossing money down a pit.

She discussed this in the office with Nadia, who thought Teresa ought to offer to help write the application.

'They'd think I was going for a high status role. I'll do it if they ask me.'

'It might make a good feature, actually. Creative fund raising.' Teresa, Nadia and the other *New Atalanta* women, Brenda excluded, were sitting in the boardroom waiting for a meeting to start. It was to be a long-term planning meeting. They had some long-term planning of their own to do. Brenda's secretary Jessica announced that Brenda had it in mind to do something on job-sharing: interviews with two women with domestic responsibilities who worked together part-time.

'What about two men with domestic responsibilities working part-time?' said Nadia.

'Are there two men with domestic responsibilities?' said Jessica. 'Anywhere?'

'We might find a man and a woman,' said Teresa. 'I think New Atalanta Man knows a couple of bank managers. Mr Bank Manager goes to the bank in the mornings, and Mrs goes in the afternoons. Shall we let him think of it?'

'Yes, Teresa, you be difficult – '

'I was difficult last time.'

'You're good at it. You be difficult and say it has to be two men. Greg can say – '

' "We can't change the world overnight." '

'Teresa can say, "But I want to" and then Greg'll think of his bank managers and we can all say, "I say, Greg! Do they really?" '

'And I can get the bank to buy an ad,' said Teresa. 'Sssh, they're coming. He's looking very perky today, isn't he? I wonder what he's got for us.'

What he had for them was a plan for a supplement to the magazine called *New Atalanta Man*. It would contain articles by and for New Atalanta Men, with advertising to match, which he was confident Teresa could handle.

Teresa was glad of this because she was not herself confident that she could handle anything. She was about to have the giggles. She glanced at Nadia who seemed to be in a similar condition. Teresa took a grip on herself. 'Would it be a pull-out supplement, Greg?'

'I saw it more as something separate, bound to the main magazine – '

'With an umbilicus?'

'With some sort of coloured binding, free, of course.'

'Of course.'

'But it could be a pull-out, I'll leave you to look into the costings. Can you give me – give Brenda – a report by Monday?'

'How shall we cost a New Atalanta Man?' Teresa murmured. 'For his price is above rubies . . .'

'Thank you, Teresa. We just thought we'd run it up the flagpole, didn't we, Brenda?' Brenda nodded and Greg expanded on his plans. The more he talked, the clearer it became that the idea had already been run up his flagpole several times and saluted by everyone who counted, namely himself and Brenda. Brenda had already commissioned features on 'Why Feminists Make Men Feel Guilty', 'Getting In Touch With Our Gentleness' and 'Team Sports Reconsidered'. There was to be fashion, of course, and cosmetics: holidays, cars and culture, including fiction, an extract from a shortly-to-be-published novel about a male tycoon having a nervous breakdown. *Burnout!*, it was called, and it promised to be a best seller.

Hysteria was lapping at the edge of Teresa's consciousness. 'The magazine for the man who thinks the battle's over and he's lost. Who'll advertise in that? I know, the Samaritans.' She ran her eyes round the table, wondering who had known about this. Nobody had, judging from the numb expressions on the faces of everybody except Greg and Brenda and Nadia . . . *Nadia*! Nadia was looking wise and interested. 'Are you sure the timing's right for this, Greg?' she said. Teresa eyed her closely and decided that she was indeed very wise and was only pretending to be interested. When the Sargents had a baby together there was only one thing to do with it: admire it, and then distract attention from it in the hope of quietly wheeling it away. 'It would be a shame to waste an idea like this with the wrong timing.'

'I think it's a good time,' said Brenda.

'Why?'

'The other women's magazines have done it.'

Teresa decided to take a leaf out of Nadia's book and act sensibly. 'Isn't that a good reason for us not to? We'll be accused of jumping on the bandwagon. Couldn't we do something else? Something essentially similar but somehow different. . . .' She was struggling and the Sargents knew it.

'Such as?'

'*New Atalanta Teenager*?' she said. *New Atalanta Dog?* she thought. If her memory of the readership survey served her correctly, fifty-six per cent of New Atalanta Women had pets at home, though she could not remember how that compared with the number who had men at home. *New Atalanta Pot Plant? New Atalanta Gerbil?*

'I think a supplement for teenagers of both sexes is something to think about for the future,' said Greg. 'Thank you, Teresa.'

Did she imagine the distilled malevolence in his eyes as he said this? She said quietly, 'So it's to be a free leisure magazine for New Atalanta Man.'

'I think he's earned it, don't you?' said Greg, and Teresa knew that the malevolence was real.

'I won't do it,' she said.

'I see,' said Greg.

Brenda gave a little trill of laughter to draw attention to the undoubted jocularity of Teresa's remark. Nadia kicked Teresa's ankle. She heard the message of Nadia's kick as clearly as if it had been put into words. *Don't say anything now. We've scuppered him before, we'll do it again.* But they would not scupper this. It was settled. Teresa felt as if she had just acquired a sixth sense, not one that she would have sought, not one that was going to add anything to her peace of mind, but one that she was stuck with and would have to live with from now on. The sixth sense was somewhere between sight and smell . . . no, not smell, stink. A sense of stink. This stank. New Atalanta Man did not buy general interest magazines so New Atalanta Man was to be given his free of charge. When were women ever given something free of charge because they refused to pay for it, *could not* pay for it? And it would not be free, of course it would not. It would be paid for by advertising, advertising which it would be Teresa's job to sell. It had given her pleasure to sell advertising, even somewhat dubious advertising, when she could know that she was thereby helping to finance good, positive articles for women to read, and for New Atalanta Man to read too, if he wanted to. But New Atalanta Man wanted articles of his own. He wanted to agonize over his guilt, his burnout and his team sports, but he was not prepared to pay to do so. It was not that important to him. He could take it or leave it alone. Women did not have that luxury. They needed *New Atalanta* and they needed it to be theirs, exclusively theirs. Of that Teresa was certain. *New Atalanta*'s success was women's success. Women brought it out; women bought it; women's hard-earned purchasing power encouraged companies to advertise in it. And there were a dozen special categories of women who might welcome a special supplement if special supplements were under discussion. But there was to be no discussion. New Atalanta Man was to have his *New Atalanta Man* because that was what New Atalanta Man wanted. She said again, 'I won't do it.'

*

'If you didn't want to live with me,' said Sam, 'you only had to say.'

What was he talking about?

'We're all set to buy a flat and you chuck your job in.'

Across her numbness she registered a flicker of surprise that he seemed to see what had happened entirely in terms of himself. *Surprise* was perhaps putting it a bit strongly. She was beyond surprise. It was interesting, nonetheless. It was an aspect of the situation which she had not considered. It did not matter, in any case. She would find another job.

She applied to be a representative with a company that sold school textbooks. She applied to be advertising manager with an antiques magazine. She could not expect necessarily to stay in the world of the media – did not necessarily want to stay in it – so she cast her net more widely. She applied to sell steel shelving to factories. She applied to sell office equipment, greetings cards, gloves.

'Come back,' said Nadia. 'We need you to help fight him.'

'There's no point in fighting him.'

'You think we should all leave?'

'Don't ask me.'

'You're very principled, Teresa, and I admire that. But I feel I can do more good by staying – '

It was Teresa herself talking to the *Atalanta* collective. But she felt no inclination to criticize Nadia as she herself had been criticized. Nadia thought her principled. She wished she could agree, and take some credit for it. 'It doesn't feel like principles. It's just that some things are impossible. I physically could not work on something called *New Atalanta Man*. He might as well tell me to cut my heart out and eat it. Even if I wanted to, I wouldn't know where to start.'

'There's some post for you,' said Nadia. 'Meet us for a drink after work and I'll give it to you.'

'I'd prefer you to send it.'

It was an invitation to a party to launch a new company: Daphne Barclay Business Training. In the corner of the printed card, the words 'I do hope you can come, Daphne' had been written in ink. Cynically, Teresa licked her finger and rubbed at the ink.

To her surprise the ink ran. Daphne wanted Teresa to come to her party. Daphne probably thought that Teresa had a sales force in need of training. To seek to re-establish the acquaintance in such circumstances was exactly the sort of thing Daphne would do, would advise others to do.

Daphne's setting up of her own business would explain the

reluctance of the START Selling telephonist to acknowledge her existence. They would not want her pinching their customers.

Daphne would be disappointed to discover that Teresa had no sales force, had no job. But she decided to go to the party anyway. It would be a chance to go out and mingle with people who knew nothing about her. She might even meet someone there who would employ her.

She spent a long time deciding what to wear. Her morale was low, she was nervous, she thought she looked horrible in everything. She settled for a short black evening frock with lacy sleeves, and borrowed some jewellery from her mother.

The party, 6.30 pm to 9.00, was held at a businessmen's club in Central London. She could not remember when she had last seen so many men in one place without any women. White triangles of bisected shirt-fronts danced before her eyes like the teeth of sharks . . . but where were the cleaner-fish? She herself was dressed quite wrongly, she realized. All these men – the assembled sales managers of the capital, if not the nation – had obviously come straight from work. Dressed as she was, Teresa could not possibly have come from work: she was announcing to her possible sources of future employment that she had no work to come from.

One of the shirt-fronts approached her: a white-haired man with a slight paunch and a pleasant smile, somebody's uncle. 'I'm Alistair Brunt, Daphne's partner. Glad you could come.'

'I'm Teresa Beal, from, er – I'm Teresa Beal.'

'Let me get you a drink.' While he was doing this she looked round again for women and spotted four, not counting waitresses. She could not believe how conventional all the men looked, after the media parties she was used to. She felt as if she had gone back twenty years. They looked like little boys pretending to be grownups . . . no, they looked like the opposite, they looked like men from fifties' films when even college students appeared middle-aged.

'I'm a great admirer of *New Atalanta*,' said Alistair Brunt, returning with her drink. On reflex she felt pleasure. Then she thought, *Come on. He's researched his guests, he knows what to say. Anyway, little does he know.*

A flash of blue caught her eye. Draped in turquoise, Daphne was holding court to a circle of men. She was laughingly laying down the law to them, her thin white arm waving gracefully. Something glittered at her shoulder; her glossy brown hair framed a face lit up with hospitality and witty determination to get her point across. Charmed, the men listened. An outsider broke the circle, arms wide in the obvious expectation of an embrace. Alistair Brunt looked as if he too expected this to happen and did not approve . . . but with a deft piece of body language which Teresa could not identify but admired anyway, Daphne caused the arms to be lowered to the man's sides, and accepted a peck on the cheek. Her display of untrammelled joy at seeing the man could not be faulted; but she had left him in no doubt as to what she would and would not do to express it. Seeing this, Alistair Brunt relaxed slightly. Teresa wondered if he were in love with Daphne. She doubted that there were many rewards to be drawn from the condition.

'Come and see Daphne,' he said. She felt reluctant, shy. She did not imagine that Daphne would appreciate being interrupted in mid-conversation with people who were or might be her clients by the arrival of someone who could not be. But Teresa knew no one else here and so had no excuse to offer Alistair Brunt who seemed determined to break up Daphne's circle of admirers.

'Daphne, here's Teresa Beal.'

'Teresa,' Daphne cried, 'How sweet of you to come!'

39

Daphne was disappointed to see Teresa arriving by herself. She had invited Brenda Sargent as well, and had assumed that they would come together.

A number of other journalists were here, but not as many as she had hoped for. They were mainly from the trade press and Daphne wanted to publicize her company more widely than that. She had been hoping to plant in Brenda Sargent's mind the idea that if it was women setting up businesses in a man's world that interested her, she need look no further for an interesting feature than Daphne Barclay Business Training.

Daphne did not begrudge Ann Mitchison her little publicity coup, but really. A teenage toy-maker and his mother in Tyne and Wear.

Teresa had come to the party alone, and Daphne would have to make the best of it. Teresa might serve a purpose. It was unlikely to be coincidental that Ann Mitchison had been featured in the magazine of which Teresa was business manager. Ann Mitchison obviously had the ear of Teresa, and Teresa had the ear of her editor.

'I'm a great admirer of your magazine and what you and your editor have done for it,' she said, taking Teresa lightly by the elbow and steering her a few paces away from the men so that they might talk in private. She gave Alistair a discreet Do Not Disturb look. 'Will Mrs Sargent be coming this evening?'

'I don't know,' said Teresa.

Strange, Daphne thought. 'It's changed, granted,' she said. 'And yet somehow it's the same. It's bright, it's lively, it's informative and readable, but the overall spirit of idealism remains. *New Atalanta* speaks the language of women like me. You deserve a round of applause.'

Teresa laughed. 'It's nothing to do with me.'

'Nonsense!' Daphne replied in a very forthright way, knowing that a display of forthrightness, even if it verged upon rudeness, was beguiling to many people, particularly if it was accompanied by a smile and followed by flattery. 'You know me better than to say that. The editorial and design staff may have done some of the work, but who pays for it? Who pays for *them*? Was it very difficult to persuade your colleagues to sell to Our Ways?'

'We had no option,' said Teresa. 'We were going bust. That was why I left early from the course. There was nothing I could do, but I wanted to be there.'

Daphne remembered how irritated she had been by Teresa's early and unexplained departure. She had drafted a brisk letter in her mind, for writing and sending should Teresa ever enquire after her diploma, but Teresa had not done this. 'I wish I'd known,' said Daphne now. 'I might have been able to help.' Over Teresa's shoulder she saw Bill Groves arrive, from Groves' Breweries. She particularly wanted to talk to Bill. She saw Alistair greet him and start shepherding him around. Alistair would know to bring Bill over as soon as Daphne had finished with Teresa. Teresa was looking very glum. 'I wish I'd known, and then I wouldn't have withheld your START diploma. From the looks of your magazine, you deserve one. I'll give you one of mine, an honorary one.' Teresa did not appear to appreciate this offer, and Daphne realized that all her congratulations might be misplaced. Were the unthinkable one day to happen, were she to be forced to sell Daphne Barclay Business Training to a large corporation, sympathy and reassurance might be preferable to congratulations. 'I'm sure you did the right thing,' she murmured. Then she decided to be vulnerable, since Teresa was obviously not in full agreement with the 'battle's over and we've won' approach of her employers. 'I, of course, have just done the opposite of what you have done. You have left the world of small businesses for the safety of a large corporation, whereas I . . . so if you were right, I may be wrong. I hope I haven't bitten off more than I can chew.'

'I'm sure you haven't,' said Teresa reassuringly.

'How sweet of you.'

'I mean I'm sure you wouldn't have bitten it off in the first place if you didn't know you could chew it. Actually, Daphne, I'm not working at *New Atalanta* any more. I've left.'

Daphne swallowed but did not miss a beat. 'And where are you working now?'

'I'm not. I haven't got a job.'

'Bill!' cried Daphne. 'How lovely to see you! Do you know Teresa Beal? Bill Groves from Groves' Breweries. Now, Bill,' she said firmly, taking his hand, 'you and I are going to have a little chat.' She edged him into a corner.

Daphne would not normally approach the delicate business of collecting debts from important clients with such directness. Far from buttonholing them at parties, she would normally prefer to leave individual clients themselves out of the matter for as long as possible while she fought it out with their underlings. Thus she kept in reserve the possibility of escalating her complaint to higher levels. But Daphne had already exchanged sharp words with the Groves' accounts department, to no avail. And Bill Groves, who had created his own business, knew the score. It was because he knew the score that he had transferred his business from START Selling to Daphne Barclay Business Training in the first place.

Meeting him at the Pastures New Health Farm, and going quietly out of her mind for want of something to do, Daphne had immediately recognized him as a potential source of business for START Selling, of which she was, at the time, an employee. After talking to him, she had recognized him as a potential source of business for herself.

Groves' Breweries had a large sales force, sixty pubs and a nation-wide chain of off licences which were, at the time of Daphne's first meeting with Bill Groves, about to undergo refurbishment. There was no point, she had told him, in refurbishing your shops if you did not refurbish your shop assistants to match. As the daughter of shopkeepers herself, she knew this.

Bill had raised a number of objections, mostly to do with the price. It was one thing to send his representatives to a four-star hotel for a week in the hope that they might, in odd moments between eating and drinking at his expense, pick up a few tips that would raise them from their present level of incompetence ... it would be quite another to do the same for shop assistants who did not stay five minutes in their jobs in any case.

'Who says you have to send them away?' Daphne had said. 'I would come to them.' START Selling did not operate on that basis, but Daphne did. She could spend a day in each region. It would have to be at the weekend (Daphne had not yet resigned from START

Selling), but that could be all to the good. If the training were carried out on a Sunday, the minimum amount of staff working time would be lost. 'You wouldn't even be paying for accommodation,' she had said. 'It will be on-the-job training, the best kind.' She had gone on to list her experience of work in the retail trade, from her parents' shop to the many nationally known chains whose staff had been delegates on her START courses.

Terms had been agreed between Bill Groves and Daphne, terms at once economical for him and profitable for her. It was out of her success in gaining such freelance work, her knowledge of the number of START clients who asked for her by name, her increasing dislike of most of her START Selling colleagues, and Alistair's announcement that he intended to remove himself from her life altogether if she did not make some kind of commitment to him, that Daphne Barclay Business Training had been born.

'Bill, let me ask you this,' she said now, taking a bottle from the hand of a passing waitress and topping up his glass. 'What would *you* have done, when your business was young and small . . .' Daphne eschewed pathos, but she would not mind if Bill noticed that she too was young and small, ' . . . if one of your most valued clients made difficulties about paying his bills?'

'I'd have sent the lads round.'

'I can't do that, I've only got Alistair.'

Bill looked comically innocent. 'To whom are you referring to, Daphne? We paid, didn't we? I'm sure I can remember authorizing the cheque. I've definitely seen it.'

'Oh good,' she said. 'I expect we'll receive it tomorrow, then. Thank you so much.'

'Give it a week,' he suggested.

Give it a week, she thought bitterly. *If you've authorized payment, why do I have to do that?*

Give it a week. As if debt were some kind of illness which must be given a chance to cure itself spontaneously before drastic remedies were tried. *I've seen it . . . so with a bit of luck it'll put itself into an envelope and fly down to the post office . . .* She let the matter drop for now. Bill's response had ensured that there was nowhere for the conversation to go other than into the realms of accusations of lying. At least she had let Bill know that she knew he was not playing fair. In the context of the personal rapport that existed between them, such knowledge should embarrass him into action.

40

Daphne wandered amongst her guests, shaking hands, smiling at
them, and, where appropriate, kissing them or suffering herself to
be kissed. It was nearly time for her speech, and she looked round
for Alistair, hoping he had not forgotten his duty to gather everybody
together and call for silence.

He was still locked in conversation with Teresa Beal, whom he
had borne away when Daphne wanted to talk to Bill Groves. Daphne
had to admit that Teresa looked quite nice this evening, particularly
now that she had cheered up, and she wondered what the two of
them were talking about. She wished them joy of each other. Teresa
was probably giving Alistair a blow-by-blow account of how she had
come to lose her job. Alistair was probably telling Teresa about his
intended good works.

Before Daphne had persuaded him to go into partnership with
her, she had had to counter his plans to go to Cardiff to work with
the unemployed. Daphne had pointed out that there were a great
many people unemployed in parts of the country other than Cardiff,
and had suggested that his talents might be better used in helping
to set up a company that would attack the causes of unemployment
at their roots.

'What have you got in mind?' he had said.

'The best way to help the unemployed is to help employers.'

'Yes, up to a point, but –'

'Our training services will make businesses so profitable that they'll
take on more staff.'

'Yes, I know all that, Daphne, but what I'm saying is that I want
to do something for the unemployed now.'

'So do I,' she had said, 'and so we will, but we'll have to do some profitable business first to pay for it.'

START Selling were, in their petty, jealous way, doing their best to prevent *that* happening. They had sent an extremely rude letter. They seemed to think that they had the right to tell her with whom she could and could not trade. They had ordered her to solicit no more business from their customers, and to return any documentation concerning such customers that she had removed from their premises. They had quoted clauses from her and Alistair's erstwhile contracts of employment, to the effect that ex-employees of START were not allowed to compete with START within two years of leaving the company.

Left to herself, Daphne would have taken no notice. She had been, and still was, sure that they were bluffing. Had they been serious, the letter would have come from a solicitor. If they did involve solicitors, it would take more than two years to sort the matter out, and then she could do as she pleased. Left to herself, she would do as she pleased anyway. She could not believe that her contract of employment could be used against her once she had left the company. It would go against the whole spirit of government thinking on the importance of competition. It would be a restraint of trade.

The solicitor whom Alistair had consulted (without Daphne's prior agreement, which had annoyed her: they were supposed to be part-ners) had agreed that, should the matter ever come to court, Daphne Barclay Business Training could indeed argue that the relevant clauses in the contracts of employment constituted unreasonably restrictive covenants; but, should the courts not accept that argument, an injunction might be served on DBBT, stopping it from doing business with START clients. Damages and costs might have to be paid. 'I'd like to see them try it,' Daphne had said, but Alistair had declared that he, on the contrary, would *not* like to see them try it. He would prefer that he and Daphne concentrated on looking for new business. 'There is no point in setting up a new business unless there is new business to be done.'

This was one of Daphne's own maxims, so she could not argue with it. 'Business training for people who think they don't need business training' was all right as far as it went: the business world was full of people who stood in sore need of training and were not getting it from START or from anyone else. But it was much harder to sell to them than to people who already believed in training as such and needed only to be convinced of the superiority of the kind offered by DBBT. Daphne was exasperated by Alistair's lily-livered reluctance to approach people who used to use START and had, when all was said and done, asked for her, Daphne, by name.

Alistair and Teresa appeared to be having a wonderful time exchanging their life stories. Daphne decided to break them up and remind Alistair to get everybody organized to listen to her speech.

'Right, Daphne.' He stepped back from Teresa and put his hand lightly on Daphne's shoulder, a gesture he often used to signify concurrence. Then, seeming to change his mind, and in a spirit of raillery that she had not encountered in him before, he took his hand away and said, 'How would we feel about putting on courses for feminists?'

'For what?' she said. 'Oh yes. Yes, for anybody. What would that consist of, exactly?'

'START Selling – Women!, plus some politics,' said Teresa. 'I didn't know you were into community work, Daphne.'

Daphne wondered whether Teresa were drunk, and decided that she must be. Teresa was teasing Daphne, laughing at her, the two of them were laughing at her. What on earth had Alistair been saying? Daphne thought she realized what was going on. Alistair was not very happy with her at the moment. He tried not to let it show – he was a professional – but she knew. He had been expecting their partnership to be more than a business partnership. And it might become more: Daphne was fond of him, and ruled nothing out. But there had not so far been time, and he ought to know that as well as she did, instead of sulking and doing what he was doing now which was to pretend to make a play for Teresa in the hope of making Daphne jealous. It would be funny if it were not pathetic.

'Alistair, *what* are you doing?' she said, drawing him aside. 'It's hardly fair to talk this way, you know these people haven't got any money.'

'Apparently someone in the EEC is giving money to women's groups on a this-is-your-last-chance basis.'

'Really? See if you can find out who they are. But first I want to make my speech.'

It was not a long speech. People knew why they were there, and they would not listen anyway. It was a formality, time was better spent in personal conversation than in a long harangue. She welcomed everybody and thanked them for finding time in their busy schedules to come and celebrate with her, her and her partner Alistair, that was. She ventured to suggest that one of the reasons why their schedules *were* so busy was that their subordinates in their companies were not always as efficient and productive as they might be. Daphne Barclay Business Training had the answer to the problem, and nobody was going to be allowed to leave the party (here Daphne adopted a manner parodying herself at her sternest) without a Prospectus of Courses: sales training courses, management courses, use-of-telephone courses . . . her guests could, in fact, name it, and Daphne Barclay Business Training would be offering a course in it. This produced some ribaldry which Daphne had not sought, and she moved swiftly on to invite everyone to drink a toast with her to the new company, which they did. Then Alistair presented her with a bunch of flowers, which was sweet of him.

Later, Daphne stood at the exit, thanking, smiling at, and pressing prospectuses upon her departing guests. Alistair was supposed to be helping with this, but he was still amusing himself with Teresa Beal. 'Have you got one of these?' she said. 'I'm so glad you could come, please take one.' She wondered how far the law went that supposedly stopped her from soliciting custom from START clients. What was a START client, and how was she to know who was and who was not? If these people, to whom she was giving prospectuses, had ever in their lives used START courses or considered doing so, had she rendered herself liable to the full penalties of the law by inviting them to her party? It was ridiculous. Daphne was not afraid of START. That the powers that be at START Selling UK disliked and were jealous of her, she knew perfectly well. But START Selling UK was only part of START Selling International, and a very small part at that.

Dear Miss Barclay, [Lindbergh Stanley had written]

As you know, I take a personal interest in the progress and welfare of every member of our worldwide community of professional sales trainers.

You will have been informed, on appointment, of our formal Grievance Procedure, under which any employee who is in doubt about the fairness or propriety of any other employee's treatment of him or her, or any aspect of company policy or practice, may refer the matter for my personal arbitration.

In my distress on learning of your resignation from START Selling UK, I was perplexed to discover that no such application for arbitration has ever been received from you.

As a START Selling employee, your salary and conditions of employment were in accordance with standard company terms which were communicated to you at the time of your appointment.

I am at a loss, therefore, to know why you have resigned your position. I would consider myself privileged to be taken into your confidence as to why you have felt it necessary to take this step. Such enlightenment could serve only to assist me in my task of improving staff care procedures in such a way as to ensure that a person of your calibre is never again lost to the START Selling family, of which I am proud (though also a little sad, I must confess, at this time) to be world president.

Cordially,

J. LINDBERGH STANLEY.

Was that a letter from a man who would stand by while his UK company persecuted her? Daphne was sure that it was not. It was a reasonable, regretful, even affectionate letter from a man who was big enough to respect her, rivals though they might be. If there were any further trouble from START Selling UK, she would let them know that Lindbergh Stanley had specifically asked her to let him know about their shortcomings. For now, she had simply written back explaining her view that when entrepreneurship beckoned, one had no choice but to follow, and her certainty that he, of all people, would understand this and wish her well. 'It is in my blood,' she had said, adding that she was sorry that they had been unable to arrange a meeting when he was last in the UK, but if he came again she would be happy to give him lunch.

Alistair had advised her against sending this or any reply. He had thought it possible that Lindbergh Stanley was trying to trap her into saying something libellous against her former colleagues, the more thoroughly to enable them to sue. Daphne had replied that Lindbergh Stanley might be many things but he was not petty. It would be beneath him to conduct such a charade. Alistair had insisted that Lindbergh Stanley's letter looked pretty sinister to him, but then Alistair would say that. Lindbergh Stanley had not written to *him*, expressing regret over his departure from the company, and Alistair was jealous.

41

Daphne cleared her throat and began.

'Sometimes I open my sessions by inviting delegates to give themselves a round of applause for being here. On this occasion I have only one thing to say on that subject. It is this. Booo!' The sound was a practised one, deep and resonant, and she sustained it beyond the end of the nervous laughter of her audience of trainee supermarket managers on day-release, brought together for a session on Dealing with Customer Complaints.

'Boo! You shouldn't be here! You shouldn't need to be here! Your customers shouldn't have any complaints!

'But they have, haven't they, and that is why you *are* here. Because of your companies' failings, you must carry the can.' Pleased with her pun, she produced a can of lamb stew and set it down where everybody could see her press on the bulging ends, which dented and sprang back into place. 'A blown tin. Disgraceful. A risk to health and a risk to our companies' reputations. What should be our first concern when the customer returns it to the shop?'

'To apologize?' suggested a delegate, examining the tin, which Daphne had passed round, with an expression of great sadness.

'Our *first* concern.'

'To give her a replacement?'

'Is that all?'

'Two replacements?'

'Are none of you concerned,' said Daphne patiently, 'to prevent her reporting the matter to the Environmental Health Office of the local authority? That would be my main concern. My actions might be the same as yours, but I didn't ask about actions, I asked about concerns. Think before you act. Please listen carefully to the way I phrase my questions and answer them as they have been put, not as you think they ought to have been put.

'Remember, please, that your customer is doing you a favour by bringing a complaint to your attention. She could just as easily make a private decision never to shop with you again, and go around blackening your name for ever more. . . .'

Was somebody blackening her name, the name of her company? She could think of no other reason for the paucity of bookings. This Friday afternoon session was the first time she had been out all week. On Monday, Alistair had given a day-school on Techniques of Leadership. Apart from that, the two of them had sat in the office, he calm and hopeful, she in a state of irritable terror, listening to a faint ticking sound in her brain, the sound of the overheads going up and up like the figures on a meter in a taxi.

'Remember too that ordinary members of the public love to tell stories of battles won with what they perceive – or used to perceive, until they encountered you – as heartless bureaucracies. I once overheard a woman returning a faulty kettle to an electrical goods shop. "I only bought it last week," she said. "But it's leaking rather fast." Her tone implied that, had she bought it last month or had it only been leaking slowly, she would not have troubled the shop about it. But she will have told a different story to her friends later. "I told them," she will have said. "Replace my kettle or I take my custom elsewhere. And they replaced it." Instead of feeling aggrieved, she will have felt important. The shop assistant made her feel important. Which, of course, she was.'

Daphne had a number of plans for making her company important. For clients already sold on the idea of residential courses, she was looking for a hotel that would give block bookings at a favourable rate. For the 'training for people who think they don't need training' end of things, she wanted to rent a grand hall or lavish conference centre and organize a day-long Daphne Barclay Festival of Selling with food and wine and music and entertainment all leading up to a virtuoso performance by herself. Delegates would leave with light in their eyes and a spring in their step . . . satisfied, yet craving more.

For now all she had was a group of embryonic managerial clones putting together an embarrassed and embarrassing role-play in a draughty classroom in a polytechnic. '*Take that tin off her!*' she cried. She did not like to raise her voice to delegates, but her patience was not unlimited. 'As long as she has that tin in her possession, she has a gun at your head. She can walk out at any time and take it to the

Environmental Health Officer who will be fascinated to learn where she bought it. No, don't *snatch* it . . .' Daphne strode into the middle of the role-play and took the part of the manager. ' "A blown tin, madam? Dear oh dear, may I see? Thank you . . . " ' She took the tin and examined it. ' "Well, I'm sorry you're dissatisfied, madam, let me give you another tin . . . " Note that I haven't admitted anything, I have simply diverted attention away from the tin and towards the customer's feelings with positive phrases like "I am sorry" and "Let me give". Note also that I have *not replaced the faulty tin on the shelf*.' Everybody chuckled at this, as if it were too obvious to need saying, but if Daphne had in her possession the amount of money the average shopkeeper lost by failing to see the obvious, she could pay off the overdraft which currently represented her share of Daphne Barclay Business Training.

A handwritten sign in the window of the small general store invited potential customers to 'Try Our New Delicatessen Counter'. Daphne went in, sniffing the cheesy air with distaste. With the exception of the delicatessen counter, the shop was laid out for self-service. The delicatessen was all behind glass with no obvious means of access, but it hardly mattered. Despite it being Saturday morning and the Suffolk town being a busy one, the shop was quite innocent of customers.

Daphne did a brief tour of inspection and approached the single checkout where a man sat scraping the covers off the numbers on instant bingo cards with the side of a 10p coin. Absorbed in this, he did not look up. Daphne shifted from foot to foot. She glanced at the confectionery counter. It was correctly placed near where queues, if any, would form; but it was too high to catch the eye of children. She reached out and casually shoplifted a bar of chocolate. The man looked up. 'Gawd, it's not that time again, is it? Hide the books, Mother! The VAT inspector's here.' He put down his bingo card and made to leapfrog the counter. He said, 'Perhaps not,' and rushed round instead, taking Daphne in his arms and waltzing her about, singing: 'Clare, I'm so happy you are there, with the rosebuds in your hair – '

'All right, Dad. It's nice to see you.'

'Let me take you to the fair – '

A customer came in and started reading magazines on the magazine shelf, but Daphne's father was nothing daunted. ' – but you'll have to lend me the money 'cos I can't afford the *fare*, oh Clare, oh Clare, oh Clare – '

The customer appeared to be under the impression that she was in a public reference library. Daphne wriggled free from her father's grasp and looked over the woman's shoulder, admiring the contents of the magazine. 'Such lovely pictures,' Daphne murmured. 'It seems only yesterday that she was shy Di, and now look at her.'

The woman ignored Daphne and said to her father, 'I'm just having a look, Mr Barclay, before I make up my mind.'

'That's all right, Mrs Dankworth. Take your time. This is my daughter, she likes to keep my customers in line.'

Daphne gave her father a furious glance, but it was intercepted by a smile from Mrs Dankworth. 'Clare, is it? You must be Daphne's sister.'

'I'm Daphne. There's no Clare. Why do you keep calling me Clare, Dad?'

'Because Daphne doesn't rhyme with anything.'

'You're doing very well, aren't you, Daphne?' said Mrs Dankworth. 'Is Clare older or younger than you?' She put the magazine back in the wrong place. 'Aren't you a vet or something?'

'Some time ago,' said Daphne, replacing the magazine where it belonged, 'I worked in veterinary pharmaceuticals.'

'And here's us can't even spell it, Mrs Dankworth.'

There was no point in trying to talk sensibly to her father in this mood. Daphne went through to the back of the shop to look for her mother. She was not really looking forward to this weekend. She generally visited her parents on a quarterly basis, to do their VAT return and check that things were all right. This time she had left it a little longer, and this time she had another task. Her parents owed her money, and she had come to make arrangements to collect it.

Mrs Dankworth was still passing the time of day with Daphne's father. She showed no sign of buying anything until she said, 'What's that nice cheese I can smell?'

'It's Italian,' said Daphne's father, as proud as if he were the sole importer. 'It's got walnuts in it. No, I'm lying. Mustachio nuts.'

'Pistachio nuts,' said Daphne.

'Want a taste, Mrs Dankworth?' Daphne's father went behind the delicatessen counter and took a knife out of the salami tray. He inspected it, shrugged and wiped it on a cloth. He cut Mrs Dankworth a generous sample of the cheese. 'Very nice,' she said. 'Give me a quarter-pound.'

'Did you say something, Daphne?'

I said, wonders will never cease. 'No,' she said. Her father weighed out a piece of the cheese which had already been cut and was wrapped in cling-film. 'Bit over, Mrs D, is that all right?' He glanced at Daphne as if to say, *I got that right, didn't I?*

'I'll just take the four ounces, thank you, Mr Barclay,' said Mrs Dankworth in a tone at once hurt and firm.

He cut a piece which, as was perfectly obvious to Daphne even before he weighed it, was only three ounces. Mrs Dankworth was satisfied. Daphne's father scurried back to the checkout and took Mrs Dankworth's money. Mrs Dankworth left. Daphne turned on her father. 'What about her magazine? That's what she came in for. You should have reminded her. There's no point in a shop of this size having a delicatessen counter. The shelf life of that type of product is too short, the hygiene requirements too costly in terms of staff time, and –'

'Daphne –'

'What?'

'I know it's a lot to ask, but would it be possible for you just to come and see us once in a while? You know, for a visit? As if you were our daughter? And not tell us what to do?'

'I'm not telling you what to do. But you might as well take advantage of me while I'm here.' Daphne sighed. 'Where's Mum?'

'She's gone to Tesco's.'

'You'll have to get rid of it,' said Daphne, meaning the delicatessen counter. Without even looking at the accounts (a thing she would do later when she had built up her strength) she knew that it was losing money hand over fist. The whole business was going off more quickly than the cheese. 'I've told you before to check with me if someone tries to –'

'We never see you,' her father retorted.

'I've been busy.'

'We had to do our own VAT return.'

'Oh God.'

'You didn't come and you didn't come and they seemed quite keen that we should send them something, so one evening we thought, well, it can't be that difficult. Let's have a go.'

'Have you kept a copy?'

'There might be one there somewhere . . . but don't *fuss*, Daphne. I'm sure they'll tell us if they find any mistakes.'

Daphne shuddered.

42

Her mother came back from Tesco's with bulging bags. In honour of Daphne's visit, Mr and Mrs Barclay wanted to shut the shop and have a proper lunch hour, but Daphne insisted that it be kept open. 'Shops should be open when people want to buy things.' She did not mind placing herself at the table so as to ensure that if anyone came into the shop she could get up and serve them. 'No one comes in at lunch time anyway,' her mother confided.

'Why not? I said why not?'

'Because they're having lunch, of course, silly,' said her father.

'Do you normally close for lunch? You do, don't you? Well, I suppose I must be grateful this isn't a restaurant. You'd probably close that for lunch too, and don't think I haven't seen it done because I have.'

'We don't always,' said her mother. 'Not if there's a rush.'

Which is not often, thought Daphne grimly, eating her lunch undisturbed by customers but deeply disturbed by her own thoughts. With interest, her parents owed her nearly two thousand pounds. The loan had been towards the cost of converting the shop to self-service. She had felt it only fair to contribute, partly because she would, in the fullness of time, inherit the shop whose value was to be enhanced by the conversion, and partly to encourage them to go ahead. 'Would I risk my own money if I didn't think it worthwhile?' she had said, and her parents had agreed that she probably would not. 'I'll want it back, mind,' she had said. She had definitely said that she would want the money back, there had been no room for misunderstanding on that score, she had even given the reason: 'I'll want to set up my own business one day.' But over the years the quarterly VAT returns had told their own sad, exasperating story, and in her misguidedly kind-hearted way she had allowed the matter to drop and the interest to accumulate.

Her parents settled in to lunch time conversation so familiar from her childhood that she might never have been away. Her mother rehearsed a census of who had moved to the area recently and who had left. Her father made jokes. Boredom settled round Daphne's heart like a boa constrictor, throttling even her little flurries of anger. It had always been like this, always, always. Her parents had married late and had had her in their middle age. 'To prove we could,' her father used to say. He used to say it in front of people: 'We had Daphne to prove we could.' As a child, Daphne had sometimes wondered why they had bothered, why they had not left the begetting of her to a younger, more dynamic couple. It had never occurred to her that, in those circumstances, she might be a different person. Her own birth, as herself, had seemed inevitable. She had a fantasy of the parents to whom she might have been born. Preparing for her three-monthly visits, the fantasy sometimes became a wish whose fulfilment was well within the bounds of possibility. This time they would have got it together. This time they would have smartened up, shaped up. This time the shop would be the thriving little enterprise of her dreams, profitable and restless to expand.

The clock ticked, her mother continued with her digest of local events, her father chewed food and read the paper. Daphne might just as well not be here. She might just as well be another daughter, the non-existent Clare, for example. 'Aren't you a vet or something?' that woman in the shop, Mrs Dankworth, had asked. Daphne kept her parents informed as to what she was doing, but they did not listen. Neither of them had asked how things were going at Daphne Barclay Business Training, or expressed any satisfaction at the extension of the family name into another area of commerce. Grimly, Daphne remembered the last time her parents had expressed satisfaction over something she had achieved. She had come second in the school trading competition to raise money for a wheelchair, and they had behaved as if she had won a Queen's Award for Industry. She had listened to their congratulations in pained silence. She had not told them of the cutting misery in her heart at not having come first. Even if she had wanted to, she would not have been able to find the words without crying, and Daphne had resolved long before that never to let her parents see her cry.

We had Daphne to prove that we could. She guessed that they had got married to prove that they could do that too, falling into each other's arms with cries of relief from the shelves to which the world had rightly consigned them as punishment for being so dull. Their wedding photographs (one stood on the mantelpiece here in the kitchen in a frame of tarnished silver) were a travesty and an embarrassment. Grotesque: plump, plodding figures, so unlike her friends' parents in their wedding pictures. Expecting school friends to tea, Daphne had once tried to hide the wedding photographs, but her father had caught her and drawn special attention to them. 'Happiest day of my life, that was, when Daphne's mother said yes.'

Daphne knew that it was not uncommon for children to be embarrassed by anything that might suggest sexual contact between their parents; but she also knew that it was not this that had caused, or still caused, her unease. Her parents could do, or had done, whatever they liked in that department. She doubted that it was very much. What she resented was their lifelessness. Having had her to prove that they could, and having failed to pick up the skills of raising a gifted and sensitive child at the time when their contemporaries were learning them, they had left Daphne to raise herself. They had fed her and educated her, but that was no more than their obligation and her right. They had failed to inspire her, failed to present life to her as it should have been presented, should be presented to all children: as a rich challenge, to be met head-on.

She had had to work out for herself that this was what it was. She had had to work everything out for herself. Her parents had waited for her to grow up as they might wait for a kettle to boil, having filled it with water and turned it on. Daphne remembered her childhood as a period of waiting: waiting to go out and take on anyone or anything that wanted to take *her* on. Finding herself old enough legally to leave school, Daphne had left, ignoring her parents' pleas that she stay on and go to university. To hell with university. Daphne had wanted to earn her living. And now that she had been earning it for as long as she legally could have been, and knew nobody of her own age whose progress in their chosen activities was further advanced than hers, she still had the feeling that she would have achieved even more if she had had proper encouragement at home, and she resented this.

'Mum! Dad! Wake up!'
  'What's wrong?'
  'It's twenty-five past eight.'
  'It's Sunday,' her father muttered, turning over.
  Daphne decided to go downstairs and open the shop herself. She

realized that there was probably not much point; if they had given up opening on Sundays, there would be no newspapers or fresh milk, but there was a principle at stake here. There was more than that. If her parents were not planning to work today they probably had some 'treat', some outing planned: one of their tedious picnics. And, tedium aside, Daphne would find it difficult in such circumstances to raise the subject of the money she was owed.

She burst bad-temperedly into the shop from the back, only to find the lights on, the shutters open and a steady stream of customers being served with newspapers, tobacco, sweets and miscellaneous groceries by a smart Asian teenager who kept up a continuous patter of polite, soft-voiced chat as he took the customers' money. 'Good morning. Yes, we have. Yes it is, isn't it? Yes, let me find it for you. Good morning, no, it isn't, is it?' On his lapel was a badge that said: 'How May I Help You?' Daphne had brought two such badges on her previous visit. They and she had been mocked.

Daphne swallowed her fury at her parents' deliberate attempt to wind her up – it could not be accidental that they had not mentioned employing an assistant – and pretended to be unsurprised. 'I am Mr and Mrs Barclay's daughter. I thought I'd come and give you a hand, for old times' sake.'

'Good morning, Miss Barclay.'

'Daphne.'

'I am Farrukh.'

'Yes, of course, Farrukh.' Daphne had a great deal of respect for the entrepreneurial skills of Farrukh's race, and he seemed to be getting on quite well, so she went to the kitchen and made coffee.

'Are you enjoying working here?' she asked, hoping to get some idea of how long this had been going on and what it was costing.

'It is the best way to learn,' said Farrukh. 'And it is a change from my studies.'

'Studies, eh? What are you studying?'

'Commerce and business management. I hope to have my own shop one day.'

Yes, thought Daphne. *And I expect you will.*

'Excuse me, please,' said Farrukh, and he went to help a customer. Daphne's father called: 'Do I smell coffee down there?' Daphne sighed and took up a tray. The shop was quiet when she returned, and Farrukh was taking advantage of the lull to clean the delicatessen counter. Helping him, Daphne said, 'Tell me, Farrukh. As one student of commerce to another. Do you think this was a good idea?'

Her gesture took in the German sausages, the ends of cheese. 'Speak freely.'

'Oh yes, Miss Barclay. Daphne. If the corner store is to survive, it must take on the supermarkets on their own terms.'

'Hm.'

'It may appear, from the accounts – '

'Oh, you do the accounts as well, do you?'

'Excuse me for saying this, but I am not sure that your parents have fully grasped the principles of Value Added Tax.'

'You were saying about the delicatessen?'

'I was saying that it may appear, from the accounts, to be undergoing teething troubles. That is quite normal, and as soon as word gets round it will take off. My father has been supplying gourmet foods to small retailers for seventeen years, and if you ask them they will all say the same.'

'These people will rob you blind!' she raged.

'He's a very nice boy,' said her father.

'I expect he can afford to be. What are you paying him?'

'Twenty pounds for the day.'

'*Twenty pounds!*'

'Cash in hand,' her father explained. 'Nudge nudge, wink wink, say no more.'

'Twenty pounds is far too much. But it's all to the good. If you can afford to pay twenty pounds a week to have someone do what you ought to be doing yourselves, you can get rid of him, him and his delicatessen counter, and give *me* twenty pounds a week.' It would cover the Daphne Barclay Business Training telephone bills, she thought. Or the payments for the office computer.

Her parents looked shocked, hurt and guilty as she had known they would. But along with her dread of the unpleasantness that was to follow, she felt satisfaction at having aroused strong emotion in them, a thing not easily done.

Her father said pompously, 'Your allegations are quite unfounded.'

'I made no allegations, but I want my money. I need it.'

'Farrukh is an investment.'

'According to whom? According to Farrukh.'

'The delicatessen brings people into the shop – '

' – when it's open!'

' – and it'll be showing a profit by the end of the financial year and that's when you'll get your money. That's why we got it. I said to you, didn't I, Mother, we mustn't forget the money we owe to Daphne. It's not fair to expect her to support us.'

Daphne's mother sighed. 'I knew she'd be hurt if we got Farrukh to do the VAT.'

'If we'd waited for her to do it,' Daphne's father retorted, 'We'd all be in prison.'

'Let's spend the day painting,' cried Daphne, in the hope of lightening the atmosphere.

'Painting what?'

'The front of the shop. It could do with it.'

'But we only did it . . .'

'When?'

'Quite recently.'

Daphne bundled her parents into her car and drove them to the Do It Yourself Hypermarket on the bypass. She selected paint, paint removers, primers and brushes, and waited while they paid. They complained that they were too old to climb ladders so she did the high bits, calling out cheerful warnings to customers who walked beneath her on their way into and out of the shop. It was fun. 'This is fun, isn't it?' Removing the loose paint and generally making good took longer than she had expected and they did not get beyond applying undercoat before it was time for her to leave. 'I want to see this as good as new next time I come,' she said. 'Or else.'

'I will come every evening this week and do it,' said Farrukh.

'How sweet of you,' Daphne retorted. 'But we mustn't keep you from your studies.'

She had not been in her own flat since Friday morning. After her session teaching supermarket trainees on how to deal with customer complaints, she had driven twenty miles in order to ring up what she considered to be a hopeful prospect, a START Selling client, an old friend, and say, 'I'm just passing through. Any chance of us getting together for a quick drink?. . . . Now I don't want you to think I'm trying to do business with you,' she had laughingly said as they had their drink, 'because *that* would be illegal, apparently.' 'That's all right, Daphne,' he had replied. 'We're quite happy with START, especially now that they've got these new discounts for established clients.' She had spent the night in a gloomy hotel before proceeding to visit her parents. One way and another, she was glad to be home and looked forward to sleeping in her own bed.

Her gladness, as always, was mixed with anxiety. She checked to see that her cleaning lady had been in and burglars had not. If business did not pick up soon, the services of the cleaning lady might have to be dispensed with, which would be a pity for both of them. But for now, everything was as it should be. She picked up her post.

Dear Miss Barclay,

As you know, I take a warm personal interest in the welfare and progress of my former employees, particularly when the circumstances of their departure from the START Selling family have been such as to cause me to ask myself what shortcomings in my performance of my duties have brought this about.

Finding myself unexpectedly in London for a few days, I intend to take the liberty of telephoning you at your home number over the weekend in the hope that I may have the privilege of expressing in person my appreciation of the contribution you made to the work of START Selling International when you were in its employ.

I have neither the right nor the wish to intrude upon your well-earned leisure, and the purpose of our meeting would be primarily social, but I have a proposal to put to you which, I hope you will agree, will be of mutual benefit, concerning as it does the possibility of future co-operation between the company of which you are part-owner, and the international community of professional sales trainers of which I am world president.

Cordially,

J. LINDBERGH STANLEY.

Daphne did not often curse, but she cursed now. What was the time? Nine forty-five. Damn and blast the man, where was he? The letter was handwritten on plain paper. She switched on her answering machine, but it contained only trivial messages, clicks and silences. She picked up the envelope in the hope that it would provide a clue. It was unstamped. It had been delivered by hand.

43

'I forbid it! I mean, I strongly advise against it.'

'Oh Alistair, don't be so prim.' She had simply phoned him to find out where Lindbergh Stanley normally stayed when he came to London. Alistair had given her the name of a block of private apartments in Mayfair, adding, 'Why?' She had told him why, and he had got into a great state: 'You can't go round there on your own at this time of night.'

'What do you think I am?'

'I'm coming with you.'

'Why? Did he write to you as well?'

'I'll meet you at Green Park tube.'

'Alistair, he wants to talk to me.'

'I am your partner,' he said.

'I'm not going to sign anything.'

'I don't suppose he's got anything for you to sign. Daphne, use your brains. He's not some cuddly old grandfather – '

Unlike you, she thought contemptuously. 'How do you know?' she said. 'You've never met him.'

'What could he possibly have to offer you – to offer us – that would be to our advantage? We're in competition with his company and they're sending us threatening letters – '

'Yes,' she said. 'I must have a word with him about that.' She put the phone down. There was no point in trying to explain to Alistair about the certainty with which she knew that START Selling UK's harassment of Daphne Barclay Business Training was being conducted without Lindbergh Stanley's approval or even knowledge. The two companies were in competition, but that was not the point.

Competition did not necessarily imply spite or lack of regard. Daphne herself, for example, felt no spite or lack of regard for her parents' assistant Farrukh or his father the delicatessen supplier. She knew that the two of them were puttting one over on her parents – and so, by implication, on her; but she did not wish harm to them as a result. On the contrary, she respected them. And so it was between her and Lindbergh Stanley. He respected her and wanted her back. He was not going to get her back, but she wanted to hear him try. And she wanted to hear what alternatives he would propose, once he realized he was not going to have things all his own way.

She had a rapid shower and put on clean underclothes. She put on a suit and a blouse with frilly cuffs. Then she decided that this was too obvious. He would know that she was trying to impress him, since nobody dressed like this on a Sunday night, particularly if, as she would explain to him, they had just got back from a relaxing weekend with their parents. She changed into navy blue tailored slacks and a top of lighter blue. She brushed her hair and reapplied light make-up. She drove to Mayfair, making good time through the quiet streets. She parked her car in the underground car park at Park Lane. She brushed her hair again and touched up her lipstick. She walked across the road in the darkness towards the apartment block.

Alistair leaped out of the shadows. 'I'm coming in with you.'

'Alistair, this is quite intolerable. Would you please let go of my arm? Thank you. This is a private matter between me and Mr Stanley. If it turns out to concern you as my partner, you will be the first to know.' Nervous excitement was making her speak more sharply to Alistair than she might have intended. He drooped off into the shadows, muttering. She felt apologetic and lonely. She called after him, but he did not turn round.

The entry-phone bells were not labelled. She tried one, then another. She tried them all. She waited. She heard the sound of a receiver being lifted. She heard a faint rumble, as of a male throat being unhurriedly cleared. The rumble ended on an interrogative note. 'Mr Stanley? This is Daphne Barclay.'

The door buzzed. She pushed it and entered. The door slammed hard behind her. 'Warning to Intruders,' said a sign. 'All Arrivals Are Filmed.' She looked round the lobby for a camera, considered dropping a little curtsey, decided not to. There was nothing to indicate which floor she should go to, but a lift arrived and opened. It was empty. She stepped inside. The doors closed and the lift ascended. It stopped, opened, and a man with a crew cut and no neck offered his hand. 'Miss Barclay?'

'Mr Stanley?'

'I am Mr Stanley's aide, Buck Castle.'

'Buck Castle . . . ?'

'My parents loved your country.'

'Yes, but –'

'Yeah,' he said. 'I know.'

The dim corridor was thickly carpeted and the doors and walls appeared substantial. It was to this, and the fact that it was Sunday evening, a time for globe-trotting businessmen to rest quietly, that she put down the silence, the eerie sense that she and Buck Castle were the only people in the building. He unlocked the door of one of the flats and led her inside, fixing a bolt and three chains behind her. She entered a room that was a cross between a sitting room and an office. At one end was an enormous desk with a computer terminal and a bank of phones. A map of the world gleamed from the wall, with little lights showing the many locations of START Selling branches and subsidiaries. Behind it, through a panoramic window, twinkled London. Daphne had not realized that the building was so tall.

'Lindy was sorry to miss you,' said Buck Castle, when he had poured her a cup of coffee from a Cona jug. He himself drank what she thought she had heard him call wholefood mineral cola but she might have got that wrong. 'I was visiting my parents,' she said. She was not nervous, exactly; but it seemed important that Buck Castle should know that she was not alone in the world: that there were people who might worry about her.

'Very sorry indeed. Lindy's not used to calling on people and finding them not at home. He's a very busy man.'

'And I,' said Daphne with some spirit, 'am a very busy woman.' She was beginning to realize that she was not going to meet Lindbergh Stanley this evening, and was in no mood to be patronized by the disappointing Mr Castle. 'Had I known that Mr Stanley was coming to London, I would of course have made space in my diary.'

'You have allowed an important opportunity to slip through your fingers, Miss Barclay. You could be on your way to the sunshine. He had a seat booked for you on the plane.'

'I beg your pardon?'

Buck Castle finished his drink and lumbered over to the map of the world. 'Do you notice anything about the continent of Africa, Miss Barclay?'

'It hasn't got any of those little lights on it.'

'And what does that say to you?'

'That START Selling International has no branches there?'

'At this time,' Buck Castle said, 'START Selling Africa is still a dream. Wouldn't you like to be involved in making that dream come true? For Lindy?'

'Let me see if I've got this right,' said Daphne. 'Mr Stanley had it in mind to spirit me away to Africa this evening, to . . . to do what, exactly? To meet Dr Livingstone? Or to set up a branch of START Selling first thing tomorrow morning?'

It was wasted. 'Lindy is not often wrong,' Buck Castle said, 'in his assessment of a man or woman's potential.'

'He has never set eyes on me!' She hoped for Buck Castle's confirmation that this was true, but he said nothing. Earlier this evening she had been flattered to think that Lindbergh Stanley had come personally to her home to deliver his note. Now she wondered if he had been there on other occasions, and did not feel flattered at all. 'Is Mr Stanley aware that I have my own business? That, unlike him, I am not free to fly round the world at a minute's notice whenever I feel like it?'

'It is as owner of your business that you would be going to Africa, Miss Barclay.'

'I don't understand.'

'Your business would retain its name and identity. You would be required to include on your official company documentation the words "A member of the worldwide community of professional sales trainers, START Selling International." You would be fully independent, but you would benefit from the back-up of – '

'And you would have me out of the way!'

'Miss Barclay?'

'Excuse me, Mr Castle. I have taken up quite enough of your time. Please tell Mr Stanley that I have at present no plans for leaving the United Kingdom, but I appreciate his kindness in thinking of me. If Mr Stanley cares to inform me of when he next plans to visit our shores, I shall be delighted to express my appreciation in person. Over lunch.'

'Lindy's not accustomed to receiving messages of that kind, Miss Barclay.'

'Then it will be a new experience for him.'

44

The following morning, Alistair was surly. Daphne tried to jolly him out of it. 'You were quite right,' she said. 'I was lucky to get away with my life.'

Alistair picked up the phone and dialled. 'Good morning,' he said. 'Can you give me the correct spelling of the name of the sales manager in your specialist supplies division?'

This was one of Daphne's ideas. First he had gone through three-month-old Situations Vacant columns to find out who, three months ago, had been looking for a new sales manager. Three months was a reasonable estimate of how long it would have taken to find the man, appoint him and get him started. Now Alistair was phoning to find the new sales manager's name. 'That's Smith with an "i", is it? Not a "y"? Thank you so much, we'll be writing to him. Goodbye.'

'Getting out of there,' said Daphne, 'was like getting out of Fort Knox.'

'Into.'

'Sorry?'

'The expression is, getting into Fort Knox.'

'Well, I expect it's quite difficult to get out of as well.'

'Good morning, can you give me the correct spelling of the name of the sales manager of your accessories department?'

Daphne muttered, 'Jones, with an "x".'

'Thank you. I'll be writing to him.'

'We don't want to go to Africa, do we?'

'We?' said Alistair, not looking up.

'It would be the company that would be transferring. Buck Castle – did I tell you what his name was? – '

264

'Yes.'

' – he left me in no doubt about that.'

'The continent of Africa stands in need of a great many things, Daphne, but I don't think it needs anything that Lindbergh Stanley has to offer.'

What had happened to this man? Would it happen to her when she grew old? She hoped not. She hoped it was just a phase Alistair was going through, otherwise she might start to have serious doubts about having him as her partner. For now she needed him as her partner. She needed his money but she did not need his moralizing. 'They're not all starving in Africa, you know. I once met an African man who was very wealthy. His name was Arthur and he came from Gambia.' Daphne smiled reminiscently. Nothing had in fact taken place between her and Arthur, but she was trying to tease Alistair out of his coldness, in order then to establish some serious points of principle. 'Let me see if I've got this right, Alistair. You don't like the idea of teaching business skills to Africans because they're poor – '

'That wasn't – '

'But you want us to teach them to poor people in Britain free of charge.'

'I never said free of charge. Well, it should be, of course, but I'm not impractical.'

'Oh good.'

'I want us to have a sliding scale of charges, and that means that, as you say so rightly and so often, we have to do some profitable business first, so if I can just get on with this? '

'What about these friends of Teresa Beal who are going to get money from – who was it? The European – ?'

'She doesn't know who's giving away the money, but it's a second-hand clothes shop that wants to go up-market a bit so that their real customers won't feel stigmatized by using them.'

'Fascinating.'

'And Teresa doesn't think that even if they get the money there's a cat in hell's chance that they'll want to spend it on anything we have to offer.'

'More fool them,' she said. She took from Alistair's desk the list he was compiling of newly appointed sales managers. He protested, but she said, 'Don't be silly, Alistair, the switchboard would recognize your voice. We're partners. Ah, good morning. May I speak to Mr Smith in your accessories division? Good morning, Mr Smith! This is Daphne Barclay from Daphne Barclay Business Training, and I'm phoning first of all to congratulate you personally on your new appointment. I'm sure you have a hundred and one other things to think about, and I won't take up more than a few moments of your time, but may I enquire as to the size of your sales force and what arrangements your company currently makes for their training . . . ?'

'Daphne, we agreed that I would do this,' Alistair grumbled, when she had put the phone down after ascertaining that Mr Smith would be training newcomers to his sales force himself, in so far as this was necessary, salesmen being born, not trained. 'You're supposed to be finding us a venue.'

Daphne sighed. He was right. There was a limit to the amount of business that could be done by training small numbers of staff on their company premises. Daphne Barclay Business Training needed a place like the Donian Hotel, a Mecca to which people would gladly send their staff from all over the country. Such places were easy to find, more difficult to pay for. The unit costs for a small or short-term booking were enormous; but so were the risks of a larger commitment. The discounts did not start to sound interesting until she was talking in the region of about two thousand delegate days per year – ten courses of four days with fifty delegates at each – and when she was talking along these lines, she did not know which terrified her more: the thought of the outlay involved, or the thought that, for all her high hopes and hard work (and Alistair's) Daphne Barclay Business Training might not be able to find the delegates it needed.

At midday, Alistair went for some sandwiches, with which he continued work. He did not follow his usual practice of asking her if she wanted any sandwiches and giving her a little lecture on the importance of eating, so she realized that she was still in the doghouse. This did not matter for herself, but it was a rather silly way of working with a partner. When he again started to get ready to go out, she said cheerfully: 'And where are you off to?' He did not answer, just nodded coldly at the office diary in which, it had been agreed, each of them was to record their movements.

'Are we only to communicate in writing, then?' she said.

'It was your idea.'

She went ostentatiously to the diary. She talked to herself out loud. 'Where is my partner going this afternoon? Ah. I see. He is going to the Maple Road Unemployed Workers Centre. I wonder why he's going there. I wish I could ask him why he's going there – '

'You know perfectly well – '

'I think it's a very good idea that we should make some kind of approach to Teresa Beal's friends in the second-hand clothes business.'

'Well, that's one you're going to have to do yourself,' he said with an ironic little laugh.

'I intend to,' she said. 'Where are they?'

They had agreed that, as far as possible, the office should never be left unstaffed during normal working hours. This was proving alarmingly easy to arrange, even following the departure of the late lamented Samantha, the full-time secretary whom Daphne Barclay Business Training had started off by employing and then found that it could not afford to pay. Daphne had three bookings for later in the week, but for now nobody needed her. *They do need me*, she thought. *They just don't know it yet. I want something big to happen. This wasn't what I had in mind, counting pennies, begging for customers. How can I get the world to notice me? Lindbergh Stanley sees my worth and plots and schemes to get me back, to get me out of the way . . . For everyone else, I am here, waiting for their call, so why don't they call?*

She put these negative thoughts from her mind. One of her favourite 'How not to do it' sketches was of a salesman sitting by a telephone wondering why nobody rings him up.

You are losing your nerve, Daphne, she thought. *Shame on you.* She telephoned the hotel and confirmed a booking for two thousand delegate-days over the next twelve months. Then she set about filling them, with a degree of success which she could only describe as moderate.

She was not unduly worried about having to postpone her visit to Collindeane Tower until after five o'clock. It did not sound to her like the kind of place that kept normal office hours.

She wondered whether she should go home first and change her clothes. Her image of feminists was predominantly one of scruffiness, but she decided against anything that would be seen as dressing down or slumming. She wished, when she got there, that she had changed her shoes at least. The courtyard outside the tower was cracked and uneven, awash with litter and rubble. When she left her car, she did so with anxiety. This was not a nice area, and Collindeane Tower was not a nice place. Were it not for the lights she could see gleaming through holes in the walls, it would be difficult to believe that the tower was inhabited by humans. It looked, on the contrary, as if it had been overrun by triffids, with foliage spilling from window boxes all the way up; and there appeared to be some kind of roof garden. Looking at the roof made her dizzy. It was probably an optical illusion that the tower appeared to be moving, swaying against the darkening clouds; but the tilt in its structure was not so easily dismissed.

For the second time that day, Daphne came close to losing her nerve. But she saw the sign – 'ALL WOMEN WELCOME' – so she went inside.

A woman said, 'Hello, have you come for lunch?' At least, that was what Daphne thought she had said, and she looked at her watch in bewilderment and was about to turn tail as from a madhouse when she realized that the woman had in fact said, 'Have you come for the launch?' Daphne had never heard of 'launching' second-hand clothes, but clearly other things were going on. 'Yes. Yes, I have.'

'It's on the fourth floor.'

She climbed the broken stairs, glancing nervously at the flats she passed. Some had their front doors open and looked lived-in, poor but cosy. She heard music and conversation. A mother pursued a child who did not want to be put to bed. Other flats were locked, or contained offices. 'PEACE CAMPS ACTION.' 'ACTION AGAINST RACISM.' There was not much sign of any action until she reached the fourth floor. 'JOANNA PRESS'. A party was going on. Which was to say, various women stood about with glasses of wine or fruit juice, and there was a table covered with sandwiches, salads, nuts and quiches. 'Hello,' said a woman. 'Are you a journalist? Would you like a drink?'

'Thank you,' said Daphne, accepting wine.

'Where are you from?'

Daphne did not want to say anything which would later be revealed as untrue. But she wanted to orientate herself to place and people before deciding on her approach. 'I was just passing,' she said, 'and I saw the sign.'

'Great,' said the woman. 'That's what it's there for. Make yourself at home.'

Drifting about, smiling, listening, and reading notices on the wall, she gathered that the Joanna Press was a part-time, voluntary and highly political enterprise. *Women Speak From the Peace Camps* was its first pamphlet for two years. It had been held back for financial reasons, and even now the printing bill had not been paid. Donations were sought. 'Help yourself to food,' Daphne was told. 'It's all on the house.'

The pamphlet itself was not in evidence, and Daphne gathered that a certain amount of singing for one's supper would be called for . . . or rather, listening. No one sang, but the women who had written the pamphlet read aloud their contributions to it, and questions and discussion followed. A few chairs and cushions were available, but for the most part people sat on the floor or stood at the back. Daphne joined the ones who were standing at the back and gave the speakers her full attention. One of them seemed very concerned about the precise location of American cruise missiles in Britain. 'The missiles we've all seen at Greenham are dummies, decoys,' she said. 'It's to fool us and fool the Russians. The Greenham campers are wasting their time.'

This brought protest. 'I've done time in Holloway for Greenham actions,' said one woman. Daphne looked at her curiously. She appeared quite normal . . . as normal as anyone here.

The speaker was sticking to her guns. 'The real missiles are at Peaston Hill. We know that. That's where the womanpower's needed. Anyone who puts energy into Greenham is playing into the government's hands.'

'Thanks a lot,' said the woman who had done time in Holloway.

'Yeah, thanks,' said someone else. 'I wish I'd known when that policeman put his boot in my face.'

It was all getting a bit out of hand. Everyone was talking at once. Daphne fought off an impulse to call the meeting to order. That was someone else's job. Whose, though? At last a woman whom Daphne took to be a member of the Joanna Press's staff (she was standing guard over a pile of sealed boxes marked with the name of the pamphlet) said: 'Do we have to be so competitive about this? Sort of more-nuclear-than-thou? Even if the Greenham missiles are just models, there's been a lot of good done there, drawing public attention – '

'But we want to draw public attention to Peaston Hill.'

'Peaston Hill's a playground,' said someone. 'It hasn't been in proper military use since the Second World War. It's just for air shows and stuff like that.'

'Yeah, that's what they want you to think.'

The discussion became more and more acrimonious. People started to leave. Daphne walked forward. She smiled at the woman with the boxes of pamphlets. 'May I?' she said, ripping open the first box with her fingernails. She took an armful of the pamphlets. She positioned herself by the door – not blocking anyone's way, but requiring them to walk round her. 'It's an interesting discussion, isn't it?' she said. 'Would you like to take one of these and think about it some more?'

'How much are they?'

'How much are they?' Daphne called to the Joanna Press woman, there being no price on the covers of the pamphlets.

'£2.50.'

'Just £2.50,' said Daphne. 'Thank you so much. Thank you so much for coming,' she said to another woman who was trying to leave. 'I hope you enjoyed the party, would you like to take one of these with you?'

Everything was happening at once. The Joanna Press women were seeking to re-establish order and encourage people to stay by filling up their glasses. Various schools of thought on various issues were putting their points across. Daphne was selling pamphlets. For convenience she put the money in her pocket, but, realizing that this might be open to misunderstanding, she emptied one of the boxes and put the money in there instead. The unsold pamphlets she arranged in an attractive display on the end of the food table, propping them up against piles of napkins and clean glasses. 'Hello,' she said. 'Would you like one of these?' 'Goodbye,' she said. 'Would you like one of these?' She opened another box.

Gradually the room emptied, save for about half a dozen women who stood staring at her, her empty boxes and her pile of money, seemingly at a loss for words.

She was at a loss herself. The time had come for introductions, but how?

She smiled, gave a little wave and walked out.

Alone on the stairs, her heart failed her. Had she timed that wrongly, judged it wrongly?

She was halfway down the second flight by the time they called her back.

'Who are you?' they said.

'Let me give you my card,' she replied, returning.

45

Ann had had a teacher called Mrs Mars. She taught history and arithmetic, subjects at which Ann had been average, as she had been average at most things. Ann had been the sort of child whom teachers were happy to ignore, upon whose reports they wrote 'Good' and 'Fair progress'. Mrs Mars had written that kind of thing on Ann's reports and never, to her recollection, spoken sharply to her on any matter. Yet Ann had always, as a schoolgirl, felt uneasy with her.

There had been other teachers – irascible, scornful, demanding – whom she had had good reason to dislike, but she had feared Mrs Mars more. She had not known why this was until she met Miss Hutton, the accountant, and became her client. On the surface, the comparison was an unlikely one. Physically the two women were dissimilar. Mrs Mars had been a square woman of military bearing; Miss Hutton had obviously had a lovely figure in her day, and even now, in her sixties, was elegant and well proportioned. Mrs Mars's hair had looked as if she cut it herself. It had bound her head like an iron bar, adding further meaning to the inevitable nickname. Miss Hutton had the kind of hair that might never have been cut at all: she wore it in a thick, grey coil, which looked as if it would reach her waist were she ever to undo it.

The similarity lay in the command the two women had of themselves, and of what they said. Neither of them ever wasted a word. Just as Mrs Mars used to begin lessons, even after a holiday, exactly where she had left off, and would synchronize her final remarks with the end-of-lesson bell, so Miss Hutton would coolly cut Ann off at the first sign of what Ann thought of as good manners but Miss Hutton evidently saw as a waste of time. 'Good morning, Miss

Hutton, this is Ann Mitchison, how are you keeping?' Ann used to say before she knew better, and still said sometimes when she forgot herself. 'Very well, thank you,' Miss Hutton would reply, waiting.

Miss Hutton could outwait anybody. Ann wondered whether, when she was negotiating on behalf of her clients with the Inland Revenue or the VAT people, she intimidated the tax inspectors with her waiting. Ann consoled herself with the thought that, should she herself ever get into trouble with her tax affairs (and the chance would be a fine thing) it would be nice to have such a person on her side. If ever Ann was in conversation with someone who seemed to have difficulty expressing themselves, it would come naturally to her to help out, to say 'Hm?' or 'Go on' or 'Do you mean . . . ?' Not so Miss Hutton. Miss Hutton just waited. On one of her rare visits to Miss Hutton's office – a room in her home, the first door on the right after the front door, carefully chosen, Ann guessed, so that clients would have no reason to see the rest of the house, and she was always careful to go to the lavatory before visiting Miss Hutton, rather than run the risk of having to ask – Miss Hutton had asked for a figure for her monthly turnover. Ann had brought out her accounts book and searched for it. She had held the book in such a way that Miss Hutton could take it from her and find the answer to her question at a glance . . . but Miss Hutton had just waited, while Ann's carefully written numbers danced meaninglessly before her eyes.

There was nothing to feel aggrieved about. This was not a social relationship. Miss Hutton was retired. She helped small businesses at first on an unpaid basis and then on a sliding scale of charges. Ann just wished that she would not make it so obvious that, if time were money, Ann had very little claim on her time. She supposed it showed how professional Miss Hutton was, and she ought to be glad of it. But it made Ann feel despised. It made her feel that Miss Hutton saw her as the kind of person who, given an inch, would take a yard; who, politely asked 'How are *you*?', would not content herself with 'Very well, thank you,' but would go into details.

'Good morning, Miss Hutton, this is Ann Mitchison.'

Miss Hutton waited.

'I've got a little . . . there's something I'd like to discuss with you.' *I didn't need to say that*, Ann thought. *If I didn't have something to discuss with her, I wouldn't have rung her up.* She had practised this call, trying to keep the anxiety out of her voice. Now, hearing it loud and clear, she knew it was vain to hope that if Miss Hutton heard it she would soften. She would, on the contrary, harden; fearing, perhaps, that Ann might be on the verge of tears.

'You remember I told you about Rideemus?'

'Yes.'

'The voluntary group that agreed to help us out – ?'

'Yes.'

What did all these yesses mean? That Miss Hutton was taking in what Ann was telling her, or that Miss Hutton remembered who Rideemus were and was impatient at being told again?

'They've sent me a bill.'

'You said they were working free of charge.'

She did remember. In the rush of orders that had followed the *New Atalanta* feature, Tom had mentioned a group he knew that did things to help the unemployed and needy. Ann had been sceptical. It could hardly mean putting labour into businesses set up for commercial reasons. It did not even seem right to ask for it. But Tom had insisted. They were needy, weren't they? Mitchison's Working Models was all that stood between him and unemployment, wasn't it? The Rideemus people were looking for things to do, ways to help. They had confirmed this. They would enjoy making models and it would be useful for them to learn another skill, with which they could help others. There would be no charge, though they expected to be kept going in tea and coffee.

'There's obviously been a misunderstanding,' said Miss Hutton. 'Write politely and tell them that you're not going to pay.'

Write neatly, boys and girls – Ann could have worked it out for herself that she should refuse to pay. She could not pay £1,100 even if she wanted to. She realized that she had phoned Miss Hutton in the hope that Miss Hutton would offer to write the letter herself, giving it more authority.

'Did you sign a contract with this organization, Mrs Mitchison?'

'No . . . they said it was exciting to be involved in something that was just taking off and we should remember them when we made our first million, but . . .'

Miss Hutton waited for her to get to the end of her sentence.

' . . . they said they go round the country helping unemployed people.' What they had in fact said was, 'The Lord has been listening to you,' but she could not repeat that to Miss Hutton.

'It sounds to me as if you have nothing to worry about. It is a genuine misunderstanding. Do as I say and let me know if they contact you again. Goodbye.'

The phone clicked before Ann could say 'Goodbye' in return. But this was one of the longest, most informal telephone conversations they had ever had. Ann remembered going back to school once for a Christmas Fair. She had found Mrs Mars transformed: friendly, chatty and funny. Ann wondered what she had to do to bring about such a transformation in Miss Hutton. Become successful, so that Miss Hutton would value her as a client? But Miss Hutton was not looking for valuable clients. She was retired, and did her work out of the goodness of her heart.

With the Rideemus people gone and the Enterprise Allowance run out, financial and production problems had returned. The priority was to give Tom an income, to keep him off the dole. She did not tell him how little of his tiny wage came from profit on his work and how much from the wooden toys that she bought by the gross from an importer in Hartlepool, how much from Ann Mitchison Craft Distribution. Ann Mitchison Craft Distribution was what she called herself when she represented other craftsmen and women, toiling around by bus, on foot, or in the car when Pat was free to come with her, keeping shops supplied with soft toys, polished stone jewellery, blown glass ornaments, fudge, made by people who were more interested in making things than in what had been described as 'the social side' of selling them.

Her enquiries to craft fair organizers had revealed that most of them did not take kindly to professional agents. The purpose of the fairs was to provide a place for individual craftspeople to demonstrate their skills and sell their wares without incurring the overheads of a shop . . . their wares, and the wares of their families. Ann would have to pretend that she had a very versatile family when she started going to the fairs. Her conscience would be clear. Her craft was selling. She had a right to claim a space for it.

The craft fairs she was particularly interested in were the ones held at air force and army bases. American servicemen and their families were often found there in large numbers, and they had plenty of money to spend on souvenirs. But that was for the future: the unknowable future beyond the thick high wall of her driving test. She had not told her present clients that the reason she could only distribute locally was that she had yet to pass her driving test. It might appear unprofessional.

She walked into a sweet shop with a holdall full of fudge, wrapped, at her suggestion, in half-pound bags made of cellophane and tied with pink ribbon. She undid one of the ribbons and offered the bag to the man behind the counter. 'I'm Ann Mitchison from Ann Mitchison Craft Distribution. Would you like to try one of these?'

'What's that, toffees? Not with my teeth.' He displayed them. 'You'll have to ask the wife.'

The wife said, 'No reps on Thursdays.'

'I'll make a note of that for the future. But now that I'm here, would you like to take a dozen packs and see how they go?'

The woman examined the label. ' "Home-made fudge from Granny Skean's Country Kitchen." That's never Vera Skean from number 49?'

'That's her.'

'I didn't know she made sweets to sell.'

The husband said, 'Got a rep, and all.'

'Is Terry Skean off work again?'

'Country kitchen, eh? I hope it's in a better state than her garden.'

Ann went away without success. She wished everyone else were as professional as she was.

She returned the bill to Rideemus with a letter saying that she would not pay. She resolved to put the matter from her mind. Another copy of the bill arrived. There was nothing to indicate that her letter had been received. She hoped that this meant it had not been. She preferred to think that she had been sent a reminder as part of a normal procedure for dealing with unpaid bills, rather than that her protest was being ignored.

She considered telephoning Miss Hutton but decided instead to send her the second bill with a covering letter reminding her that she had said she should be informed if Rideemus got in touch again. This way, the ball would be in Miss Hutton's court. She would have ways of dealing with the matter, and she might decide that it was as easy to deal with it herself as go through the business of telling Ann what she should do.

If I don't hear anything further, I'll take it that everything's all right, she thought, turning her attention to her Highway Code.

' . . . on a bend, on the brow of a hill, approaching a roundabout or junction, approaching a pedestrian crossing,' she said.

'One more,' said Tom.

'What?'

'One more.'

'Oh Tom – '

' "Where it is unsafe to do so," ' he said.

'That's obvious. It doesn't need saying.'

'Suit yourself.'

'How am I doing?'

'Improving. Got the date for your test yet?'

'No,' she lied. They shared most things but there was no way she was going to share this.

One thing he was not sharing with her was the true state of his feelings over Michelle, or Shelly, as Ann had come to call her during the brief period when it had looked as if Ann might become her mother-in-law. Since their break-up, he had been moody and withdrawn and had shown no sign of wanting to go out and find himself another girlfriend. This surprised her almost as much as she had been surprised by the engagement itself. She had known that Tom was fond of Shelly, but she had not realized that she was special enough for him to want to marry her. And she had not been, of course. His proposal to Shelly had been an attempt to make a convenience of her, no more and no less. Ann had not known whether to laugh or cry.

'You can't say that to a lass!'

'Why not? I was honest.'

'Does Shelly see it like that?'

'Look Mam, if I say one thing and she hears another, that's not my fault, is it?'

They had not got the job at the museum. There had never been the slightest chance of it, in Ann's view. They were much too young for the responsibility, whatever their other qualities. The museum's manager had said as much. He had written Tom a very nice letter saying that he must be sure and apply for such other, more suitable vacancies as might arise, and adding that if, in a few years' time, a vacancy arose for a couple, Tom and his future wife would be given favourable consideration. He sent his best wishes for their married life in the meantime.

There had followed a period during which Tom and Shelly had remained engaged – had not, at least, announced that they were not engaged – and Ann had resigned herself to having Shelly move into the flat after the wedding. But tensions had arisen; Shelly's visits and Tom's references to her had become less and less frequent; and now Ann took it that the grudging and conditional nature of Tom's proposal had finally made itself clear to Shelly and offended her beyond bearing. The relationship was at an end, and this was certainly not Tom's doing, if his obvious misery was anything to go by.

When the phone rang, he raced for it.

'It's for you, Mam.' He did not even do his usual *It's for you-hoo!* joke.

'Who is it?'

'Our accountant.'

'I'm sorry to trouble you in the evening, Mrs Mitchison, but I've been thinking,' said Miss Hutton.

'That's all right,' said Ann in wonderment.

'It's about this invoice. May I speak frankly?'

'Of course. . . .'

'My status is an odd one, particularly when I am working with people whose business experience is not – forgive me – wide. I am their servant. I am on their side. They pay me to be on their side.' Ann wondered in alarm whether she owed Miss Hutton money, but Miss Hutton continued as if she wanted to get something off her chest. 'And yet they perceive me as an authority figure. A person from whom things must be concealed, lest I should tell them they have done wrong, think less of them, or report them to the authorities. Lest I *be* one of the authorities.'

'Oh no, Miss Hutton, I never – '

'If you have signed something in the nature of an agreement with this organization, all may not be lost. But it is important that I know about it at once.'

'No I haven't. Just one moment please, Miss Hutton. Tom. Did you sign anything with Rideemus?'

'No, Mam. I told you.'

'Sorry about that, Miss Hutton. I was checking with my son. We've not signed anything.'

'What about verbal agreements?'

'Well . . . there was a joke about when we get our first million, but . . .'

Miss Hutton did not wait. She interrupted. 'I'm not talking about that. But verbal agreements are binding, you know. Is there anyone else who might have given some kind of undertaking? Someone whom they might have thought was authorized to . . .' *Shelly?* thought Ann. Shelly being stupid? Shelly being spiteful? Getting back at Tom? ' . . . please search your records and your memory, Mrs Mitchison, and telephone me as soon as possible. Before I write officially to these people, I must be sure that the money is not, in fact, payable. Goodbye.'

Ann talked to Tom. He was hot in his defence of Shelly. She would not do such a thing. She was neither stupid nor spiteful and he was surprised that his mother should think it of her. But Ann persisted. 'One or other of us has got to talk to her. It's not fair to Miss Hutton – '

'Bugger Miss Hutton.'

'Be quiet. I'll go and see Shelly tomorrow.'

'I'll go,' he said. Despite her anxiety, she recognized that he would be glad of the excuse, and was touched.

But it was all very well for him, she thought later. While he was using this business as a way of making things up with Shelly, Ann had earned at least her accountant's suspicion, and at worst – if it turned out that Shelly had in fact promised that Rideemus would be paid – Miss Hutton's contempt for wasting her time with family problems. Miss Hutton might even be thinking that Ann had deliberately lied to her. Anyone who, trusting their accountant as Ann trusted Miss Hutton, lied to them, was a fool, so Miss Hutton must either think herself untrusted or Ann a fool: like someone going to the doctor with a lump, talking to the doctor about something else, and coming away kidding themselves that the doctor had told them there was nothing to worry about. Doctors were right to think their patients foolish in such circumstances; but Ann wanted Miss Hutton to respect her.

46

He was glad to have an excuse to go and see Shelly. He saved it, like a windfall of money that he had not yet decided how to spend. He savoured it. *Today I'll go*, he thought. And then, when he did not, he thought, *Tomorrow*.

He did not want to waste it. If Shelly were serious about never wanting to see him again, this might be his last chance. He would never have believed how much he would miss her. He would never have believed how guilty he would be made to feel, just because he had been honest. It did not pay to be honest. He would have done better to have given her the romantic, no-holds-barred proposal that she had wanted, and then, when he did not get the job, changed his mind. He would have done better. He could not have done worse. At least he would have felt in control of the situation if he had been the one to change his mind. He would have kept open his option to change it again. But Shelly had changed *her* mind.

'If you think I'm going to drag you to the altar just to make you keep your word, you can think on.'

'But Shelly, I've no place to take a wife.'

'If you wanted to, we'd find a way.'

Miss Hutton in the meantime had been busy finding out about Rideemus. His mother was in a state about it, though whether because of what Miss Hutton thought she had found or because of what she would charge for doing so, Tom was not sure.

'She's got a friend who's a bishop.'

'Oh aye – '

'She used to do his books.'

'Blessed are the accountants. For they shall rake it in.'

'I think she's quite worried,' said his mother. 'She never usually goes to this trouble.' She sounded almost proud, as if, along with her anxiety, she was flattered by all this attention from accountants and bishops. The bishop had arranged for Tom and his mother to be sent a leaflet from something called 'CULT CAUTION'.

HAS A MEMBER OF YOUR FAMILY FALLEN VICTIM TO THE MIND-BEND CULTS? WATCH OUT FOR THE TELLTALE SIGNS.

1. A formerly home-loving youngster or spouse, perhaps at a moment of personal crisis, goes away for some course or seminar. The exact nature of the event is ill-defined, but he returns claiming to have found the answer to all his problems.

2. Peculiar clothing. Some cults require their disciples to wear a particular colour. Others insist on special jewellery, badges, or, in the case of women, veils. . . .

He said, 'At Rideemus, it's the fellers who have to wear veils. We'd not be safe on the streets otherwise.' His mother ignored him.

3. A staring expression in the eyes, brought about by lack of sleep and prolonged indoctrination.

4. Obsessive and seemingly tireless working for some ill-defined good cause.

5. Shortage of cash. Cults make heavy financial demands on their members.

6. Slavish obsession with some mysterious guru, a charismatic individual who . . .

Judith? he thought.

. . . who is rarely seen (he is elsewhere, lining his pockets) but whose words are frequently quoted. These are rarely more than platitudes, but to the cult member –

'Sounds like you and our accountant.'
'There's no talking to you.'
'Well, be your age, Mam. They're not after our minds, they're after our money.'
'Have you talked to Shelly?'
He decided to talk to Rideemus first. That might give him something to go on. When he went to Shelly, he preferred not to go with questions that might sound like accusations. He preferred to sort this out himself, without involving Shelly, or accountants, or bishops.

'It's not a bill,' said Judith. The people on the Rideemus barge seemed busy today, but Judith was her usual friendly self. 'It's an invitation to contribute.'

'I-n-v-o-i-c-e. That spells "invitation to contribute", does it? I'll remember that next time we get one from the gas board. My mam's in a right state.'

'Why?'

'Because we can't pay this.'

'Don't, then. There's no problem. The people we worked for before you contributed, and their contribution covered our costs to move on and help you. We thought you might like the opportunity to keep the chain of good will going, but if you can't, you can't. Tell your mother she has no cause to feel guilty.'

'She's not feeling guilty,' he said, though he suspected that she was, and he certainly was, now. 'You didn't say anything about paying or contributing. She's written to you about it and you sent another bill.'

'Oh, that's just Rideemus House. They couldn't organize a . . . well, you know.'

'Can I have that in writing?'

'What?'

'That we don't have to pay?'

Judith looked hurt. 'Are you *serious*?'

'Just to keep things straight.'

She rolled her eyes and shrugged. She fetched a sheet of paper headed 'The Rideemus Institute for the Study of Psychotheolistics' and fed it into a typewriter which she had had to haul down from a shelf in a cupboard. A man said, 'I thought you were washing up, Jude.'

'Sorry, Dan. I have to do this, I won't be a minute.'

'Well, we ought to get a move on. We don't want to miss the tide.'

' "This is to certify," ' typed Judith, ' "that Mr Tom and Mrs Ann Mitchison are a genuinely needy family and are not required to pay for any services provided by Institute members" . . . All right?' she said, signing it.

'Well,' he said.

'Now what?'

'We might be able to give you something.'

'You said you couldn't.'

'A token,' he said. 'I'll make you a model. How about that?' From the depths of the barge he heard a loud bang, followed by the throb of an engine. Judith pretended to rush for the shore. 'Quick, Tom, get off. We might kidnap you.'

'Well,' he said, aggrieved. 'What did you expect us to think?'

'What *do* you think?' She waved in the direction of the engine – 'Don't worry about that, they're just testing' – and sat down at the table as if for a long talk. 'You come to our disco, we help you with your business, we're glad to do it . . . then there's some small misunderstanding over an invoice and you come here as if . . . what *do* you think we are? Tell me. I'm curious.'

Tom told her what the bishop had said to the accountant, and the accountant had said to his mother. Judith did not appear surprised. 'The thing about bishops,' she said, 'the thing about all the established churches is that they don't want anyone getting in on their act. If there's to be any brainwashing, they want to be the ones to do it. I bet these Cult Caution people don't lose a lot of sleep over people wanting to become monks or nuns.'

Tom nodded. 'Everyone's entitled to their point of view.'

'Tell that to the BBC.'

'What have they done?'

'We tried to get a slot on "Thought for the Day".'

'No dice, eh?'

'No dice.'

'Where are you off to, anyway?' People were stowing things into cupboards as if in preparation for a rough sea voyage.

'Just down the coast. Our work here's finished, we won't be . . . but you still haven't answered my question. You're a fair-minded person. Do you think we've tried to make you do anything you didn't want to do?'

'No.'

'Does Shelly?'

'I don't know . . .'

'Of course, you're not going out together any more, are you?'

'How do you know?'

'Sorry if I've said the wrong thing. I hope you sort it out. We're all very fond of Shelly, and you too . . .' The *you too* was an afterthought. He wanted to know how Judith knew about him and Shelly breaking up, but she was saying, 'Now you really will have to get off if you don't want to be shanghaied.' She walked with him to the exit. Someone was starting to untie the gangplank but Judith told them to wait. He thought she would say 'Laugh with the Lord' but she just shook hands.

'What's it mean, anyway?' he said. ' "Laugh with the Lord." '

'This is a fine time to ask.'

'I just wondered.'

'Well, thanks for everything, Tom.'

'It's me who should thank you.'

'Good luck with your business.'

'Er . . . aye. Good luck with whatever it is that you do.'

The gangplank was pulled in and the barge chugged out into the middle of the river. He watched it go, puzzled. Judith waved and called something.

'What?'

'Love to Shelly.'

47

She looked so pinched up with unhappiness when she came to the door and saw him that he almost forgot that he himself was the cause. He almost put his arms round her to console her.

'How are you doing, Shell?'

'All right. How are you?'

'Can I come in?'

'Suppose so.'

Her father and her brother were at work. Her mother had gone shopping, leaving her with a pile of dishes to wash. He felt indignant that they should make a drudge of her. She got on with the dishes while they talked. He guessed that this was because she did not want him to see her face. He decided to give her time.

'So what have you been doing since I saw you?'

'I had an interview,' she said.

'Great. What for?'

'Admissions clerk at the hospital.'

'And when are they letting you know?'

'Yesterday.'

'Oh. Still, you had the interview, eh? So they must have liked the sound of you.'

'They just didn't like the look of me.'

'I like the look of you,' he said, approaching cautiously.

She walked past him and picked up the bread knife. She washed it. 'To what do I owe the honour?' she enquired.

'Does there have to be a reason? Shell . . . have you been hanging around with Judith and them . . . ?'

'Who wants to know?'

'Tell me. Please.'

'No, I haven't. Why?'

'Just wondered.'

'Good conversation, this.'

'Just what I was thinking.' He was about to tell her about the bill and ask if she could throw any light on it when he remembered that, unaided by bishops and accountants, he had sorted the matter out. He had a written statement from Judith confirming that nobody owed anybody anything. Instead of talking about the bill, he said, 'They've gone. Did you know?'

'No. Should I?'

'I went there this morning.'

'Did you?'

'And Judith was talking about you as if you and she were old pals.'

'Well. I had a few chats with her when they were working for you.'

'But she seemed to know . . . seemed to think that we'd broken up.'

'You probably told her.'

'I didn't say a word.'

Shelly turned round from the sink. 'You probably told her from the way you look. Cares of the world on your shoulders.' She smiled shyly, blinking hard.

'I thought the same about you when you opened the door. Daft, isn't it?'

'What?'

'Well, here's you and me chewing ourselves up because we're not together, and – '

'Speak for yourself,' she said, yielding to his hug.

'All right, here's me chewing myself up – and here's you putting up with me out of kindness – '

'That's right,' she said, between kisses.

'I didn't mean to hurt you, Shell.'

'I know you didn't. That's what I've been thinking. You were right. What's the point in getting married if we've nowhere to live?'

'No, but I shouldn't have . . . I mean, it's an important day when someone asks you to marry them. It's an important day when you ask, come to that. Christ. I was that nervous, and it came out wrong, and then I was all disappointed about the job . . .'

'D'you think it's always been like this?'

'What?'

'Well, in stories and films, people ask, and the next thing you know, they've got this little home . . . I mean, you never see how they get it, do you? D'you think there ever was a time when you could get married and settle down just because you want to? And the other person wants to?'

Tom knew that there had been poverty in Victorian times: worse poverty than now, if anything. But he could not get from his mind the image of the factory cottages at the museum: carefully reconstructed by craftsmen, small but snug, with their tin baths, their coalburning ranges that heated the room, cooked the food and kept a kettle constantly simmering in case anyone fancied a cup of tea . . .
'We were born in the wrong century,' he said.

'You were, you mean.'

'What time's your mam coming home?'

'She's gone to Newcastle.'

'Has she indeed?'

'Oh, Tom, not here.'

'Upstairs then.'

'I mean, not in the house.'

'Where do you fancy? The ring road?'

'I'm not – '

'Come on, Shell. I've missed you so much. I love you, Shelly, I do really.' He meant it. He was not just saying it to get what he wanted. He loved her. He loved her sweet slim body, her pink nipples, her hair . . . he loved the way she giggled in her throat as he entered her, lying on her narrow little bed while her earless old teddy bear looked on. She was only a year younger than he was, but she had been so sad before and now she appeared so happy that he felt he was giving a treat to a child. 'What are you laughing at?' he said, pretending to be stern.

'I'm laughing with the Lord.'

'They bring religion into everything these days. What does it mean, anyway?'

'I don't know.'

'You do.'

'Judith told me but I didn't understand.'

'What did she tell you?'

'God made the world because he was bored. When things go wrong, it's God playing a joke. And we should try and see the joke rather than getting upset. I've probably got it wrong. She said you have to go to Rideemus House for lectures if you want to understand.'

He propped himself up on his elbow and wagged his finger at her. 'Now you listen to me. You didn't get it wrong because there's nothing *to* get wrong. My mam's been into it, and it's dangerous.'

He did not know whether it was dangerous or not, but he did not want Shelly exposed to risk. 'You're not going to any lectures.'

'Who says?'

'Me. All right?'

'All right,' she said. 'Laugh with the Lord.'

He slapped her bottom. She slapped his, harder.

He went jauntily home, full of things to tell his mother. He had got back together with Shelly again, and he had sent Rideemus packing.

But his mother was not interested in what he had to say, and neither was his aunt. It was the middle of the afternoon and they were knocking back the sparkling wine. They had been doing it for some time, from the looks of things. 'Housewives in Drunken Brawl Drama,' he said. A flash of red caught his eye and he saw the two torn-up L-plates. 'You've never – '

'I passed!'

'I didn't even know you were taking it.'

'You'd only have made me nervous if I'd've told you.'

He resented that. He would have bought her a card. 'And if you'd failed,' he said, 'would you not have told me that either?'

'I would. But maybe not at once.'

'Who's talking about failing?' demanded Auntie Pat, fetching him a glass. 'She passed first time.'

He congratulated his mother, putting aside his resentment. He congratulated his aunt too. It was not everybody that could teach their own flesh and blood to drive. 'Ours is no ordinary flesh and blood, Tom.' Possibly not, but it was his flesh and blood too. He had thought that his mother enjoyed his teasing over her driving. Had he been making her nervous all the time? If he had known, he would not have said a word. Freed of guilt about Shelly, he now felt guilty about his mother, though it hardly mattered, now that she had passed first time.'What's it going to be, Mam? An XR4 – ?'

Auntie Pat said, 'She can treat my car as if it were her own – '

'Brave words.' He stopped himself.

' – for the time being.'

'So let's go for a drive, Mam. Where are we going?'

'Straight down to the police station to give myself up if I drive in this condition.' His mother poured more wine. 'I'd love to ring Miss Hutton up and tell her.'

'Go on then.'

'She'd just say, "Yes. Goodbye." Let's have a look at those maps.' She was working out which craft fairs she would be able to go to.

She and his aunt were like a couple of generals planning a campaign. 'I could go to this one, and this one.'

'Speaking of our accountant, I've just done her job for her.'

He flourished Judith's letter.

His mother turned up her nose. ' "Genuinely needy family." Thanks very much. Still, it's a relief.' She returned to her maps. 'I wonder if I could drive this far. I don't like the look of that junction.'

'You could stay with our Audrey if you went to that one.' Audrey was one of Tom's two married sisters. He left his mother and his aunt to get on with it and went to his workshop. With the whole country to sell to now, his mother would be more demanding than ever.

Of necessity he had given in over the matter of mass-produced parts – his mother had found a small factory to supply them to his specifications – but he fitted them together and painted them himself. He preferred to do it himself. Those Rideemus people had been willing enough, but their work had been slipshod. They had not cared. He cared. He would keep his standards up ... though he would have his work cut out to keep abreast of the ready-made toys from Taiwan that his mother thought he did not know she sold under the Mitchison's Working Models label, alongside his own craftwork.

'Mam. Letter for you, from the driving test people. There's been a mistake.'

'Failed, did I?'

'No, they've given you an award. New Driver of the Year. Feller forgot to mention it.'

Actually the letter was addressed to him. It came from Judith and it made him want to rub his eyes. They might never have had their conversation. 'Do hope you can come to our Introduction to Psychotheolistics Weekend Seminar at Rideemus House in Northumberland. Let us know if you need transport. Laugh with the Lord, Judith.'

48

'Fiacre', a French word meaning 'cab', was the name of a magazine given away in taxis. It would have to be given away. Teresa could not imagine anyone wanting to buy it, and even if they did they would not know how to pronounce it.

It was modelled on the idea of flight magazines in aeroplanes. People who made use of expensive forms of public transport could be assumed to have money to spare. They could also be assumed to have time to spare. What nicer way to pass the time, while being chauffered from A to B, than by browsing through articles on London life by famous Londoners? People in taxis had high self-esteem, particularly those who would later be claiming back the cost on an expense account. What better environment, then, for advertising prestige products?

This, broadly speaking, was the line Teresa took when selling advertising space in *Fiacre*. It was the line she urged her tele-sales team (housewives working from home) to take. She was advertising manager of *Fiacre*. (To herself she called it *Tumbril*.) She shared an office in the East End with the magazine's owner, an ambitious youth for whom *Fiacre* was one of many projects and who sought endlessly to pick her brains on what Greg Sargent, his idol and role model, would have done in this or that set of circumstances.

'Did Greg Sargent's family have money?'

'No, but they had him so I expect that made up for it.'

'Did he go to university?'

'Yes. This thing on all-night hamburgers is illiterate. Couldn't you have got a ghost-writer to do it?'

'No, she insisted on doing it herself. I'll lick it into shape.'

'Who is she again? You told me, but I've forgotten.'

'She's married to the spin bowler, Teresa.'

'Ah yes . . . I'm a bit worried about some of these escort agency ads. We might have the vice squad round.'

'You leave the vice squad to me,' he said.

He's probably got friends in it, she thought.

For this I left New Atalanta? *she thought, a dozen times a day. For this I left I left* New Atalanta *on a matter of principle?*

She had to cross London at its busiest times to get to the *Fiacre* office from her parents' home where she still lived. This enervating commuting filled her with rage. *You mean I have to work as well?* she would think when she arrived. At least at *Atalanta* and *New Atalanta* there had been something to look forward to. And in the evenings she slumped before her television, bowed down with fatigue and depression, listening to her sister Marion reporting to the nation on what Mr Gorbachev had and had not said, describing the disorders in Beirut, listening to Marion's real words for her ears only: *You don't want to grow up! You don't want to leave home!*

Sam had said much the same thing. She might have proved him wrong, but by the time she got the job at *Fiacre* things had so far deteriorated between them that living together was the last thing on their minds. Sam considered her leaving *New Atalanta* to have been much more than a pointless gesture; more, even, than an attempt to avoid living with him. He saw her hostility to the *New Atalanta Man* supplement as hostility to him personally.

She had made the mistake of referring to it as *New Atalanta Wimp*. This had really got him going.

'Wimp. Yes. Now we're getting to it. Wimp, noun, masculine, twentieth century. Meaning, a man who is making an effort.'

'Why should I applaud you for making an effort?'

'Who's asking for applause? But I don't need contempt. If you were going to despise me anyway, I might as well be a macho bruiser.'

'Oh Sam, you'd never make it as a macho bruiser.'

'Don't be so sure. Are you sure it's not what you want? You wouldn't be the first so-called feminist to get bored with her pet wimp and then go off with – '

'Has that happened to you?'

' – go off with a thug for thrills and excitement. Why the hell shouldn't you run articles on "Getting in touch with our gentleness?" Don't you want us to get in touch with our gentleness?'

'I do, yes. At your own expense.'

'And when you're not around because you don't want to see it, or read about it. You want it but you're embarrassed by it. You want everything and nothing. What do you want? I was ready to make a commitment to you. A big commitment. It's no joke having a mortgage to pay when you're freelance. I might have had to take work I didn't want to do to pay my share of it. I was prepared to risk that, and it's not very flattering that you weren't.'

'So you don't want to go out with me any more.'

'Teresa, that's what teenagers say. "Go out with me." No, I don't want to go out with you. I want to stay in with you. In our home. That's what I did want. What do you want?'

She wanted him. She wanted him as he used to be, in the relationship they used to have. But this was impossible. They could not go back to being dazzled, anxious new lovers. Nor could they go back to the early days of her working at *New Atalanta* when he had been so careful of her, so sympathetic in his questioning about the ordeals of her days, so pleased for her when they turned out not to be ordeals, so happy that *she* was happy that he had suggested that they might live together. All that was over. Chasms of suspicion had opened. The very qualities that she loved in him – his amiability, his unaffected lack of machismo – were the ones he feared she despised. She in turn feared that somewhere in him was a Greg Sargent waiting to pop out: a man awed and turned on by feminism and looking for his chance to grab a little piece of it for himself.

And there were plenty of women who would agree with her, not least at Collindeane Tower. Did she, after all, belong with them?

In the matter of sexual fantasies, Teresa followed a strict code. She could not enjoy a fantasy unless its fulfilment were within the bounds of possibility. These bounds could be liberally extended, but bounds there must be. She could not, for example, excite herself by imagining an encounter with a man from fiction, or the past, vainly though she had tried with John Stuart Mill, whom she considered to have been a bit of all right. A present-day celebrity was another matter. David Bowie existed, and it was not impossible that their paths would cross.

She could construct strangers, for it was not impossible that they too existed. She constructed any number of unknown men. Contrary to Sam's accusation, these were not bruisers or sadists, but they did have the invariable characteristic that they left the premises immediately after doing whatever it was, and did not stay to discuss it.

What she could not construct was a woman.

She went through the Collindeane women one by one: those she loved, those she liked, those she disliked. There was not a lover amongst them. It was not sex that was the obstacle. It was not intimacy. It was understanding.

She had been on the point of going to Collindeane Tower with a parcel of Goddess Garments – clean, mended and ironed – when the conception of *New Atalanta Man* had been announced. She had lost her nerve and had not gone. She had sent the clothes by post with a note to the effect that she was going away unexpectedly for a few weeks and would be in touch when she returned, to arrange to do more work. The weeks had become months and she had not been in touch. It was not that she feared she would not be made welcome. It was more that she knew she would be. She knew that, self-exiled from *New Atalanta*, defeated, unemployed, penniless and wronged, she would be easily accepted back into the ranks of the pure, the invisible pure about whom nobody knows. She was not ready for that.

And she felt guilty. She felt as she understood raped women felt: *I should have fought harder. It must have been my fault.*

If I had been raped, I could phone the Rape Crisis Line.

Beverley must have heard by now about New Atalanta Man. *She must have heard that I've left the magazine. Can't she guess what I'm going through? Doesn't she care? Why doesn't she come looking for me?*

Dear Molly, I'm going through a bit of a bad patch at the moment –

Dear Teresa, poor you.

There was no reason why Beverley should come looking for her. For all Beverley knew, Teresa might have just drifted off, as hundreds of women before her had drifted off. Beverley had done her part in patching up the quarrel over the sale of *Atalanta;* it was Teresa who had withdrawn. Beverley had other things to think about.

Teresa tried to stretch a point in the matter of John Stuart Mill, but it was no good. No one, male, female, past, present, fictional or real, was any good. The next person she loved would have to have been a founder of *Atalanta* or something similar; would have to have risked everything in fulfilment of a vow to look after it; would have to have surrendered, would have to have left.

When she was not designing her perfect lover, Teresa sometimes set herself the exercise of designing the perfect job. She did this at work, to console herself.

Don't worry whether this job exists, or ever could exist. Just design it, and design a life style to go with it. What would make you happy?

It would make me happy if Sam had had a perfect understanding of why I left New Atalanta. It would make me happy if we lived together in a little flat and did things to it in the evenings.

That doesn't answer the question. We were talking about jobs, not lovers.

I want to work in a feminist business

You have already worked in two feminist businesses. One of them failed and the other is a success. You couldn't cope in either case.

New Atalanta *is not a success.*

Isn't it? It's still there, but where are you?

She was in the office of *Fiacre*, waiting for her home-based team of saleswomen to phone in their space bookings for the day. She was building up her strength for the journey home. She was reading the typescript of an article by a quiz-show panellist on places where it was possible for a couple to enjoy a nice dinner for under £30. She was marking the names of the chosen restaurants with a yellow felt-tip pen and looking up their telephone numbers. She was reading a woman film star's account of shopping in London for second-hand clothes. It was highly rewarding, she said: she had picked up an Edwardian cocktail gown and a lace wrap on the Covent Garden piazza; she had found an elegant beaded evening bag at an Oxfam shop.

'And speaking of good causes,' the film star wrote, or perhaps her ghost-writer wrote, 'would you believe that women's lib is now in the business of supplying beautiful women with beautiful things? You have to search for it, mind, and GODDESS GARMENTS (Collindeane Tower, Collindeane Estate, SE) doesn't provide the most salubrious setting for bargain-hunting, but for all that, it's well worth a visit. I found a backless diamanté ball gown, worn once only, I was assured by the very helpful assistant, and that by a titled undergraduate at a May Ball at Cambridge. . . .'

Teresa's boss was speaking from very far away.

'That's more of a fun piece,' he said.

'Yes.'

'Don't waste your time on Oxfam.'

'Right.'

'Some of the antique shops in Camden Passage, though – '

'Some of the antique shops in Camden Passage.'

'And Covent Garden.'

'Could you remind me what you're talking about? My mind's gone blank.'

'Advertisements? Space? Money? Ring any bells?'

'Ah yes,' she said. 'I remember.'

*

293

'It all comes down to marketing,' said Beverley.

Teresa could see that it did.

'We're not just marketing clothes here. We're marketing an idea. We're closing the gap between people who think it's clever to get a second-hand bargain, and people who think it's degrading.'

All over the estate were signs reading: 'THIS WAY TO GODDESS GARMENTS. OUR NEW AND SECOND-HAND CLOTHES ARE DIVINE!' Goddess Garments had expanded out of the single room it used to occupy and now filled an entire flat, clean and newly painted, on the ground floor. One room in the flat next door was marked 'Men's Department', with a sign politely explaining that men were not welcome anywhere else in the building.

The *Fiacre* contributor had obviously found her backless gown on the rail marked 'YOU *SHALL* GO TO THE BALL!' It seemed alive with glitter and feathers and silk, and attracted the attention not only of customers who looked as if they might have serious reasons for wearing such things, but also of children and impoverished-looking mothers who admired and laughed over the ball gowns before moving on to look at more serviceable items. 'FULL OF WOOL' was the woollens section: there were jumpers, cardigans, jersey dresses, scarves and hats. Some looked recently manufactured, some home-made, some new, some second-hand, but most would need a second glance to establish what they were, so nicely were they packaged and set out in the softly lit room. And second glances for that purpose were not encouraged. 'PLEASE DON'T ASK WHAT'S NEW AND WHAT'S BEEN WORN,' advised the sign on the wall. 'IF YOU LIKE IT, BUY IT.'

'PLEASE DO TOUCH AND TRY ON.'

'GODDESS GARMENTS. IF YOU CAN GET IT CHEAPER SOMEWHERE ELSE . . . PLEASE DO.'

'IF YOUR CHILDREN ARE BORED PLEASE SEND THEM TO THE CRÈCHE. IF THEY ARE STILL BORED PLEASE ACCEPT OUR APOLOGIES.'

'PRICING POLICY: WAGED, PAY THE BLUE PRICE. UNWAGED, PAY THE RED PRICE.'

There was a denim section, a school uniforms section and a section marked 'GREAT COATS'. There were Asian, African and Caribbean clothes. Jewellery ranged from plastic to antique. There were baby clothes, there were shoes for all ages, there were handbags, there were hats.

'Would you like to try it on?' smiled Beverley to a customer who approached with a sweater. Beverley's hair was a complex and elegant arrangement of braids, dotted with beads that matched her earrings and her long, full, flame-coloured skirt.

The customer said: 'I don't understand about the prices.'

'Are you waged or unwaged?' said Beverley.

'I don't understand.'

Beverley said patiently: 'Do you work for a wage?'

'No, I'm a housewife, but my husband does.'

'Unwaged, then. You pay the lower price.'

The woman insisted on paying the higher price. 'Don't forget to sign the wall,' said Beverley. Everyone who bought clothes from, or gave clothes to, Goddess Garments, was invited to sign the wall. There were some famous names there: names of women who had once been referred to as cleaner-fish.

Searching for words, Teresa said to Beverley: 'Why did she pay the higher price?'

'They always do. It's never occurred to some of these middle-class housewives that they're unwaged. But she'll think about it.'

'Beverley. What can I say?'

'You like it?'

'I love it. I take it you got that grant from Europe?'

'Not a penny,' said Beverley, firmly but without bitterness. 'But we got the next best thing. We got a feminist business consultant in, a woman called Daphne Barclay. She's – '

'How much is she charging you?'

Beverley looked hurt. 'She believes in what we're doing, so she gives her services free. Do you know her?'

'Our paths have crossed. Bev, are you sure you've got that right? Are you sure she's not going to send in some huge bill?'

'Thank you, Teresa. You disappear into the sunset and then you come back and tell us we've got it all wrong.'

'If Daphne Barclay's a feminist,' said Teresa, 'then I'm – ' she tried to think of something sufficiently ludicrous, ' – a Thatcherite.' On this, Beverley made no comment.

49

Dear Ms Heriot –

Who? thought Gina, who no longer reacted to her maiden name, and who considered 'Ms' an affectation.

> We are writing to you as a woman prominent in your field to offer you the opportunity to become involved in an entirely new concept –

It did not look like the kind of document that would invite her to peel off the YES! sticker and return the card as a way of having her name included in a free draw for half a million pounds. That was what it usually was when strangers wrote breathlessly offering opportunities to become involved in entirely new concepts. Strangers they might be, but they might have bothered to get her name right, and, before turning on the flattery about prominence in one's field, they might have checked to see where she worked: the letter had been forwarded to her from Franson & Franson.

She was feeling nostalgic about Franson & Franson these days. Small it might have been, and she had earned less money there than she did now at Stalton Industries. But she had been happier there, and had liked her colleagues. There had been none there such as Hilary and Trevor Foreman.

> Goddess Garments began as an informal arrangement among women living, squatting and working on a South London estate. It was concerned mainly to pass on children's clothes that had been outgrown, and to supply other good-quality second-hand

clothing to families suffering from unemployment, low incomes and –

And melted sinks?

– Goddess Garments has now formed itself into an all-women Co-operative which exists to:

(i)   supply disadvantaged families with low-cost, good-quality clothing, new and second-hand.
(ii) combat the waste caused by a fashion industry which encourages people to discard serviceable clothes for no better reason than that they are last year's style.
(iii) provide a retail outlet for clothes made under non-exploitative conditions by radical businesses and community workshops.
(iv) offer an opportunity for financial involvement to women who prefer to know that their money is being used to promote socially responsible trading practices rather than –

Ah yes, thought Gina. *Here it comes. I'm supposed to buy shares in this jumble sale?* On reflection it seemed like a good cause, and she would like to help. But she and Oliver were paying out heavily on their mortgage and had little left over for investments which, far from promising fat returns, appeared to be trying to make a virtue of doing the opposite. 'This should not be looked upon as an investment for profit. The payment of fair prices to suppliers and wages to workers will take priority over the payment of interest on the loans, which is not guaranteed. We believe that this is what you would want.'

Why not just ask for a donation and be done with it? Gina did not intend to send a donation, but Goddess Garments were not finished with her yet. They wanted every recipient of this letter to send one item of clothing. The only stipulation was that it be clean and in wearable condition. They wanted people to rummage through their wardrobes, not their dustbins. Every woman had something in her wardrobe that she no longer wore. Perhaps she had bought it on impulse and changed her mind. Perhaps it was an unwanted gift. Perhaps it had been bought for a special occasion, and the occasion had passed. Alternatively, recipients of the letter who were skilled at sewing or knitting might like to make something themselves and send it, or buy something new. Their generosity would be acknowledged by having their names written on the wall in the Goddess Garments shop. Among the names already so immortalized were . . . and here, Gina started to be impressed. She recognized a great many names – businesswomen like herself; university lecturers; writers; politicians;

actresses; Brenda Sargent, wife of the tycoon; Marion Henley, the newsreader; Daphne Barclay . . . *Daphne Barclay?* If Daphne Barclay were involved in this, it might explain the mistake over Gina's name and current place of employment, for she had been Gina Heriot when she went on Daphne's course, and still on the staff of Franson & Franson.

Well, why not? she thought. She curbed an urge to send money. Her future was uncertain. She was looking for a way to move out of Bitumen Products, in the hope of never again setting eyes on Hilary Foreman. Ideally she would transfer to a sales job in another department, but her exasperation with Hilary was such that she thought she would accept anything – even a downgrading and a cut in salary – though that would be drastic and damaging and she hoped it would not prove necessary.

It was true that she had things in her wardrobe that she never wore . . . her wedding dress, for one, though perhaps that was not quite what Goddess Garments had in mind. There were a couple of skirts and that absurd scarlet pantsuit thing that she had worn – had she really worn it? She had – at her Graduation Ball. Goddess Garments were welcome to that. Was it the sort of thing they wanted? It would not be of much use to low-income families. Children might like to dress up in it, but it seemed a bit mean to send something that was of no practical use. She got it cleaned, along with the skirts, and bought a sweater from Marks & Spencer's. She parcelled everything up and sent it off with her best wishes. Gina was not a women's libber, but Goddess Garments sounded like something that deserved encouragement.

Gina was most certainly not a women's libber. If her working arrangement with Hilary was an example of new opportunities for women, you could keep it. Since the birth of Hilary's second baby, Sally, things had got worse and worse, though they might have been expected, with the advent of Monique from Grenoble, the au pair, to have got better.

Monique's alleged virtues were such that Gina wondered how Grenoble had spared her. Hilary remained based at home, but she was able to come into headquarters more often. When she did so, she used Gina's desk. 'Only when you're not here, Gina,' she said, and this was true, so it was hard to raise objections. It was petty to mind about papers being rearranged or, once, a dummy in her in-tray, encrusted with dried slime. (Monique was perfect, but baby Sally was not; she had demanded to accompany her mother, apparently; Trevor's secretary had not minded sitting with Sally in the representatives' office while Hilary and Gina and the Beach Boys were in their meeting.)

But why MY desk? Gina had raged inside. *Why is it always ME that gets phoned in the middle of the night? Why is it always me who arrives at a hotel after a day of calls and finds that the booking has not been made? Why do her mistakes always relate to MY customers?*

Hilary did not make many mistakes – she was her usual manically efficient self – and the mistakes she did make were usually so minor (a name spelled wrongly; an unimportant inaccuracy in a calculation; a message garbled by Monique when Hilary could not come to the phone) as to make Gina feel petulant indeed for even mentioning them. But this made it worse. If Hilary were obviously out of her depth, everyone would suffer, everyone would know, and something would be done about it. Gina did not concern herself with what this 'something' would be. Were Hilary to be dismissed from Stalton's, Gina would be genuinely sorry, for her dislike of the woman did not prevent her admiring the energy and determination with which she insisted on her right to her career while looking after a toddler and a baby. A mutual dismissal, though – of Hilary from Gina's life, and Gina from Hilary's – would be a different matter, one that would fill Gina with joy.

But no one was being dismissed from anything. Covert questioning of the Beach Boys revealed that they had no complaints about Hilary's handling of their work. And this made Gina wonder all the more whether Hilary's little slips were deliberate: her way of reminding Gina that two could play at mistake-making. Paperclips aside, Hilary had not accused Gina of making any specific mistakes; but she missed no opportunity to remind Gina of her lack of experience in sales administration, a lack which Gina could have made up if she had been willing to adopt Hilary's suggestion that they swap jobs once in a while.

Hilary had not asked any of the Beach Boys to swap with her. She did not phone them after hours. On the contrary, they marvelled at how she managed not to do this. Gina knew how Hilary managed it. She managed it by putting Gina last. She managed it by dealing with the Beach Boys when she was fresh and with Gina when she was tired.

She managed it by assuming that, in the name of some imagined sisterhood between them, Gina's tolerance and adaptability were without limit. If that was sisterhood, you could keep it; but Gina did not mind making a small contribution to Goddess Garments.

*

She tried to arrange things so that her application for a transfer would be dealt with in Personnel by somebody other than Trevor. She could hardly say, 'Actually, Trevor, the real reason I want to move is that I can't stand your wife.'

She did not say that, of course. She wrote an eager memo about wanting to vary her experience within the company, laying it on with a trowel about her passionate fascination for fertilizers, the product in whose division a vacancy had arisen.

She was called in to see Trevor. He greeted her pleasantly and invited her to sit down. 'You're very ambitious, aren't you, Gina?' he beamed.

'Of course I am. That's why I'm here.'

'And do you really feel that you've learned all there is for you to learn in the short time you've been in Bitumen Products?'

'Yes,' she said. 'Has anyone seriously suggested that I haven't?' She laid a light stress on 'seriously'. She was quite ready for what Trevor was saying. She had done her homework and had the names of three young men who, over the last couple of years, had sought and obtained transfers after being in their initial sales jobs for shorter periods than Gina had been in Bitumen Products.

'I see,' said Trevor. 'Your mind's made up. I just wanted to be sure of that, before I put your application forward.'

'It should have gone forward already! I mean . . . surely it should.'

'There's plenty of time,' said Trevor. 'I wanted to be sure that you've considered the implications of what you're doing, or what you would be doing if you moved now.'

She guessed that he meant the implications for Hilary. Another mug would have to be found for Hilary. Another Stalton Industries equivalent of Monique.

Trevor was saying: 'We do have a provisional career plan drafted for you, as we do for everybody. We didn't envisage a move for you just yet.'

'May I see this plan?'

'I don't have it here. It's confidential and it's not binding on anyone, you least of all. A great many people have felt as you obviously feel and have preferred to carve out their own careers within the company, going to wherever they think they'll get on best. Sometimes they're right. You may be right. I just wondered whether you and Oliver – maybe we ought to get Oliver up here.' Trevor lifted his phone.

'This is nothing to do with Oliver.' Gina restrained the sharpness in her voice. She could not afford to anger Trevor. 'I would like – please, Trevor – to have my application considered on its merits.'

Trevor shrugged and abandoned his call. 'We have to take account of the likelihood that you'll want to start a family at some point. In about four years' time, I think Oliver said. After that, you're not going to want to go back to square one, are you? Surely you'll want an arrangement along the lines of what Hilary's doing. You'll find it easier to fix that up in Bitumen Products, now that Hilary's blazed the trail for you, so to speak, than if you're in one of our, well, more traditionally minded departments where they think careers and motherhood shouldn't mix.'

'What – did – you – say?'

Trevor laughed. 'Some men do still think that. They're not all like me and Oliver.'

Gina was so angry that she could hardly see. 'What did you say before that? About starting a family in – ?'

'Four years' time?'

'*Oliver* said that?' Oliver had said that to *Trevor*? The subject was closed between Gina and Oliver at the moment. They had agreed on a truce. Oliver no longer made his airy-fairy comments on the presumed joys of family life; Gina kept to a minimum her remarks about her profound lack of envy for Hilary and her lot. Had Oliver in the meantime been keeping the Foremans posted of specific dates?

'Only in a general way, Gina. Come to think of it, he hasn't mentioned it for some time, so I wonder where I got the idea ... I know what it is. When you were first married, he talked – you both talked – about having children in five years. And that's about a year ago, so – '

'And you've been doing a countdown?'

'Well, no, of course not, but obviously we have to – ' Trevor sighed. 'I knew we ought to have had Oliver in on this.'

'Don't worry. I'll tell him.'

'They've been planning our family for us.'

'Don't be silly.'

'They have! They've got it all worked out!'

'I thought *we* had it all worked out,' Oliver retorted. 'I didn't realize it was a secret. We decided we'd have children in about five years. I've heard you say that.'

'*About* five years. That's just an expression. He didn't say "about five years". He said "about four years". That's like saying "about twenty-nine minutes". People don't say "about twenty-nine

301

minutes". If it's approximate, they say "about half an hour". If they say "twenty-nine minutes" they're being exact.'

'You want to have a baby in twenty-nine minutes? We'd better get moving.'

'They've got it all worked out, Oliver. Hilary gets her child-bearing over in one fell swoop. I wait five years . . . four years. As soon as their kids are in their nursery schools or whatever the hell they're going to send them to, I drop out and Hilary comes back! I'm just keeping her place warm for her!'

'And what's wrong with that?'

'What's *wrong* with it?' As an arrangement freely entered into, there was nothing wrong with it, Gina supposed. It was the sort of thing that friends might agree on. 'What's wrong with it is that they've got a bloody cheek!'

She mused on the way she was using pronouns instead of naming names. THEY'VE *got a bloody cheek.* THEY'VE *been planning our family for us.* Trevor had been just the same. WE *have a career plan drafted for you.* WE *have to take account of the possibility.* WE *weren't envisaging moving you yet.* Who? The Board of Stalton Industries? Stalton Industries Personnel? Or Mr and Mrs Trevor Foreman?

The vacancy in Fertilizers was filled by a young man who had been in Fertilizers all along. Where possible, the company preferred to do this. But they had noted Gina's request to move and they would keep her in mind if anything suitable arose.

Oh yeah? thought Gina, looking for vacancies in other companies.

But it did not come to that. The curtain fell on Hilary Foreman's career in rather tragic circumstances.

Monique had returned to Grenoble in tears. It was not known what had brought this about. There had been a row. What was known was that Hilary had been left alone with two young children during a busy time for the Bitumen Products Division. An accident had occurred. Hilary had been doing something with the baby upstairs when the telephone had rung. Gina and the Beach Boys wondered gloomily which of them it had been who had made the fateful call. None of them could remember having done so at the relevant time. Rushing downstairs, Hilary had missed her footing and dropped the baby. Hilary was unhurt, but Sally had suffered a fractured skull.

Sally had survived, but Hilary had been closely questioned by a hospital social worker as to the cause of the accident. The social worker had not been satisfied. There had been marks on the baby's body which the accident did not explain. 'They think I did it on purpose.'

'Of course they don't,' said Gina. 'But they have to be careful.'

Hilary resigned from her job to care for her injured baby and to receive a steady stream of visitors: health visitors and social workers who, according to Trevor, deliberately humiliated her with their unnecessary calls and insulting questions. Trevor struggled manfully to get Hilary's resignation commuted to indefinite unpaid leave of absence, but Stalton's were adamant. Such irregularities would interfere with the smooth running of the company. Hilary had been under a lot of pressure and needed a rest. Once she had had this, and sorted out her domestic arrangements, any application she chose to make for re-employment – perhaps on a part-time basis – would be sympathetically considered.

Now that she had no further reason to be angry with Hilary, Gina felt deeply sorry for her. She renewed her offer to babysit at weekends so that Hilary might develop new interests. But Hilary wanted no new interests. She became inert and lethargic. Sometimes she did not even bother to get dressed. Going round to babysit one Saturday afternoon when Oliver was playing squash with Trevor, Gina found Hilary in her dressing gown. 'Aren't you going out?' Gina said.

'I can't be bothered.'

'Come on. You'll be all right. It's not the end of the world.'

'Isn't it?' said Hilary bitterly. 'Come with me, Gina, I've got something for you.' She took Gina to her and Trevor's bedroom. On the unmade bed was a pile of clothes: smart dresses, skirts, suits. 'I won't be needing these any more. You might like to give them to your friends in the women's movement.'

50

Ann's first long-distance craft fair was to be held near where her daughter Audrey lived with her family, so Ann arranged to spend the weekend with them.

Audrey's five-year-old son was adamant that Ann should dress up for the fair, Ann having let slip that this was suggested by the organizers. Stall-holders were supposed to come in the traditional costume of their craft, or dressed as any character from English history or literature. This would give atmosphere to the event, and make it more interesting for the American servicemen and their families.

'You could go as a pheasant, Gran,' said Ricky.

'And what do pheasants wear?'

'Rags.'

'I'll be fine as I am, then.' If Pat or Tom had agreed to come to the craft fair with her, they might have dressed up as the two Ugly Sisters or Jack-and-the-Beanstalk and his mother, but she could not see herself running her stall on her own, wearing fancy dress. She was going to be quite self-conscious enough, and worried in case anyone noticed that not all her Working Models were working models, or asked straight out whether everything she was selling had in fact been made by herself and members of her family.

Ricky did not intend to give up. 'You could go as a queen!' He brought a picture book and found a picture of a medieval lady in a long dress and a pointed hat with a veil attached. His father, David, fetched a sheet of cardboard and rolled it into a cone. They stuck a tea towel into the top of the cone and put the resultant contraption on Ann's head. 'Long live the queen, long live the queen!' Ricky shouted, dancing round her and bowing; but she insisted that she would go to the fair in her ordinary clothes. 'It doesn't say you have to dress up.'

'But you can if you want to,' said Ricky.

'I *don't* want to.'

'I do! I want to dress up and help you with the stall, Gran!'

'You'd be a big help,' said Audrey. 'Leave your gran alone.'

The plan was for Audrey and David to bring Ricky and his baby sister to the fair in the afternoon, to look around and see how Ann was getting on.

The RAF base was about half an hour's drive from Audrey and David's home in Carlisle. Ann gave herself plenty of time, allowing for the possibility that she might get lost on the way. But she found the place easily. Almost as surprising as the fact that she could drive – had driven all the way to Carlisle from Sunderland, through the Friday traffic – was the fact that she could find her way to individual places. As a passenger, she had never taken much notice of road numbers, but now it fascinated her how it all worked: how the numbers formed a system that was easy to follow, and how, if you followed the system, you ended up where you wanted to be.

It helped that someone had stuck 'This way to the craft fair' signs under the RAF ones. Some of the RAF signs were illegible because of graffiti. 'RAF' had been changed to 'USAF.'

'BEWARE OF ENGINE BLASTS AND FLYING OBJECTS FROM AIRCRAFT OPERATING IN THIS AREA.'

Thanks very much, thought Ann, slowing down. *But then I'm no less likely to be hit by a flying object when I'm going slowly than when I'm going fast, am I?* She went back up to fifty. *They tell you what to beware of. They don't tell you what to do about it.*

She had thought that once she found the base she would have found the Recreation Centre where the craft fair was being held, but the base went on and on, flat, open land with no sign of buildings other than the occasional collection of hangars, sheds and fuel storage tanks.

'THIS IS A PROHIBITED PLACE WITHIN THE MEANING OF THE OFFICIAL SECRETS ACT. PHOTOGRAPHY STRICTLY FORBIDDEN.'

It can't be all that secret. They wouldn't be holding public events in it. I could be a Russian spy, dressed up as a saleswoman.

'THIS WAY TO THE CRAFT FAIR.'

Behind the wire, the open grass and runways gave place to office buildings and houses, square, grey blocks that you would recognize wherever you saw them as being temporary quarters rather than proper homes. 'NO SOLICITATION ON THE BASE WITHOUT THE APPROVAL OF THE COMMANDER.' The different-coloured curtains took nothing from the sense of regimentation; the long, flat American cars with the unfamiliar numberplates looked incongruous and yet somehow at home, as if Ann were arriving in a foreign country while still being obliged to feel hospitable in her thoughts towards visitors. She drove through the base's main entrance. It was wide open: sentries were on duty, but they took no notice. Outside the Recreation Centre (spelled 'Center') people were wandering about dressed as Cavaliers and Roundheads, and she thought she spotted Henry VIII parking his dormobile.

There was a stage at one end of the large hall, and a snack bar at the other. Snacks could be paid for in pounds or dollars. Off-duty servicemen lounged about, fit as tigers, watching the craftsmen and women setting up their stalls, some of which were quite elaborate: there were castle battlements, fairy grottos and workshops with work in progress, wood-turning, leatherwork, portrait-painting and quilting. Ann realized that she had been wrong to avoid coming in fancy dress out of fear of being conspicuous. She would be more conspicuous without it.

She looked for the organizer, who was dressed as a pantomine dame but recognizable by his badge. He showed her to her place, which was a table on the left-hand corner of the stage, and asked if she needed anything, electricity supply, tools? She said no. An obliging man, he offered to help her carry her stock in from the car, but she did not want him looking at it too closely. Managing by herself, she had to make several treks.

She put a tablecloth from home on the table and fixed her sign with drawing pins: 'MITCHISON'S WORKING MODELS'. Closest to the sign she put a couple of Tom's perpetual-motion fountains and hurried off to the cloakroom for water to get them going. They would catch the eye. She added windmills, a model colliery and half a dozen brightly clad Mitchison's Working Women. There were fewer of these than there had been, now that the Rideemus people no longer helped, but they were of better quality. They worked. The bus driver drove a bus. The accountant sat at a desk and, when you turned the handle, shook her head over a page of figures.

Further away (*Well, I never said they were ALL Mitchison's Working Models, did I?*) she put clay cottages, ornaments made of polished stone, doggy door-stops, Adam-and-Eve cruets and then, furthest of all from the sign, the items that most troubled her conscience: a range of novelty animals, their 'MADE IN TAIWAN' labels carefully removed with white spirit.

The hall filled up with visitors, some of whom looked as if they were from the base and others who looked as if they had come in from outside. They seemed very distant. People were reluctant to climb the stairs to the stage. The couple on Ann's left, whose stall was a fluffy array of fairy-dolls and bride-dolls, and who were themselves dressed as a fairy and a gnome, were very angry about the location they had been given. They were going to put in a complaint. On Ann's right was a man who did not seem too bothered one way or the other. He was selling hand-made pipes and smoked one (to the obvious annoyance of the doll people, fearful for their lace) while he read a book.

Ann dusted her stock, rearranged it and dusted it again. She felt exposed and wished she had somebody to talk to. *Don't stare at people, it's intimidating*, Daphne Barclay had said. *Look busy, but be ready to stop what you're doing if they want to talk. Don't say 'Can I help you?' It's the most aggressive question in the English language.*

The doll woman said to a lone customer: 'Don't be afraid to pick them up. Everything that comes off is washable. It's all made of Northumberland lace.'

A little American girl approached Ann's table with her mother. She showed no interest in Tom's models. She went straight for the Taiwanese cats.

'Have you got a cat at home?' Ann asked.

The child replied precisely, 'I had one at my home in New Jersey, but I haven't got one at my home in England.'

'What a shame. What's his name?'

'His name was Tips. He hasn't got a name any more because he's dead.'

'We couldn't really bring him,' the mother explained. 'Is the paint non-toxic?'

Ann said it was, though she did not know. The mother bought the cat and went off with the child to look at the lacy dolls. Ann put the money in her cash box and wrote down the sale in a notebook. 'Congratulations,' said the man with the pipe, not looking up from his reading.

A court jester bounded up the steps of the stage and came towards Ann, shaking a stick covered with bells. He did a theatrical bow. 'Good morrow, Mistress.' She recognized the glass-blower from the Sunderland craft fair who, with his wife, enjoyed the social side of

the fairs and so did not want to use her services as an agent. He
looked at her stock. 'Got your distribution agency going, then?'

She looked round in alarm, hoping nobody had heard. 'How's
your wife? Everything all right with the new baby? What was it, a
boy or a girl?'

'Boy,' said the glass-blower, winking as he got the message. He
went away. Someone else came, and bought a Taiwanese elephant.
These animals were proving very popular, but she hoped someone
would buy one of Tom's models soon. The man with the pipes asked
her if she would mind keeping an eye on his stall while he went for
a bite of lunch. She decided to postpone her own lunch until she
had taken enough money to cover the cost of hiring the stall and her
petrol for getting here. It would give her something to work towards,
because after that everything she took would be profit, or nearly
everything. The man with the pipes came back. She reached her
target, but she was too excited to be hungry, so she stayed.

Audrey entered the hall with her family. They waved to Ann and
started to make their way through the crowds and towards the stage.
Ricky's eyes were popping. They stopped to watch a medieval fire-
eater, whose display caused Ann some anxiety until she saw the fair
organizer, the pantomine dame, approach the man between bursts
of flame and order him outside. An argument ensued, but the dame
won. He looked as if he did not have arguments very often but
expected to win them when he did. And, having sorted out the fire-
eater, he was bustling self-importantly towards the stage, coming to
talk to Ann. He reached her stall ahead of the family, and waited
for some people who had been examining her stock to move away.
Beneath his padded bosom and scarlet make-up, he was clearly very
upset.

'Could I have a word with you, Mrs Mitchison?'

'Of course.'

'I'm sure there's some perfectly innocent explanation,' he said, in
a tone suggesting that he was nothing of the kind. 'But could you
please tell me what this is?' From the deep pocket of his skirt he
produced the cat that she had sold to the American girl. In the same
moment she saw the girl herself, and the mother, watching from the
foot of the stage, looking both innocent and smug.

Audrey, David and the children were approaching. Ricky was
staring hard at the man who, dressed as a woman, was drawing his
grandmother's attention to a wooden cat with a 'MADE IN TAIWAN'
label on its left inner thigh.

Audrey called cheerfully: 'Hiya, Mam! Made your first million yet?'

The pantomime dame said, 'This is a craft fair. For home-made crafts. If people want imported junk, they can go to imported junk shops.'

51

'It is against our terms and conditions,' the dame continued. 'And it puts the origin of everyone's work under suspicion.'

Ann cringed under the inescapable justice of what he was saying. She felt as if she were twelve years old, called out in front of the class. The man with the pipes had heard everything and was trying not to smile. He was smiling. Ann could not tell whether the smile was one of amusement or sympathy . . . or indignant satisfaction on behalf of all bona-fide stall-holders that she had got her comeuppance.

All this was happening in front of her family. She had been looking forward to their arrival, looking forward to being seen by them not just as their mother, mother-in-law, grandmother, but as a saleswoman, a professional . . . instead, they were about to witness her being ordered from the fair in disgrace.

The pantomime dame was waiting for his answer.

Ann's daughter Audrey took the Taiwanese cat out of his hand. 'Well I never. That's where it got to. Ricky, here's your cat.'

Ricky began, 'It's not – '

'I told you,' his mother said, 'not to get your own toys mixed up with your gran's stock. It's lucky we arrived when we did, or she might have sold Brownie to this lady, er, gentleman.'

'But – '

David said, 'Hey, Rick. Look at those lovely dolls over there.'

'Dolls,' muttered Ricky scornfully as he was hustled away by his father.

The dame was still suspicious. If the Taiwanese cat had not been intended for sale as part of Ann's stock, how come there were other identical cats on her table?

'They're copies,' said Audrey. 'We get the originals from Taiwan and I copy them at home. That's allowed, isn't it?'

'Well, please give this lady a refund,' said the dame, walking off grumbling, swinging his hips. Ann leaned over the front of the stage to apologize to the woman for the misunderstanding and repay the money. 'Or would you rather have one of the other cats? The ones my, er, daughter made?'

The little girl said, 'I want *that* cat.'

'Well you can't have it. I mean, sorry, pet. It belongs to my grandson . . . If she wanted it, what did she complain for?' Ann muttered to Audrey when the mother and child had gone. 'I know what I'd do to her if she were mine.'

'Who's your friend, Mam? The transvestite?'

'D'you think he is? I think he's just dressed up for the day.'

'Any excuse.' Audrey stayed to chat, then went off to rejoin her family. The man with the pipes came over, laughing. 'Bit of quick thinking there.' He seemed amused rather than indignant, but she found herself blushing: a delayed reaction, perhaps, after the accusations of the dame. Or was it his good looks that were making her blush? He was tall and lean with thinning grey hair, twinkly eyes and a face lined from smiling. 'Everybody does it,' he said.

'Do you?' she said, with a glance at his pipes.

'Well, no, but it's just a hobby for me. If it were my living . . . Toby Hamilton, by the way.' He offered his hand. 'Don't tell me all that lace – ' he nodded in the direction of the dolls ' – doesn't come in bales from a factory, because I won't believe you.'

The doll woman overheard and was outraged. 'I make it myself.'

Toby Hamilton apologized solemnly and returned with a wink to chatting with Ann. He was a retired civil servant who made pipes for something to do, and brought them to craft fairs mainly to cover his costs and have a bit of social life. He did not get much social life otherwise, following the death of his wife. Ann made a sympathetic sound, and he asked about her husband. She explained and he said, 'I am sorry.' They agreed that there was no need to be embarrassed or apologetic. It was not this that was upsetting – people's casual assumption that one had a husband or wife still living, and the need to correct them – so much as the strategies people used who already knew what had happened but wanted to avoid talking about it. 'You want to talk about it,' she said. 'That's what they don't realize.'

'Do you live round here?'

She explained that she was staying with her family and asked about his. They were all grown-up and far away, he said. He saw them occasionally, but they had lives of their own to lead. 'I'd like to hear more about your distribution service.'

'What distribution service?'

'Sorry . . . do you fancy going for a cup of tea? Somewhere away from here, where you could tell me?'

'Well, I'm working.'

'Of course you are. Still, I think I'm going to call it a day.' He started to clear up his things. Some of the other stall-holders were doing the same, but while there was a single customer left in the hall Ann did not intend to budge. 'It's been nice talking to you,' said Toby.

'It was nice talking to you.'

'Perhaps I'll see you again. What other fairs will you be going to?'

She mentioned a couple. 'I'll be there,' he said. 'See you then. Unless you'd like to have dinner with me tonight?'

First there had been that policeman: PC Victor Summers, whose job it had been to bring her the news of her husband's death. He had come to the door with her next-door neighbour: the wrong thing to do, as it happened. The neighbour had been a newcomer to the block and Ann had had an argument with her the previous day about her leaving rubbish in the corridor instead of taking it out to the bins. It had not been a major argument, but, opening her front door and seeing the neighbour there with a policeman, Ann had thought the worst.

Well, no. Not quite the worst, as it had turned out.

'I always do that,' Vic had said later, when they knew each other better. 'I go to the neighbours and say, "Look, I've got a bit of bad news for the people next door. Will you come with me so that you can be there while I break it to them?"'

'It must be hard for you,' she had said, marvelling without pride at the way, in the midst of her own loss, she had sympathy for other people. 'Knocking on strangers' doors and telling them the world's fallen in.'

But he liked being in the traffic division, he had said. At least you weren't dealing with people who hurt each other deliberately. Not usually. You raged at the waste, of course. And you saw some horrors. But if you couldn't cope with seeing horrors, you didn't join the force. Someone had to do it. He had told her about being called once to an accident where there were fingers all over the road. 'You don't want to hear this.' 'You've told me now. What did you do with the fingers?' 'I picked them up and put them in a bag.' One of the cars had been so badly smashed up that no one could get inside it to turn off the radio which was working perfectly, blaring out classical music through the carnage. When Vic had finished collecting up the fingers, he had put his arms round one of his mates and they had waltzed a few steps to the music, killing themselves laughing until their sergeant told them to stop.

She had enjoyed his stories, even the grisly ones, reminding her as they did that Neale, her husband, had been killed instantly, reminding her of how normal and relaxed he had looked in the morgue, fingers intact. Vic's calls over the ensuing weeks and months, first on business and then 'to see how you are', 'to see how you're getting on and take a cup of tea off you' had been a pleasant feature of her dreary life. Then he had been transferred south. He had written a couple of times and then there had been silence.

With a young family to bring up, she had had little opportunity to meet men, even if she had been looking for one. Pat had asked her if she thought she would ever marry again. Ann had considered the question as if it applied to someone else, which it did: it applied to a woman who could feel things for men, things beyond friendship; it applied to a woman who had some choice in the matter of whether she would marry again. 'You mustn't shut yourself away. Neale would want you to be happy.' This had hardly needed saying as far as Ann was concerned, particularly in that tone that implied that Neale no longer existed. How could he not exist when she had his photograph and his children, his name and some of his old clothes? *Neale WOULD want you to be happy*. He did want her to be happy, while he waited out there somewhere for her to turn up. He would have preferred to make her happy himself, but since that was no longer possible, anything she decided to do was fine with him. Pat and her husband were always asking her round to meet their friends, not in a crude, match-making way, but to get her out of the house and into circulation. 'If you ever want a babysitter, Ann, just say the word.' She had met people, she had gone out, but not often and not recently.

And nothing had ever come of it. She would go out with someone once or twice, and then he would disappear, leaving her to wonder if it was something that she had said. Sometimes she had known exactly what it was that she had said. It had astonished and infuriated her how insensitive some men could be, the things they thought you would agree to in exchange for a ticket to the cinema or a few drinks.

They had not all been like that, but they had all drifted away after a couple of dates. She had concluded that she was not very good company. They had not wanted to hear about her housework, her neighbours, her family . . . and she had had no other conversation.

' . . . unless you'd like to have dinner with me tonight?'

'Well. I'm staying at my daughter's.' She was shocked and wanted time to think.

'Bring her along,' said Toby. 'I'd be glad of the company, I hate eating alone.'

52

'Oh aye,' said Audrey ironically. 'We'll bring the baby and all.'

'But he said –'

'Mam –' Audrey put her hands on her hips and looked tolerant. 'He's lonely. He wants to be with a family again.'

'Does he hell. He fancies you.'

'Do you think so?'

'When he said I could come, did he mean on my own? I've often thought I needed an older man.'

'She'd finish him off,' said David.

'Go on, Mam. Be a devil.'

'But I've nothing to wear.'

'Wear something of mine, then. What about this?' said Audrey when they reached home, Ann having told Toby that he should pick her up at half past seven. Audrey held out a short green dress with a low-cut front.

'I can't wear that.'

'Try it on. We're the same size.'

'We're not the same shape, though.' Ann looked at herself in the mirror, showing everything she had got. 'No, I brought a dress to wear tomorrow. I'll go in that. He knows I'm away from home, so if I go looking too glamorous he'll think I was expecting someone to ask me out to dinner. He'll think I do it all the time.'

'I want you home by ten-thirty, mind,' Audrey mimicked, wagging her finger, giving her mother a key.

Toby took her to an Italian restaurant in Carlisle. She had avocado pear followed by Chicken *alla Romagna*. He had spaghetti. She would have liked to have the same, but she feared she looked a terrible sight when eating spaghetti. He did not, but she would have.

Toby wanted to hear about everything: Tom, the business, her learning to sell, her learning to drive. She was in danger of talking too much. But he was genuinely interested, she decided. He was not just questioning her out of politeness.

The restaurant was nearly empty. The busiest thing about it was its staff, hundreds of waiters, it seemed, topping up Ann's and Toby's wine, whisking away their plates . . . in other circumstances this might have made her feel special, pleasantly looked after in a way she was not used to . . . but she was alarmed at how quickly they were getting through the meal, how soon the evening would be over. She was enjoying herself. She ought not really to have a sweet, but he said he was going to have profiteroles with extra cream, so she had fresh fruit salad, envying him his profiteroles. They ordered coffee and, to spin things out further, she had a crème de menthe while he had a brandy.

'Now, Mr Hamilton,' she said humorously, 'how would you feel about having me take your pipes round the tobacconists' shops for you, and you can concentrate on what you're good at, which is making them?'

'Don't you think I'm good at selling, then?'

'No. You're not supposed to read a book when you get bored and you're not supposed to pack up and leave early either.'

'Oh.' He looked solemn. 'What am I supposed to do?'

'You're supposed to look alert and approachable.'

'Like this?'

'Not bad.'

'But look at it this way, Ann. If I'd had an agent selling my pipes, I wouldn't have met you.'

'You would if the agent was me.'

'I'm not in that league.'

'You could be.'

'I don't think so. You must come and see my workshop some time, and you'll see what I mean. I don't have the facilities for producing more than I can sell myself. It's a thing I've often thought about craft fairs. People say things like "hand-crafted" and "home workshop" as if they were a boast. I've heard myself say them. But what I'm really saying is, mine are better because they've been made inefficiently. I'm making a virtue of the fact that I've put so much time into them that nobody could afford to buy them if I wanted paying for my time. You're a brave woman, Ann, trying to make a living out of work that most people do as a hobby. You are, you're brave – you and your son.'

Ann looked at the tablecloth.

'Did you like your husband?'

'What?'

'Forgive me. I forgot we'd only just met, we're so – may I go on with what I was going to say?'

'I loved him.'

'Of course, but that's not what I asked. It's a theory I've got. I want to test. When you get to my age – '

'Your age?'

'I'm older than you. I know a lot of people who've been widowed. Everyone takes it hard, of course, but it seems to me that the ones who take it hardest – it's a paradox, but it still seems to me that the ones who take it hardest are the ones who – if they're honest – didn't really like the person who's gone.'

She was shocked but she thought she understood what he meant. She had never heard it put into words before. It was not romance with Neale that she missed, or had missed. It was not even sex. It was more the sort of day-to-day having him around: someone to talk to. He had got on her nerves – the way she had had to smile at the same old stories, which would be even older now; and she had got on his – the way she never quite finished a cup of coffee or tea, poured away the dregs and started another one. But they had been companions, parents to the children and sometimes to each other; friends.

'I liked him.'

'I liked my wife, and somehow that makes it easier. There's no reproaches. There's none of this "What did she mean by that?" or "Why didn't I say this to her?" Whatever needed saying, we said. It was all . . . settled. I miss her, but I can get on with my life.'

What else was there to do? she thought. But she liked what he had said.

They left the restaurant. It was still early. Audrey and David would not have gone to bed. The hospitable thing would be to invite Toby home to meet them, but she did not do it. She assumed that he would take her back to their house, and she could do it when they arrived.

She did not recognize the streets through which he drove her, but then she did not know the neighbourhood. He stopped outside a strange house. She felt she ought to say something, but he said, 'Come in for a minute. I want to show you my workshop.'

'Why?'

'Well, if you want to be my distributor, you'll want to do a quality control check.'

Was he laughing at her? He was. He had no right to. Could he not see that this was difficult for her? Did he make a habit of this? Did he think that she did?

'I don't,' she said.

'Don't what?'

'Want to do a quality control check.'

'All right,' he said. 'But come in anyway.'

She entered the house behind him. He turned on the light in the hall and, as if for the first time, she saw the fabric of his jacket, the stitches weaving in and out of each other, appearing to move (was it the wine? the crème de menthe?) like waves on the sea; she thought of how it would feel to have that fabric close to her, on her face, under her hands – soft and substantial and slightly scratchy. She wanted a cuddle. She wanted him to cuddle her. Perhaps a little kiss too, but the thought of that made her feel shy. What she really wanted was a cuddle. If they had a cuddle, would she have to kiss him too? Which came first, the kiss or the cuddle? She did not know the rules. He closed the front door and turned to her, resting his arms on her shoulders as if all he wanted was some assistance in bearing his arms' weight. 'There aren't any rules,' he said. 'We're grown-up. We can do whatever we want.'

She felt herself flinch. He felt it too. He took his arms away. 'And we don't have to do anything we don't want.'

'And what if – '

'What?'

'What if we don't know what we want?'

'If we don't know what we want, we can have fun finding out. I know what I want. I want to kiss you.'

Go on, then, she thought.

He must have heard her, because he did. First he just brushed her with closed lips and then he was licking the inside of her mouth. She remembered when Neale had first done this, her first kiss from her first boyfriend, her only love. She remembered how surprised she had been, *what a funny thing to do, sticking his tongue in my mouth, is it his way of saying what he really wants to do, if I let him do this, am I agreeing – ?* She had agreed to nothing with Neale until they were married, and he had respected this.

'I'll make some coffee,' said Toby.

She waited in his living room. Waited for ever, wanting him to return. Wanting him. She did not want coffee, she wanted him to kiss her again and hold her, hold her all over. *What am I doing here?* she thought. She knew what she was doing. Waiting for a strange man to return and make love to her, a man who had taken her out to dinner and brought her home and kissed her. She could not pretend not to know what she was doing. But what would she do? When he came back, what would she do? *I don't have to decide*, she thought. *He can do what he wants to do and I can stop him, he's not some maniac.*

But that's not fair to him.

It's not fair to me either, I have to decide.

I do have to decide.

By the time he came back with the coffee, she had decided to stay, and with the decision came a great lightening of her spirits as if the matter had passed out of her control and all she had to do was enjoy herself and be happy, which she did and was.

53

Gina was not really a women's magazine person but, having been given a copy of the edition of *New Atalanta* containing the interview with Ann Mitchison, she had found it more to her taste than any of the others and had taken to buying it now and again. Overestimating her interest in it, Oliver had bought her a year's subscription for her birthday. It was nice to relax with.

It arrived one Saturday morning when they were having a lie-in before setting off for the wedding of one of Gina's cousins. She opened the envelope and the magazine came apart in her hands. She picked up the bit that had fallen to the floor, examined it and handed it to Oliver. 'I think this is yours.'

'I'm not a New Atalanta Man, thank you very much,' he said, making a camp gesture.

'Of course you are. You're married to me.'

' "BURNOUT!" ' he read dramatically.

'Eh?'

'It's an extract from a novel about a man who . . . oh, *yes*. How true.'

She tried to read over his shoulder. He pushed her away. '*New Atalanta Man*,' he said. 'M-A-N. That means it's mine.'

'How is your burnout these days, anyway?' she said, slipping her hand inside his pyjamas. To her astonishment, he was hard.

'It's burned out,' he said. 'Or at least I thought it had. Now look what you've done. Get out. Or don't. The way this fellow deals with his burnout, I'll have to think about getting it again.'

'What does he do?'

'Develops an overwhelming lust for women.'

'Which he satisfies?'

'Whenever he can, from the looks of things. And wherever . . . and however . . .' He flicked through the pages, stopping occasionally to concentrate on a paragraph.

'Be my guest,' said Gina, picking up her own magazine.

'Eh?'

'Lie next to your wife in bed and give yourself erections from reading pornography.'

'It's not pornography, it's erotica.'

'Oliver, either you stop reading that thing or I'm getting up.'

'But you gave it to me. Perhaps you're right, though.' He dropped his magazine on to the floor beside the bed. 'Why read about it when you can do it?' He was trying to move her into position to make love to her from behind, a thing she quite liked on some occasions. This was not one of the occasions. Neither of them spoke. With the utmost tenderness, grace and display of good manners, they fought. Oliver crawled round behind Gina and put his hand up her nightie. Gina faked a moan of ecstasy and fell on her back. Oliver's arms went under her shoulders, hauling her up and round while he kissed her mouth. Gina pushed him off balance and sat with her full weight on his stomach while she stroked his face. He bucked her off. She wondered why they were not speaking. Each of them knew what the other was up to. They were capable of the most ribald conversations, in bed and out of it. They were capable of speaking their desires and usually sought to accommodate them. The romantic explanation for this silence was that they were listening to the language of their bodies. Less comfortable was the possibility that Oliver was as embarrassed as Gina was. She wanted this to stop. She could not find a way to stop it. She lay on her side, sideways and facing would be best. It was awkward, but for now it would be best. He started to climb over her. She pushed him back and got on top. *Well, if you really want to make an issue of it*, said his face. She had won – she supposed she had won – but she was glad when it was over. They did not complete their planned lie-in. By silent mutual consent, they got out of bed. Oliver went to the bathroom, slamming the door. Gina made the bed, tidied up and tore *New Atalanta Man* in half.

'That's what fascists do,' said Oliver.

'You made me jump – '

'Censor stuff that they don't approve of. Whether or not they've read it. If you're turning into one of these women who think there's some great principle at stake when you make love, for heaven's sake tell me what the principle is.'

'Sorry,' she said. She had been wrong to destroy his magazine. As he said, she had not read it.

He kissed her gently. 'If you want to fight battles, fight *real* battles,' he said.

They had breakfast in their dressing gowns, not wanting to put on their wedding clothes until it was time to leave. Oliver had hired a morning suit. Gina had bought a dress the colour of marigolds and a rather *outré* hat. She modelled it. Oliver said, 'My God.'

'Why not?' she replied. 'My cousin doesn't get married every day.'

'One or other of them seems to.'

The phone rang. 'Isn't that a sweet sound?' Gina sighed, getting up to answer it. 'Now that we know it won't be Hilary?' Hilary had been replaced by a new young graduate, pleasant, efficient, office-based and a strict adherent (at the insistence of his wife, who was at home all week with their baby) to the doctrine that a weekend was a weekend.

It was Trevor.

'I really hate to bother you on a Saturday, Gina, but we've got a bit of a problem here.'

For Oliver's amusement, she nodded her head about to the rhythm of Trevor's hedging and hinting. *Wants a babysitter*, she mouthed, rolling her eyes.

'You see, what's happened is this.'

Gina waited.

'Could you just get here?'

'Trevor, I'd love to help, but we're off to a wedding. Sorry, I'm not laughing at you, it's just that I've got the hat on.'

'It's a bit more complicated than that, I'm afraid.'

'Sorry?'

'Look,' said Trevor. 'You're not going to like this. In fact, you're going to be furious and I won't blame you. But could we make an agreement that you'll be angry later, and for now you'll do what has to be done to put the situation right? In the interests of the company?'

'What situation?'

'I'd rather you just got here.'

'I'm not moving an inch.'

'Hilary hasn't been well as you know – '

'I'm saving my anger for later, Trevor. Could you save the excuses and tell me what you want?'

'Hilary's been setting up calls for herself.'

'She has been what?'

'She's been . . . well, sometimes she thinks she's still at work.'

'Jesus.'

'I only found out today, otherwise I'd have stopped her. Fortunately it hasn't got out of hand. She hasn't actually been anywhere yet. She's just been making appointments.'

'With my customers?'

'No, it's not that bad. I got that out of her. She's been phoning round her old customers – people who've left Stalton's for one reason or another. She thinks she can win them back. She got this idea that if she did it informally and they didn't come back, nothing would be lost, whereas if they did – as a result of her efforts – it would stand her in good stead when she applies for – it's crazy, of course, and very wrong of her. She sees that now. But she's arranged to see someone today, and now she's ill.'

'She'd better ring him up and put him off.'

'That's what I mean about it being complicated,' said Trevor. 'He's made a special arrangement to see her on a Saturday – they're old friends – and it's a biggie. His company's involved in a new flyover project – '

'Trevor, I – '

'I know, I know. She's not an employee of Stalton's, and the customer is in your territory. She would have told you, mind. She was looking forward to it, ringing up on Monday and telling you she'd got you an order.'

'Well, that was very big of her.' Gina raged and blustered, but it was no good. The customer was in her territory and so he was her responsibility. If he were let down by a person with whom he had, in good faith, made an appointment, it would not interest him to know that that person had had no right to make the appointment. At best the order would go to a competitor, and the man's opinion of Stalton's would fall. He would tell his friends. He would talk about the unreliability of Stalton's in general, and its women employees in particular. At worst, he would put in a complaint. The complaint could not, with any justice, be levelled against Gina . . . but who was talking about justice? Some of the mud would stick to her.

'You'll have to go to the wedding on your own,' she told Oliver.

'What? It's your family.'

'I thought you liked families!' she screamed, pulling off her wedding hat.

54

The Foremans' front door was open when she arrived. Trevor rushed out as Gina went in. 'Bless you, Gina.' He got into his car and drove away.

Gina had already decided on the attitude she was going to adopt towards Hilary. If ever she had been a professional, she would be a professional today. If you had to do business with somebody, you put aside your feelings and conducted yourself with courtesy and efficiency . . . and speed. Your thoughts were your own.

'Just coming,' called Hilary from upstairs. Gina went into the sitting room, which looked as if it had recently been lifted up and shaken. The tiny figure of Jeremy slouched in the armchair, staring at an Open University programme on the television. He was moodily licking the side of a plastic cup which contained a bright yellow milk drink. Much of the drink had gone into the upholstery. *It's not his fault*, she thought. 'Hullo, Jeremy. When do you sit for your degree?' He ignored her.

Hilary appeared wearing a suit that Gina recognized as one of the items that she had succeeded in dissuading Hilary from sending to Goddess Garments. Gina had thought Hilary's announced intention to send all her business clothes a somewhat theatrical gesture, put on for Gina's benefit. Hilary's hair looked in serious need of a wash, but apart from that she was unusually smart: bright-eyed, made up and with a new Stalton Industries folder in her hand, the information on the cover recently filled in. 'This is so good of you, Gina. Trevor said you were going to a wedding.'

Gina made a noncommittal sound and put out her hand for the folder.

'The gods have smiled on your kindness. Sally's asleep.'

'Are those the notes on the customer?'

'Yes, he's such a darling. I'd have hated to miss him. Now, where's my briefcase – ?'

'Just a minute, Hilary. Where do you think you're going?'

'To see my customer.'

'You're not going anywhere. You haven't got a customer.'

'I have, I have, and I've got to see him. You're staying here with the children.'

'No, Hilary. That was not the arrangement.'

'But Trevor said – '

'I don't think he did, and if he did there's been a misunderstanding. This is my customer and I'm going to see him. I thought you were ill.'

'I got better.'

'Good. Now, if you'll just give me the notes on my customer – '
There was a long pause, after which Hilary handed over the folder with an expression suggesting a hope that it would blow up in Gina's face.

'You're very angry with me, aren't you, Gina? I can tell. You think I shouldn't have done this.'

'I think that, yes. But as a matter of interest – ' Gina stopped, remembering her resolution not to enter into discussion or recriminations. Anger got the better of her. 'As a matter of interest, given that you did set up the appointment, and given your miraculous recovery from your illness, why couldn't Trevor have stayed here with the children?'

'I thought he would. I didn't know he'd arranged to go and see his mother.'

'Doesn't his mother like to see her grandchildren? He could have taken them.'

'He won't!'

'I see. Well, I'll be off.'

'Gina – '

'What?'

'Are you going to report me to Stalton's?'

'I don't know.'

'It'll ruin my chances if you do.'

Gina said nothing. Impulsively, Hilary picked up her son and cuddled him. As a display of executive smartness coupled with maternal affection, it was grotesque. Jeremy did not want to be picked up. He pummelled his mother with his fists and screamed. Hilary put him down, roughly and with disgust.

'When you get back, Gina, will you come and see me? There's something I have to tell you before you make your decision.'

'Decision?'

'About putting in a report.'

Gina sighed. 'I'm not going to report you to make trouble for you. But I'm not going to let you make trouble for me.'

'So you'll come and see me?'

'I might.'

Hilary said nastily, 'You'll have to come. I've been a very bad girl, I've made some other appointments. If I'm not allowed to keep them, you'll have to. And you won't be able to if you don't know when they are, will you?' Gina made no comment. Hilary became sweet and sunny. 'We'll see you off,' she said, as if her threat had not been uttered. 'Come on, Jeremy, let's go and see Gina off. Good luck, Gina. Give my love to Harry.'

Gina thought she would not have minded giving Hilary's love to Harry, or even some of her own, had she met him in different circumstances. He was, as Hilary had said, a darling: in his forties, cuddly, chestnut-haired, bedroom-eyed, good-humoured. She doubted that he had in fact come into work on a Saturday especially to receive a call from Stalton's. He looked as if he would have been glad of the excuse. He looked as if he worked a nine-day week and throve on it. 'Hullo,' he said, as she entered the prefabricated shed that was his office, in a goods yard behind a railway station. 'Do you want me?'

Gina introduced herself.

'What happened to Hilary?'

'Didn't she phone to say I was coming instead?'

'No . . . are you the girl she works with?'

'Not exactly.' Gina did not go into details. She might have liked to: Harry looked as if his would be a sympathetic ear, even if he were a friend of Hilary's . . . not that good a friend, surely, if he did not know that Hilary had left the company and was barking mad . . . Gina took a grip of herself and tried to stop staring at his hypnotic, quizzical eyes. It was difficult to miss the eyes. They remained on her as if he had never heard anything so new or fascinating as her recital of the features and benefits of Stalton Industries' bitumen, its many grades, its competitive prices, its reliable deliveries to site, the back-up advisory service . . . he interrupted her only when somebody interrupted him, snatching up his phone with: 'Do you want me?' This seemed to be a catch phrase of his. He did not say his name or number, he said, 'Do you want me?' He said it when one of his drivers came in with a query and he said it when his wife put her head round the door – apologizing to Gina for intruding – to leave some shopping for Harry to bring home later. Gina was rather sorry to see the wife. She had just been starting to wonder dreamily whether 'Do you want me?' was a sign of a secret insecurity, one that could only be cured by . . . but he seemed fond of his wife, reaching out to squeeze her hand as she passed by his desk to leave the shopping.

'Thank you, Gina,' he said, when she had finished her presentation . . . a presentation which, she might suppose from the look upon his face, had been unique among its kind. 'I knew all that,' he said.

'You did?'

'Yes, that's word for word what Hilary told me over the phone. And I told her that I've got a special deal lined up with BP, and, frankly, you're nowhere near it.'

There had been no mention of this in Hilary's notes. Hilary had filled in Harry's Customer Record Form – and, presumably, the forms of all her other imagined customers – with a meticulousness that would have been pathetic if it were not so terrifying. She had chronicled Harry's long record as a Stalton's customer in erstwhile days, and described his being lured away by BP (before Gina's time, she had been relieved to note), but she had not mentioned any special deal relating to the flyover project currently under discussion. Under 'comments', Hilary had described her certainty that the 'close personal rapport' she had with Harry would lead him to see the error of his ways in the matter of BP, whom Hilary knew, from private research, to be making problems for him.

Gina wondered if she should try a bit of reckless discounting. She was not supposed to do this without prior authorization, but if her sales manager cut up rough she could say, 'I'm sorry, Paul, but he had such nice eyes.'

'So you're quite happy with BP?' she asked.

'We're practically in bed together.'

'So why – ?' She could not say it.

He laughed, but pleasantly. 'Why are you here? Don't ask me, Gina. I told Hilary she'd be wasting her time, but she said she wanted to come, and it's a weakness of mine. I can't say no to a lady.'

'But you're saying no to me?' she teased. 'I know, I know, don't say it – that's no lady, that's a rep.'

She drove straight home. In the matter of Hilary, she had decided on a compromise. She would not put in a formal complaint against her – she doubted that a procedure existed for doing so against someone who was not a member of staff but only thought they were – but she would tell Paul what had happened. This would cover Gina against any similar oddities in Hilary's behaviour in the future. Having decided to do this, she had nothing to discuss with Hilary.

The house was empty and quiet. She guessed that Oliver had gone, after all, to the wedding. She hoped he had enjoyed himself. She went upstairs to collect her copy of *New Atalanta*, her reading of which had been so rudely interrupted that morning. She put some music on, poured herself a gin and tonic, and relaxed.

She must subconsciously have known that Hilary would come round. When she heard her car draw up, she knew who it was, even though she was not aware of there being anything distinctive about the sound the car made. She was surprised that Hilary had brought the children, though. It was long past their bedtime. Hilary left Sally sleeping in the car and brought Jeremy in, yawning and rubbing his eyes.

'How did it go?' said Hilary, who was still wearing her suit but who appeared to have been doing some cooking in it, minus an apron. 'Did you get the order?'

'There was no order to get.'

'Never mind. Better luck next time. That's right, you have a drink.'

'Would you like a drink, Hilary?'

'Please. And could Jeremy have some milk?'

'Sure . . . is Sally all right out there?'

''Course. My God, you're going to make a fussy mother, Gina. They're tough. Aren't you, Jeremy, eh?' She hit him playfully. He dropped his cup of milk and hit her back with all his strength. 'See what I mean? They grow up anyway, you know. Get it over in one fell swoop, that's my advice.'

'I'll remember,' said Gina, going for a cloth.

'Are you going to?' said Hilary, when Gina returned. 'Is it still plan A? Babies in four years?'

'Not necessarily, and it's none of your business. Do you want to lie down on the sofa, Jeremy? You look tired. And I'm tired too, so if you –'

'*Tired?*' The word came out of Hilary's throat like a bark from a dog. 'Tired? You don't know the meaning of – ' she took a sip at her gin and resumed her normal voice. 'It'll work out perfectly, Gina. Sally's obviously going to be very bright, so she can go to school early. I'll look after your customers and you'll be looking after me and the Beach Boys.'

'I said, not necessarily.'

'Why not?' said Hilary, turning savage again. 'It's not natural. What about Oliver? I know what it is. You've been using me, haven't you? You've been watching me because you wanted to know what it was like. You never wanted to help me. You've obstructed me all the way. When your turn comes you'll want people to adapt, but you've never heard of adapting.'

'May I remind you of what I've just done today? For you?' It was no use. It was noncommunication time again. The noncommunication of the insane. Hilary looked like a ghost. Jeremy lay on the sofa, eyes closed, still as a corpse. 'Don't you think you've said enough? Don't you think you'd better take him home?'

'I'd rather leave him here.'

Now we're getting to it, Gina thought. 'Don't you . . . like having them?'

'I hate it.'

'I see.'

'I didn't think it would be like this. All the fuss and never being able to get anything finished and never being on my own and the mess – I mean, you just went bananas about a drop of milk on your carpet, for me it's like that *all the time* – ' Hilary was on the verge of tears; suddenly she was rational and charming again. 'Gina, listen. Suppose you were going on a flight. You're sitting there waiting to take off and a voice comes over the intercom: "Good morning, this is your captain, Lorraine Smith, speaking – " ' Hilary's voice was a cruel imitation of Lorraine, a secretary in the Stalton's travel department.

'As long as Lorraine knew her stuff, I wouldn't give it a second thought.'

' "And I am flying this plane as part of a special positive discrimination work experience programme for dimwit women – " '

'Stop the plane, I want to get off.'

'Of course you do. But this is the sort of thing that can happen. And people like us get tarred with the same brush. The law says Stalton's have to hire women, so they do. They're not allowed to fire us for getting pregnant, so they don't. But that doesn't mean they like it. They hate it. They hate pregnancy. It's untidy. They'd like us to go away and produce fully formed chemistry graduates from an injection moulder. They watch out for the first excuse to downgrade us or get rid of us – they did it to me and they'll do it to you. If we let them. If we don't stick together. We have a responsibility to stick together – so why are you making all this fuss about stains on the carpet, why are you trying to cut my throat? Whoops.' Hilary spilled gin. It was deliberate.

'Give me that and get out.' Gina made a grab for the glass. Hilary dodged her and dropped it. It hit the side of a bookshelf and smashed. Glinting slivers rained down on to the cover of *New Atalanta*. Gin soaked it. Gina was afraid. Hilary picked up the jagged stump of the glass. Jeremy started to scream. Gina backed away and fell into an armchair. Hilary held her there, bringing the glass closer and closer to her face. Gina heard her say, 'You're trying to cut my throat, Gina. We have a responsibility,' and then there was nothing but the bite of glass into her neck, pain, blood and the smell of gin.

Closing

55

Dear Mrs Mitchison, I am giving a small party at my home for some of my clients and friends. I would be delighted if you and your son could come along. Yours sincerely, Gwendoline Hutton.

At her home? thought Ann. *I thought I wasn't allowed to see the rest of it.*

'Gwendoline, eh?' said Tom. 'I thought her name was "Yes. Goodbye." '

'You'll come, won't you?'

'If I have to.'

'I'd like you to.'

But he did not. He said he would, but Shelly rang up at the last minute wanting to see him. Disgusted, Ann mimed summoning a dog: 'Come here, boy! What's she got that I haven't?'

'You really want to know?'

'No. But it's bad manners to accept an invitation and not turn up. When did I last ask you to go anywhere with me?' She abandoned her nagging. It was not his fault that she felt shy and anxious. *Some of my clients and friends.* That would include men. Would it include the bishop? Would he be able to tell that Ann was the kind of woman who went to craft fairs for the social side, meaning the sexual side?

That was all it had been for Toby. She saw this clearly now. He was not serious about selling his pipes. He had said as much. He went to craft fairs to get over the loss of his wife. He had already got over it because he had 'liked' her. He had said that too, worming it out of Ann that, although she still grieved quietly for Neale, she had no sense of unfinished business with him, she had laid his memory to rest and had no obligations.

Having established that, he had taken her home and made love to her, and had not been in touch with her since.

She had made sure that he knew how he could get in touch. She had given it a great deal of thought. She remembered lying in bed beside him while he slept. *I can't stay out all night*, she had thought. *I've got to get back to Audrey's.*

It would have felt bad-mannered to wake him. She had wished that she had brought her car. (Would that have been bad-mannered? To insist on going out to dinner with him in her own car?) It would not have done much good even if she had brought it. She had not known where she was.

She had moved about and made a few sounds in the hope that he would wake up naturally. Neale used to be like this: full of the joys of spring before sex, dead as winter after it – but it did not matter when you were man and wife. The two of you would still be there in the morning.

Finally she had got up and looked for a telephone and a Yellow Pages to call a taxi.

'What address, madam?'

She had given Audrey's address.

'But what address do you want to be picked up from?'

'I don't know – ' she had realized. She had banged down the phone in embarrassment. She imagined the taxi people guessing the situation and sniggering. *Still, they don't know who I am*, she had thought. *They don't know who I am, but I've just given them our Audrey's address. Just my luck if they know her.*

She had searched around for an envelope or something giving the address of where she was. If he woke up now, he might think she was having a snoop . . . if he woke up. He had not woken up and she had not found the address. She had opened the front door to check the number. 53. Number fifty-three, what? She had put her clothes on properly and hurried to the end of the road to find its name. She had left the front door open – keeping an eye on it – so that she could get back in without waking him. He might be angry if she woke him. She had returned and called another taxi company. Still he had slept.

'Dear Toby, I had to get back to my daughter's as she might be worried – '

Worried about what, exactly?

' – sorry for – '

Sorry for leaving you?

He might have been counting on it.

Don't be silly, she had thought, though she did not think that now, not after three weeks.

She had thought herself clever, writing her message on the back of a Mitchison's Working Models business card, as if it were the only thing to hand, as if giving him her address were a secondary matter.

Maybe that's what's wrong, she thought. *Maybe he thought it was a bit cold. Three weeks? Three weeks is nothing.*

Her message had not been cold at all. She had thanked him for a lovely evening – not specifying what she meant – and signed 'Love, Ann.' She had not meant to imply anything or jump the gun, but . . . well, what else was there? Best wishes? Yours sincerely?

Miss Hutton's living room was not at all spinsterish, as Ann had expected. It was furnished as for a person who had money and intended to enjoy it. The armchairs were of the old-fashioned type, large and deep and soft, but freshly covered. There was a television, a video recorder, a hi-fi system that would have had Tom writhing with envy, and more books than Ann had ever seen outside a library. They were not all about accountancy. Miss Hutton appeared to have wide interests; art and history, travel and novels. The only odd thing about the room was that there were lumps of rock everywhere.

Miss Hutton wore a long, colourful print frock. Her hair was still pinned up, but it was looser than Ann had seen it. She served drinks with a generous hand and introduced Ann to some of her other small-business clients. When these were men, she found herself tongue-tied. She could not think what she had said to Toby to lead him on, so what if she said it again? When they were couples, it was even worse. The wives might see her as a predatory widow. Wives might have been seeing her as that all these years.

'Is it still orange juice?' said Miss Hutton, moving towards her with a crystal jug.

'Yes please.'

'I'd like you to meet some friends of mine. Susan Clark and Adela Griffiths-Robins. Ann Mitchison.'

Adela Griffiths-Robins was about Ann's age and one of those people whom fat seemed to suit. 'Are you both accountants too?'

'For my sins,' said Adela Griffiths-Robins. 'Sue's a builder.'

'What do you build?'

'I don't do it personally,' said Susan Clark, who was in her late thirties and red-haired. 'Are you one of Gwen's businesses?'

'She's helped me a lot.'

'Ann's in craft distribution.'

'My God, is there a living in that?'

'Well, it's difficult, because you're competing with people who do it as a hobby, and – '

'You're brave,' said Adela Griffiths-Robins.

Miss Hutton told everyone to help themselves from the buffet, which looked wonderful. Ann was not hungry, but she took the opportunity to move away from Miss Hutton's friends. She had run out of things to say to them. They were kind, but she thought she was probably supposed to talk to the other small-business people.

'Sorry your son couldn't make it,' said Miss Hutton, seeing her standing alone.

'He's sorry too. His girlfriend – '

'He could have brought her along. Still, as long as he hasn't gone off with those Rideemus people – ' she left the sentence hanging, the first time Ann had ever heard her do this.

'No, we've not had any more trouble from them.'

'It's odd, very odd. Adela – ' Adela came over, chewing a piece of pork pie. 'Adela's a very keen churchgoer. Have you heard of Rideemus?'

'No, what is it?'

'Bunch of Christians who go around trying to part people from their money.'

'So-called Christians, then. Gwen is very cynical about God, Ann, but He tells me it's mutual.'

'If He knew what I know about bishops – '

Ann wondered what she had done to earn the right to see Miss Hutton in this mood. Perhaps it was just that she kept her social self and her work self separate. That was the professional thing to do. It was the thing that Ann had failed to do at the Carlisle craft fair.

'Any time I want to know anything about God, I look at one of these.' She picked up a piece of rock. It shone like gold and had a tiny shell embedded in it. 'A pyritized ammonite.'

'But Miss Hutton, it's beautiful.'

'Please call me Gwen. I found it in Dorset.'

'She means she hacked it out of a cliff face with her bare hands while suspended from a rope,' said Adela.

Gwen smiled benignly. 'Are you interested in geology, Ann?'

'Don't say yes unless you're an acrobat. Remember that weekend in Northumberland, Sue? My back's still not right.'

'Well –'

'It's fascinating,' said Gwen. 'I sometimes think I'll give up accountancy and concentrate on it.'

Ann said, 'I don't know where I'd – where we'd all be without you.'

'How nice of you to say that. I won't give up yet. Now this is a schist. You see those little black specks? We need a lens. Adela, could I borrow your glasses? Thank you.' Gwen held one of the lenses over the rock. Ann gasped. 'What are they?'

'That's mica and those are garnets.'

'Garnets? I've got a client who makes jewellery. You could sell this. I could sell it for you.'

'*Sell it?*'

Adela choked on her pork pie. 'You didn't mean sell that particular one, did you, Ann? You were just speaking in a general way.'

'In a general way, yes,' said Ann.

She went home feeling cheerful. She always went home feeling cheerful these days, particularly if Tom too had been out in her absence. The possibility that the phone had been ringing and ringing and would soon ring again would keep her cheerful for at least half an hour.

Tom was watching television, drinking lager. 'You're back early,' she said.

'Aye.'

'Had a row with Shelly?' She should not have said that. She might once have said that theirs was a relationship in which private affairs could safely be discussed, but that belonged to the days when she had had no private affairs. She had not told Tom about Toby. She had told him that she had met a man and had had dinner with him – he would have got that from Audrey if he had not got it from her – but she had stressed Toby's role as a potential client. Whether Tom believed this or not she did not know; but he had not mentioned it, so Toby remained her secret. And if she was keeping secrets from him, she had no right to probe into his secrets.

'Anyone phone?'

'No. Mam, I've got to tell you something. Shelly's pregnant.'

'You bloody fool!'

'It's not my fault.'

'Who else's?'

'She always said she was on the pill.'

'She always – what do you mean, always? *Always?* How long have you been – ?'

'Ah, Mam, come on. We're not living in the Victorian age.'

She could hit him. She had not hit him since he was seven years old but she could hit him now.

'Bloody right we're not living in the Victorian age, when a man knew how to respect a woman and a woman knew how to respect herself.' She heard what she was saying. 'Well, what's done's done,' she said. It had been on the cards that Tom would marry Shelly anyway. 'What have you said to her?'

'I said I'd marry her if she wanted me to.'

'I hope you didn't say it like that.'

Tom did not reply.

'I said I hope you didn't say it like that, Tom! What did she say? When will you be getting married?'

'She doesn't want to.'

'*What?* She's going to have an abortion?'

'No, Mam.' Tom looked bitter. 'No, she's not going to have an abortion. She says if I don't want the baby she'll have it by herself.'

'She's just saying that. Where did she get the idea that you didn't want . . . ah, Tom, come on. You've been going out with that lass for some time now, you must be fond of her.'

'Of course I'm fond of her but she's gone all funny.'

'*She*'s gone all funny! Tom, listen. I don't care what you say. Victorian age or not, pills or not, sex is . . . well, it's different for a woman . . .'

'There's no need to cry, Mam.'

' . . . it's important. Shelly's not the sort of lass to do it if she didn't think you were going to . . . if she didn't think you meant . . .'

'Tell *her* that! I've offered to marry her.'

'But you don't *offer* to marry someone, Tom. As if you were doing them a favour. You should want to!'

'Mam, I've told you. It's her that doesn't want to.'

56

She was being absurdly old-fashioned about this. It was in a business context that she had met him, so there was no reason why she should not write him a business letter. Or even make a business phone call.

If it came to that, there was no reason why she should not write him a personal letter. *Look at it this way, Ann. Suppose you're right. Suppose he does it all the time. Suppose you're nothing to him.*

I'm not nothing. I may not be the love of his life but I am not nothing. Shelly doesn't think she's nothing.

Ann had been brought up on a strict code of morals. You did not do it until you were married, and that was that. It was more than morals, it was practical. You had your reputation to consider, and the risk of pregnancy. There was also the matter of keeping something to bargain with. *Why buy a book when you can borrow it from the library?*

Shelly did not consider herself a library book. If anyone was being treated as a library book in that little business, it was Tom. Shelly was keeping her options open.

Ann did not believe that Shelly really meant to turn Tom down and have the baby on her own. Her parents would never stand for it, for one thing. They were furious about the whole situation: furious with Shelly, furious with Tom, furious, by implication, with Ann.

No, Shelly was flirting. She was making Tom want her with her pretended coolness. Was Toby playing the same game with Ann? Did he not realize that it was unnecessary, since she wanted him anyway?

She was not nothing and she was not a library book. She and Toby were friends. For heaven's sake. They had been out to dinner together, at his invitation. They had chatted as friends. Never mind what else they had done. It was immaterial. (It was not immaterial to her, but it might be to him.) All right. Fair enough. If that was the way he wanted it. But they could still be friends, couldn't they? Colleagues?

She went to see a few tobacconists and asked if they were interested in craftsman-made pipes. They said they might be, if they could see them.

She knew it was wrong to do this – waste time trying to sell something that she had not got and might never get – and she missed an appointment on behalf of one of her real clients to do it; but it seemed important.

'Dear Toby,' she wrote. 'I have a number of retail outlets who would be interested in seeing samples of your pipes – ' she finished the letter ' – hope you are well, see you soon, yours sincerely Ann, Ann Mitchison, Ann Mitchison Craft Distribution.' She did not re-read it. She posted it. It was done. The ball was in his court now. If he did not respond, well, she could take a hint.

The ball had been in his court all along. He would see through this. He had said that he did not want her to distribute his pipes. No, he had not said that. He had said that, once she saw his workshop (she had not seen his workshop) she herself would be the one who would not want to distribute them because she would see how amateurish he was.

She was like the condemned man, allowed to write one letter. She had written it. Had it been the right one? She could do no more. That knowledge gave her a kind of peace.

His phone call did not interrupt that peace. She had herself rigidly under control.

'Ann! Lovely to hear from you!'

She waited.

'Look, you've persuaded me,' he said. 'I've put a couple of pipes in the post to you, all right?'

All right? she thought. *I was hoping you might want to give them to me personally.*

'How *are* you?' he said.

'Very well, thank you.'

'We must get together soon. Did you get home all right?'

'Looks like it.'

'Sorry I didn't get up.' He spoke as if it were yesterday that it had happened. 'I was dead to the world.'

The world can take care of itself, she thought. *You were dead to me.*

'Are you going to the York craft fair?' he said.

'Yes,' she said.

'I'll see you there, then.'

'Yes,' she said. 'Goodbye.' *Two can play the yes-goodbye game,* thought. But she could not stop herself replaying the conversation endlessly in her mind. *Lovely to hear from you,* he had said. *We must get together soon. See you at the craft fair in York.* He had also said that he had sent her some pipes, which came, in a parcel postmarked the day after his phone call. That was very interesting. He had not needed to make the phone call at all, so he must have wanted to.

She went back to work and looked forward to the craft fair in York. A letter came from Customs and Excise. They wanted to know why she was not registered for VAT. *Come round here and I'll tell you,* she thought. Gwen Hutton had explained the regulations to her. Ann knew from talking to other self-employed people that VAT inspectors had a reputation for enthusiasm: kicking your front door down at 4 am. They were welcome, as far as Ann was concerned. If ever her turnover reached the astonishing figure that made VAT registration compulsory, she would be able to afford several new doors.

'Are you saying you want to register voluntarily?' said Gwen. 'There are some advantages, but it would involve a lot more paperwork and you would have to put your prices up. I thought we'd been into all that.'

'But why do they keep asking me?'

'It's probably routine. Write and explain the situation.'

'You think it's a mistake?'

'Yes,' said Gwen Hutton. 'Goodbye.'

'Thought I might come with you tomorrow, Mam,' said Tom the night before the craft fair.

'What?'

'Meet the customers. Pick up a few ideas.'

'Well, if you'd wanted to do that, why didn't you come to Carlisle? You could have seen your sister.'

'Don't you want me to come?'

'Suit yourself, but there'll not be a lot of room in the car.'

He raised his eyebrows. She had to laugh. 'Don't look at me in that tone of voice.'

'Have a good time at the craft fair, Mam.'

'Why shouldn't I?'

The doorbell rang. It was Terry Ainsworth, Shelly's father. 'Is Shelly here?'

'No.'

'Is Tom?'

'He is, aye, but – ' Ann felt protective of her son. She had said everything to him that needed saying, and the situation was not entirely of his making, not by any means.

'Oh, hello, Mr Ainsworth,' said Tom.

'Evening. Where is she?'

'How should I know?'

'Have you seen her today?'

'I've not seen her for weeks.'

'Is that true?'

'If he says it, it's true. What's happened, Terry? You'd better come in.'

'She had a row with her mother,' said Terry, sitting down, his anger fading behind his anxiety. 'I wasn't there, but from the sound of things they both said things they shouldn't. Shelly walked out and she's not been back.'

'I haven't seen her, honestly, Mr Ainsworth.'

'No, well, I was hoping – '

'Have any of her things gone?' Ann asked.

'A few. Enough to tell us she's not been taken anywhere against her will. Not enough to say it's permanent. As if she'd gone away for the weekend. You know?'

Tom swore. Ann did not react, guessing that he was thinking what she was thinking. If Shelly had another man in her life, that would explain a great deal.

'Have you been to the police?'

'Not yet. Her mother's phoning round her friends.'

Tom said, 'I know where she might have gone.'

'Where?'

'Rideemus House.'

'Where's that?' said Terry.

'It's these church people that helped us out with the models when me and Shelly were – '

'When you and Shelly were engaged, you mean? So that you could apply for a job?' Terry shook his head, as if it were beyond his understanding. 'Well, if it's something to do with the church – '

'Tell him, Mam.'

'They're not a proper church. We don't know that much about them. Our accountant's got a friend who's a bishop, and he says they might be a cult. Tom, why would Shelly – ?'

'Search me. She was interested. They invited the two of us to go

on a course, this weekend. I told her to have nothing to do
it – '

'That'll be why she's gone, then,' said Terry grimly. 'Where is
this place?'

Tom fetched the invitation. A phone number was given, but when
they rang it there was no reply. The address was vague: just
'Rideemus House' and the name of a town in Northumberland
which, when they found it on a map, turned out to be eight miles
from the nearest railway station. 'So how would she have got there?'

' "Let us know if you need transport." '

'Bloody hell.'

'Terry, she'd surely not have gone off without saying – ' *not perfect
little Michelle*, Ann added to herself.

'She's done a number of things lately that I thought she'd never
do. I'm going there in the morning.'

Tom said, 'I want to come.'

'You! She'll take one look at you and sign on for life.'

'I want to come.'

Ann said, as gently as she could, 'It might be better if you didn't.'

Terry tried to take the invitation off Tom. 'Give me that address.'

'I'll give it to you in the morning when you pick me up.'

'I've got the address, Terry,' said Ann, remembering the invoices.
She felt treacherous but she had to do it. Tom became desperate.
'I want to come, damn it. I don't want anything to happen to Shelly.'

'When she's got your baby in her.'

'Please, Mr Ainsworth.'

Ann took Terry to the door. 'He really wants to come.'

'He only appreciates her when he thinks he's lost her.'

'And that's a thing that never happened before between a man
and a woman.'

Terry Ainsworth shrugged and sighed. 'Tell him to be up and
ready at six o'clock, then. But he's staying in the car when we get
there.'

The York craft fair was held in an Arts Centre. Unlike the fair at
Carlisle, where everyone had been in one big hall, today the stalls
were arranged throughout the building in rooms. There was a plan in
the front lobby showing where everybody was: Mitchison's Working
Models in the dance studio, Toby Hamilton Pipes in the theatre
space. She made her way to the dance studio with brisk footsteps.

She could not expect him to come looking for her during the first
hour or two of the fair. He would be doing business, as she was,

and how well you did in the first hour or two often set the tone for the day. She sold so many models that she hardly gave him a thought. She wondered if he might come along and suggest lunch (having asked whoever was next to him to mind his stock), and she could offer to share her sandwiches with him.

He kissed her on the mouth in front of her customers and ruffled her hair. 'Ann, how lovely to see you. How long has it been?'

If he really wanted to know, she could tell him. To the minute. 'How's business going?' she said.

'Well, you know how it is.'

'Got any pipes for me?'

'There might be one or two left over.'

'I've got customers waiting for them.'

'Sssh,' he said. 'You're not an agent, remember?'

'I'd forgotten.'

'May I say something personal?'

She waited.

'I knew I missed you,' he said. 'But I hadn't realized how much until I saw you.'

She replied cautiously, 'Absence makes the heart grow fonder.'

It was only when he had eaten his sandwiches and returned to his selling that she realized that this was, in fact, the opposite of what he had said.

'Oh good, I'm glad I caught you before you left,' he said, when evening came. 'Can you sell these for me?' He offered her a dozen of the pipes.

'We haven't discussed my terms.'

'That's all right. Whatever arrangement you have with your other clients.' *It's just a hobby for him. But am I?* 'I'm sure it's fair. Look, I'd love for us to have dinner tonight, but . . .' *Did I say we had to have dinner? I said we hadn't discussed my terms.* ' . . . but I've promised to visit an old friend.'

'I have to get home,' she said.

'Home . . . that's Sunderland, isn't it?'

'Yes.'

'I thought so. I'll be out that way in a few weeks. Can we have a night on the town?'

'I'd love to.'

'It's a date, then?'

'It's a date.' *What date?*

57

Shelly said, 'I'm sorry if you were worried, Mrs Mitchison.'

'Tom was too.'

'Good.'

Ann sighed. 'So you were at your friend's all along?'

'I'm still here. I'm living here.'

'Oh, Shelly – ' It was none of Ann's business. The fact that Shelly was pregnant with her grandchild did not make it her business. ' – and your dad and Tom have gone all that way to look for you.'

'My dad hasn't gone anywhere. I rang them up last night.'

'So where's Tom?'

'I don't know.'

And you don't care. 'You might have let us know.'

'I expect my dad thought it wouldn't hurt Tom to stew for a bit.'

'He'll be back,' said Pat.

'But what if he's gone to Rideemus House? Terry didn't come for him so he decided to go by himself?'

'How would he have got there?'

'Hitching. Train.'

'I thought you said there was no station.'

'There's one eight miles away. Pat, I hate to ask you this, but can I keep the car tomorrow?'

'He'll be back tonight. You'll see.'

'If he's not.'

'Keep it,' said Pat. 'I never see it these days anyway. You be careful.'

*

Ann set off in the early morning. She did not know whether to be afraid or angry. Either was better than being sad. She ached with disappointment. *This time yesterday*, she kept thinking. *This time yesterday I was on my way to the craft fair. This time yesterday I knew I was going to see him. I thought I was going to know. One way or the other, I thought. By the way he looks at me, by the way he talks to me, Toby'll let me know how things are between us. And even if it's bad news, I'll have my peace of mind back.*

And I wasn't expecting bad news. I wasn't, was I? I believed what I wanted to believe. I thought we'd have gone out together last night. I don't know what I thought we'd have done afterwards. I don't know if I'd have brought him home or gone home with him. But I thought we'd be together, I thought I'd KNOW. *I can't stand this not knowing. What about the next craft fair? And the one after that?*

It was a bright, windy day. She tried to see how beautiful the countryside was. She was driving through a valley with high tree-covered slopes and outcrops of rock. What would she find at Rideemus House? Would Tom be there? She did not know whether she wanted him to be there or not. If he was not there, where would he be?

Approaching a blind corner, she slowed down. She was glad she had. Beyond the bend, a group of hikers straddled the road as if it were their own. She pressed her horn and her brake. The hikers scattered as she skidded through them, missing, though one of them tripped and fell. Ann pulled in to the side of the road and watched in her mirror as the one who had fallen picked herself up and collected the helmet – a miner's helmet, it looked like – that had come off her head. Ann supposed she ought to go back and see that everyone was all right. 'You should keep in on a bend!' she shouted.

'Oh! Hello, Ann.'

'Miss Hut – Gwen! I didn't recognize you with your helmet on.' *I didn't recognize you with it off, either. It was the boots and the anorak that fooled me.* 'You nearly got me that time!'

'I'm sorry . . . what are you . . . ?'

'I'm on a geology weekend. May I introduce my friends? James, Alice, Muriel, David, Sue . . .'

'We met at Gwen's party,' said Sue. 'How are you, Ann?'

'Is Adela here too?'

'She's on kitchen fatigues back at the Centre,' said Sue.

'Her back,' Gwen explained. 'Are you off to one of your craft fairs?'

'No, that was yesterday.' Ann started to explain where she was going. She tried to be matter-of-fact about it, but her distress must have shown, because the geologists suddenly became fascinated by something sticking out of a slope beside the road and hurried off to examine it with magnifying glasses, leaving Ann to talk to Gwen alone.

Gwen said, 'You think he might have *joined*?'

The idea was embarrassing. 'No, he's too sensible. He hadn't a good word to say about them. If he was going to join them he's had plenty of opportunity without – ' she counted off the reasons why Tom would never join a thing like Rideemus. 'But he didn't come home last night and that's not like him.'

'I don't want *you* joining them,' said Gwen.

'Me?'

'These people have ways, as the bishop said to the accountant.'

'I'm glad I've seen you, then,' said Ann. 'If I don't come back, you'll know what's happened.'

'It might save time in the long run if I come with you now. Keep an eye on you.'

Ann thought wildly, *Would I have to pay?*

'Unless you prefer to go on your own.'

'Would you . . . ?'

'I should love to. How far is it from here?'

'About fifteen miles I think. The map's confusing.'

'I shall navigate.'

'But I'd be interrupting your geology.'

'It's all right. I hate these people.' Gwen did not look as if she hated them, striding off to explain to her geology friends what was happening. When she got into the car and started talking, Ann realized that it was not the geologists that she hated: it was Rideemus. 'Cults, religions, call them what you like. Stick to rocks and figures, that's my advice. You can't go far wrong with rocks and figures. Turn left here and we'll pick Adela up from the Centre. She'll know how to talk to these people.'

Adela was lying on a bottom bunk in an upstairs room at the Centre, resting her back. She got up wincing, but willing to come. She got into the passenger seat while Gwen sat in the back, and the two of them argued while Ann drove.

'There's little enough people like Ann's son have to call their own. Why can't they leave their minds alone?'

'That's the worst kind of bigotry, Gwen. To say that anyone who takes a view contrary to yours has lost their mind.'

'Is it . . . brainwashing?' Ann ventured.

347

'You flatter them,' Gwen retorted. 'All it takes is a bit of group pressure, mass hysteria, half-baked psychiatry . . . and, of course, a charismatic leader. Some crank at the seaside going up to fishermen and rolling his eyes. "Come. Follow me." Ought to be locked up.'

'He was. You don't shock me with your blasphemy.'

'*Please don't*,' said Ann. 'I'm sorry, but – '

Adela laughed. 'Take no notice. We enjoy it.'

'Enjoy it! This is Ann's son we're talking about.'

'Tom never mentioned a leader. There was a lass called Judith but he thought she was a bit of a joke.'

'She probably is. You know how it is at pop concerts?'

'Do you go to pop concerts?'

'Now and again, don't we, Adela? When it's somebody we like. They save them for last, of course. They start you off on novices and then the real thing seems all the more attractive by comparison. We go right here, Ann.' There was a brief silence while Ann negotiated the corner. Adela had said that she and Gwen enjoyed arguing like this, but Ann found it embarrassing. And when Adela spoke again, it was in a conciliatory tone. 'The established churches must bear some of the blame, granted. Young people don't – ' Ann looked at Gwen in her mirror. She still looked angry and argumentative and quite unlike the woman Ann had known as her accountant: long hair coming out of its pins in wisps, cheeks pink from fresh air and strong emotion, and (Ann could not see, but remembered) enormous muddy boots.

'Public confessions! Self-flagellations! Visions, visitations, miracles, relics – '

'Dear oh dear, where have you been all these years?'

'It's the modern equivalent. You get a group of vulnerable people together. Isolate them. Control their food supply and their sleep. Some of them even control going to the loo.' Ann thought of the way she herself had been afraid to ask for the loo in Gwen's house, but decided not to say anything. 'You get them to talk about their problems. If you tell your problems to a stranger you're a fool because you become their hostage.'

'Tell that to your clients,' said Adela.

'You know that's entirely different. We're professionals, and if we and the clients have any sense we restrict ourselves to professional matters.' *So what are you doing now?* thought Ann. *Coming with me to find Tom?* 'If you tell someone what you need and they can fool you that they're the only person who can give it to you, they become

348

omnipotent. There's too much omnipotence around. Psychiatrists call it transference. Other people call it charisma. I call it – '

'Love?' said Ann.

'I call it a rip-off. That so-called bill they sent you, Ann – I should have realized – it was just to get your attention. Or Tom's. When they cancelled it, he was supposed to feel guilty and grateful. Indebted. What you said before about love is wrong. Love's different. Love's mutual.'

'Is it?' Ann sighed as she drove on. She wondered how much Gwen Hutton knew about love, mutual or otherwise.

Rideemus House looked a bit like the Geology Centre from which they had collected Adela. It was a square grey mansion far from anywhere, old but well maintained. 'I wonder how they pay for this,' said Gwen grimly.

'Well, how do they?' said Adela, bending her back painfully as she got out of the car.

'I expect we'll find out.' Gwen was last out of the car but she did not wait while Ann locked it. She strode towards the front door. Ann matched her pace to Adela's, who was limping.

Gwen did not knock. She turned the handle. 'Surprise, surprise, it's open,' she called.

'Gwen – '

'What?'

'Don't you think we should – ?'

'Desperate cases need desperate remedies.'

'Hello,' said a young man in jeans. 'Can I help you?'
The most aggressive question in the English language.

'We're looking for my friend's son.'

'Right. What's his name? I'm Gareth. And you are – ?'

'His name's Tom Mitchison.'

'Would you mind?' said Gareth. 'Your boots – '

'Nonsense,' said Gwen. 'Or is this a mosque?'

'I think he's worried about the carpet, aren't you?' said Ann, looking at the trail of mud. *I'd say the same if it were my carpet. Or perhaps I wouldn't.*

'We don't have a Tom Mitchison on the list of enrolments.'

'He wasn't enrolled,' said Ann. 'He came here looking for someone.'

'I see. Well, they'll be having a break soon.'

'You allow that, do you?' said Gwen.

'Of course. Would you like to take a seat and I'll get you something to drink.'

'No, we wouldn't. We want to see what's going on.'

'Great. I can enrol you for our next course. If you went in now, you wouldn't understand.'

'I think we would,' said Gwen, opening and closing doors. All the rooms were empty.

Gareth said, 'I can't let you.'

'Adela, take the basement. Ann, come upstairs with me.' Adela did not want to move. Ann said to Gareth, 'Could you bring a chair?'

'It's not a chair I need. I need to lie down flat.'

'Feel free,' said Gareth.

'Stay on your feet, both of you,' ordered Gwen, racing up the stairs with heavy footsteps.

Gareth said, 'Do you want to lie down, Mrs, er – ?'

'I do but I won't,' gasped Adela. From upstairs came a series of bangs, more doors. Gareth looked unruffled. 'She *is* worried, isn't she? I thought she said it was *your* son.' He seemed a nice enough lad and Ann felt she should explain. 'She thinks – '

'I know what they think. If your son's here, you'll see him in half an hour. Have you come far?'

'From Sunderland.'

'That's miles. Why didn't you phone?'

'There was no reply.'

'That's funny, there's always someone here.' Gwen came clattering down the stairs. Gareth looked at her with mild curiosity. 'Is she an old friend of the family, something like that?'

'Don't tell him anything, Ann. Down to the basement with me, both of you.'

'I'll stay here,' said Adela.

'Not on your own,' said Gwen.

For the first time, Gareth looked alarmed. He tried to stop them going to the basement, so Ann realized that that was where Tom would be.

' . . . know you are very special people, otherwise you wouldn't be here,' said the speaker as Ann and Gwen helped Adela into the back of the small hall. 'What each and every one of you has to decide is what you are going to do with that knowledge.' The speaker was a spotless man in a sharp-edged suit, addressing a mixed group of about forty people, old and young, male and female, some quite well dressed. Ann recognized Tom's back. He was sitting in the middle

of a row, inaccessible. ' . . . Are you going to go away from here
thinking, well, I'm special, that's nice. Or are you going to . . . hello.
We have some visitors.'

'Hello,' said Gwen. 'We'd just like to sit in.'

'I'm so sorry, that won't be possible. Have you talked to Gareth?'

'We're staying here till the break.'

'In that case,' said the speaker, 'we'll take the break now.'

For the first time, Gwen looked discomfited. The speaker was
sharper than she was. Ann did not mind. Tom was here and was to
be given a break so she would be able to talk to him and take him
home. But she was disturbed by something else. In spite of the
interruption, he had not turned round. None of them had. Ann
herself had not spoken, and there was no reason why he should
recognize Gwen's voice – Gwen had said nothing to identify herself
or indicate why she was here – but to sit in a meeting and not turn
round when someone came in and started arguing with the speaker?
It was unnatural.

'Mam! What are you doing here?'

'What are you, is more to the point. We've found Shelly, she's
fine. This is Miss Hutton, our accountant, and this is Miss Griffiths-
Robins, a friend.'

'Bloody hell.'

'Tom – '

Gwen put her arm around Adela's shoulders to help her move out
of hearing, though the two of them remained within calling distance.

'What did you bring them here for?'

'It was very kind of them.'

'They look like a couple of – '

'Tom. What is this?'

He stopped staring at Gwen and Adela, who were pointedly
rejecting the attempts of Rideemus members to engage them in
conversation and bring them chairs or tea. He smiled, looked over
his shoulder and looked mischievous. 'They're a bunch of nutters.'

She was relieved. He was his old self. 'So why are you still here?'

'I didn't get here till late. I got a lift from a feller who took me to
the wrong place. By the time I realized Shelly wasn't here – I didn't
believe them at first – I'd missed the last train.'

'There must have been trains this morning.'

'I think I can get a job out of them.'

'I doubt that very much.'

'I think I can. I'm working on it. We were talking about model-

351

making. They said God's the original model-maker. That's how they talk. They said they've been looking for someone who can make a model of God making the world. A big one. A sort of sculpture to go in front of the house. If I play my cards right, I think I can get the commission.'

58

Daphne, thought Teresa. *You've done it. It could not be done, and you have done it. Daphne Barclay Business Training. Miracles we work at once. The impossible takes a little longer.*

'We weren't too happy about all the signs on the wall,' said Beverley. 'Some of us wanted to put, "If you can get it cheaper somewhere else, it's probably been made in a sweatshop." '

'But you settled for, "If you can get it cheaper somewhere else, please do." '

'Yes. We're not in the business of guilt-tripping our customers. We decided that looking after them was our priority. Clothing workers have other people to look after them. Unions. They don't, but they're there. Who have mothers on social security got?'

'You're right,' said Teresa.

'You have to decide what your priorities are, Teresa. You might want to do everything at once, but if you try that you might end up doing nothing.'

'It was just another job,' said Daphne modestly.

'Don't give me that.' It felt easy to talk to Daphne in such a bantering way. She was her usual slick, cool self, but Teresa knew that they were friends. 'You once said to me, "If you want people to pay for something, don't let them see you giving it away free." ' She was no longer sceptical about Beverley's claim that Daphne had offered consultancy services to Goddess Garments gratis. Even if one put the most cynical interpretation on this – and Teresa hated to do it, but she had to, to try it out – the possibility that Daphne would wait until Goddess Garments was dependent on her and then send in a bill did not bear examination. The know-how and advice that Daphne had provided could not be taken away.

Still less could her inspiration be taken away. Much of what had been done had been obvious. It should not take a business consultant, or even an entire feminist collective, to work out that a shop in a derelict flat could be rendered less depressing by a few tins of paint, a professional layout and cheerful posters on the walls. That was common sense. Common sense and a dash of honesty would lead all but the most ideologically prim women to the realization that even cleaner-fish had their uses: customers who felt stigmatized by going to Goddess Garments for clothes – with its air of being a welfare service – would at least have their curiosity aroused by news that famous celebrities went there too, bought, gave, and signed the wall. And for those who thought this an elitist concept – well, everyone should sign the wall. All women are celebrities.

Coming to the shop out of curiosity, customers found not rubbish tossed away in disgust, but thoughtfully chosen gifts. (There was a section called 'RUBBISH' – tastefully displayed in a row of spotless dustbins – 'RUBBISH BUT CLEAN RUBBISH'. People could help themselves to rubbish. It emphasized the superior quality of everything else. And fewer and fewer items were coming in that fell into this category.) Customers who still disliked second-hand clothes would often find that the two-tier pricing structure enabled them to buy something new. The 'waged' and 'unwaged' prices were nothing to do with Daphne. This was a normal practice at feminist events.

It was nothing to do with Daphne. It was everything to do with Daphne. It was one thing to see what needed doing. It was quite another to believe it could be done. Daphne exuded belief. *If it weren't the best, you wouldn't be selling it. If it weren't a good idea, capable of fulfilment, you wouldn't be wasting your time on it. I wouldn't be wasting MY time.*

She had come as an outsider. She had never heard of cleaner-fish so she had no hesitation about saying things that might lead her to be called one. In her dress and manner she made no concessions. She wore high heels and make-up and ordered people about. And since she did not see herself as a cleaner-fish, no one else did either. Or, if they did, they thought, *Maybe cleaner-fish aren't so bad after all. This one may spend her days picking the teeth of sharks; but in the evenings, she comes to us.*

Daphne had never heard of the idea that meetings should not start on time or be chaired; and so, under her, they did and were. She had not the remotest interest in the difference between radical feminists, socialist feminists, bourgeois feminists, lesbian separatists; she was interested in profit and loss. She did not see black women, white women; she saw only saleswomen. An entrepreneur and a lover of beautiful clothes, she herself felt no anger against the fashion industry – grinding poverty at one end, vanity and waste at the other – but she recognized that anger in others and saw in it a marketing opportunity. Not an opportunity for great wealth to be made, but an opportunity to be efficient and of service; an opportunity to show respect and be respected; an opportunity for Goddess Garments to make a few choices about the direction in which it would go.

She lectured on management, marketing and investment. She did not know that these words were rude, so she used them. She talked about the Business Expansion Scheme. She described the process whereby a company could go public and issue a prospectus to potential shareholders. This drew gasps. She was ready for them. She had instances of charities that had set up public companies and solicited investment on the understanding that large profits would not be made. And, where suspicion still reigned, she declared, 'I am not here to be keeper of your conscience. I am here to tell you what is possible – what *I believe* to be possible.'

'I'm not doing it for nothing,' she said.

'You're not?' said Teresa one day when they were alone.

'It has been a two-way exchange. I have learned a great deal from them.'

'Such as?' Teresa hoped she knew the answer to this, but she wanted to hear Daphne say it.

'Such as that some people think it wrong to invest for profit...' Yes, that would have been hard for Daphne to swallow. Or had it been? The hallmark of Daphne's approach was that nothing should be hard to swallow. *You need it, I've got it, you can have it...*

'... not least the investors themselves.'

Teresa wished she had been there. She wished it with all her heart. Still, she could take some credit, for was it not her conversation with Daphne's partner which had arrived half-jokingly at the startling possibility that, were Goddess Garments to receive money from Europe, they might use some of it to pay for consultancy services from Daphne Barclay Business Training? 'Sounds just up my street,' Alistair had said solemnly, and Teresa had said, 'It would have to be Daphne, I'm afraid,' and they had laughed a laugh of resignation and tolerance, the laugh of parents at a wilful child.

All of which proved how wrong you could be, and Teresa wished she had witnessed Daphne's virtuoso performance at the Joanna Press pamphlet launch which, catching the attention of the buyers as all good sales presentations should, had led to the women of Collindeane Tower sitting down and listening to Daphne. They had made no promises, but they had listened. And she had listened to them. This excited Teresa almost as much as did the transformation of Goddess Garments. Daphne had listened to their accounts of their pennilessness and the reasons for it. She had gone through the books with them. She had started by saying that things were probably not as bad as they looked. After auditing the figures she had conceded that they probably were, but, she had said, rather than feel defeated by thoughts of resources they did not have, why not make the most of what they did have? What had they? They had a building. It was only a squat, but a long-term squat, and there was no sign of anyone disturbing them for the time being. They had themselves. Each woman represented a wealth of energy, skill, knowledge and experience. Teresa wished she had been there when Daphne had sat them in a circle with pieces of paper for each woman to make a list of the things she personally was good at. Daphne had not known that feminists were not supposed to talk about the things they were good at.

And they had the mailing lists. Every group had a list of supporters and former supporters, some going back many years. These, said Daphne, could be enormously valuable. Possibly, the women had retorted, but they are a trust and they are not for sale. Daphne had not been planning to sell them. She had been planning to use them.

She had taken away a copy of the Goddess Garments grant application for detailed study, this being the best available statement of the group's aims and principles, principles that made it impossible for them to apply for money from conventional sources. They were not prepared to pay interest to financial institutions while they themselves worked unpaid and garment workers earned peanuts. The good will of donors had run out. Europe was their last hope.

Having read the application, Daphne had declared herself utterly convinced by it. So convinced had she been that they would get the money that she had started work at once. 'If you get it, you pay me. If not, not.' They had not. In their disappointment, they had assumed that they would lose Daphne, but no. 'I've got my teeth into it now,' she had said.

The sinking of Daphne's teeth into the ideology of Goddess Garments had brought up a collectively designed profile of Goddess Garments' ideal investor. This woman had been actively involved in the women's movement in her youth, and was still sympathetic with its aims. Alternatively, she was 'not a feminist but . . .'; she was a beneficiary who felt gratitude from time to time. She was perplexed and sometimes irritated by the direction the movement had taken. She had money but saw no way of using it to get results. She wanted results. But the results need not be financially advantageous to her. She would probably be as uneasy about making a profit out of Goddess Garments as the Goddess Garments collective would be about allowing her to.

'Call it a loan,' said Daphne. 'A five-year loan with no guarantee of interest. Anyone who lends money on that basis has already written it off. She knows it's a donation, you know it's a donation, but don't call it that. Everybody saves face and you get the money.' *Oh GOD, I wish I'd been there*, Teresa thought.

Her sister Marion had sent money, as had, at Marion's persuasion, a number of her friends. 'Cleaner-fish are like that, Teresa. We're mean as hell, as you know, when it comes to bailing out magazines with a death-wish . . . but if something looks as if it's trying, and doesn't call us names . . .'

Beverley too made reference to the fate of *Atalanta*. While appreciative of Daphne, she denied that the transformation of Goddess Garments had been all Daphne's doing. 'It's no more than the sort of compromises we'd already agreed to make at *Atalanta*. Before you – '

'I had to.'

'Yeah, well. And then we heard about the Boys' Own supplement, and we thought, shit. We've got to do something, before Greg Sargent buys us too and turns us into a chain of gents' outfitters called New Atalanta God or something.'

It was water off a duck's back as far as Teresa was concerned. Her days at *Fiacre* were numbered, she decided. She would make herself unemployed, go on social security and work full-time for Goddess Garments, for Daphne. Daphne, whom she had, however indirectly, brought to the women's movement. Daphne, about whom women's groups all over the country were writing to Collindeane Tower saying who was she and when could they borrow her? Daphne Barclay who had come to Collindeane Tower to sell, and had stayed to give.

59

Her period of unemployment had left her broke and further indebted to her parents. She decided to put up with *Fiacre* for a bit longer. Nasty though the job was, she had been lucky to get it. It might be the last paid job she would ever have. There would be something final about giving up. To give it up would be to say to her parents – and to Marion – *I am here, for ever*. It would be to say to Sam – not that he was around to hear, but she thought of him constantly – *I will never live with you*. It would be to say to the women's movement: *Take me. I'm yours*.

Take me, I'm ours.

She contented herself with working at Goddess Garments at weekends and on as many evenings as she could manage. She took to arriving early at the *Fiacre* office so that she could leave promptly. Her boss uttered all the usual bromides at finding her at her desk before he was at his. 'Couldn't you sleep?' And when she rushed away at five o'clock, he said, 'What's his name?'

She told him about Goddess Garments. She told him that Greg Sargent's wife had sent money and clothes and signed the wall. Within days, his own wife had done the same.

It was a slow Sunday. The sky outside the window was grey; Teresa was tired of rearranging stock, of looking alert but approachable when occasional customers drifted in. A new rail caught their eye: '101 THINGS YOU CAN DO WITH A WEDDING DRESS'. The 101 things included slitting the dress down the front, affixing buttons and using it as a house-coat; dyeing it for wear at parties; or turning it into an angel costume for a child's play. Some astonishing people had sent wedding dresses, people who, to hear them talk, had never owned one. The wedding dresses were in good condition, but then they would be. A few had been left as they were, and hung from a rail marked: 'YOU CAN EVEN GET MARRIED IN IT.'

The customer who came in was not interested in wedding dresses. She hurried to 'GREAT COATS', head bent, shoulders hunched, as if she did not want to be seen. She put on the first coat that she touched, covering a suit that looked expensive but wet, as if she had been out in last night's rain. She buttoned up the coat and approached the counter. She was a large-boned, distracted-looking woman with dirty hair and a voice that expected to be obeyed. 'Do you take American Express?'

Teresa glanced at Linda, the woman with whom she was sharing the shift. Linda smiled and looked away.

Teresa said, 'No.'

'I haven't got any cash on me.' Teresa looked sceptically at the leather handbag. 'Well, I have,' the woman admitted, as if telling lies degraded her. 'But I need it.'

If you've got American Express, you don't need a hand-out. 'Are you waged or unwaged?'

'Unwaged.'

'If you really can't pay for the coat, take it.'

'Thank you for helping me,' said the woman. 'You think women should help each other, don't you?'

'Yes . . .'

'I thought so. I think that too.'

Teresa said with sudden concern, 'Are you all right?'

The woman did not answer. Linda came over and said gently, 'Do you want a cup of tea? What's your name? I'm Linda, this is Teresa. Tell us your first name?'

'Do you have to have it?'

'No,' said Teresa and Linda together. Teresa added, 'We'd just like to know what to call you.'

Still managing to be both arrogant and forlorn, the woman said, 'I suppose you'd have to have my name if you were going to give me my clothes back.'

'What?'

'To prove it was me that sent them. I sent some but it was a mistake. I need them back. I want to make a fresh start.'

'Come on,' said Linda. 'Let's get you a cup of tea.' She led her away in the direction of the flat that housed the Survivor Centre, where victims of male violence were cared for. Teresa stayed in the shop. Linda told her later 'There's blood all over her suit. She won't say what happened, but she's been out all night.'

'Is she going to stay?'

'We've told her she can.'

Over the next couple of days, Teresa both saw and tried not to see press reports to the effect that a woman called Gina Linton, a sales representative at Stalton Industries, had been found unconscious in her home, bleeding from wounds in her face and neck; and police were looking for another woman, a former colleague. *It could be anyone*, she thought, deliberately avoiding the photographs. The woman who was being sought, Hilary Foreman, had recently lost her job. Gina Linton's distraught husband had indignantly denied that his wife had had anything to do with this; but one of the tabloids had traced an au pair to Grenoble (the photograph of *her* was unavoidable) who had confirmed that yes, there had been animosity and professional jealousy between the two women.

Teresa was too busy to go into Collindeane Tower, but she reassured herself with the knowledge that Linda, who lived there, would also have read the papers and would know what to do. But this was a cop-out, she realized, and phoned. Linda was cautious, cutting Teresa off. 'I think I know what you've called about. She's gone.'

'Good.'

Linda laughed. 'Yeah. It is, isn't it?'

Hilary Foreman was reported arrested. The owner of a fish and chip shop had become suspicious when she tried to pay for her purchases with an American Express card.

'Still doesn't mean it was her,' said Linda. 'Necessarily.'

'Right,' said Teresa.

With a suspect charged, the sub judice rules silenced comment on the case; but they did not silence sudden media interest in the general topic of the inability of women to work harmoniously together; the prevalence of stress in female executives; its effect upon their children.

'On their *children?*'

'Yes. Apparently Hilary Foreman's toddler was there when it happened; and there was a baby outside in the car.'

'She probably couldn't get a babysitter.'

'That's not very funny, Teresa,' said Linda.

It was only when a press photographer was stopped, in the nick of time, from taking pictures of the Goddess Garments wall – having come in by chance, she said – that the women realized that not just Hilary Foreman but Gina Linton as well had, at different times, sent clothes and had the signatures from their letters put up.

To discourage ghoulishness, the women took the names down. It went against the grain to do this and, to make up for it, they decided to send a Get Well card to Gina Linton. By common, unspoken consent they had this discussion when Daphne was not around, Daphne having been opposed to the taking down of the names, believing that any publicity was good publicity.

Some of the women wanted to send some kind of message to Hilary Foreman as well: not support, not solidarity, but the equivalent of a wordless squeeze of the hand, a token of trust that there was more to recent events than met the eye. It was agreed that any woman who felt moved to do this should do it in her personal capacity only, while Gina Linton's card should come from the collective as a whole. Teresa did not write to Hilary Foreman. She had – if she were honest – met her, helped her, felt sorry for her; but her real sympathy was with the woman who had been attacked, albeit she was a stranger.

A handwritten sign on the door of her flat said, 'There is a man inside. Do not be alarmed, it is me, Sam.'

She was alarmed: horribly alarmed at the thought of that pain starting again. Gina Linton and Hilary Foreman aside, she was happy in her work at Collindeane Tower. It was her real work; *Fiacre* was tolerable as a short-term means to an end; sometimes she went whole hours without thinking of Sam. And now he was in her flat.

'Who let you in?'

'Your mother. I told her you'd said she should.'

Indignation warred with joy, and lost. She wanted to kiss him but he was not even smiling. His face was calm and stern. But his eyes glinted in the way they used to when he was fooling around, playing at being tough. She glinted back. 'I suppose your landlady's thrown you out.' She sat in the armchair.

'I haven't got a landlady,' he said with great dignity. 'I'm buying a flat with a friend.'

'You mean – '

'I am buying a flat with another friend.'

Was this what he had come to tell her? Was he a sadist after all? 'It's nice to see you,' she said. 'But this is my place. You can't just barge in – '

'I can.' He pulled up a hard-backed chair, sitting astride it and wagging his finger to emphasize his words. 'This is the sort of thing that wimps do. We go trundling along with our wimpish ways until something snaps. The Wimps' Code of Conduct allows for one act of machismo every seven years and this is mine.' He walked over to her, slowly and deliberately. He looked arrogantly down his nose and curled his lip. 'You are my woman, Teresa, and I have come to claim you.' His voice smouldered.

'Gosh. How thrilling.' It was, actually. 'What if I don't want to be claimed?'

'I'd have to look that up. Besides which, the friend I'm buying the flat with – whose name is Kenneth, in case you're interested – has just got himself a job in Portsmouth. So I thought to myself, who do I know who's in gainful employment and is looking for a place to live? I know, old whassname.'

'What happened to "You are my woman and I have come to claim you"?'

'Oh, you liked that, did you?'

'It was all right. On a septennial basis.'

'Can I kiss you, then?'

She put her arms round him and it was as if he had never been away. 'You can ditch your Code of Conduct if it says you have to ask.'

'I couldn't wait to ask you,' he said, when they lay relaxed and naked, stroking each other. 'I couldn't bear not knowing what you'd say. I don't really approve of conning my way into people's flats, even if they do work for *Fiacre*.' He giggled. '*Fiacre*! Is that how you pronounce it?

'Oh shut up.'

'Anyway, I won't have to con my way into your flat when your flat is my flat.' She gave him a very long kiss, to change the subject. After it, he said, 'How much are you earning, if I may make so bold?'

'Not enough.'

'I haven't told you what the payments are yet.'

'I mean not enough for what I do. I hate it, and to be honest I was thinking of leaving.'

'What? Oh no. Oh, shit, Teresa, not this again – '

'I said I *was* thinking of leaving. You've sprung this on me.'

'But you do want to live with me?' He was like some terrified woman who has given her all: *You do want to marry me?*

'Yes. I do.' She soothed him. 'I do.' *I do. But it's not all I want. While Daphne's at Collindeane, I want to be there too. Seeing what she does, and how she does it.*

Sam seemed satisfied with Teresa's answer and fell asleep, holding her. She thought it was just as well that she had forgotten how it felt to be held by Sam in his sleep; having the memory and lacking the reality, she might have died. She looked round the sitting room turned bedroom by the opening of the settee: the granny flat in her parents' house. *If I were a granny, I'd have a pension; I could do what I wanted. If I were living here because I was a child, my parents would look after me. It's the bit in between that's so difficult.*

60

For the first few days they had kept Gina in a private ward, a policewoman at her bedside; and then, when her condition had improved and Hilary had been caught, charged and released on bail on the understanding that she would not go near Gina, they had moved her to a ward of six women.

One of them had cancer but seemed very cheerful about it. A second thought she had cancer but turned out not to have. A third was senile, a fourth had been knocked off her bicycle by a newspaper delivery van and appeared more angry than hurt, and the fifth woman died, quietly and to the obvious perplexity of the staff who had been getting ready to discharge her.

'What a rotten thing to happen,' said Oliver, when he came on his daily visit. 'As if you didn't have enough to worry about. They should separate people.'

'Why?' It hurt to talk, but she wanted to. 'I could be dead, you know.' Her voice sounded strange, but it was not just the wound in her neck that made it so. *I could be dead.* It sounded like a boast, though she did not feel boastful: just wondering. *I could be dead. This person who I am could be having the experience of being dead.*

'But you're not.'

'Would I know I was dead? Would I be able to watch you having fun?'

'I wouldn't be having fun.'

She had not meant that. He had suffered too; was suffering. 'I meant, would I know that everything was over for me?'

'I don't think so.' He obviously did not want to talk about it but he knew that she did. 'I think it would be like being asleep.'

You hope.

'The first time I thought about death,' she said, 'really thought about it, as something that could happen to me – was when I went on that course. A Stalton's driver ran me off the road. They didn't get me that time so they tried again.'

'Gina, it was Hilary. Hilary herself. Hilary gone crazy. She was nothing to do with the company. It was nothing to do with the company. Everyone's terribly upset.'

The board of directors of Stalton Industries were so upset that they sent Gina a dozen red roses, a note confirming her right to sick leave on full pay and a reminder that she must not discuss company business with journalists without prior authorization from the press office. The woman who had been knocked off her bicycle said that if any journalists came from the paper whose van had done the deed, Gina should refer them to her.

Hilary would be pleading guilty to Malicious Wounding. In mitigation she would say that she was under stress at the time and that the attack had not been premeditated. The court would believe this latter point, according to the police solicitor who visited Gina once she had returned home. He believed it himself. If Hilary had planned the attack, she would have come equipped with a weapon and would not have relied on there being a glass conveniently to hand. She would not have timed her visit to coincide with Oliver's expected arrival home – the arrival which had saved Gina from bleeding to death. Hilary would have made more effective arrangements for her getaway. It was not known where she had been during her three days on the run; but she had had hardly any cash on her. Above all, had she been intending to commit a crime, she would not have brought her children along. 'She'll say it was a fight.'

Gina sat in the armchair that Oliver had bought while she was in hospital to replace the one that had been soaked with her blood. 'It was not a fight. I don't fight. There was an argument and she attacked me.'

'Did you and Mrs Foreman have many arguments? Did you get on?'

She fingered the long scar on her neck and chin. Time and plastic surgery would restore her good looks, she had been told. 'Does it look as if we got on?'

'Would you like to tell me what the argument was about?'

'It's in my statement.'

'Please tell me again.'

'She's insane.'

'You don't have to decide that, Mrs Linton.'

'She'd got this idea into her head that there was an arrangement between us. I'd be a sort of backstop for her while her children were small, and then we'd swap over.'

'Good idea . . .'

'I beg your pardon?'

'My wife did something similar when ours were young. She had a friend with kids of the same age, so – '

'And did your wife know about it in advance?'

'What? Oh, I see. And Mrs Foreman accused you of not keeping to your side?'

'I never had a side. It was a fantasy of hers. Her and her husband – '

'Wait a minute. Isn't he in Personnel?'

'He *is* Personnel. He thinks he is.'

'Are you saying this arrangement had some kind of official backing from the company?'

'I don't know.'

'I'll have to find out.'

'Don't ask him.'

'Whom do you suggest?'

'Somebody senior. Somebody who isn't in Trevor's pocket.'

She was well, she was not well. She was free of pain and fear; then whole nights and days would be haunted by the sensation of glass biting through flesh, the sight of Hilary's hate-filled face. She was lethargic, could not even find the energy to raise her hand from under the bed-covers to drink the coffee she craved. Oliver fed her with a spoon, teasing and scolding. 'It's like having a baby.'

She got out of bed, full of energy. 'I want to have a baby.'

'What?'

'I do. You do too, don't you?'

'Well yes, but – '

She smiled. The scar tissue made smiling difficult but she smiled. 'Don't say "in about four years", or I'll – ' She stopped. She had been going to say 'or I'll kill you'.

'Is this a good time for making decisions?' he said.

'I've made it,' she said. 'I can't stop thinking about being dead. I want to think about life. I want to know that my body works – '

'Of course it works,' he said, with only the faintest of kindly suggestive smiles to remind her that they had not made love since the incident, that he wanted her but was content to wait, that he understood.

'I want to carry on,' she said.

What she meant was that she did not want to carry on. She saw no way that she could carry on as an employee of Stalton Industries. Everyone would be kind, of course. They would pretend not to see her scars until one day when she would come back from the plastic surgeons as good as new and they would compliment her on the improvement . . . the improvement on the grotesque sight that they had never acknowledged when they could see it.

She would make the most of her time on sick pay, and then she would leave.

Leave – and go where? Who would want her, with her name now a national byword for the inability of women executives to cope? (An international byword – for had not Monique in Grenoble had her three francs' worth?) And even if some other company did want her – she could change her name, go back to her old name, *it's been in the Heriot family for generations* – even if some other company did want her, would she want them? How could she walk into a new office on her first day, looking at her new colleagues and wondering whether, wondering which of them . . .

Wondering which of them was wondering, *Did she ask for it? It takes two to have an argument.*

She needed a break.

She needed to do something different. She would not make Hilary's mistake. She would not try to do everything at once. She would give herself fully to her maternity, enjoy it, do it well, keep up with her reading, stay in touch and then, when the time came, patch her career together as best she could.

In about five years . . .

'I'd love for us to have a baby,' said Oliver. 'I'd really love it. It would help us to put all this behind us. But I'm not going to let you make a decision until you're well.'

He was right, of course. He was always right. He had been right to say that she was a complacent person who thought nothing bad could ever happen to her. Nothing bad, except death. . . . She was not complacent any more. Life's tennis balls could not always be fished out.

Would having a baby be a way of trying to fish out a tennis ball? She searched her conscience. It would not be fair to the child to lay upon it the responsibility of making up to her for something that had happened before it was even conceived, even thought of . . .

something that had happened at a time when she had started to think that she never would conceive a child.

So why the sudden change? Was she simply fooling herself, covering up for a loss of nerve?

She did not think so.

She would not be the first woman who, thinking she did not want to have children, suddenly wanted one with great, aching passion. But might it not just be that she was at home all day with nothing to do?

She did not think so. She remembered how, after her wedding, she had suddenly felt older, more responsible, more wise. If a ceremony in which she did not fully believe could do that, how much more strongly and truthfully she could be affected by a brush with death, in which she had no choice but to believe. Which was more important, really – selling bitumen, which anyone could do? Or having her and Oliver's baby, which only she could do? Climbing up a career structure designed by somebody like Trevor Foreman – or carrying on the human race?

'She's changing her tune on the mitigation plea,' said the police solicitor.

'Oh?'

'If she blames her stress on you and Stalton Industries breaking your word to her, we can bring in the entire top brass to say that there was no arrangement of any kind other than that she could do her job from home for as long as she could handle it. Anything else was, as you say, her fantasy. Your appointment was quite separate, and coincidental.'

They would say that, wouldn't they? They wouldn't say, 'Well yes, of course. We were worried that we were about to lose one of our bright young women and then we heard that one of our bright young men was about to marry another bright young woman. So we seized our opportunity and we didn't tell her because she might have said no.'

'She's getting a psychiatrist to speak for her. A top man who knows everything there is to know about post-natal depression.'

'Does he?' said Gina.

Trevor would have put a stop to it, of course. Well and truly though Hilary had burned her boats at Stalton's, Trevor's boats were still afloat . . . just. The last thing he would want would be his wife getting up in court and tossing shit into the company fan. Far better for everyone if Hilary said, 'Yes. I'm a nutcase. And here's a famous doctor to prove it.' Far better for everyone . . . far better for Gina than if she had to go through cross-examination about who said what to whom.

Let me get this straight, Mrs Linton. You do think you might have made remarks that would lead Mrs Foreman to suppose that your plans for having a family would dovetail nicely with hers?

You babysat for her – at your own suggestion?

You covered up mistakes for her? You worked in your off-duty hours when she was under pressure? Did the other representatives do that? Why not, do you think? Are you saying that you didn't feel a special bond with her? Was she wrong to suppose that, as two women working together in one of the last bastions of – that silky smile. The word 'bastion' seemed made for men to say with a self-deprecating smile in the phrase 'last bastion of male dominance'. She had never heard it used in any other context. What did it mean, anyway?

Rampart. Fortification. Defence.

It was nothing to do with men. Hilary had tried to kill her. She wanted the trial over and Hilary behind bars. She wanted something else to happen too. She wanted Stalton Industries to snap her out of her daze by telling her to stop malingering or else. Alternatively, she wanted to find herself pregnant . . . but that was unlikely as she was still taking the pill. She examined the little dots of chemical in the packet, wondering which one would be her last. If she had died, she wondered how soon Oliver would have thrown away the pill packet – immediately? Or never?

Oliver. She trusted him. He was her husband, her love. He had stuck by her. (*Why shouldn't he stick by me? I haven't done anything wrong. No, but other men might have found it an embarrassment. He has never been embarrassed.*) But one thing she must ask, or she would always wonder.

'Love, can we just go through something?'

'Sure.'

'It was while I was away on that course that Stalton's made their first approach to me. Through the agency. It was on the tape.'

'Yes?'

'But you hadn't asked me to marry you then.'

'No.'

'Had you told anyone that you were going to?'

'I can't remember. I don't think I would have.' He laughed and stroked her injured face. 'You might have said no. I'd have looked a right berk.'

She might have said no and he would have looked a berk. Of

course. So Stalton's offer to employ her had had nothing to do with her marrying Oliver. There had been no cosy little planning meeting between Oliver and the Foremans: *Great, Oliver. You marry her. We'll get our kids over in one fell swoop and you can wait about five years.*

Get Well cards continued to flow in. Roy and Alex Franson sent one, full of outrage and concern and a promise to come and see her soon. And Goddess Garments sent a card: a tangle of handwritten greetings. 'Get well soon, Lynn.' 'Best wishes, Beverley.' 'Thinking of you, Marsha.' 'Love and sisterhood, Kim.' She stopped reading. It was a kind thought, but the sentimentality was embarrassing. Who were these people to send love when they did not know her? What was sisterhood? In the name of sisterhood would they call her a coward for considering giving up and having a baby? In the name of sisterhood, would they have sent a card to Hilary as well? What did they know, selling off second-hand clothes in a slum? What did they know of what it was like at the sharp end, in real industry with real products and real money? Like everyone else, they would probably think that, in the name of sisterhood, she should have fallen in with Hilary's deluded plans.

'Oliver, will you do me a favour?'

'What?'

'Would you write to these people and tell them I don't want my name on their bloody wall?'

61

When Daphne Barclay said that she had got a lot out of her involvement with the feminist movement, she was telling no more than the
truth. Specifically, she had got a grant from the European
Community to establish the Daphne Barclay Business Training
Women's Project.

She had not made her first visit to Collindeane Tower with this
in mind. It was as she had always said: she had gone there as a
saleswoman in the belief that here were people who needed what
she had to offer and might have the means to pay for it.

It was only later, when she was looking through the Goddess
Garments grant application – which they had been kind enough to
allow her to take away with her, for research purposes – that it had
occurred to her that everybody's best interests would be served if
she, rather than they, got the money.

Reading the application, she had not known whether to laugh or
cry. She had done neither. She had seethed, comparing the pathetic
document with the careful business plan that she and Alistair had
had to put together to get their bank loan. She had seethed as a
businesswoman and she had seethed as a taxpayer.

The DBBT business plan had succeeded as a tempting invitation
to invest for profit. The Goddess Garments application was an invitation to tear up bank notes, tempting only to those whose hobby
that was.

The aims and scope of Daphne Barclay Business Training had
been described in a single, well-phrased paragraph. 'Goddess
Garments – Introduction' had gone on for three pages in prose
notable only for the dearth of clear, unambiguous statements, and

the tendency, when these did appear, for them to be followed by another statement clearly and unambiguously saying the opposite. 'We demand an end to sweatshop conditions for garment workers' appeared in the same paragraph as: 'We refuse to charge prices that claimant families cannot afford.' Close on the heels of: 'We intend to run the shop with maximum efficiency' came: 'We are opposed to hierarchical styles of management.' And finally, the classic: 'As part of the Women's Liberation Movement, Goddess Garments is committed to the international struggle against capitalism and patriarchy – ' . . . but . . . ' – we hope that you will feel able to give us a grant.'

Give us a grant. *Give* us a grant. Nobody had given Daphne Barclay Business Training anything. Daphne's flat and Alistair's house stood as security for their loan. Daphne's career, Alistair's hope of retirement in a few years, were on the line. They personally were on the line. Who was on the line at Goddess Garments? 'As a collective, we do not have leaders . . .' Twenty names had followed, and not a qualification amongst them. It was not that they had no qualifications; it was that they had not thought it nice to mention them. They had thought it would appear boastful. 'Elitist' was the word they used.

'They are elitist to the core,' she had told Alistair. 'The best decision I ever made was not to go to university.'

'Have they all got degrees, then?'

'Not all of them, but they all know something I don't know. About the unregenerate wickedness of commerce. People who go around satisfying customers ought to be locked up. It is *not funny*.'

'Daphne, you are so innocent. I love it.' Alistair had looked away, as if this was not quite what he had meant. 'If you're going to venture out into the radical fringe, you're going to meet quite a lot of this sort of thing. You'll have to transform it.'

'I intend to. If groups like this get one sou out of Europe, it will be an international scandal. It won't be, of course; but it should.'

Alistair had himself been rather scandalized by Daphne's plan to send in an application of her own.

'Since when were you a women's liberation group?'

' "All Women Welcome." '

'Yes, but – '

'I can ask, can't I? I'm not going to say anything that's not true.'

And she had not, in her application, said anything that was not true. It was, for example, true that 'the partners in Daphne Barclay Business Training share a belief that efficiency and profitability, so far from being obstacles to social justice, are essential for it.' It was perfectly true. Alistair believed in social justice and Daphne believed in efficiency and profitability and they were partners who shared everything.

'The Women's Liberation Movement in Britain is at a crossroads. Will it go forward and take its rightful place in the business, political and social community, or will it dwindle into the fringe of the bankrupt . . . ?'

'You seem to know a lot about it all of a sudden.'

'I have been listening to my customers, Alistair. One should always do that.'

The cheque, when it arrived, came not a day too soon. Daphne and Alistair had not had their salaries for two months. A couple of freelance trainers of whom they made use were pressing for their fees and being told to give it a week; a hotel was demanding a deposit to confirm a block booking, Daphne was looking for a venue sufficiently grand for the forthcoming day-long Daphne Barclay Festival of Selling, and START Selling UK was up to its old tricks.

'I thought we'd agreed that we wouldn't use our START contacts,' said Alistair, frowning over the solicitor's letter.

'We've got to fill that hotel somehow.'

'They seem to know what we're up to.'

'Show me . . .'

START's solicitors wanted all their papers returned and a firm undertaking that no copies had been kept, otherwise 'we will have no alternative but to seek remedies through the courts.'

Goddess Garments had finished with the delegates' list from START Selling – Women!, so Daphne had returned that, along with a few other bits and pieces and a letter of obsequious apology for the misunderstanding.

Then she had sat down to write a rather different letter to Lindbergh Stanley.

As you know, my partner and I share a belief that efficiency and profitability, so far from being obstacles to social justice, are essential for it.

It is hard for me to understand why our work of inculcating this belief amongst the unemployed and other disadvantaged groups should be seen as a threat to START Selling UK, but so it would appear.

It seems to me that your UK subsidiary must be in a parlous

state if it finds it necessary to instruct solicitors to harass me for doing no more than inviting comfortably off women to send unwanted clothes for the use of those less fortunate. Such petty-minded behaviour has no place, I am sure you will agree, in the international community of professional sales trainers of which you are world president. Yours sincerely,

Daphne Barclay.

'I'm sure you enjoyed writing it, but I don't think you should send it.'

'Of course I shall send it. At worst, he will be amused.'

'And what are you going to do about this money from Europe?'

'The first thing I am going to do,' said Daphne, 'is pay myself a salary for the work I have been doing at Collindeane Tower. And you, for the back-up.'

Alistair put his head in his hands. 'They'll hit the roof when they find out.'

'That will make very little difference to the roof, or to me. They won't find out. They will, because I shall tell them, but not yet. Once I have got them to the point where they don't need to go crawling to Europe for hand-outs, I will tell them, and, so far from hitting roofs, they will thank me.'

'It's shabby. I'm embarrassed to be associated with it.'

'All right.' She flung up her hands. 'Off you go – down to the Tower – if they'll let you in – and tell them what I've done. Hand over the money, they'll be happy to spend it. Or offer your services. My services will not be acceptable, but I'm sure they'll be delighted to continue their education at your hands and will do everything you say.'

She was sincere in her intention to tell the Collindeane women what had happened to the money. She was sincere in her belief that they would thank her. Not at once, but after their anger had died down. She would use the incident as an exemplary tale of how to apply for money and how not to. She would point out that, in view of the 'All Women Welcome' policy, they could count themselves lucky that it had been she who had got the money, rather than somebody unscrupulous.

She was scrupulous in her attentions to Goddess Garments. She intended to give good value. It amused her to see what could be done: turning nothing into something gave her a pleasing sense of her own power. The belief of the women that she had been giving, rather than selling, her services, had been essential for her (and their) success. She would challenge them on this. The more honest among them would admit that it was so. Teresa Beal at least would admit it; and she could persuade the others.

'I have to admit to having played a little trick on you.' Daphne was coming to the end of a day-course in a secondary school. She had been brought in as part of the borough's Enterprise Education Week. 'The trading competition that I mentioned at the beginning of the day was my way of ensuring that you did not waste time during the breaks. There are no prizes because prizes imply winners, and if somebody is a winner, somebody else has to come second. Nobody comes second on a Daphne Barclay Business Training Course.'

'Aw, Miss – '

Too late, she realized her mistake. Her delegates were fifteen and sixteen years old. She had decided that the little joke about the competition, which always amused adult delegates, would not be appreciated by the young. She had in fact brought prizes for every-body – an assortment of Daphne Barclay Sales Stationery for them to practise with – but she had fluffed her lines. She wondered if she might admit this – saving face by saying that they had all been so brilliant that she had given them the adult version of her script without thinking – but one or two of them were quite bright and would recognize patronage when they heard it. 'The prizes,' she said, 'are in the world outside, and I look forward to hearing, in future years, of how you have won them. Will somebody please collect up the bank notes?'

Later she drank tea with the headmistress, who said, 'Well, they seem to have enjoyed it.'

'So have I, Mrs McTavish. They are a credit to you. Before I go, let me ask you this. Is there anything about my conduct of the day that you are *not* satisfied with?'

'I think they were a bit disappointed about the competition.'

Daphne herself was a bit disappointed about the condition in which her bank notes had been returned to her. She had had them specially made, plastic-backed so that they could be used again. She had asked that they should not be written on or marked in any way.

'Apart from that you've been quite happy? I'm so pleased. You above all know that Enterprise Education is not just a one-week-a-year affair. Are there any other schools in the area to whom you might recommend me? A colleague whom you might perhaps phone now, while I'm here . . . ?'

Mrs McTavish said that all the borough's schools were listed in the telephone directory. Daphne recognized a brush-off. She hoped that her oversight regarding the competition was not to blame. It was probably not. Mrs McTavish's reluctance to phone fellow head-teachers could probably be put down to embarrassment over her inability to do so: they would have already gone home, the time being ten past four.

School work was not highly paid, but Daphne could not afford to let anything go. She could afford even less to get her scripts mixed up. She was tired. She was doing too much. Next time it might be worse. She might find herself speaking to sales directors as if they were schoolchildren, car salesmen as if they were telephonists, personnel managers as if they were feminists in a tower block . . . or even vice versa.

She must slow down. She could not afford to slow down. She must speed up. What should it be this evening? Collindeane Tower or the office? She felt a brief and treacherous yearning for her days at START when she had had only to conduct courses, not sell them and do administration as well. She suppressed it. She had been an employee then. A person who had had to do what she was told. A person who had had to tolerate nicknames, unkindness and being disliked.

She hated being in the presence of people who disliked her. It filled her with fear. This was one of the reasons why she had minded so much about disappointing the children. They had looked at her with frank dislike. Fortunately this did not happen often. She was rarely in the company of people who disliked her. They might, like Alistair, think her ruthless at times, but she had to be. His underlying fondness for her was not in doubt. Nor did she doubt that the Collindeane feminists liked her. They found her odd – she *was* odd, to them. They had never met anyone like her before. That was part of their problem. But they respected her forthrightness, her determination to finish what she had started. Even those who made it clear that they abhorred everything she stood for (and there would always be some) liked her as a person, appreciated her generosity.

Her generosity. She sighed as she entered her office. She did not care what anyone said. She had done the right thing concerning the European money. Would Goddess Garments have got it if she had not? It seemed unlikely. As a taxpayer she hoped it was unlikely. Would Goddess Garments have let her into the building if she had gone to them announcing the truth? On the contrary. 'All Women Welcome' would have come down at once.

She believed this. She truly believed it. The problem would lie in making others believe it. She was going to have to do this sooner than she had hoped. The sigh that she had let out as she entered the office became a groan as she saw what lay on her desk: a letter postmarked Brussels. The Eurocrats were coming to town. They wanted to visit her project.

62

Every woman is frightened of rape, Teresa thought. *Margaret Thatcher never goes anywhere without her detectives. The Queen woke up one night to find a strange man sitting on her bed. That's why Daphne, not content with transforming Goddess Garments, wants to transform the whole of Collindeane Tower, starting with the services to rape victims.*

The collective were sceptical, but they listened. Everyone made time to listen to Daphne, for Daphne's time was her own time, scarce and valuable.

'We can't charge fees and that's flat.'

'Not at the moment of counselling, perhaps,' said Daphne. 'Have you considered insurance? People take out insurance against other kinds of misfortune. So if women who feel themselves to be at risk paid so much per year – '

There was derision. Polite derision, but derision. ' "Help, I've been raped." "May I have your policy number?" '

Daphne nodded as at a fair point that she had not thought of. 'No, you wouldn't want to say that. Well, let's be systematic about this.' She brought forth from her briefcase a sheaf of Daphne Barclay Problem Solving Exercise Sheets. Everyone was used to these now. They quite liked them. Containing problems, they made them seem manageable. With their columns and flow charts, their multiple choices and boxes to be filled in, they allowed for solutions to be declared imperfect; but they did not allow for no solution to be found.

The Exercise Sheets focused attention on the question 'Who is the customer?' – rephrased, at the women's insistence, as 'Who needs a rape crisis line?' The answer was rape victims: (a) actual, and (b) potential. All women, in other words. 'What about men?' said Daphne. 'They're the ones who do all the raping. Why shouldn't they pay for it?' The justice of this was acknowledged but someone raised an objection: 'If they think they've bought shares in a rape crisis line, they might think they're allowed to.'

Teresa froze but Daphne joined in the laughter. Teresa was the only one not laughing; she had been too fearful of Daphne's reaction. Daphne was lovely when she let herself go and laughed. She did not do it often. Usually she had herself under tight control; but she was not a cold person, of that Teresa was sure.

Daphne resumed speaking. 'If the people who need a service can't or won't pay for it, somebody else will have to or the service will disappear.' She must have said this a thousand times, in this building alone. Yet she made it sound fresh. 'Have you considered looking for commercial sponsorship?'

'You mean – like – we'd have to call it the Benson and Hedges Rape Crisis Line?'

Why didn't they just listen to her?

'Since you bring it up, Benson and Hedges is a very good example. They sponsor cricket matches because they see cricket matches as a good thing – '

' – in their wisdom – '

'In their wisdom. Put it to them that as many people are against rape as are in favour of cricket matches. Possibly more.'

'Rape is not cricket.'

'A very good slogan. And what about your Safe Lifts service? Get on to the car companies, tell them your minibus has broken down, tell them what it's for and ask them to give you another one. *Ask.* Not like this.' Daphne drooped her shoulders, became shy, unassertive, hopeless. ' "Please, may we have a minibus?" "No." "Oh. Sorry." ' She brought the house down. 'Ask as if you believe you are going to get what you want, and the reason you are going to get it is that you are *offering something in return.* You are offering the chance to be associated with something good. Do you think all those people who went on sponsored runs for famine relief cared about famine relief before the run, or after it?'

'No.'

'No, but they did it. Something exciting was happening and they wanted to be associated with it. Did the famine victims care? If you were saved from rape by a lift in a minibus, would you care that the people who gave the minibus have their name on the side for public relations purposes? You have brought rape to public attention as a crime and a problem and a burden on women, something all decent people are against. You did that. Be proud of it, and for heaven's sake use it.' Daphne shrugged, appearing to lose interest. 'Or don't. Far be it from me to tell you what do to. I'm just telling you what's possible, if you'll only believe in yourselves. If you don't ask, you don't get. You asked for me, and look at what you did get.' The Collindeane women had not actually asked for Daphne, but the point was a fair one. It might sound like arrogance, but it was not. Daphne's words were, Teresa guessed, as much for Daphne herself as for the other women in the room. Like many seemingly arrogant people feeling themselves to be under attack, she had to keep reminding herself of her own worth.

And Daphne was under attack. Her relentless honesty made it impossible for everybody to regard her as highly as Teresa regarded her. The women from the Peace Camps' Support Group gave her a challenge: 'You tell us how we can get women to stop spending so much time at Greenham Common and get down to RAF Peaston Hill which is where the cruise missiles really are.'

'I'm sorry,' said Daphne. 'I know nothing about politics. All I know about is selling.'

'What about world peace?'

'Are you selling that? I know you think I'm flippant, but please, hear me out. I don't know what makes thirty thousand women stand around in the rain at Greenham Common –'

'We'll tell you.'

' – and I don't know how to make them do it at this other place of yours. The only way I know to persuade people to do something is to offer them something in return. What are you offering?'

They were offering the truth, they said. The cynical truth that the missile-shaped objects that had been seen at Greenham were non-working models: perfect in every detail but lacking warheads, they were there as decoys, to fool the Russians and fool the peace movement. The real things were at the last place where anyone would expect to find them: at a base turned playground, home of air shows, craft fairs and other hearts-and-minds events.

'There you are, then,' said Daphne. 'Book a stand at a craft fair there and sell your pamphlets. Go to where the people are who need what you have, and sell it to them.'

'You don't understand.'

'Possibly not.'

A woman who did not contribute to the women's movement was a cleaner-fish. A woman who did was part of the movement, and no more deserving of votes of thanks than anyone else.

Fair enough – but could not exceptions be made? Did the other women not realize – dared they not admit – what they had in Daphne? The fleshly embodiment of the ghost who lurks at every unstructured meeting of every open collective, hovering now at one woman's shoulder, now at another, whispering, *Go on. I dare you. Say it: we can await the emergence of perfect decisions and die waiting. Or we can be brave enough to make imperfect ones, and take action.*

Daphne was that ghost. She was the missing member of the *Atalanta* collective. The alternative they – she, Teresa – had cravenly postponed taking until it was too late. The ghost had remained a ghost. They had got Greg Sargent instead. 'Daphne, I think what you're doing is wonderful.'

'Not everyone would agree with you.'

'Not openly, perhaps. But everyone appreciates the way you're putting in time for nothing.'

'It's not for nothing. I've got a lot out of it.'

'I know, but you've got a business to run.'

'You really think I've made a difference?'

'*A difference* – ?'

'And would others feel as you feel?'

'As I say – '

'*Other* others. People away from here. If we had a sort of open day and let them come on a visit?'

' "All Women Welcome." Oh. I see. You mean men.'

'Women and men. From all over the country, and perhaps Europe.'

'I don't see why not. But you're not really asking the right person.'

'I know. I'm just sounding you out.' *That's funny*, thought Teresa. *I thought I started this conversation.* 'They can be rather intimidating.'

'Beverley's not intimidating.' *Not much, she's not. But I wouldn't have thought she could intimidate Daphne. Nobody could. That's the whole point.*

'That's true. I'm very fond of Beverley.'

In her jealousy, Teresa heard Daphne say, 'I have a little confession to make to you.'

'Well, don't make it here.'

'What?'

'Let's go for a drink.'

'But I have work to do.'

'You've done enough for one day.' Why should Teresa not take

Daphne for a drink? Why should she not make overtures of friendship? The other women did not own Daphne, did they?

'When I said I'd got a lot out of it,' said Daphne, sipping grapefruit juice with ice, 'I should have said that I hope to get a lot out of it. A lot more than I have already got.'

'Such as?'

'As you know, my partner and I are very keen on extending the side of our business which deals with organizations concerned not solely with profit.'

'Yes, it's great.'

'My confession is that I saw Goddess Garments as an experiment and, if successful, a showcase. Now that it is successful, I want to show it.'

Having been slightly alarmed at Daphne's use of the word 'confession', Teresa felt relieved. There might be the odd cynical sniff but she doubted that the Goddess Garments women would object en masse to a brief visit by a few radically minded men and women who wanted to flatter by imitating. 'I don't think they'd want men in the rape crisis line office –'

'Eavesdropping? Dear me, no. They wouldn't need to go in. There's nothing to see. We could show them the new rotas – the efforts we're making to get sponsorship –'

WE could show them?

We the women of Collindeane Tower.

'I'm sure they'll agree, but –'

'I know, I know,' said Daphne. 'It's not for you to say. But you'll be on my side?'

'Oh yes. I'm on your side.'

'How sweet of you.'

63

They were nutters. He must take care not to get drawn in. That was what his mother obviously feared would happen.

She had not needed to turn up like that, though, bringing our accountant with her, and the other one. They had made him look a fool himself. They had insulted the Rideemus people, who had said, 'You'd better go with your mother, Tom.'

'Tom, come on.'

She had looked so worried that he might have gone, to please her. He might have gone and come back. But he had his pride. It was one thing to be kind to his widowed mother. He had not needed three of them bursting in like the police.

Miss Hutton was not what he had imagined: a spinster accountant who never said anything except 'Yes. Goodbye.' She had had lots to say, and all of it with a sneer. 'What is this, higher consciousness?'

'Something like that,' the Rideemus people had replied politely.

'And when do we get the bill?'

Someone had asked Miss Hutton's friend, Miss Griffiths-whatsit, what was wrong with her back. 'Have you tried Theolistics Therapy?'

'That being – ?'

'It's a bit complicated to explain. I'll put it as simply as I can. Oxygen is the basis of life, right – ?'

Miss Hutton had muttered: 'Forget DNA.'

'Oxygen is the basis of life and if oxygen doesn't reach the cells of the body in sufficient quantities, they die or malfunction. Theolistics Therapy stimulates the circulation of the blood by controlling the breathing in a natural way – '

'There you are, Adela. You've never got the hang of it, have you? Breathing in a natural way.'

'You'd better go with your mother and her friends, Tom.'

'Mam,' he whispered. 'You're fouling up a deal here. I've got to stay till the end of the course. I'll be home tomorrow.'

It turned out that he had got it wrong about the meaning of 'Weekend Course'. 'It's more of a sort of long weekend, Tom. We go on till Monday evening.'

Some of the others on the course had misunderstood too. They had to get back to work.

'Will your work really not spare you for one day, for something as important as this?'

The Rideemus House telephone being out of order, lifts were offered into the village for those who wished to phone home to say they were staying another day. Tom did not go; his mother would not be back yet. He could phone her tomorrow.

He sat alone at the long table in the dining room. He was hungry, but they did not eat till late.

'Sorry we've had to interrupt the course,' said one of the Rideemus people, Lena or Jackie or Christine, whatever her name was. They were all very nice but he could hardly tell them apart. 'We prefer not to start again until everyone gets back. It gives us a chance for a chat. Is there anything you haven't understood?'

Where should he start? He ran over in his mind what he had understood, what he thought he had understood.

The course was about jokes. When he had first been told this, he had thought that someone was playing a joke on him. This was true, they had acknowledged, but only in the sense that a joke is a very serious matter. 'Man is the only animal that laughs.'

When Tom had sought to raise objections to this – hyenas and kookaburras – they had been ready for him. Everybody brought up hyenas and kookaburras. 'Hyenas and kookaburras don't laugh, any more than parrots have conversations. They don't laugh, they just make their natural animal sounds which remind us of ourselves laughing. And that in itself makes *us* laugh, reminding us as it does of the animal in ourselves. Will you go along with that?'

Tom had nodded and they had pounced. It was a thing he was starting to notice about them: the way they pounced. Lectures got boring; he preferred the discussions in between; but it made his head spin, the way they got you to agree with something quite ordinary and then pounced and turned it into something else and left you wondering which were your ideas and which were theirs. 'Why do we laugh when an animal reminds us of ourselves? Are we really amused? Or are we uneasy?'

'I saw a gorilla once. At the zoo. It was – ' *wanking as if it had invented it* ' – picking its nose.'

'And you didn't like that, did you? So you laughed.'

Since man was the only animal that laughed, it followed that God must have had a special purpose in creating laughter, a meaning applicable only to His chosen species. Psychotheolistics – of which Rideemus was the missionary and recruiting wing – was an enquiry into that purpose. It was international and multidisciplinary; multi-denominational and scientific. 'We don't make the mistake of separating science from theology, Tom; though we do use the Bible.'

Their Bible. Other Bibles had got it wrong, apparently. There were mistakes, mistranslations, deliberate cuts. Most versions of Genesis had something along the lines of 'God made man in His own image.' In its complete form, the passage should read: 'God made man in His own image, *that man might laugh with the Lord at the latter day*.' 'God laughs, Tom. At the moment, He's laughing *at* us, but He wants to laugh *with* us. Isn't that exciting?'

'Is there anything you haven't understood?'

'No. It's all pretty clear.'

'Didn't you want to go with the others?'

'My mam knows where I am.'

'And Shelly?'

'Why do you keep talking about Shelly?' he said. *As if you knew her*, he thought.

'*You* keep talking about her. You came looking for her. She's obviously very important. But there are problems, aren't there? Tom, you're a Tynesider – '

'Wearside.'

'Do you know the Geordie joke about the two old women in the bingo queue?'

He knew it. A funeral procession went by and one of the women left the queue, went to a flower stall, bought a bunch of flowers and put it on the coffin. Then she went back to her place in the queue. Her friend said, 'Ee, pet, that were a nice gesture,' and she said, 'Aye, well, we'd been married forty years.'

'It's not really funny, is it, Tom?'

'It's all right.'

'We laugh at the unexpectedness of the punch line – it throws us off balance – but it's a cruel joke. Think of what that marriage must have been like, over forty years, to produce such a level of indifference. An unhappy marriage is no joke – but sexual relationships are the basis of most jokes in most cultures. Why do you think that is?'

'I'll tell you what I do think,' he said. 'Jokes are just a bit of fun. You're not supposed to take them apart and look at them like that. It's like cutting a cat open to see how it works.'

'Did you ever do that?'

'No.' He had wanted to, though. A friend of his had suggested it. 'It would have died. It wouldn't have been what we'd thought. And that's what you do to jokes. Kill them.'

The Rideemus girl smiled at him as the people who had been into the village returned and got ready for the next session. 'See if you still feel the same after Tuesday's session,' she said.

He was free to leave at any time. The doors were not locked. He tested them. If he wanted to go home by train (his mother had given him money for this) he would need a lift to the station; but if there were any difficulty, it would not kill him to walk eight miles, or hitch. Not tonight, though. It was dark and he did not know the road.

He was all right. He was safe and warm and dry, and the food, when he got it, was not bad. Upstairs there was a bed for him, a top bunk in a room with eleven other men. They were a mixed group: some unemployed, some in good jobs, some, like him, halfway between the two. He did not want the Rideemus people to forget what they had said about giving him a commission to make a model of God creating the world, but he preferred, as far as possible, to keep off the subject of work. A bank teller, who had just got back from phoning his wife to ask her to phone the bank tomorrow and say that he was ill, got up at the end of the evening session on the Value of Psychotheolistics and said, 'You can't put a value on it! Money's the biggest joke there is and that's all there's been in my life up till now, money, money, money. I'll give £500.'

Everyone cheered. He was hugged by Rideemus members, male and female. Tom thought the man must be out of his mind. It was late, everyone was tired and the speaker had been laying it on with a trowel about what special people they all were, this smaller group who were strong enough and had their lives sufficiently under control to be able to stay the extra day. Flattery would get them nowhere. Tom sat silent, exchanging significant glances with those he knew to be unemployed while those who had jobs emptied their bank accounts. He wasn't falling for this. But no one was trying to make him fall for anything. No one put pressure on him to give money, to say anything, to do anything. He, like everybody else, could leave whenever he wanted.

64

The Collindeane women did not object to Daphne's plan as such.
With or without Daphne, all women were welcome, at any time; and
male visitors could go to the men's room at Goddess Garments. But
Collindeane Tower was not a zoo. 'We'll want to ask them things as
well. Swap ideas . . .'

It appeared that what Daphne had in mind was a quick tour, with
her doing most of the talking. 'You're busy. You won't want to stop
what you're doing.'

'We will. We'll give them lunch – '

'I haven't time.'

'Fine. Leave them with us. We'll look after them.'

Not for the first time in her life, Teresa found herself on both
sides. There was something arrogant about Daphne's apparent belief
that she was the only person who could give a proper account of
what had been happening. But did it matter? Daphne would be trying
to sell to these people. Could she not be left to do it in the way she
thought best? Could she not, just this once, be indulged?

'Teresa, I owe you a meal.'

You do? I only bought you a grapefruit juice.

'I love cooking for friends, but I do it so rarely.'

Daphne was inviting her to her flat? For a party, surely. She waited
to hear whether Sam was included. Teresa was practically living with
Sam now. Kenneth was yet to move to Portsmouth, so she had not
transferred her things; but she had started to think of Sam's flat as
home.

Sam was not included. Neither were any of the Collindeane

women. Teresa was the only guest. Daphne's flat was small but cleverly furnished to make the most of the space. Geometric structures – of the kind mendaciously described in advertisements as 'easy to assemble' – filled alcoves in the walls with shelves, in which Teresa recognized a number of Book Club monthly selections. Ornaments looked expensive and carefully chosen. The air was warm, the carpets thick, the lighting subtle. On a table, placed as if casually, was a hand-out announcing 'The Daphne Barclay Festival of Selling'.

'That's just the mock-up,' said Daphne.

Teresa marvelled at the choice of venue. 'You really think you can fill a place that size?'

'I shall have to. I've booked it.' Daphne took the piece of paper away, politely, but as if she had not meant Teresa to see it, which Teresa did not believe. She marvelled again at the gritty ego, the unstoppable self-confidence. 'Nice flat,' she said, shy suddenly.

'Thank you.' Daphne too seemed ill at ease. What was the purpose of this occasion? Daphne was looking lovely, in silky culottes the colour of a tropical sea and a black blouse with a high neck. 'I only hope I shall be able to hold on to it.'

'Why wouldn't you?'

'You don't want to hear about my business worries.'

Teresa did. She wanted to hear everything. She would understand. She was not the country cousin that Daphne seemed to think her. The experience of setting up a business and having it slip from her fingers was not foreign to her. Nor was the experience of hearing a wolf pawing at the office door. 'My former employers are trying to close me down. They have threatened to sue me for letting Goddess Garments use one of their precious mailing lists.'

'Tell Beverley and the others that.' *Stop being omnipotent, Daphne. Let yourself be vulnerable. They'll like you better for it.*

'I may not be here much longer.'

'What?'

'I've been given the opportunity to work abroad for a while,' said Daphne, coolly unaware of the anguish in Teresa's heart. At least, Teresa hoped she was unaware of it. 'It might be best.'

'What about the Daphne Barclay Festival of Selling?'

'I'm afraid it may be a *folie de grandeur*.'

'I bet it's not,' said Teresa stoutly.

'My parents are long overdue for retirement,' said Daphne. 'I want to be in a position to help them.'

'You make me feel about six years old. You talk about supporting your parents, and mine are only just about to stop supporting me.'

'Let's eat,' said Daphne, bringing a glass dish of fried whitebait with fingers of brown bread and slivers of lemon. 'Please start.' Teresa helped herself. 'You don't get in to Collindeane Tower much during the week, do you?'

'I'm working.'

'But you could slip away.'

'Why?'

'I have something rather naughty in mind.'

So have I, thought Teresa. *I want to touch your hair. I want to know if it feels as it looks.*

'I was wondering whether it might be possible for me to bring my visitors in when only you were on duty. When everyone else was in a meeting, perhaps.'

'Why?'

'You know why.'

'Do I? Is there more to it than you've said?'

Daphne was sitting opposite Teresa at the little table, so close that they could touch. She was eating whitebait. She raised a forkful of the little fishes to her lips, swallowed delicately, drank wine. And then she started to speak, and turned into a monster.

The monster said, 'Did I do wrong?'

'Did you really say that?'

'I phrased it wrongly. Do you believe I did wrong? Knowing what you know? Knowing what I have achieved?'

I will not be a monster too, just to keep you company. 'What *you* have achieved? What those women achieved.'

'I see. Why didn't they achieve it before?'

'What do you propose to do?'

'I was hoping you would advise me.'

'Leave me out of this. You'll have to tell them.'

'We will, yes.'

'And if they decide to sabotage the visit, they won't do it by halves.'

'They mustn't.' Nothing daunted Daphne. Her voice was the voice of pure will. *I say they mustn't; so they won't.* 'They will be the sufferers. Even if the Europeans ask me to pay the money back – and they have no reason to, I am using it for precisely the purpose I said I would use it for – they would hardly give it to *them*, if they show how easily they can be – if that is how they see it – taken for a ride.'

You've got it all worked out, haven't you? Except that I bet you couldn't pay it back. It's all gone. Sunk into your business which you are afraid

390

someone is trying to close down. Your Festival of Selling, which you are afraid people won't come to. You are not afraid. You are not afraid of anything. You are manipulating me. I am in your mind. Are you in mine? The thoughts I am having now – did you put them there? I know what I have to do.

'I'll share the blame.'

She waited for Daphne to toss her a crumb ... *how sweet of you* ... but she just nodded. She nodded as if she had expected it ... more than expected it, agreed with it. Agreed that Teresa was entitled to a share of the blame. And perhaps she was. Perhaps she was. Had she not been the means whereby Daphne had come to Collindeane Tower? Had she not thought cynical thoughts, uttered cynical words, about the unlikelihood of Goddess Garments getting the money, the unlikelihood of them making good use of it if they did? Had she not uttered these words to Alistair Brunt, Daphne's partner? Might she not have uttered them for the specific purpose of having them reported back to Daphne, and planting in Daphne's mind the idea of doing what she had in fact done?

Teresa tried to remember. The conversation with Alistair was a blur, getting fainter. What had she *said*? Surely it had only been one of those conversations that you have at parties, that feminists who like men have with the men they like? She had liked Alistair: a tired old liberal with a conscience, a man approaching retirement with dread, desperately and (Teresa had thought) inexplicably in love with Daphne. Had she really said something disloyal? She had mentioned Europe, she had mentioned Goddess Garments, but they were not secrets. She had mentioned the endless contradictions between being good and being rich, but they were not secrets either. She had not betrayed anything, anyone. But she could pretend to have done so.

Sharing the blame would not be enough. She must shoulder all of it. She would say that she had been Daphne's *éminence grise* throughout. That, knowing nothing of feminism, Daphne had allowed herself to be led. But Daphne was not going to have things all her own way. Teresa had her now. Teresa was in control, Daphne was dependent. *Your real job is to bear the guilt, carry it away.* Teresa would do that, if it meant that the association between Daphne and Collindeane Tower could continue. But if it were to continue, Daphne must know what she was doing and give herself to it. She must never again do such an appalling thing as she had done.

'The women's movement is built on trust.' She stopped as if Daphne would argue, but Daphne finished off her whitebait, put her head to one side and said, 'Yes?'

'That's why we don't have structures and leaders and security passes for getting into the building. Being a woman is enough. It should be enough.' *Go on, say it. Much good has it done you.* 'I've got a friend who's dying.'

'I'm sorry to hear that,' said Daphne.

'Molly's not really a friend.' It would be demeaning to appear to be seeking sympathy. 'I don't know her surname and she doesn't know mine. She lives in Suffolk and she's dying. I send her a postcard once a week because that's what she wants. For all I know she's dead already, but until I know for sure I won't stop.' Why was she dragging Molly's ravaged body into this? Molly was a private matter. The only other person Teresa had ever discussed Molly with was Beverley. She had been trying to convince Beverley that she was a good person really and so had told her about Molly.

Molly is my proof that I'm good. Writing to Molly is the sort of thing that feminists do, Daphne; we are good; and you must be too.

'My former boss used to call me Evita.'

'What?' said Teresa irritably.

'I took it to mean that he and his cronies would laugh at my deathbed. Death one accepts – though one would rather not. But one wants to be remembered with affection and respect. One would want to know that one was not forgotten at the end. What you are doing is very good, Teresa. I don't know that I . . . if I saw such an appeal, I might prefer not to think about it.'

Don't flatter me. Don't change the subject, or come the little waif. I ought to hand you over to the police for impersonating the women's movement. Trouble is, I doubt if there's any such offence.

She told Beverley that, for reasons which had seemed good at the time but which she now recognized as wrong, she had advised Daphne to apply for the European money and keep quiet about it.

'I don't believe you.'

'Why would I make it up?'

'Why would you *do* it?'

This conversation is grotesque. But they must go on using Daphne, as she has used us, they mustn't throw her away. She's good at making things happen. I'm good at taking blame. And we should all do what we're good at. 'I thought I knew best. I thought you wouldn't get the money anyway, or, if you did, you'd waste it. I didn't want you going down the same road as *Atalanta* . . .' Teresa was coming dangerously near to defending herself. Any more of this, and she might, in the face of Beverley's loyal disbelief, tell the truth. It was time for the *coup*

392

de grâce. 'Because I didn't think that anything could work unless I, directly or indirectly, was in charge of it. Because I thought you might take from Daphne what you wouldn't take from me. Because I come from the class that is used to ruling empires. Daphne doesn't. She hasn't got a degree. She hasn't got anything that she hasn't earned, and neither have her parents.'

'We've heard about them.'

'I fight it in myself, Beverley. I try to hide it. But that's the kind of person I am, and have been all along, whether you know it or not.'

Know it or not? Beverley? What Teresa had just said was Beverley's own analysis of elitism within the women's movement, spoken back to her. That was the way to get people to pay attention to you: speak their own beliefs back to them. Teresa watched the perplexity in Beverley's dark face turn to cold certainty, and knew that Beverley believed her.

Well, that wasn't difficult. Beverley's never liked me, and people are always ready to believe bad things about people they don't like. See if I care. Teresa did not care. She had done the right thing. She had other matters to think about. She was looking for a new job. She would not leave *Fiacre* until she found one because soon she would have a mortgage to pay.

The news that Teresa was soon to fly the nest and live with Sam brought about an improvement in her relationship with her sister Marion, who started inviting them round for dinner. Teresa used the opportunity to extract from Marion, an uninvolved supporter of Goddess Garments, news that would enable her to guess whether or not Daphne was still there.

Marion said, 'They've sent me a share prospectus – '

Daphne was still there.

' – but you must know this?'

'I haven't been in for a while.'

Marion asked, 'Is it true that those two Stalton's women had their names on the wall?'

'Is this on or off the record?'

'Off. Don't tell me, then. It's a nasty one, isn't it?' Marion's face took on an expression of unease, one of the few expressions with which the television-watching public were unfamiliar. It vanished into flippancy for the joky item at the end of the news. 'It's made me look at some of my colleagues with new eyes, I can tell you.' She made a throat-slitting gesture.

'That's not very funny, Marion.'

'It wasn't, was it? I'm sorry.' Marion's unease was genuine. Everyone's unease was genuine. Were career women all over the country thinking, *There but for the grace of God*? And if they were, with which of the two Stalton's women were they identifying? Gina Foreman or Hilary Linton? Or was it the other way round? Were career men thinking it too? Marion's husband and Sam were listening politely to the conversation, but their expressions betrayed nothing.

'She's mad, of course,' said Marion with relief.

'Which one?'

'Hilary Foreman. The one who did it. Apparently – this may not come out in court – but what I've heard is that she'd set up this cosy little arrangement whereby she'd have children and the other one – Gina Linton – would fit in, and then they'd swap.'

'What's wrong with that?' said Marion's husband in puzzlement. 'You did that with Rowena.'

'What's wrong with it is that she didn't tell her!'

Teresa said jovially, 'Who does this Hilary Foreman think she is – Mr Linton?' Oliver Linton had sent an extremely shirty letter to Goddess Garments asking that his wife's name be taken down from the wall. The women's indignation had not been mitigated by the fact that they had already, for different reasons, done this. Teresa had taken a deep dislike to this unseen man. 'I mean, surely the only person who's allowed to take it for granted that some woman will adapt her career to fit in with their family plans, is that woman's husband.'

'That's not very funny, Teresa,' said Marion.

65

It was one of the worst estates in town. Ann took a quick sniff at the lift and chose the stairs.

Her knock at the door of the flat was answered by a young man with a ponytail and earrings. If he had leaned forward and knifed her, she could not have been more shocked. She had understood Shelly to say that she had moved in with an old school friend, a girl, Barbara.

'Is Michelle Ainsworth here?'

What she had wanted to say was, *Is Tom here?* but she saw no reason to involve this man in her business.

'She lives here. Who wants her?'

'Who is it?' called a female voice, not Shelly's voice.

'Someone for Shell.'

Barbara appeared, buttoning up her clothes, blatant, unashamed.

'I'm Tom's mother.'

'Lucky you.' Barbara laughed.

'If Shelly's not here, can I come in and wait for her?' The pair of them seemed none too keen, but Ann smiled as if she had something to sell and walked past them.

The living room was stuffy and untidy. Three bars of an electric fire burned. The extravagance of this irritated Ann. The day was not cold. A three-year-old was playing with bricks. 'And who's this?' she said, with false heartiness.

'David,' said Barbara. 'My son.'

'David's my son-in-law's name.' It was something to say.

'What a coincidence,' said the man with the earrings. He had a giggle and Barbara joined him.

Did they dislike her as the mother of Tom who would not do the right thing by their friend, or was it that they guessed her intention to break up their cosy little household?

'Will Shelly be long?'

' 'bout five foot six," ' said Earrings, and there were more giggles. It had not been funny, and Ann wondered what they had been doing, apart from the obvious.

Whatever they had been doing, they went away, after a brief 'All right, Dave?' to continue doing it.

She asked David if she could join him in playing with his bricks. He said she could if she wanted to. He seemed a happy little boy and when her towers fell over he was very kind about it.

Through the thin walls she could hear people in the flat next door, talking in normal voices. Cold came in from outside . . . she shivered and drew closer to the fire.

'Shelly, Shelly, Shelly!' cried the little boy in delight.

'Oh, hello, Mrs Mitchison.' Shelly picked him up, hugged him and put him down again. She took off her coat to reveal a pathetic attempt to hide her pregnancy: a tight skirt and a big jumper. Perhaps she was not trying to hide it. Perhaps she could not afford maternity clothes. Ann would buy her some. She would take her shopping, like a daughter.

'Have you seen Tom?' Ann had not meant to ask this at once. She had meant to save it until she was strong enough to hear the answer. 'You don't have to tell me where he is, just tell me if you've seen him.'

'What's happened?'

'I've not seen him for a month. He didn't come back from Rideemus House – '

'I thought I was the one who was supposed to have gone there.'

'He went looking for you.'

'I suppose that's my fault.'

Ann thought it was but she did not say. It was Shelly's fault – and her father's – that they had not phoned and stopped Tom setting off. It was not their fault that Tom had fallen for Rideemus's line about giving him a commission. It was not their fault that Ann had failed to take the advice of Cult Caution, which was never to argue with cultists.

I'll be back on Thursday, Mam.

Which Thursday?

This Thursday.

You said that last Thursday. I want you back here.

You have to let me go, Mam, I know it's hard for you as a parent but you have to let me lead my own life.

She had hung up on him in disgust. These were not his words. They had been planted on him. *'As a parent.' I'm his mam! Bloody hell, Mam, leave me alone! That's how he talks. What are they doing to him?*

She had heard nothing since. She had allowed herself to believe that this meant he would be home soon. In the three weeks between his going to Rideemus House and that last call, he had been good about phoning. Every time he extended his stay – the van had broken down; he had missed the train; someone was coming from London who wanted to meet him – he had phoned to tell her not to worry. She had worried both more and less after the phone calls. Now there were no phone calls, and this was her fault, not Shelly's. Nor was it Shelly's fault that Ann had made up a little story about how he had left Rideemus but, still angry with his mother, had come to Shelly instead, to be reconciled. It was not Shelly's fault that Ann had believed this.

'Where have you been?' she said, for conversation.

'Interview.'

'That's good . . . isn't it?'

'No.'

'Ah well. At least you had the interview.' *No one's going to give you a job with that belly on you, especially if you try to hide it.*

'I'm going to get a job, Mrs Mitchison.'

'That's the spirit.'

'If my baby's not going to have a father, he's going to have everything else.'

Here? thought Ann. Shelly said she would make tea and Ann followed her into the kitchen. There was not a clean cup, plate or pan in sight. The bin was full of tins and old kitchen towels. Shelly looked like a husband, come home exasperated after a hard day's work: *Where is everybody? What is this mess? Where's my tea?*

'Come home with me, pet. I'll make your tea.'

'Tom knows where I am. I don't need to be dragged to him by his mother.'

'He's not *at* home. I told you.'

'That's his business.'

'It's your business. It's our business. If you really don't want him there's nothing I can do about it. But if this is some game the two of you are playing, you ought to know it's gone beyond a game.'

'It's not a game. He doesn't want me. He doesn't want the baby.'

'He does.'

'He's got a funny way of showing it.'

'It's the oldest way in the world. It's called hard to get. Isn't that what you're doing?' She knew she was taking a risk, saying this. She and Shelly were not all that close. But she wanted to get close.

Shelly said, 'I get my own giro, living here. I wouldn't get one if I was married.'

'You'll not go on getting it if you have men here.' Ann nodded in the direction of the bedroom.

'He's with Barbara.'

'And with a bit of luck the social security'll believe that. What are you, the cover story?'

David clamoured round Shelly's legs. 'I want hoops.'

Shelly said, 'Tell your mam to get them for you, then.' Ann wondered whether this had been said for her benefit: whether Shelly had guessed that *she* had guessed that Shelly was being made use of.

Shelly read her mind. 'She lets me live here, I help out. Fair's fair.'

'And you're happy with that, are you?'

'Yes.'

'And if I told you I could get a place for you and Tom to live you wouldn't want to know?'

'Can you?' Shelly's eyes were wide.

'Let's stay with the "ifs", I'm making no promises. But I haven't just arrived, you know. I know what you want. And you're only pretending you don't want it because you think you can't have it.' She took Shelly home, gave her her tea, and they talked.

She had worked it out as a sales strategy. The first thing to do was to identify the problem, the need.

Tom and Shelly wanted to marry each other. She knew that. All that stood in the way was pride. Each of them had, in their own way and at different times, turned the other down. Pride prevented them from admitting that they had been wrong. Pride, and the lack of anything to get married with: money, a home.

They could live with Ann while waiting for their names to come up on the housing list, but they would not want that. It was understandable. She was not all that keen on the idea herself. For all the shortcomings of Barbara's flat, Shelly saw it as her own place, and preferable to the alternative.

But there were other alternatives. 'All over the country, there's people making crafts as a hobby. Selling them for less than they cost to make. What does that say to you?'

'Says they're daft.'

'Thank you. What I'm getting at is, people who've got time to spare have usually got money to spare. Well, sometimes. And if they've got money to spare they've often got space to spare in their homes . . . living in a place that's too big for them . . .' Ann thought of Toby with a whole house to live in, to bring people back to . . . 'Retired people whose families have moved away, or people who know people who've got somewhere. Now they don't always like to advertise for tenants because they don't know who they'll get and they might not be able to get rid of them. But these people are my clients. I know them and they know me. That's how it's done. Personal contacts. Don't look like that, Shelly. We can *try*, can't we?'

'Mrs Mitchison, I'm sorry to say this, but even if you get us a flat in Buckingham Palace I'm not going to beg Tom to marry me.'

'Who's begging? We'll put it to him. "There's a home for you, there's a lass wants to marry you if you want to marry her and there's a baby on the way." ' *Arguing with cultists may turn out to be fruitless. Their twisted logic has an answer for everything. It is vital that the family remain cohesive. Let the cultist son or daughter see that the 'family' he thinks he has joined is no substitute for* . . . 'We'll put it to him and let him make up his mind.'

'From the sound of things he's already made it up.'

'His mind's not his own, pet.'

It was the hardest sale Ann had ever made.

They would apply for advertised accommodation, of course, but so would hundreds of other people. Real hope lay in personal letters to everyone Ann knew. Assurances that Tom and Shelly were responsible and honest. Shelly was good in the house, Tom was clever with his hands. Someone must know of a live-in job for a couple, or a few rooms going spare, rooms that could be paid for with housing benefit if Tom could not afford them.

If Tom were in a fit state to afford anything. Who would give a home or a job to a blank-eyed cultist?

Shelly was stiff with pride. It was no bad thing, Ann had to acknowledge. She could do with a bit of pride herself. Toby had not fulfilled his promise of a night on the town, but she was looking forward to the Newcastle craft fair with a nervousness and excitement that kept her awake at night. When she wrote to him about his pipes, she did so in formal tones – *best wishes, Ann* – but for all her anxiety about Tom she could not avoid the realization that if she found him and Shelly somewhere to live, she would have her flat to herself. If she found them somewhere to live . . . or if Tom did not come home.

66

'Gina, darling! What have they been doing to you?'

'Hello, Roy.'

'I'm here too,' said Alex on the extension.

'Have they locked her up yet?'

'This could be her last night in the bosom of her family for some time.' Gina felt no remorse speaking this way about Hilary's probable impending imprisonment. Nor did she feel particularly vindictive. It slipped out of her quite naturally. It was her normal manner of speaking: casual, flippant, outrageous. The manner of speaking of a complacent person who had once had her own tennis court . . . a clear-eyed, straight-necked, I-belong-here manner of speaking.

A clear-eyed, slit-necked . . .

A few inches to the north, and she'd have blinded me.

'We want to come and see you.'

'I'm not a pretty sight.'

'I doubt that.'

'And we don't care. Shall we come to the court and make noises in the gallery?'

'I don't really want you there. It's awful.'

'Afterwards, then?'

They met her afterwards. They hugged her and made no pretence of not seeing her scars. Roy made a special point of kissing the one on her cheek. Alex said, 'You had good looks to spare anyway. You're still ahead.'

'I'll be having plastic surgery.'

'You want that?'

'I don't want to go into hospital again.'

'Don't then. You've survived. Be proud of your battle scars.'

Oliver had taken time off work to be with her at the trial, but now he needed to get back to the office. 'Is that all right?'

'Sure.' She did not mind. It was lovely to see Roy and Alex again and she liked the idea of being alone with them. They took her for a late and expensive lunch.

'Deep remorse,' she said. 'Enormous stress. Out of character.' She counted on her fingers. 'Upright citizen. Helpful husband. Children need their mother. No purpose would be served. Psychiatric treatment. Sentence suspended.'

'I'll give her psychiatric treatment,' said Roy.

'I have heard,' said Alex, 'that women prisoners all over the country got up a petition saying, "Don't send her here." '

'Right,' said Roy. 'Or they'd all have asked to be put in solitary confinement and the system would have broken down.'

'The thing I can't take in,' said Gina, 'is that she'll just be walking about. I might meet her coming out of the cleaner's.'

'She ought to be run out of town.'

'Tied to the back of a horse.'

'Why don't you come back and work for us?' said Roy.

Was he joking? He must be; if he were serious, he would have discussed it with his brother in advance. Alex said, 'What are you talking about? We haven't got any vacancies.'

'We've always got a vacancy for Gina.'

'We could fire somebody, I suppose.'

'I've never liked that fellow you got to replace her.'

'Me? I thought it was you – '

She started to laugh uncontrollably. 'Stop it.' It was pleasure, not hysteria, and her face hardly hurt at all. She felt so safe with these two kind men who kept topping up her wine glass, fussing about her smoking and urging her to eat. 'I might take you at your word.'

'Go on then.'

'You were joking.'

'We were, but we needn't be. First vacancy that comes up, you can have it.'

She retreated. It sounded definite. It was appealing. It was too appealing. She was afraid. She had laughed when she thought they were joking, and now she was afraid. 'I may be giving up work for a while,' she said. 'Oliver and I are thinking of having a baby.'

'Put that thing out, then,' said Alex irritably, passing an ash tray.

'I'll give up when I'm pregnant.'

*

Oliver came home with a bunch of flowers and an array of treats from the delicatessen. 'So you won't have to cook. I'll give you a pasting at Scrabble, and then we can have an early night. How about that?'

'Roy and Alex have offered me a job.'

'Oh?'

'Not yet. But they said there'd probably be a vacancy within a few months.'

'You couldn't commute from here.'

'No . . . will you sit down for a minute?' She outlined what she had been thinking since the departure of the Franson brothers.

She did not want to return to Stalton's. She did want to have a baby. She did not want to have a baby in conditions that might lead her down the path trodden by Hilary. Hilary had thought that Gina would help her. She had been wrong to take that for granted, but she had been right to think that she could not do everything herself.

'I was thinking about sharing a job. Properly, with everything worked out in advance.'

'You mean Roy and Alex have got another woman who – ?'

'I meant sharing the job with you.'

'It's an interesting idea, but I've never worked with plastics.' He sounded relieved.

'So? I'd never worked with bitumen. Franson & Franson isn't like Stalton's. They don't make this big division between sales and admin. Everyone does everything. One of us would be out on the road, one of us would be at home with the telephone, the paperclips and the baby. Take turns.'

'Have you worked all this out?' said Oliver suspiciously.

'Only to myself, but I think they'd agree. They want me. They don't know you that well, but they know how well you're doing. I could put in a word for you – '

'That's big of you.'

'Just a joke.'

'What, the whole thing?'

'No. I'm serious. What do you think?'

'I think it's crazy. I'm well in at Stalton's. Nobody leaves a company like that to go to . . . well, I like Roy and Alex, but . . . and changing two good salaries for one small one?'

'People manage. People work for Roy and Alex and support a family. We might not have such a big house. Everything might not fit and match and shine . . .'

'Darling, don't use that against me. I said that in quite different circumstances.'

'I remember,' said Gina. 'It was our wedding day.'

He went out to the kitchen with his packages. She wondered whether he would notice that she had in fact started to prepare tonight's meal. If he did, he did not say, returning with a great fuss and a selection of cold meats, fancy cheeses, ready-mixed salads, and wine, which Gina declined. She had already drunk wine today and wanted to keep her head clear. 'Oliver, how did you think we'd manage?'

'Manage what? Try some of this.'

'You always said you wanted a family, didn't you? Even before you met me, you thought you'd get married and have children.'

'Of course. Doesn't everybody?'

'But how did you think you'd manage? Did you think you'd marry a little mouse who'd stay at home?'

'I can't have thought that, can I? I married you.'

'I'm not asking what you can have thought or couldn't have thought. I'm asking what you did think.'

'I don't think I did.'

'No. I don't think you did either. I think you've been putting one over on me. All that talk about how I was complacent, I took it for granted that I belonged, I took it for granted that I could have everything. You're the one who's been taking things for granted. And even more recently – when I started to say I wanted a baby – you didn't say, "How will we manage?" "What about your career?" '

'But you wanted to.'

'*You* wanted to. You always wanted to. I thought – at the worst times, I thought, maybe he's in this too. You. I thought maybe you'd got together with Hilary and Trevor and planned a nice neat arrangement that would suit everybody. Meaning, would suit you, Trevor, Stalton Industries and the Beach Boys. "Sure, let the girls have their babies. We'll carry on as before." '

'I didn't.' He scurried away to fetch the Scrabble board. He issued her with letters.

'You didn't need to! That's the missing bit. That's what I've only just realized. I couldn't really see you and Trevor planning it, but it had to have been planned. You didn't need to plan it. It was there all around you for you to assume, and you went ahead and assumed it.'

'Are we playing Scrabble or not?'

'We can play and talk. OZONE.'

'That old favourite.'

'So what do you say? Job sharing at Franson & Franson?'

'It would be a step down for me.'

'Yes. That quite often happens. When a couple have a baby, one or other of them has to take a step down in their career. But it won't be for ever. In five years – '

The prospect of leaving Stalton Industries appeared to have hit Oliver like a bereavement. He was speechless, and his letters, when he arranged them on the board, formed gibberish, ALTX ... 'What's Altx?' she said. 'You could have Lax,' she added helpfully. 'Or Tax.'

'Thank you.' He took his turn. 'Trevor's looking for a transfer,' he said, as if this were in some way material.

'I'm not surprised,' she said. The only thing that surprised her about the thoughts she had just thought and the words she had just said was that they had taken so long to come to her.

'You always worried about burnout,' she reminded him. 'You worried about getting stressed. We've seen what stress can do. Is that what you want? No one gets burned out at Franson & Franson. No one gets rich either but that's not important to you. You don't want to be the kind of person who talks about objects all the time. You grew up in a council flat. At Franson & Franson, it's just one big happy family. And that's what you want, isn't it? It's what you've always wanted. A happy family.'

'You're looking at my letters!'

'I'd change them if I were you. Anyway, we've got lots of time to think. And I'll keep taking the tablets. My sick leave ends from Monday. I'm going back to Stalton's. They're not going to get rid of me. When I'm ready, I'll get rid of them.'

'Is this an ultimatum?'

She had not thought of it as one. It had just been an idea when she had first mentioned it. But the way Oliver had reacted told her that it was an ultimatum. She saw him as two men. She saw the man she loved and had married ... and she saw Trevor Foreman, a complacent man who took everything for granted. She saw Oliver and Trevor as interchangeable, just as Trevor had seen her as interchangeable, for domestic purposes, with his wife.

Oliver need not know yet that it was an ultimatum. But when the vacancy came up at Franson & Franson, he would know. With or without him, she would go to them. 'Let's not talk about ultimatums. Let's talk about fairness.'

'Life isn't always fair.' He was trapped. He changed his letters.

'Ours is going to be. But that's enough for now. Whose turn?'

He looked at her ruefully, but not without affection or humour. 'I've just had to change my letters,' he said, 'so I think it's yours.'

67

It had taken him a long time to admit that some of it made sense.

Take away pain and cruelty from jokes, and what are you left with? Very little. Think of one joke that isn't about someone being hurt or killed, embarrassed or thought inferior, misunderstood or badly treated. Just one. You can't.

'Take banana skins,' said Professor Richardson. He was Visiting Professor of Psychotheolistics, up from London on a visit. ' "Falling on a banana skin" is a catch phrase for a certain type of joke. There are equivalents in other languages, which is revealing. Have any of you ever fallen on a banana skin? Was it really funny? Of course it wasn't.

'And why a banana skin, anyway? It's slippery, granted. But it's not the only thing that's slippery. You could just as easily fall on ice. More easily, there's more of it. But no. Banana skins it is. Bananas have a characteristic shape with sexual associations. Which brings us to the Flesh . . .'

Which brings us to the Flesh. Everything brought them to something else, and sooner or later it was the Flesh, or Authority, or Eternity. Tom still found the lectures boring, but not as boring as he had found them when he had not understood them, when he had been resisting their meaning.

'You're resisting the meaning, Tom. Why? What have you got to lose? Have you got the answer? Do you understand the mind of God, His purposes? If you've got an answer that's better than ours, I'll gladly listen to it,' said Professor Richardson in one of their moments alone, walking on the moor. Tom tried sometimes to go for a walk on his own, to think, but one or other of his new friends always came with him. He had felt honoured when Professor Richardson offered to come.

'I don't know if I believe in God.'

'Fine. Have you got an explanation that excludes God? I know you're resisting, because I resisted myself. I didn't want to believe in a God who's playing jokes on us, particularly when I realized how much cruelty there is in humour. But God doesn't mean to be cruel. He isn't cruel. We perceive His ways as cruel sometimes because we haven't fully understood that what He wants is to laugh with us, not at us.'

Tom remembered religious instruction lessons at school. He remembered how irritated he used to get with teachers who said, *It's true because it's in the Bible, and it's in the Bible because it's true.* He had had a friend once who had felt the same about Karl Marx: *As Marx correctly said . . .* These people were just the same. They kept coming back to the same phrases. But how could he argue with a professor? A man the same age as his father would have been, a man who singled him out to go for walks, a man who had heard of A. J. Ribson?

'A very great man, Tom.'

'What's your theory on Sally, then?'

'Sally? Remind me . . .'

'The automaton. How did he do it?'

'Ribson had special powers. There's no doubt about that.'

'I reckon it was a hoax,' said Tom. In fact, he had an open mind on the subject. But he did not think that Professor Richardson knew as much as he did about Ribson, and he wanted to impress him. 'I reckon he knew a few things no one else knew about magnets and electricity.'

' "Hoax" is a very interesting word. It comes from the same root as "Hocus" which is widely used in witchcraft.'

'There's no witchcraft in my models. Simple mechanical principles. Once I get started – '

'Oh yes, I heard about that. You're going to make a model of God creating the world – '

'As soon as I can get started,' Tom repeated. 'As soon as I can get some tools. I could go home and get my own – ' They had reached the top of the hill that they had agreed to walk to before turning round. It was a clear day and they could see for miles, as far as the nearest town, the town with the station, eight miles. *I could go home.*

Professor Richardson was looking at him in a queer way. Not *queer*

queer: Tom could recognize that a mile off and would have nothing to do with it. This was different. There was a fondness there, of a kind he had never had . . . or had lost before he could remember having it. 'I thought we were supplying you with tools.'

'Well, they did say, but they seem to have forgotten.'

'Typical. They have a skilled craftsman staying with them and they don't make use of him. Didn't you go into town yesterday?'

'Aye, but that was for recruiting.' He had thought that it was to get him some tools, but he had ended up recruiting.

Excuse me, sir, do you have a few minutes to answer some questions?
Go on.

Has anything made you laugh today?

Eh?

Anything at all. I'm part of a multicultural research institute and we're collecting examples of regional humour –

Sometimes he had got an answer, sometimes not. Whatever he got, he had to write it down and move on to, *Can you tell me, in your own words, why you thought that was funny?*

It's hard to say. Seemed funny at the time, but now you mention it –

Would you agree that there's a lot of cruelty in humour? Would you agree that there's a lot of cruelty in the world? If there were an explanation of that – one that offered hope – would you be interested in hearing it?

He was supposed to enrol them for a seminar, and take a deposit off them. It amazed him how many people showed interest in the seminar, even if it was just to get rid of him. *Aye, well, maybe . . .* He had his response ready: his own response, and his official Rideemus response. His own response he silenced: *Look, I'm not a nutter. There's something in this.* There had to be something in it, or he would not be doing it. The official response was to ask for a deposit. If they jibbed at that, he had to say, *I'll enrol you anyway, sir, or madam.* He must always call them sir or madam, even if they were his own age. He avoided people his own age. *I'll enrol you anyway and I'll pay your deposit myself. Don't worry about it. We have to do that, to keep the books straight. You can give it back to me when you come to the seminar.*

He did not pay their deposits for them, of course. He had no money. It was not a con, his Rideemus friends assured him. People valued things that others paid for, for them. That was why the deposits, if paid, were refundable on request if, at the end of the seminar, the person did not feel they had enhanced their potential for living life more fully. That was why nobody paid for their own seminar or service. They were invited to contribute so that someone else could benefit. *A chain of giving, Tom. Kindness to make up for the cruelty in the world. You think that's funny?*

He might have, once. But 'funny' no longer meant what he had thought it meant.

They had urged him, in town yesterday, to sign on for social security. They would give him an address. It was not that they minded paying for his bed and board, it was just that he was depriving someone else.

He had said that he would sign on, thinking that they would leave him to do it on his own and he could give them the slip and get himself on to a train. He had no money – he had donated the fare money that his mother had given him – but he could tell the ticket collector that his mother would pay. His mother. She thought he was in a cult. He had told her that he had got a job. What a fool he would look when he confirmed that he had got a job all right: stopping people in the street and asking them to tell jokes.

I can't sign on, I'm employed, self-employed, I've got my own business.

Have it your own way.

And I'll be going home soon.

'There's one thing that puzzles me,' said Professor Richardson. 'If you don't believe in God, how do you think you can make a model of Him creating the world?'

They were walking back down the hill towards Rideemus House. How could Tom argue with a professor? He did not even want to. 'I don't not believe in Him. But it's neither here nor there, is it, Professor Richardson? It's just a model, a commission. I'll do it in accordance with your beliefs.'

'So you'll need to find out more about what those beliefs are, won't you?'

It all came back to the Flesh. Authority, Eternity and the Flesh. All jokes were on one or other of these themes. The Flesh covered sex jokes and jokes about illness and bodily functions. Authority was anything to do with judges, policemen, teachers, bosses, mothers-in-law and, of course, God. Eternity was . . . Eternity.

The significant thing about Authority, Eternity and the Flesh was that they corresponded to the three aspects of the triple godhead, best known in Western society as Father, Holy Spirit and Son.

There was an angler who died. He had been a sinner. He had neglected his wife and children to go fishing, taken time off work, poached. He was anxious, but it seemed to be all right when a figure whom he took to be an angel (Authority) met him at the pearly gates, took him into a field and sat him down to fish. He had all the right equipment – no sandwiches, but he was not hungry – it was a lovely sunny day and the fish were biting. He caught fish after fish, bright-eyed, plump, shiny. (The Flesh.) He filled his net. The angel took it away and brought him another one. He filled it. Same thing happened. On and on it went. He started to get bored, but he did not like to say anything, this place was all he had ever wanted. At last he plucked up courage to say to the angel – just casually – 'What time does the sun go down?' The angel said, 'It doesn't,' and took away the net. Next time the angel came back, the man said, 'When's the close season?' 'There's no close season,' said the angel. The man said, 'Oh hell.' The angel said, 'Exactly.' (Eternity.)

Tom shivered. It was too real. Things going on for ever, even things you liked . . . but a girl said, 'That's the perfect theme for Tom's model.'

At last they were talking about it.

'Fishing. Maybe that's how God created the world. He cast His line into the firmament and drew it out.'

'That's an interesting idea, Lucy,' said Professor Richardson. 'What do you think, Tom?'

'If that's what you want.' It sounded daft to him. If God had a line and a firmament to cast it in, creation must have already begun. Whatever He drew out must have been there before. But Tom could do it, if that was what they wanted. He could make an old man fishing, with the world on His hook. It could be a perpetual-motion machine along the lines of the peacock fountain. He could make the water gurgle through the old man with a sound like laughter if that was what they wanted.

'Never mind what *we* want.' The professor looked at Tom as if they were the only two people in the room. As if he would wait patiently for as long as it took for Tom to say what he, the professor, wanted to hear. 'This is your model, and you've got to believe in it. How do you believe the world began?'

'Energy. An explosion of natural energy.'

'And that was it?'

'That was it.'

'Can you make that?'

No one could make a model of natural energy. He had another idea: one that he would like and they would like. One that they would let him get on with. It came out of one of the lecturers. It was funny – funny in the true sense of being deeply serious – that one third of the world had too much to eat and not enough to do, while the other two thirds had the opposite.

'If there were a way to transfer energy – human energy – '

'Yes? Yes, Tom?' They were breathless, eager in the way they became eager when someone got up to offer money, eager to know how much he would offer. They knew Tom had no money to offer. They wanted to hear his idea. He was the most important person in the room.

'Like – a wheel – as big as the world. Turned by us. Making energy for them.' Energy to fuel machines for those who tilled the soil by hand. Energy to move water along pipes into the homes of those who had to walk miles for it. Unemployed energy. A wheel.

'We have a wheel and we have a fisherman,' said the professor. 'Have we any other ideas?'

Why was he asking for other ideas? Tom wanted to get started on his world and his wheel. He felt light-headed, alert. Others had talked about this moment: the moment when you stopped resisting meaning and were rewarded with an insight into the mind of God. The moment when you saw the joke. He had seen people in tears of laughter, like nutters. He had not become a nutter, he just wanted to get started on his model. If tears burned his eyes, it was because he missed his model-making. It was weeks since he had made anything. He coughed and swallowed. 'I'll need some tools.'

'What about the tools in the shed?' said Lucy.

No one had mentioned tools or sheds. Lucy took him to look at them. They were old but serviceable: saws, planes, gougers, screws. 'Why didn't you tell me you had these? I could have got started.'

'Could you? You didn't know what you were going to make before.'

'I thought you'd tell me.'

'God has told you.'

'What about wood?'

'God will give you what you need. We'll all go for a walk tomorrow and let Him show you what He wants you to do.'

He thought it had already been decided what he was to do.

Back in the lecture room, discussion still raged on what God had looked like, creating the world. Wheels and fishermen had gone by the board. Someone thought God had laid the world like an egg and that was why hens made a laughing sound when they laid eggs. Tom listened politely, but he was set on his wheel. He was not sure how he would do it, but wheels and energy came into it. He did not want to listen to any more, he wanted to get started. 'Maybe God gave birth,' said someone. Professor Richardson nodded. 'God as female.

Yes, that's interesting.' Shelly came into Tom's mind. Shelly, with his baby growing inside her. Never mind models of God, never mind automatons, Tom had made a person. He might never meet that person, but without him that person would not exist. (The Flesh. You couldn't take it in, so you laughed. . . .) Why was he assuming that he would never see the baby? Of course he would see it, he would be home by the time it was born. He would be allowed to see it, wouldn't he? Even if Shelly did not want to marry him, he would be allowed to see his son, his daughter.

68

Alistair was worried about the Daphne Barclay Festival of Selling. Correction. He was jealous about the Daphne Barclay Festival of Selling. It was her idea, her project; why shouldn't she have her name on it? 'We haven't got enough bookings.'

'I've hardly begun.'

'And you're not going to be able to, are you? You were counting on using the START mailing lists – '

Of course she was using the lists. What did he think she was, stupid? She had copies of the lists at home. Who was to know? 'They'll be hanging from the chandeliers.'

'That venue is ridiculous.'

'Where would you prefer? Ambridge Parish Hall?'

'I think we should cancel.'

'It's too late,' said Daphne. 'The cancellation fees would be – '

' – peanuts, compared with what we stand to lose, both financially and in terms of prestige, if we have you and a couple of hundred delegates rattling around in – '

'I never rattle around.'

'Daphne. I want to cancel.'

Alistair was richer than Daphne so his holding in their partnership was greater than hers. But she worked harder. It had been agreed that she would. She had more energy than he had, for travelling and speaking. Technically, his was the final say on matters of controversy. Morally, hers was.

They had never had a matter of serious controversy before. Their different qualities complemented each other and they worked in harmony. She could not believe that they were going to fall out over this.

'Daphne, don't you think we should have a talk? About this, about everything?'

They went out for dinner. They went to a small fish restaurant – Alistair was counting pennies – where the low prices were reflected in the urgency with which the waiters pressed them to order, eat, pay and go.

'As you know,' he said, 'I only saw my involvement – my active involvement – in DBBT as a short-term thing.'

As you know. That's what Lindbergh Stanley says. 'He's probably watching us,' Alistair had said, that night at the bistro. *'By satellite.'*

'I thought I'd help set you up, do a few of the things I wanted to do and then find someone suitable to buy me out, someone you liked and could work with.'

'You are the only person I can work with.' She was sincere about this. She had never met anyone else whom she could imagine having even technical control over her.

'Thank you for that, but can we keep to the point? I'm not denying that I wanted more out of this than I've . . . than has turned out to be the case. I told you that. I told you that I wanted to be close to you in more than a professional way, but that was foolish and unfair of me as I see now.'

'It wasn't foolish. It wasn't unfair. I have no interest in young men.'

'It wasn't my age I was referring to.'

'Sorry,' she said, meaning it. When old age came to her she intended to accept it with grace and dignity, but she would not appreciate constant references to it. Alistair was in an unusual mood tonight. It was a long time since they had had any purely social contact . . . but this was not social. Alistair had brought her here to read the riot act. She was impressed.

'I was referring to the fact that Daphne Barclay Business Training was set up with two purposes in mind, one of which was to help the unemployed – '

'And the second was to earn money to make that possible.'

'But that's all we do do, and it never becomes possible.'

This was an outrageous lie, but there was no point in reminding him about her work with Goddess Garments, of which he disapproved, and not just for the reasons to which he admitted. Casually mentioning one day that some of the women there were lesbians but very nice, she was sure she had seen him flinch.

'It never will become possible if you go around wanting to cancel the sort of event that will put us on the map. I'm going to give free tickets to the unemployed.' She planned to send a sheaf of the tickets to Collindeane Tower, to the value of the unspent grant.

'Whether they want them or not.'

'That's up to them. What is this, Alistair? Are you pulling out on me?'

'I think it's time you looked around for another partner.'

Daphne had never had sex with a man as a way of getting something out of him. She was not going to give anyone reason to say that she had slept her way to the top.

She had not held to strict virginity, though she might as well have done, for all the pleasure sex had given her. She had never enjoyed sex because she had never respected the men she had had it with. She had respected them before – it could not have happened otherwise – but not afterwards. The only thing she had felt for them afterwards had been comradely pity, lest their embarrassment be as great as her own. The things one did. The things one said. The things one allowed to be done to one.

But Alistair was not his usual self this evening. He was giving her an ultimatum, and she was not used to that, from him, from anyone. Excitement mingled with outrage and anxiety. She had met her match. And with the thought came longing: if she had really met her match in Alistair, she might yield a little, rest in him. She might have the burden taken off her shoulders of always being in charge, always having to be right.

'I don't think I've always appreciated you, Alistair.'

'I agree, but that's my fault. I'm not asking you to feel things you don't feel.'

'Why do you think I don't feel them?' She was going carefully. This man was no fool and she had hurt his pride. She had done this inadvertently, but she had done it. 'I'm not always very good at expressing what I do feel.' *And that's probably just as well*, she thought, while the waiters dumped down cups of frothy coffee, slopping the saucers. Her body was alert with anticipation. What would he be like? He was old but fit: slightly on the plump side, but the flesh on those parts of him that she could see was reasonably firm and no more wrinkled than one would expect. Her own flesh was taut and spare and smooth. The thought of the two kinds of flesh coming together made her feel sick with excitement and curiosity; but she must go carefully. 'If you leave, I shall leave too. I shall cut my losses and place myself in the hands of Lindbergh Stanley.' She smiled. 'I speak metaphorically.'

'What do you feel about me, Daphne? Really?'

'I'm very fond of you and I'm sorry that you should have to ask.'

'And the future – ?'

She shrugged. 'As you know, START Selling International – '

'No. Your future. When you're my age, will you be happy to think that all you've done is – '

'Your bill, sir.'

' – don't you want to settle down? Don't you want to have children? I don't mean mine, I'm past that, but ... isn't there a woman in you?'

Not for nothing had Daphne served her time at Collindeane Tower. 'There is a woman, but perhaps not the one you'd like there to be.' *All Women Welcome.* With precise and icy courtesy the feminists had welcomed the European delegation. Through gritted teeth they had answered their questions. They had taken Daphne's point that to tell the truth about her and Teresa's small, well-meant deception – no, omission – would not simply make them look fools, it would make the Europeans look fools too. People who had been made to look foolish did not think kindly of those who had achieved this. The coffers of this particular European committee were, for the moment, empty, but its individual members would move on, and if they took with them a favourable impression of Collindeane Tower as a thriving hive of alternative enterprise, what largesse might not come its way in the future? Besides, to prove that Daphne Barclay Business Training was not a bona fide women's liberation group, they would have to define what that was; and they could not.

After the Europeans had gone, Daphne had explained to the women that they were still entitled to many days of her consultancy services. They had told her to get out and stay out. 'Not All Women Welcome, then?' she had said. 'You're not one of us,' they had replied.

An expectant queue of diners was forming near Daphne and Alistair's table. 'Can we go somewhere and talk about this?' she said.

'Where did you have in mind?'

'My place.' She had never allowed a man into her flat on his own. It had always been their place, so that she could escape.

Alistair looked so suspicious that she almost felt she should assure him that her intentions were honourable. It seemed an amusing thing to say, so she said it. 'So are mine,' he said.

In olden days when a man said that, it meant that he did not intend to make love to the woman. In these more permissive times it meant that he did not intend to do so without her full-hearted consent . . . or his own. He followed her home like a dog, sat himself coldly in a chair, demanded coffee and did what he had come to do, which was talk. He would have talked all night if she had let him: about friendships and partnerships, realism and hubris, honesty and ethics. He talked as the Collindeane women talked, and her response, though unspoken, was the same. There was only one ethic and that was the ethic of providing people with what they needed. Any other ethics were a luxury, exclusive to those who did not have to struggle: those who lived in safe, self-contained worlds, whether of wealth or of ideology. What gave Alistair, what gave the Collindeane women, the right to opt out of what lesser mortals had to do, which was to make compromises in order to be effective? Why should they opt out of the obligation to be effective? The Daphne Barclay Festival of Selling would put DBBT on the map, and then it could do whatever it wanted.

Alistair wanted to talk about ethics but Daphne wanted to take him to bed. And, when it came to it, it was easy, because he loved her.

It took her breath away, the way he loved her. Her experience was of tussles and violence (for not even the most delicate and courteous entry into her body could be seen by Daphne as other than violent) followed by indifference and regret. This was different and new. He sat on the edge of the bed. He could have been sitting at his desk, but for the fact that he was naked and smiling a smile halfway between affection and mischief. He pulled her towards him and administered love with his hand. Not even his whole hand, his finger and his thumb. She was under his thumb. They were both naked but he was sitting while she lay, gasping. It took her breath away.

She thought at first that it was a prelude. She had experienced such things and knew how to get it over with, for in her experience men did not like this any more than she liked it, any more than she wanted to like it. She made appropriate noises and movements of appreciation and waited for him to lie down on top of her and do what she was used to. But he did not. He was searching for something and had not found it yet. He found it and went on with his search. She found it, and found it again. She was breaking down. She was appalled at her own delight.

'Come in me.' It was the first time she had ever asked.

'Are you on the pill?'

Why would she be? She muttered something about it being all right, the time being all right.

'Better not risk it,' he said. 'Time was I'd have come equipped, but it never occurred to me . . . oh, Daphne, you're crying, have I hurt you?' He stopped sitting there, stopped looking down at her and took her in his arms. She had not been aware of crying, but she felt him kiss away something wet. Of course he had not hurt her. Would she allow him to hurt her? How dare he ask, in his power, as if he had it in his gift to hurt her or not hurt her?

'What about you?' she said.

'What *about* me?' he said genially, lying down beside her, placing himself in her hands.

This was something she had not encountered since her school days; and, having encountered it once then, had resolved never to encounter it again. All or nothing would be her approach to sex, she had decided: mostly, nothing. Between teenagers, this was undignified; between a grown man and woman . . .

But she obliged. She could hardly not, and at least it ended the disturbing business that had been going on before.

69

Sunrise over industrial landscape filled Daphne with awe. Pylons strode through mist. This was a depressed area. Speeding along the motorway, Daphne found nothing depressing about it. Daphne was never depressed. She did not allow it, and neither should anyone else: not people, not areas, not countries.

An empty factory could be filled up. Tarpaulins could be pulled back off heaps of bricks and the bricks used. Broken windows could be mended. Silent machinery could be turned on again, providing employment perhaps for the misguided youngster who had broken the window, employment and rehabilitation.

It was a depressed area. It was nothing of the kind. There was no such thing as an unemployed person. There was a person looking for an opportunity. This was an Opportunity Area and the local authority were putting on an Opportunity Day. Businessmen had been invited in from all over the country, and from abroad, to view the opportunities. Daphne turned left, following the signs to the industrial estate.

'Although we have a high level of unemployment, this in no way reflects on the qualities of the workforce, which is skilled, eager and adaptable. Many companies have found that the area provides a refuge from the wage-inflation spiral . . .' She walked past the video, the officials eager to answer her questions. 'I'm a speaker,' she explained. She was not an exhibitor. She did not need to be an exhibitor, she had been invited to speak. START Selling, she noted, had rented space for an exhibition stand. 'I'm a speaker,' she said again, loudly. START Selling would not like that. START Selling liked to be the ones to provide speakers. But the local authority had wanted a woman and had asked for Daphne by name.

She was to appear on a panel to discuss 'Training for Competitiveness', with a local industrialist, a junior minister from the government and a trade union official. 'That was your bread and butter,' said the chairman jovially to the audience when these three had spoken their pieces. 'Now for your cake.' Daphne did not mind being called cake. They could call her whatever they liked, as long as they listened to her.

This was the start of a busy week for Daphne. She liked to be busy. Things did not always work out so neatly, with bookings and meetings in the same part of the country, East Anglia in this case. Tomorrow she was at Chestnut Computers. On Wednesday she would be seeing a number of people about block bookings for the Daphne Barclay Festival of Selling. On Thursday she was booked to lecture to trainee sales managers at a factory near Ipswich, and, this being conveniently close to where her parents lived, she would go to them to spend the night and pick up the last three instalments of the money they owed her.

'Women,' she said now as the applause died down, 'are the nation's greatest under-used resource.' She ignored the smattering of ribaldry. She was used to it, she hardly heard it. 'Women are one-third of the workforce, and the industry that ignores them does so at its peril.' She made a few more remarks along these lines from the notes prepared for her by Alistair, and then moved on with relief to her main topic which was the value of sales training in general, her kind in particular. 'Your salesmen and saleswomen are the best. If they are not the best, why are they on your staff? If they are the best, give them the best.' *Give them me. You can afford me. You can't afford to be without me.* 'Give them the chance to do their best, for you. Perhaps you don't want to spare them for long, expensive residential courses. But can't you spare them for one day? The most important day of their lives?' Daphne Barclay Business Training had not been able to afford an exhibition stand at the Opportunity Day, but this was better. She was not paying them, they were paying her to speak.

'On the general subject of women in industry, Daphne,' said the chairman, 'I wonder if you'd agree that – '

'Yes of course.'

'What I was going to say – '

'I am so sorry.'

' – women aren't their own worst enemies – ?'

'As a woman I have no enemies. As a saleswoman I have no enemies either. I see only two kinds of people: customers and competitors. That is the approach that I will be encouraging delegates to adopt at my forthcoming – '

The government minister interrupted her, obviously feeling upstaged. His party political broadcast concerned fascinating new developments in tax laws concerning investment and employment subsidies. 'The Prime Minister has said – ' *The Prime Minister has said. The Prime Minister has sent this nonentity along. The Prime Minister should be here herself.* Daphne longed to meet the Prime Minister and knew that one day she would. They would have so much to talk about. In the meantime, she let the underling speak. She had acquitted herself well. Let the audience form its own conclusions. On their seats were booking forms for the Daphne Barclay Festival of Selling. She had put them there herself, along with their official literature. The event organizers might not like that; they might think that she should book an exhibition stand if she wanted to exhibit; but nobody had stopped her. One advantage of being a woman was that if you did menial things, everybody assumed that you were an officially authorized menial and left you to get on with it.

At Chestnut Computers there was a message for her to phone Alistair urgently. She did not do so. It could only mean trouble, and it was as much his job to deal with trouble as it was hers, while he was her partner. He had yielded on the matter of the Festival of Selling – Daphne having convinced him that she could fill the venue – but had not changed his mind about wanting to retire as soon as a replacement could be found. Daphne accepted this philosophically and with a certain amount of embarrassment. She could not now remember what had led her to go to bed with Alistair, but, he having made it clear that he had not seen it as part of any kind of deal – would, indeed, regard it as an insult to both of them if it had been – Daphne could hardly suggest that it was. Had it been? She could not remember. All she could remember was grief and fear at the thought that she might lose him: a grief and fear that had expressed itself as fondness, a fondness that had got out of control.

'I'm not going anywhere, Daphne,' he had said. 'I had thought I might have another try at the Cardiff project, but now – ' he had taken her hand, squeezed it, as if to remind her of what she had not forgotten ' – I want to be with you but I don't want to be arguing with you.'

'We never argue. Hardly ever.'

'When I wasn't arguing with you, I was putting up with you. I want to love you. Save the arguing for your new partner, and then when we're together I'll always be on your side.'

Very cosy, she thought.

'You can use the phone in my office, Miss Barclay,' said her host at Chestnut Computers.

'No, no,' she said. 'Your staff are waiting for me, and I am here for them.'

On Wednesday, Alistair was unable to reach her. He tried desperately, as she was later to discover. He could not reach her because he did not know where she was. She had not told him that she was visiting former START clients because, unnerved by the threat of legal action, he would have stopped her. Daphne still did not take START's threats seriously, for how could you prove in court who 'owned' a customer and who was to know that she still had the mailing lists? She was wrong. She discovered how wrong she was in the worst possible place: at her parents' home with her parents listening in. Alistair knew she was there and phoned her there. He was phoning from a friend's house. His own phone was out of order, having been accidentally ripped from the wall by bailiffs with a warrant to search for START property. A similar accident had occurred at the office. 'They've been very thorough,' said Alistair grimly. 'They've had the floorboards up, they've cleaned out our cupboards and they've taken away our papers. Oh, and they've frozen our bank account.'

'What papers?'

'Accounts, address lists, you name it.' Alistair was very calm and very angry. 'But we don't have to worry too much.' He did not mean this. 'It could be all right, according to my solicitor. This sort of thing could close a business down and the courts don't do it lightly. START had to give an undertaking to compensate us when they're proved wrong, which they will be, won't they, Daphne? We're under an injunction not to trade with our START contacts, but that's all right, isn't it, because we haven't been, have we? They're suing us for lost business, but they haven't lost any business to us, have they? You're probably right not to answer. Get yourself a solicitor.'

She found her voice. 'We've got a . . .' she would not say 'solicitor' with her parents listening. 'We've got one.'

'One for you personally, Daphne, just as I've got one for me personally. Get yours to phone mine. Goodbye.'

The knowing look that passed between her parents as she put the receiver down turned her terror into rage. 'He is my *partner*!'

'We never thought anything else.'

'Have you known him long?'

'How have you been?' she said. 'How is Farrukh?'

'He's done wonders with the delicatessen counter,' said her father. 'Here, this is for you.' He handed her a cheque made out to Daphne Barclay Business Training. 'You might as well hang on to it,' she said shortly, and her father made fainting motions, for which he was rebuked by Daphne's mother who said, 'That's very generous of you, Daphne.'

'It must be love,' said her father. Daphne turned her back on him and pumped her mother for local gossip, convincing her that she wanted to hear everything.

'Janet Moore – that's Janet Hardy – is going for a divorce, I wonder it took her so long. Mrs Dankworth's got shingles – '

'But not from our salami, in case you were wondering,' said Daphne's father.

' – and old Mrs Kerslake's died finally – '

' – as opposed to dying temporarily – '

'Ha ha. Mum, I'm sorry. Was she a friend of yours?'

'No, dear. I never saw her, never saw either of them, nobody did. I don't know what the sister'll do now.'

'I heard Mrs Kerslake had left it all to women's lib.'

'She can't have,' said Daphne.

'Hear that, Mrs Kerslake?'

'Allow me to know something about it. Women's lib is not the sort of thing to which you can leave money. It doesn't exist in that way. It should, but it won't let itself.'

'If they don't know what to do with the money, they can give it to us.'

'Is the sister still there, Mum?'

'Thelma Cook, yes. Mrs Kerslake was Molly Cook. She married a banker, they never had any children, she was supposed to have been a bit funny.'

A fly felled by insecticide will buzz and twitch for a long time. It will lie as if finished; then it will enter a frenzy as if about to resume its normal activities. Thelma Cook reminded Daphne of such a fly. She was on her feet; but energy and will came to and went from her various functions in a way that was arbitrary and disconcerting. Daphne had watched her long shuffle to the door through the frosted glass, wondering what was going on during the many pauses: rest? reflection? indecision? Now the eyes swam into and out of focus behind thick lenses as the woman inspected Daphne over the security chain; the balding head turned to hear better, and turned away again as if it did not matter.

'I've come about Molly.'

'Mrs Kerslake has passed away.'

'I'm sorry if I sounded over-familiar, but Molly was what I knew her as. I used to send postcards.'

'What?'

Daphne might be barking up the wrong tree. The only reason why the late Molly Kerslake should have been Teresa's Molly was that everything fitted. And luck was what happened when preparation met opportunity.

'*Postcards!*'

'You?'

'Yes.'

'Which one are you?'

'Teresa.'

'Teresa! Oh, come in, dear!'

Swathed in cardigans, the old lady hobbled ahead of Daphne towards the sitting room. The air was dim and slightly fishy. Under its dust the furniture was antique. With contents, £80,000 to £90,000.

'You were very faithful, weren't you, Teresa? The others came and went, but your card arrived every week. It got delayed in the post once or twice, and Molly fretted. "I hope Teresa's all right." ' This burst of coherence appeared to have worn out Thelma Cook, who sat. ' "What a dear girl she must be." '

'How sweet of her.'

'Would you like to see the room?'

'Not if it's an intrusion.'

Thelma Cook looked vague, muttered something about '. . . intrusion . . . a friend . . .'

The walls of the sick room were covered with postcards. There were flowers. 'From your family?'

'I am the last of the family . . .'

So if the will fails, it all goes to you. While you last. 'What a shame. Who is looking after you?'

'I don't need any looking after. I looked after *her*, didn't I? Don't need . . . such a comfort . . .'

'It was the least I could do,' said Daphne, 'for such an important foresister.'

'Important what, dear?'

'Fore-sister.'

'I don't know that one. We got out of touch. We stopped all our subscriptions because of the solicitor's bills.'

Hairs rose warningly on Daphne's neck at the word *solicitor;* but she wanted to know what Thelma Cook had meant. Her vagueness seemed to come in cycles; Daphne caught the next burst of coherence. 'Molly could never make up her mind which branch of the women's movement she supported. Every time another newsletter arrived, she'd change her will. She thought . . . bang their heads together . . . united. What did you say your name was? Who are you?'

'Teresa. I came to pay my respects.'

'Oh yes. You wrote to us. You never missed.'

'Would you like me to leave?'

'Tell me everything.'

She was lonely. Her age was unimaginable. Nursing her sister could not have been easy; but they had had each other for a long time.

'I'm a management consultant.'

'A what, dear?'

'I help women's groups to be efficient. To use their money wisely.'

'What makes you think I've got money?'

'I don't.'

'There's no will, you know,' said Thelma Cook. Daphne took her hand. What started as an admonitory pat became an intimate squeeze, as Daphne placed her face close enough to Thelma Cook's for her sincerity to be visible, but not so close as to arouse fear.

'Miss Cook, you must not allow strangers into your house or discuss your private affairs with them. You must take proper advice.'

'Solicitors. Arm and a leg. Men. Do you want a drink? What time is it?' They had coffee, which seemed to steady Thelma Cook's brain. 'Which is the best one?'

'Solicitor?'

'Women's group.'

'My own company.'

'You naughty girl.'

Daphne smiled. 'You asked.'

'Is it sensible?'

'Very sensible.'

'Does it have arguments?'

'No.'

'What does it do?'

'I told you. It gets people organized.'

'You're just saying that, to get my money.'

Daphne drained her coffee cup. 'I shouldn't have come,' she said in a small voice.

'Wait . . . let me see you off . . .'

Daphne waited. 'You'll come again?' said Thelma Cook.

'Only on one condition.' Daphne pointed to a cracked pane in the glass of the front door. 'That you'll let me mend this for you.'

'You are a clever girl, Teresa! Molly would have loved you. What else can you do?'

'This and that,' said Daphne, clasping the old lady's hand in both of hers, feeling her rings, smiling au revoir.

Gloom pressed in on her as she drove to London. She had to go home. She did not want to go home. They had searched Alistair's house; they would search her flat. They might already have done so. Did the warrant allow them to kick the door down or would they be waiting for her return? Must she turn her own key in her own lock and open the door to these people who would damage her home and go through her personal belongings to turn up evidence of her guilt . . . *Guilty, your honour. Guilty of trying to do business.*

70

Flat-hunting for Tom and Shelly was taking up most of Ann's time. She was neglecting her clients – all but those who showed the slightest sign of being able to help her.

Few did, and those that did were a disappointment. A retired couple in Stockton showed her and Shelly over the top half of their house. It had its own bathroom and would have been ideal. But it was a misunderstanding. They had been looking for someone who would buy the top half of their house.

'Do we look as if we've got that kind of money?' Shelly grumbled as they drove away.

'We must do. We'll take it as a compliment,' said Ann, to whom it was nothing of the kind. She was trying to keep Shelly's spirits up as a way of keeping up her own. Flat-hunting was better than worrying. Flat-hunting could be reduced to a plan on paper, a list of telephone numbers. Evidence for the existence of what was needed was all around: houses, flats, everywhere. Somewhere was the right place. If they kept on looking, they would find it, and Tom would come home.

A maker of stuffed toys in East Boldon had a sister who kept a boarding house. They went to see it. The place stank and the room was half a room with a partition. 'I'm better off where I am,' said Shelly.

The landlady said: 'Suit yourselves.'

Ann thought that she and Shelly understood each other. With a shared anxiety and a shared purpose, they were becoming friends. But something needed to be got clear right away. 'If you've made up your mind to stay at Barbara's, you'd better say so.'

'I didn't say that. Would you take a baby there?'

Ann sighed. 'No.'

'I do want him back.'

'You do, eh?'

'If he's still himself.'

Ann did not want to think about that. She preferred to go flat-hunting. 'So what was all that "get out of my sight"?'

'I bet you never said that when you didn't mean it,' said Shelly with a sly smile. She was very sure of herself, almost pert. Ann would never have talked to her mother-in-law in such a way. But she was not Shelly's mother-in-law. And anyway, she liked her.

'Sorry, Mrs Mitchison.'

'What for?'

'You might have thought I was talking about when you and Tom's dad were – '

Ann, who had been thinking no such thing, laughed. 'Neale chased me until I caught him.' Sometimes she thought she would tell Shelly about Toby. It would increase their closeness if Shelly knew that they were in the same boat. They were not, not really. Shelly admitted that she wanted Tom, whereas Ann had written Toby off.

More or less. She would probably see him at the Newcastle craft fair.

The circumstances would in fact be perfect for her to see him. He had not said that he would definitely be there, so she was not holding out any hopes. And where you did not hold out hope, you could not be disappointed. If he were there, she would be casual. Newcastle was home territory for her, so he would not have the slightest grounds for thinking she was there for any purpose other than to sell her clients' crafts. He, on the other hand, would have come a long way, especially considering it was only a hobby for him.

She would wait and see how he treated her and respond in kind. She was not going to get into a state about it. She had written him off to experience . . . an experience which, for all its limitations, many women of her age might be glad of. More or less.

Dear Ann, I had a word with Sue and she knows a block of old people's flats looking for a caretaker couple. They'd prefer someone older than T and S, but it's worth a try. Phone them as soon as possible. In haste, Gwen.

In haste, Gwen. Yes, goodbye. Ann had hesitated before asking Gwen. Gwen's own house was much too big for one person. But that was her business, and Ann would have died rather than have Gwen think she was hinting. 'I just thought you might know somebody.'

Gwen thought it was as good an idea as any, but Ann had the feeling that she was losing interest in Tom and his doings. It was understandable. Gwen was not Tom's mother. Gwen was not anyone's mother. She had only met him once and he had not made a favourable impression. Gwen was concerned for Ann, in a professional way. People were funny. They might like to help, but some of Ann's clients might take a dim view of having their distribution agent suddenly lay a family problem in their laps. 'Business first,' Gwen had said. *Business first.* Gwen's note came on her personal stationery, and Ann knew better than to phone her about housing problems when she was at work.

'There's no point,' said Shelly.

'In what?'

'Phoning these people at the old people's flats. All they'll say is, "Come and see us." '

They would need Tom for that. Tom in his right mind.

'Could you . . . could we try again?'

'You mean go to Rideemus House?'

'The two of us. We could keep an eye on each other.' Shelly laughed nervously. 'So we don't join. Your sister would let us have the car, wouldn't she?'

'She's forgotten it's hers. All right, Shelly. We'll go on Monday.' She had people to see on Monday.

'Couldn't we go over the weekend?'

Ann looked away. 'I can't manage the weekend.'

'But if we leave it till Monday we won't be able to phone them till Tuesday.'

'I can't manage the weekend. I've got to go to a craft fair in Newcastle. I've been neglecting my clients as it is.'

'Ann!' he said. 'Long time no see!'

'Is it?' she said. It was the wrong thing to say. She should have said *Long time no see* back. In pretending she did not know how long the time was, she had made it clear that she did know. She was making an issue of a casual remark, like people who answered *How are you?* by going into details.

'This is a happy coincidence, isn't it?' he said. Did he think she had arranged to have their two stands next to each other? Had he arranged it?

430

'I'd like you to meet a friend of mine. Lesley, who helps me make my pipes. Ann, who helps me sell them.'

'Pleased to meet you,' said Ann.

'Pleased to meet *you*,' said Lesley, who was in her thirties.

'She's just a friend,' he said, when Lesley had gone to fetch some boxes from the car.

How dare he say that? Did I ask? What do I look like? Why can't I hide what I feel? Look at all these people, here for the social side. It doesn't show, does it? They're just getting on with selling their stuff and talking to each other as if it were the most normal thing in the world, which it is. For them. Not for me. This isn't my world, why did I ever think it was? 'Lesley helps me make my pipes.' I'll help him make his bloody pipes. Ann stood over her stock with dignity, smiling at her customers, alert but approachable. Toby and Lesley were much too busy talking to each other to take notice of their customers, but it was just a hobby for them. Now and again, Toby would turn to Ann and try to bring her into the conversation, but she cut him off by talking to her customers. When they thinned out she talked to the stall-holder on her left, a maker of fake antique musical boxes. 'Your first time?' she asked him.

'More or less,' he said. 'Bit slow, isn't it?'

'You'll get the hang of it. Have you come far?' *And that one's very nice too*, she thought, eyeing a weaver doing his weaving. *And that one, and that one, and what about the customers – ?* She stood there, brazen, sizing them up, and then she went to the Ladies and wept.

She packed up and went home. She had been through too much and was finished. She had set up in business to help her son and had lost him. It was her fault. She had pushed him too hard. She had insulted him by bringing in inferior products. It was all very well for women like Daphne Barclay, Gwen Hutton, to say that you should be professional, make a division between your work life and your personal life, but they had no personal lives.

'Ann, it's Gwen. Are you all right?'

'Yes, why?'

'I looked for you at the craft fair. Someone said you were ill.'

Someone should ring up himself if he's worried. Or else mind his own business.

'Why were you looking for me?'

'No special reason. I was in town. You're really all right?'

Yes. Goodbye.

'Peaston Hill's your next one, am I right?'

What is this? It's Saturday. Is this my accountant or my friend? 'I've got a booking,' she said casually. 'But I might give it a miss. They're not really worth my while, craft fairs.' *That's right, Ann. Lie about your accounts to the person who knows them better than you do.*

'So you wouldn't be interested in having me come along and give you a hand?'

Of course she would be interested. She would love it. But what was this? Was Gwen looking for a new hobby, to go with the geology and the pop concerts and hating cults?

'It's not out of the goodness of my heart, Ann. I'd better come clean. There's going to be a women's peace demonstration. Sue and Adela are going, and I know from past experience that my life won't be worth living if I don't go too. I'm sympathetic, of course, but I'm not a great one for . . .'

Cults?

' . . . groups.'

Stick to rocks and figures.

'People get carried away. Do things they wouldn't do normally. They'll probably get arrested.'

'Do they often – ?'

'It's only a matter of time. I could use your stand as a sort of bolt-hole, if you don't mind me putting it like that.'

Ann was amused. 'I'd be glad of your company,' she said. 'If I go.'

'Right. Good. That's fixed, then.'

'Yes . . .'

' . . . goodbye.'

It took about two minutes to see through this. Saturday though it was, it was not Ann's friend who had called, it was her accountant. She had not necessarily guessed the reason for Ann's flight from the craft fair (please God, she had not) but she had seen it as commercially unwise. And she intended to keep an eye on her to make sure it did not occur again.

Ann might have felt indignant, but she was touched. It was nice to be looked after. As if she were a child. As if she were Tom, with a worried mother. Two days later she went with Shelly to Rideemus House.

'We want to see Tom and we want to see him alone,' she said. 'Sure,' they said, and Tom came. He was not a prisoner. He could do what he wanted, and what he wanted was to stay and find out a bit more about Psychotheolistics, which was interesting and important

– as Ann and Shelly would discover if they put aside their prejudices and came on a course – and make his model. He might be wrong, but he had thought that getting commissions to make models was what his mother wanted him to do. When he had made his model, he would come home. He seemed not to see Shelly's pregnancy. He seemed not to see Shelly at all, or Ann. He did not have a conversation with them. He just talked in circles. They left, Shelly in tears, Ann not far off. In desperation that evening Ann phoned Tom's friend Chris. She did not like him, but he might have some special knowledge of Tom, some way of getting to him. 'I could take the lads over and grab him.' Any excuse for a punch-up. 'It's his mind they've got hold of, not his body, Chris. He can leave any time he wants to. It's just that he doesn't want to.' *He doesn't want to. And he needn't think I'm going to go on trying to persuade him indefinitely, because I'm not.*

71

Your unseen friend Molly died after a long illness. Her friends and family thank you for your kindness to her, which will always be remembered, but ask that you make no further contact with them at this sad time. They know that you will understand.

The black-edged card was one of the last pieces of post Teresa received before moving from her parents' house. This was fitting but puzzling. She had not put her address on her cards to Molly.

There was no reason for the card not to be authentic. Why should anyone want her to stop writing to Molly, other than for the reason stated? She put the matter aside as one of life's mysteries. She was moving from the place where, apart from a brief break for university, she had lived all her life. The card fitted neatly into her wallet, and she carried it with her. It did not seem morbid to do this. It made her feel happy.

Fiacre remained her burden, but Sam and their life together in their new home were her joy. Sam was involved in starting a new magazine. 'It's for men who want to get in touch with their gentleness in their own time,' he explained.

The collective's inaugural meeting was held at the flat. Teresa did the decent thing and withdrew to the bedroom, addressing envelopes for her change-of-address cards. She burned with curiosity. She called: 'Do you want some coffee in there?'

'We'll make it,' Sam replied, and the other men joined in: 'No need.' 'We're all right.' 'Don't bother.'

She took in a tray. 'I was making it anyway. I won't interrupt.'

'You wouldn't be interrupting, Teresa.'

'It's nothing to do with me.'

'We have no right to ask her.'

'Ask me what?'

'Well, we haven't got much experience of the business side. Would you sit in?'

'Only if you're not doing anything.'

'I was, but it'll keep. Let me ask you a few things.' She took a chair at the head of the table. 'Who is your reader? What's he like? Which magazines does he read at the moment? What's his purchasing power?'

The men looked aghast. 'This isn't going to be a profit-making venture.'

'You can say that again.' *I'm turning into Daphne. I hated her but I can hardly remember why. She was good. Good for us. We needed her, we got her, I miss her so I'm turning into her.* 'If you don't break even, you're copping out. If you're only interested in pleasing yourselves, you might as well stay in bed.'

Later she went over their estimates while Sam addressed her envelopes for her. 'So I only please myself in bed,' he said.

'You know what I meant.'

'You shocked them.'

'Go on with you, they loved it. There's too much of this word "donation". Call it a "supporting subscription".'

Sam was getting to the end of her address book. 'I wish you weren't so popular. My arm hurts.'

'I can't help it. You didn't need to do them all.'

'Now she tells me. Are you going to post them from work?'

'Yes, he's so generous. In fact, I'll get him to take out a supporting subscription to your mag. I'll tell him it's just the sort of thing Greg will love.'

'Praise indeed.'

'Have you got a name for it?'

'*Wimps' Digest.*'

'You're never going to let me forget that, are you?'

'Not until you say something worse.'

She came in a few evenings later and he said, 'You missed a funny phone call. Mad old lady wanting to know if you just got married. I said you hadn't mentioned it.'

'Who was it?'

'Miss Cook?'

Teresa shook her head.

435

'She said the arrangement with the bank was in your old name and should she change it?'

'Sounds interesting. Is she going to call back?'

'She hung up. She sounded quite confused.'

Next day Teresa was phoned at work by a strange bank manager. 'Mrs Beal, I'm sorry to trouble you – '

'It's Ms.'

'May I ask if you have ever gone by any other name?'

'No. What's this about?'

It concerned a client of his who had recently asked him to set up an arrangement whereby a large sum of money (he did not specify) was to be paid in cash to a friend at a London branch. He had queried this – the client was old, Teresa gathered, and not in full possession of her faculties – and had been told to mind his own business.

Miss Cook knew the friend as Teresa Barclay, though a different Christian name was to be used for purposes of payment: her professional name. The bank manager had not liked the sound of this at all and had urged caution, only to be told once again to do as instructed.

But before the payment could be made, Miss Cook had received notification that someone called Teresa Beal had a new address and telephone number. Miss Cook knew only one Teresa, had become confused and upset and had called in the bank manager. 'It said *Fiacre* on the envelope,' he said now, using a pronunciation that was without precedent, 'which is how I found you. Can you shed any light on the matter?'

They had a brief talk, after which Teresa said to her boss: 'I need the rest of the day off.'

'Ah, Teresa, come on – '

'Or else I resign.'

'All right,' he said.

'Which?'

'Have the day off.'

'Tell me,' she said. 'You're a man of the world. Do you believe in evil? Do you believe it walks around on legs?'

'I've said you can have the day off,' he grumbled.

She calmed her agitation on the long train journey to Ipswich by making a commitment stronger than her commitment to Sam and her commitment to feminism rolled into one. She was going to have Daphne Barclay put in prison. This settled, she relaxed and arrived at the bank manager's office in fairly good humour. Together they went to see Thelma Cook.

'It had to be cash,' Thelma Cook wept. 'Her bank account's been closed by the male establishment.'

The bank manager said, 'I beg your pardon?' but not as if he really wanted to hear it again. 'No money has been paid, Miss Cook, so it's all right.'

'It's not all right! She's to have the money! This girl is an impostor!'

'I don't want your money, Miss Cook. But Daphne – '

'Teresa, her name's Teresa.'

'I am the Teresa who sent cards to your sister.'

'It's for her Feminist Enterprise Day!'

a.k.a. The Daphne Barclay Festival of Selling.

The bank manager said, 'How many people are we talking about?'

'Two,' said Teresa.

'One,' said Thelma Cook.

'I thought it was three,' he sighed.

Thelma Cook said savagely to Teresa, 'I've never seen you before in my life.'

'But you've seen my cards. Look. Molly's still in my address book. Was she in Daphne's? Did you check the handwriting?'

'She knew all about it!' Thelma Cook was not impressed by her sister's name in Teresa's address book. 'You could have just written that.'

'All right. What about this?' She produced the card announcing Molly's death and asking that no more cards be sent. 'Did you send this?'

'Of course I didn't. I didn't have your address.'

'Daphne did, and this was her way of stopping me sending cards. You'd have thought that very odd.'

Thelma Cook read the card several times, moving it back and forth across her field of vision, her old eyes rolling. Teresa's heart ached for what she must be going through, realizing the cynicism behind the sensitive words of bereavement. Teresa did not know what the bank manager would do if Thelma Cook spat on the card, which the working of her jaws suggested she might have in mind; but Teresa herself would follow suit.

Thelma Cook did not spit. Her sagging face broke into a smile of fondness. 'Oh, she *is* a naughty girl,' she sighed.

'And that was all?' Sam raged.

'Yes! As if Daphne had just put her tongue out, or something.

437

The bank manager was just the same. "I can see there has been an attempted fraud, Ms Beal. But I can't for the life of me say what it is." '

'What? Pretending she was you?'

'That would have to be proved. Daphne's word against a confused old lady who's obviously as besotted with her as – as other people have been. "How sweet of you to believe me, your honour." '

'Can't they trap her? Arrange to pay the money and wait in ambush?'

'But she hasn't done anything, Sam! Thelma wants her to have the money! It would have to be proved that the Daphne Barclay Festival of Selling isn't a feminist enterprise day! That she isn't management consultant to the women's movement. She's going to get away with it again!'

And she did. She made a run for it. Teresa found this out from Alistair Brunt. DBBT had been in legal trouble, apart from the trouble with Thelma Cook, about which Alistair appeared not to know. Their office and homes had been ransacked. Daphne had been offered a job in Africa. Teresa asked Alistair what he would do. He said he would clear things up as best he could and retire. He sounded sad.

Teresa was sad too, in spite of everything. But Thelma Cook's letter made her indignant.

Dear Ms Beal, I should be delighted if you would come to lunch, and please bring your friend. Yours sincerely, Thelma Cook, Miss.

Dear Miss Cook, thank you for your invitation. I'd love to come, but I'm not sure who you mean. Daphne Barclay is no friend of mine, and anyway I understand she has left the country. Best wishes, Teresa. (Teresa Beal)

Dear Teresa, of course I don't want you to bring that horrid girl. I mean the young man who must take credit for exposing her.

'Typical,' said Teresa.

'My knight in shining armour!' cried Thelma Cook, embracing Sam.

'I wouldn't say that. Teresa asked me to write to everyone in her address book. I always do as I'm told.'

On first meeting, Teresa had taken Thelma Cook to be somewhat senile. (*Daphne thought that too*, she thought grimly.) But, relieved from the burden of her nursing and recovering a little from her loss, she was alert and cheerful. Teresa said, 'You're looking well,' but did not speculate openly as to the reasons. Thelma Cook had obviously loved her sister, in a wry, tolerant way.

'Was it cancer? I always assumed it was.'

'Cancer one day. Swamp fever the next. She was old and liked attention.'

'So that advertisement –'

'What did it say, "I am dying"? She always said that. "Aren't we all?" was my reply. It's cold in here, are you cold?'

'No,' said Teresa, who was.

'No,' said Sam.

'Molly always said we should get double glazing,' said Thelma Cook, buttoning the left side of one of her cardigans to the right side of another. 'I wish Daphne were here. If she had just asked me for money for her project, I'd have given it to her. It was the sort of thing Molly would have approved of.'

Indignant again, Teresa tried to change the subject. 'You were fond of your sister.'

'They were alike in many ways. Always knew best –'

'I bet your sister didn't go around impersonating people.'

'No, dear. And that I cannot forgive.'

'Tell me about Molly.'

'Where should I start? If you'd had a sister who always outshone you –'

'Miss Cook, do you ever watch the news?'

'I try not to, dear. That's why I'm so out of touch, and don't know what to do for the best regarding Molly's money. There's a bit now, and there'll be the house when I no longer require it.'

'You ought to take advice.'

'I'd like to take yours.'

Teresa panicked. She started to tell Thelma Cook about various women's groups steering their way between rocks of finance and whirlpools of ideology. Sam's eyebrows were in his hair. He was enjoying his revenge for the things she had said to his men's group. *Take a lead, Teresa*, his face said. *Make a decision*. She could not. She heard herself wittering on. Miss Cook heard too and looked irritable. 'I wish Daphne were here.'

'Why?'

'Didn't I tell you she mended the glass in the front door? Fixed the washers on the taps? What didn't she do? I might have got her to put in double glazing.'

I'd like to fix a few washers on Daphne's taps. 'Was Molly a pacifist?'

'Not in her private life, but we won't go into that.'

'She hit people?'

'With her tongue, dear. With her tongue. Why do you ask?'

'It was just an idea I had.'

With Thelma Cook's agreement (and her money) Teresa wrote to the organizers of the forthcoming air show at Peaston Hill, booking exhibition stands. This done, she got in touch with the groups who were organizing the demonstration to draw attention to cruise missiles, telling them that space was available inside the base at no charge.

'This sounds dangerously like leadership,' said Sam.

'It's management. There's no time to faff about.'

Some of the groups thought it a great idea to take their message into enemy territory. Others would not soil themselves. But they took the point that a quarter of a million members of the public were expected at the air show, all of them with money to spend. Why not take some of that money off them? Why stand passively by with banners while they filled the coffers of militarism? Could not feminists provide snacks as well as Burger King could? Print official souvenir programmes that were not? Busk? Sell books, baby carriers, jewellery, balloons, magazines, personal alarms, greetings cards, craftwork? Might not the grassland outside the base be made as attractive as the play-acting of carnage within it? Was Daphne Barclay the only person who could put on a Festival of Selling?

72

Daphne Barclay was undergoing training. Her employers at START Selling Africa called it local orientation, but she knew what was being done to her.

'You've been away from the START organization for some time,' they said.

Yes, I presumed to leave. I set up in competition with the world president. And this is my punishment.

Working abroad was not in itself a punishment. It could be a useful experience. That was how it had been put to her. No one had said, *We have you on the ropes. Now you do as you're told.* In their serpentine way they had respected her pride. In her resourceful way, she had tried to respect theirs. Her urgent telex to Lindbergh Stanley had been couched in terms of telling him what he did not know: he had once asked her to take him into her confidence regarding the shortcomings of her erstwhile colleagues at START Selling UK; he should know that they were sueing and sabotaging her out of vindictiveness. Lindbergh Stanley himself would never (her words had implied) countenance such pettiness. She had appealed to his chivalry. The reply had come from Buck Castle. 'Mr Stanley has asked me to inform you that the opening to transfer your business to START Selling Africa no longer exists. He has, however, authorized me to offer you a vacancy . . .' Her indecision had not lasted long. She had repaired as best she could the disarray in which her flat had been left by the search, but she could no longer think of the place as home. Alistair had been communicating with her only through solicitors, and the look on the face of the bank clerk who told her that Thelma Cook's promised payment had been delayed in transit had given her the message that it was time to cut her losses.

'You'll need to study local conditions.'

Of course one had to study local conditions. She did not need START Selling International to tell her that. Know your customer, know your product, know your staff. (Daphne was staff. Clerical workers aside, she was lowest of the low.) There was not that much to know. Business was business, selling was selling. A black businessman, a white businessman, it made no difference to her. There were legal differences. There were language differences but the courses were conducted in English. There were local customs to be learned, made use of or broken down. For example, some tribes thought it rude to look an older person in the eyes. It must be explained to adherents of this view that a salesman who did not look a Western buyer in the eyes would appear shifty to him. There were codes of practice regarding bribery. There was the status of women.

'It's because I'm a woman, isn't it?'

'What is?'

'That you won't let me conduct my own courses.'

'We've got a course for you. Village girls who want to be agents for baby accessories.'

START *Selling – Women* . . .

In the meantime she was kept out of sight in the office. She was let out to attend her colleagues' courses, to see how it was done. It was done in exactly the same way here as it was done anywhere. You Need It, I've Got It, You Can Have It, Closing.

'We have no power to detain you, Daphne,' they said. 'If you're not happy.'

She was wretched. Her colleagues were men with insufferably dull wives. She was neither fish nor fowl. She missed her parents. She used not to see them that often, but it had been nice to know they were there. She missed Alistair. She regretted having impersonated Teresa Beal. Regret was an unfamiliar emotion to Daphne, and an uncomfortable one.

There was plenty to enjoy in her new surroundings. The weather was marvellous. She rented a modern three-roomed flat, and with it came a shared swimming pool and Susie who used to come in and clean for the previous occupant. To assuage her loneliness, Daphne tried to make a friend of Susie. They exchanged language lessons. And as soon as Susie's English could manage it, she was telling Daphne about a cousin of hers who would be happy to come in and clean on the days when Susie did not. 'I don't need a cleaner every day, Susie,' Daphne said, and Susie replied, 'Oh yes, madam. You need it.' Daphne insisted that she did not and the matter was dropped, but the conversation added to Daphne's feeling that scores were being settled with her by a power even greater than Lindbergh Stanley. She laughed at herself for thinking this; but the fact remained that wherever she went, people tried to sell her things.

She had her own car, but during the daytime she liked to walk. (Everyone she met told her not to walk at night, a prohibition that added to her isolation.) Within minutes of setting foot outside, it was:

'Taxi, madam?'

'Shoeshine, madam?'

'Papaya, watermelon?'

'Madam, come into my shop.'

At first she found it enchanting ... and, at the same time, humbling. Marketing was a science to which educated men devoted their lives; but were not these simple words on the lips of a small trader the law and the prophets? *Madam, come into my shop. Try that, Dad*, she thought sadly. 'My bananas are very sweet, madam,' said a market stall-holder, pressing one into her hand. 'You no like, you no pay.'

What Western greengrocer dared say *that*?

'Madam! I give you good discount.'

Sometimes she chided them. 'Never volunteer a discount. Trade it.'

'I trade with you, madam. Come into my shop.'

Even social conversations turned into attempts to sell her things, or make her give, she was not always sure which. At somebody's wife's cocktail party she met a delightful African man, a graduate of Balliol College. Next day he rang her up at work and asked if she could persuade START to pay his fare back to England to defend his thesis. Otherwise, seven years' work would be wasted. He made it sound as if it would be seven years of *her* work that would be wasted. A little boy in pants and plimsolls stopped her in the street with a bewitching smile and, 'Madam! Talk to me! Please! I am learning English.'

'You speak it very well. Who is teaching you?'

'My teacher at school. Next term I finish school.'

'But you're much too young.'

'My father cannot pay for me to go to school. I need a sponsor, madam. I need it!'

'Safari, madam?'

She went for a weekend safari and viewed a great many different kinds of horned cattle. She also saw clumps of trees which, she was told, contained elephants. (*Real ivory chess set, madam?*) Meat was placed outside the safari lodge so that lions would show themselves, but they did not fall for it. They had more dignity, Daphne decided. *Come again, madam! Two week safari, you will see everything!*

'Shoeshine!'

Joseph was her shoeshine boy. His patch was the corner of Disraeli Street and Nkrumah Street. It was much coveted, she gathered. Ownership of patches was strictly, though unofficially, policed. Were she to take her custom to another of the boys whose footstools and collections of brushes stretched as far as the eye could see, the consequences for him could be serious.

But she would not leave Joseph because Joseph was the best. She would not have chosen him otherwise. He called her by her name. He had the right coloured polishes. He remembered that she preferred to have her shoes removed for cleaning, lest she get polish on her feet. He unbuckled her high-heeled sandals with a gesture at once respectful and tender.

If enough customers shared Daphne's view that Joseph was the best, Joseph might one day leave the streets for a shop of his own. This would not happen to all of them but it would happen to the best. Joseph was the best, she would not have chosen him otherwise. He would be able to provide employment for his relatives, making shoes. He might own a shoemaking empire, for that was the way it was done. The only way it could be done. There was no alternative.

73

Everyone had a different idea of what God had looked like, creating the world. A bored clown wanting something to play with. A woman giving birth. A man giving birth. A chicken laying an egg. A model-maker in a workshop. 'Like you, Tom.' Flattery. When God created the world, He hadn't had a bloody committee telling Him how to do it.

'It's a system, right? The world's a system. We don't always under-stand it but we know it works. So I'll make a system – a clockwork system of movements – and we can add everything else on.' He was proud of his wheel: ten foot in diameter, it stood in a frame in front of Rideemus House, protected at night by tarpaulins. He wanted to be left to get on with what else he had in mind, which was a further system of wheels whereby models of rich people would transmit energy to models of poor people. God started it off with a flick of His finger and smiled at the result. But the Rideemus people rationed the time he was allowed to spend working on the model. He still had to go to lectures, otherwise he would lose the understanding that made the model possible. He still had to go out recruiting, to earn his keep. 'It's only fair, Tom.' He gave them his social security money, but that was not enough. And he had to listen to them. 'The clown should go on top, Tom.' 'Shouldn't it say "Rideemus" on it somewhere?' 'Why aren't the people smiling?'

Those that can, do. Those that can't, interrupt craftsmen.

Sometimes he arranged some peace for himself. He told the ones who were going recruiting that he was staying for a seminar, and the ones in the seminar that he was recruiting. But the ones who had gone recruiting seemed to have come back early. He cursed as they approached him. They did not look like the ones who had gone for the walk, but then they all looked the same to him. People came and went while he stayed. But he was sure that they had had some girls with them . . .

A hand gagged his mouth. His arms were pinioned, his feet lifted. He fought but he was outnumbered. He was being kidnapped. He was carried to a van. They climbed in after him and the van sped away. The hand had gone from his mouth but he was too shocked to speak. He made for the door and was stopped.

'Calm down, Tom. You're with friends.'

It was his old mate Chris. The others were strangers. Chris said, 'Nice one, lads.'

'Don't mention it.'

Tom found his voice. 'Nice one? Nice one! What are you, fucking maniacs? Oh, I see. It's Cult Caution.'

'It's the darts team, man. Cult Caution said you should do it with love and understanding, but Shelly and your mam tried that.'

'So you thought you'd try GBH? I'm bleeding to death here.' He looked at his cut knuckles.

'So am I,' said one of his captors, who had a split lip.

Tom jeered, 'You kept well out of it, didn't you, Chris?'

'You might have recognized me.'

'I need a piss.'

Chris gave him a clean pickle jar. 'We'll not look,' he said.

'You give us your word of honour you'll not make a run for it and we'll stop for a pint.'

'I give you my word of honour.'

'Think he means it?'

'No.'

'No.'

'No.'

'You could be put in prison for this.'

'Such is life,' said Chris.

'That looks like a nice pub,' said another one.

Tom had forgotten what beer tasted like. He knew but could not conjure it on to his tongue. His senses and emotions seemed to be coated with thick film. He knew he loved Shelly and his mother, but he had seen them as strangers because they did not know what he knew.

'Pity we can't go in.'

'Especially after what I've heard about the barmaid.'

'Hey, Tom, did they have group sex?'

Psychotheolistics was the study of God's purposes and all Chris could think about was group sex. There had been no sex of any kind at Rideemus House, so far as he was aware. He knew it used once to be important to him, but he could not remember how it felt. He laughed. 'Every night.'

Chris said, 'Turn the van round.'

'No,' said Tom sharply. 'Don't do that.'

'I'm your mate, Tom.' They were crossing the boundary into Tyne and Wear. 'I worry about you. I don't want your mind taken over. It was bad enough before.'

'No one'd take over your mind because you've not got one.'

'Just as well.'

'Listen. All of you. Tell me a joke. Tell me one joke that isn't about cruelty and suffering.' There was more to it than that. 'Authority, Eternity and the Flesh. *Or* the Flesh. Just one. You can't.' They tried, but he was able to bring every joke they told back to the same things.

'We'd better stop this,' said Chris. 'This is how they got him into it in the first place.'

'Having doubts, eh? Starting to think there's something in it?' He imagined persuading them to turn the van round. He imagined arriving back at Rideemus House with five new recruits. He did not want to imagine it.

'Suppose all jokes do come down to Authority, Cruelty and . . . what you said. Why does that mean you have to walk out on Shelly when she's expecting your baby?'

'You're the great moralist all of a sudden.'

'In my opinion,' said Chris, 'that lass is in grave moral danger.'

Tom looked at his friend, who might have done him a favour. Not necessarily, but possibly. The place where he had been was a hothouse. Ideas might be right, they might be wrong, but you never got the chance to test them because everyone thought the same. He could go home for a few days, think about them on his own, then stay or go back, as he chose. He had been meaning to go home on this basis ever since he went to Rideemus House, but had never got around to it. Chris had forced him to get around to it, and for that he deserved thanks. Nevertheless, there were limits. 'You be very careful with what you're going to say, Christopher.'

'It's about her living at Barbara's. It's not natural, is it? Any day now, that bairn'll be born. How do you feel about him having two mams and no dad?' The rest of the darts team nodded gravely.

'I never had a dad.'

'But you didn't have two mams, did you? You knew where you were in that department.'

'What are you saying?'

'I'm saying nothing. But women aren't what they were, Tom. If they can't have us, they'll find ways of managing without us.'

The scenery through which they drove was becoming familiar. The darts team were restive. Tom wondered if they had got involved in this out of concern for him, concern for his child or because they welcomed an excuse for a punch-up. One of them was looking for another one: 'Time to put Tom's blindfold on, Chris.'

'Piss off.'

'Promise you'll not look.'

'I don't see much to look at.'

Chris said, 'It's a mystery tour, like. We've got a surprise for you.'

'Surprise me by taking me to the nearest pub.'

Instead, they took him to the Waylands Museum.

He was still their prisoner. They surrounded him, ushering him through the turnstile and past the railway station, the sheds where the fitters worked with sleeves rolled up and heavy tools clutched in oily hands, under the eyes of awed visitors. He breathed the smells of steam and coal, the smells of energy and importance, the smells of a time when his birthplace had been important in the world, when he might have had a chance to be important himself. . . .

A model of God creating the world, Tom. . . .

His captors took him past the Working Men's Reading Room towards the reconstructed labourers' cottages in the shadow of the reconstructed colliery. Some of the cottages were open to the public, but they took him to one that was not, and the door opened, and Shelly came out, grinning above her huge pregnant stomach.

Chris pushed Tom towards her, not that he needed pushing. 'Package delivered.'

Shelly kept one arm round Tom and hugged Chris with the other. 'I never thought I'd say you were wonderful Chris, but you are.'

'I know.'

Tom said, 'Oi – '

Chris said, 'Don't try and run for it, Tom, because we'll be outside.'

He did not want to run for it. This was where he wanted to be.

'Did we get a job, Shell? Are we going to live here?'

It was nothing like that. There was no job for him or her, in the museum or out of it. Shelly had simply fixed it with one of the museum's managers, who knew Tom and was concerned for him, that they could have their reunion here. Cult Caution said it was sometimes helpful for ex-cultists to be reminded of things that had been important to them in their former lives.

'Does Mam know I'm here?'

'We didn't tell her what we were doing. We didn't want to raise her hopes. She's gone to a craft fair with her accountant.'

To sell what? he thought, with a bitterness that he knew he had no right to. *They'll find ways of managing without us. . . .*

His restless eyes took in the huge armchair, the smaller sewing-chair, the gleaming kitchen range, the tin bath. From outside he heard the whistle of a train, a real old steam train turned working model. *They'll find ways of managing without us.* He looked at Shelly who, after all he had put her through, did not want to manage without him. She had shown that she could but she did not want to. He took her in his arms. He felt her pregnancy. He should have been around to see it grow. He should have looked after her. But how could he?

'You could start by wanting to,' she said softly into his shoulder when he asked the question.

'I do want to.'

'You don't have to say that. We wanted to get you away from Rideemus. The rest is up to you.'

'I want to marry you, Shelly.'

'Just in time, or born in the vestry,' said Chris, when they told him.

'Oh shut up, Chris,' Shelly sighed.

'Out of one cult, into another,' Chris crowed to the darts team.

74

Teresa had always known that Mr Nice Guy would turn out to have feet of clay. She said this. 'It's a women's demo, Sam.'

'I won't go near the demo. I want to see the air show.'

'You what?'

'It's interesting. Don't be so prissy. You can admire machinery without approving of what it's for.'

Thelma Cook was just as bad. As aircraft buzzed and roared above the traffic jam outside the base, she kept saying, 'I haven't seen one of those since the war,' and 'What's that?'

Sam said, 'I think it's a Mustang.'

Besides paying for the renting of exhibition space inside the base for those women's groups who wanted it, Thelma Cook had, through her solicitors, set in motion the process whereby, her own needs taken care of with an annuity, the remainder of Molly Kerslake's money would be given to Goddess Garments. Teresa was keeping out of this as far as possible, but a cordial note had come from Beverley, thanking her for the role she had played and outlining plans to use the money to take on more outworkers at improved rates of pay. On Thelma Cook's death, the house would be sold, also for the benefit of Goddess Garments; Beverley had managed to convey excitement at the sense of security this offered for Goddess Garments' expansion plans, without expressing any hope that it would not be too long delayed.

The Goddess Garments women had not yet met Thelma Cook. She could not travel to London and they were very busy. They would meet at the air show, in the hangar where the craft fair was being held, inside the base.

'Who's going in?' said Adela Griffiths-Robins, 'and who's staying out?'

'I'm going in, I've got a stand booked,' said Ann.

'And I'm going in to help her,' said Gwen.

'It's funny, isn't it,' said Adela to Sue Clark. 'Ann's managed all these months without help – '

Ann was impatient to enter the base and set her things up in the hangar. 'I'm expecting a lot of customers today.'

Adela was greeting friends whose banner read: 'Lesbian Accountants Against Militarism.'

Sue said, 'I can't stand under that. I'm not an accountant.'

Ann looked nervously at the banner. She had been wondering about this for some time.

Gwen said, 'Just because we go into the base, it doesn't mean we're in favour of it.'

Not everyone agreed with this. To get into the base, Ann and Gwen had to drive past a reproachful picket line singing 'Women make your choice' and 'Which side are you on?'

'I think it's a Mustang.'

'What am I doing with you people?' grumbled Teresa from the back of the car.

'Get out and walk then.'

'I think I will, actually.' The traffic queue was under siege from saleswomen and she wanted to see how they were getting on. She wanted to see people and be seen outside the base before going in.

'Fresh fruit, 30p.'

'Official souvenir programme, madam?'

'Wholefood sandwiches . . .'

The official souvenir programme was not. Printed by the Joanna Press, it had a convincing air show cover but was packed with information about cruise missiles: number, fire power and deployment. It contained testimony from campaigners who had followed convoys from Greenham Common to Peaston Hill. They had seen the missiles go into the base but had not seen them come out. Maps showed where at RAF Peaston Hill the missiles were now thought to be located: at the far end, away from the air show, behind security fences with razor wire.

A very young woman poked her sweet face into the car and offered Thelma Cook an apple. 'It's free.'

'That's very kind of you, dear, but let me pay you.'

'This is a protest against consumerism.'

'A what, dear?'

The young woman explained that she did not think anyone should be allowed to make money out of war, not even the women's movement. She was not alone in her belief. All along the wire were women whose banners and stance proclaimed that they were here to protest. They were resolutely selling nothing. Teeth gritted, Teresa started to get out of the car. Thelma Cook said, 'Can I come with you?'

Teresa did not want her to come. She did not want her confused by the utterly convincing arguments of those who would say that a dead feminist's money would be better spent on campaigns, services and charities than on a business. Thelma Cook had asked for Teresa's advice, had got it and taken it . . . nearly. The papers were not yet signed.

'Of course you can come . . .' *You can do whatever you like. Talk to anyone. Change your mind. I can't stop you.*

The old lady's legs were unsteady. She had agreed with reluctance to Sam and Teresa's proposal that they hire a portable wheelchair for the day. Teresa struggled to get it out of the boot.

The traffic moved. A policeman said, 'You can't stop here. There's a disabled car park inside the base.'

Thelma Cook said, 'All right. I'll go into the base with Sam.' She wanted to see the air show. She was not having second thoughts about the disposal of her money. They were Teresa's fantasy.

The perimeter fence was seven miles long with six entrances. If the architects had designed RAF Peaston Hill with today in mind they could not have done a better job. Narrow roads allowed for traffic jams to build up nicely, with passengers getting very bored indeed. ('Enjoying the music? Care to make a contribution?' *What for?* was not asked, or said. People were paying for their entertainment. Teresa recognized the buskers as being from a support group for the children of a woman who was in prison for committing criminal damage at Greenham Common.) There was plenty of ground both outside and opposite the fence where people gathered who did not want to pay admission charges but wanted to see what they could of the air show. Teresa supposed that some of them were there for that. There were plane spotters, demonstrators, buyers and sellers. But which was which?

Women with banners sang: '*Building bridges between our divisions –* '
Others said, 'Wear a flower, madam? Support battered women – '
'Sunglasses to look at the planes?'
'Balloons?'
'Home-made sweets?'

452

'With all of our voices and all of our visions – '

'Something to read while you wait to go in?'

'Free apples – protest against the money economy.'

'Which side are you on?'

Ten planes screamed into the air in a perfect triangle. *I think it's the Red Arrows.* Arrows was right. They came at Teresa from all sides. *Goddess Garments is commercial. Goddess Garments is consumerist. Panders to cleaner-fish, lets men in. Has shareholders, is not revolutionary, is part of the system. Is inside the base.* Aircraft looped and rolled. They almost touched but did not. Red, white and blue smoke made gorgeous patterns in the sky. You could not deny that it was clever. You did not have to admire machinery to appreciate what it could do.

'What am I bid for this pair of braces – ?' The braces belonged to a news-reading colleague of Teresa's sister Marion. They were part of a Celebrity Auction being conducted from a bus in the overflow car park outside the base. 'I thought you'd be inside,' said Teresa.

'Why should we be?' said Marion.

The cleaner-fish were out in force, raising money for rape victims. 'Hello, Teresa,' said Brenda Sargent pleasantly.

'Teresa Beal, is that?' said another voice, its owner looking straight at Marion.

'I'm not Teresa Beal, I'm her sister.'

'How many people are you expecting here today, Ms Beal?' asked the stranger, a journalist.

'About a quarter of a million.'

'I mean for the demo.'

'Everyone's here for the demo. Aren't they?'

'You organized this?'

Good gracious no. Groups have come from all over the country and they're all autonomous. No organizers. No leaders. No spokeswomen. 'It was my idea to make money out of it,' she said. Actually it had been Daphne's idea. But Daphne had impersonated Teresa. *Am I now impersonating her?* Teresa queued up with pedestrians waiting to enter the base, entertained by feminist jugglers.

Ann parked near the hangar, in the Exhibitors' Car Park. The horizon was jagged with weapons: planes, tanks, helicopters, guns, missiles, grey and green and pencil-sharp. Replicas, for display only. A tall column of scaffolding offered visitors the chance to try para-chute jumping in a movable harness. There were roundabouts, helter-skelters, flying boats. Above them fluttered exhibitors' flags: MARLBORO. MIDLAND BANK. DONUTS. FRANSON & FRANSON PLASTICS. TELECOM. PANCAKES FOR PEACE. AUTOMOBILE ASSOCIATION. WOMEN'S WHEELS BREAKDOWN SERVICE. BRITISH RAIL, WE'RE GETTING THERE. *Women make your choice, which side are you on?* Ann was not on any side. Like most people she was here to do business. If anyone doubted that, she had Gwen with her to prove it. 'This is my accountant,' she would say, if Toby were here. Meaning: *Don't waste my time with your hobbies.* Having Gwen with her meant that she could not hope for anything from Toby and so could not be disappointed. He would not say anything in front of Gwen.

Gwen got out of the car. 'What do we do?'

'Sure you don't mind me giving you orders?'

'That's what I've come for,' said Gwen, cheerful in her chunky jumper and well-tailored jeans, but slightly ill at ease too, Ann thought.

'We'll take some of the boxes in and find out where we are . . .' Ann loaded Gwen's strong arms with boxes of craftwork made by clients of Ann Mitchison Craft Distribution, then picked up as many as she could carry herself. There were no rules at this craft fair, you could sell what you wanted, you did not have to pretend to be Mitchison's Working Models, which was just as well because this was the first craft fair she had come to with nothing to sell that had been made by Tom.

And if that was the way he wanted it, that was the way he could have it. She still worried about him, but Gwen's calm insistence that she should not abandon her work in her wish to bring him home had clarified a few things for her. She had set up the business for him, but he did not want it. He had moved away. She had moved on. She had gone to START Selling – Women! for him, but she was here at RAF Peaston Hill for herself.

You Need It, I've Got It, You Can Have It, and Closing. Ann worked for her clients, her customers and herself. And for Closing. The moment when people said yes. Yes, I'd like one. Yes, I'd like a dozen. Yes, I'd like you to be my distributor. Yes. Be professional, said Daphne Barclay. Go to where the customers are and sell to them. Anywhere. Even an aircraft hangar within walking distance of where nuclear weapons are housed? The demonstrators said they were here, but Ann had no opinion on this. She was not on any side. She was at work, in a job she had created for herself.

The hangar was huge and packed. You could hardly see one end from the other, through the throng of customers and clusters of stalls. If she had been looking for Toby, she would not have spotted him. She was not looking for him, so she did. Toby Hamilton Pipes, next to Goddess Garments. He did not see her. She noted that he was alone. But he had picked his place. Goddess Garments was a clothes stall, staffed by women dressed as goddesses: Greek goddesses in armour. Roman goddesses in togas. African goddesses in long straw skirts and beaded tops. They were dressed to be eye-catching and imposing rather than sexy, but he would find them sexy. Their stall was an elaborate representation of heaven, with cardboard pillars and arrays of flowers made of coloured tissue, and heaven was exactly what he would be in, sitting next to them. He was pretending to pay no attention. He was smoking his pipe and reading a book, biding his time.

In another time zone, Daphne Barclay woke early. She swam twenty-five lengths of her shared swimming pool. She returned to her flat, showered and sat on her verandah to dry her hair, eat mangoes and look over her notes.

Her day had come. One hour from now she would be beginning the process whereby forty young women would be transformed into agents, selling Stalton International Infant Care products around the homes and clinics of the rural areas from which they came.

A senior official of START Selling International would be present, sitting in on Daphne's first course. Very senior indeed, she gathered. He had not been named, and she had not asked.

She dressed in a suit of pale blue cotton, freshly pressed by Susie, put a gold locket on a chain round her neck and gold studs in her ears. She set out. It was a lovely day. She walked.

'Taxi, madam?'

'Pineapple, peaches?'

'Money change?'

What did he think she was, a tourist? She lived here. She worked here.

'Shoeshine, Miss Barclay?'

'Oh, thank you, Joseph.'

'You look very happy this morning, madam.'

Was she? She was excited. She was at last being allowed to do what she had come here to do, what she existed to do. There was just one small thing. Stalton International Infant Care had supplied her with the product information leaflets which its agents would be using. One of the products was a disinfectant cream for applying in the event of nappy rash. The name of the cream was familiar. It, or something like it, had been withdrawn from the market in Britain because it caused dermatitis. Daphne remembered seeing the fuss about it in the marketing press.

She wondered if she ought to mention it to someone. The cream had probably been withdrawn here too, and it would be very unprofessional to send saleswomen out with leaflets about products that they had not got.

'Thank you, Joseph.'

'Thank *you*, madam. Shoeshine, sir . . . ?'

'Madam. Look at this.'

A young man, mournful-eyed, poor, proffered a piece of paper. It confirmed that, three years previously, he had given good service as a gardener.

'I have no garden,' she explained. 'Otherwise . . .' She spoke as pleasantly as she could. He was not begging, he was not threatening her, he was selling.

'Give me money, madam.'

He *was* begging.

'I am not a thief, madam. It is better if you give me money.'

Was he threatening her?

She was not worried. There were plenty of people about. Busy people, salespeople. 'Wooden elephant, sir!' 'Lottery.' 'Come into my shop.'

Daphne said clearly, 'Go to a house where there is a garden, and ask.'

'Please give me money, madam.' He put his hand on her bag, but not as if he meant to take it. As if to show that he could, if he wanted to. As if to satisfy himself that it was real, that it could be opened and money could be taken out and given to him. Was he threatening, begging or selling? In this city of business and want, the distinction was not always clear. And if the distinction were not clear to her – her, of all people – what was she doing here? What had she been doing all her life? What was she doing now? The sun was yet to reach its full heat, but she felt dizzy.

'I may know someone who needs a gardener,' she said. 'Tell me your name and address.' Gently but firmly she reclaimed her bag and opened it to find something to write with. As her hand entered the bag, a long, silver-coloured car slid to a halt beside her. The nearside doors snapped open; two big white men in tight suits leapt out and dragged away the gardener, the beggar, as if he were a thief.

'Don't hit him! He wasn't – '

'Looks like we came along just in time, Miss Barclay.'

Buck Castle's face was at the window of the car. Behind him was another man, a shadow.

'We – ?' she stammered.

'Get in, please, Miss Barclay. There's somebody I'd like you to meet.'

75

In a lull between customers, Gwen asked Ann if she had seen what it said on Adela's friends' banner.

'Yes,' said Ann, who wanted to concentrate on her selling.

'I am a member myself,' said Gwen.

'Are you?' *Live and let live*, she thought. It was what she had always thought.

'I mean I pay my subscription. But I'm not very active.' Gwen's tone was slightly teasing.

'What do they – you – do?'

'Talk about accountancy, that sort of thing.'

A customer picked up a Taiwanese cat. 'Is this hand-made?'

'Yes,' said Ann, selling it with relief. As soon as the customer was out of hearing and before Gwen could speak again, she said in a rush: 'These are what bring the money in, and help me sell the nicer things. I shouldn't lie though, should I? What do you think?'

Gwen laughed pleasantly. 'I'm not here to be keeper of your conscience. You do know why I *am* here, don't you?'

'Because you didn't want to go to the demonstration.'

'That was an excuse. I could have stayed at home. I wanted to be with you.'

Miss Hutton, Ann thought. From *Yes, goodbye* to this. She felt honoured, embarrassed, happy and terrified. 'I'm not . . .'

'Not what?'

'A, er, lesbian.'

Gwen said evenly, 'I know you're not. I wonder why you found it necessary to say that.'

Because I don't know anything about this. Because I don't know what happens next. 'I believe in live and let live.'

'That's extremely generous of you.'

'It's not, it's –'

'Oh, but it is.' Gwen looked as if she had just been hit. 'Do you really mean it's a free country and I can be as peculiar as I like? You won't bother me if I don't bother you?'

Ann stood stunned by the realization that she had hurt Gwen by patronizing her. She would not have thought it possible. Patronizing was what the high did to the low. It was what Gwen could have done to Ann, only she never had. She had offered expertise and friendship and Ann had loved having a strong, slightly strange friend who was self-assured and never seemed to need anything. Of course Gwen needed things. She had just revealed a need and Ann had put the boot in. 'Sorry if I offended you, Gwen.'

Gwen was becoming Miss Hutton before her eyes. She straightened her shoulders. She smiled distantly, professionally. 'You didn't. You're quite right. Forget the whole conversation. I think I'll go outside for a while.' *Outside? Outside the hangar? Outside the base? Outside my life?* Appalled, Ann watched her go. She wanted to follow but she could not leave her stand, her clients' craftwork, her customers.

One of the customers was Toby. 'Ann!' he said. 'Long time no see.' He put his hand on her shoulder. 'I was hoping you'd be here,' he said.

'Were you?' She felt sarcastic, sceptical; she sounded flirtatious.

'How have you been?' he said, going for a kiss.

'Very well, thank you.' She dodged him, but carefully: not to hurt his feelings. She knew how not to hurt his feelings. She knew how to talk to a man who had aroused desire and disappointment in her and had sauntered over to humiliate her again. She knew how to behave.

'How about dinner tonight?' he said.

She had not known how to talk to a woman who had said, 'I wanted to be with you.' The words: 'Good. I feel the same,' had not come. What had she feared? That Gwen would grab her, assault her, claim her in some way? That the person whose formality had been so excruciating in the first months of their acquaintance would respond to a statement of affection by doing something unwelcome, embarrassing, indecent?

Toby said, 'How about dinner tonight?' and waited for her reply.

*

'He's been getting into helicopters,' said Thelma Cook from her wheelchair.

'Only stationary ones,' said Sam. 'Anyway, what about you? I turn my back for five minutes and you've bought a swimming pool.'

'I was only talking to them about my double glazing.'

Teresa said, 'Please don't buy double glazing at an air show, Miss Cook.'

'It wasn't that kind of double glazing, dear. It's a very respectable plastics company, and they were such a nice young couple.' She had a sheaf of leaflets: 'Franson & Franson Acrylic Sheeting For All Your Outdoor Glazing Needs.' The sudden onset of the Falklands war overhead distracted Teresa from wondering why the name rang bells. 'Harriers three, Argies nil,' crowed the commentator on the public address system as the sky darkened with planes shooting each other down in clouds of pretend smoke. Was it pretend smoke? If something went wrong, how would anyone know? Were the demonstrators right about live nuclear warheads being stored here a few thousand feet beneath this airborne atrocity?

Of course not. If it weren't safe, it wouldn't be happening.

If the base were secret, they wouldn't let us in.

Cleaner-fish are always allowed in.

What was a stunt and what was real? What was tolerance and what was camouflage? Were the exhibited weapons armed? Were they real or were they replicas? And the exhibition stands – which of those were real, and which replicas? Who was inside and who was outside? Who was making a killing and who was selling out? The Falklands charade came to an end. It had lasted just seven minutes, and during that time had probably cost more money than all the women's groups inside and outside the base had taken today . . . *We've got to have our own money. We've got to learn how to make it.*

'Shall we go and see Goddess Garments now?'

'Yes please, dear. Aren't you coming with us, Sam?'

'No, I'll go and do a parachute jump or something.'

A parachute jump. A fitting metaphor, Teresa thought as she wheeled Thelma Cook towards the hangar. *All you have to do is decide, be brave, jump, and live with the result. Or not.*

She had once, in a moment of appreciation of Daphne Barclay, thought that her main contribution had been to inspire courage to make imperfect decisions and see them through. The handing over of Molly Kerslake's entire bequest to Goddess Garments was an imperfect decision. Of course it was. Outrageously imperfect. There were a thousand arguments against it, each one of them the name of an equally good cause. And if any one of these arguments held sway, there would be a thousand against *that*, one of them being Goddess Garments.

The hangar was packed and not laid out for wheelchairs. 'Shall I park you somewhere and get them to come to you?'

'Oh no, dear, I want to see it.' Thelma Cook could not see the Goddess Garments stand, but Teresa could: it was magnificent, the most eye-catching in the place. It was set up to look like heaven. Teresa wished she believed in heaven, and heavenly signs. She wished she could see the future of Goddess Garments: a chain of clothes shops, practical, ecological, feminist and fair. Today's actions were a microcosm of feminist politics: you could stay outside the base, or you could enter, putting your fingers in your ears against the scream of warplanes and get what you could. All women welcome. It was a microcosm of the opposite too. Everyone who was selling was cashing in on a festival of death, a festival so rich in self-confidence that it tolerated, even accommodated, opposition. Would Goddess Garments grow greedy and fat? Was the progression inevitable from *Atalanta* to *New Atalanta* to *New Atalanta Man*? Voices outside the base might say it had already begun, for what had paper flowers, fancy dress and air shows to do with the needs of the poor for good clothing, the needs of garment workers for fair wages, and what had any of it to do with the horror of living in a world that could go up in flames on a man's say-so . . . or a woman's . . . ?

Rather as that bucket of paper flowers six inches from Beverley's long grass skirt was going up in flames. . . .

Beverley swore and hit out as Teresa knocked her sideways. Tables went over, pillars collapsed, clothes rained down. 'We're on fire – ' Teresa and Beverley were trapped by each other's limbs and Goddess Garments stock. Teresa waited for the pain of burning, a pain that could hardly be worse than the metallic bite into her back of whatever it was on to which she had fallen. Fire extinguishers drenched her with water and all was still.

All was still, but only for an instant. Like a disciplined army the Goddess Garments women moved into position, shielding Teresa and Beverley from onlookers as they got up and moved tables, clothes and decorations back into position to conceal the pile of bolt cutters.

Beverley said, 'Teresa, we can't go on meeting like this.'

Teresa said, 'Come and meet Thelma Cook.'

'How about dinner tonight?'

Ann felt hypnotized. She wanted to say no. She felt her lips getting ready for yes. And then a woman in a toga burst through the crowd, screaming at the astonished Toby: 'Are you a pyromaniac or what?'

Ann had been aware of the commotion around the Goddess Garments stand, but it had been far away.

'You left your pipe on our counter and it fell into the flowers – someone could have been hurt – '

'I'm most frightfully sorry. I'll pay for any damage.'

'Someone could have been hurt.' 'I'll pay for any damage.' It doesn't follow, Toby.

'What were you doing in our space anyway?' the woman raged.

Ann thought, *I expect he was looking for the social side*, but she did not say it. She decided to make use of him instead. 'Would you keep an eye on my stand for a few minutes, Toby?' She left the hangar at a run. Above her head the Dam Busters raid was being enacted, with explosions and music. *Live and let live.* Where would Gwen be? She could be anywhere. Renewing her subscription to the RAC? Buying herself an ice cream, a pancake? Watching the field-gunner race? 'Let's give them a round of applause, ladies and gentlemen, and one for the losers too.' Waiting her turn for a parachute jump? She would have left the base and rejoined her friends. Maybe she didn't like groups, but they were better than *live and let live*.

Ann left the base. She knew she was doing this because she went past an Exit sign, but outside was not all that different from inside. She could still see and hear the planes. She still had to push her way through buyers, sellers, protesters, plane spotters, ordinary members of the public, looking, amid the forest of banners, for Lesbian Accountants Against Militarism.

Gwen was not with them. Ann tried to look unconcerned.

Adela said, 'Hello, Ann. Have you come to join us?'

'She can't,' growled a voice. 'She's not an accountant.' From the other side of the fence, Gwen was pretending not to laugh.

'I am nearly. I can add up.'

'I probably shouldn't say this,' said Gwen through the wire.

'Please. Say anything.'

'It's none of my business – '

Say it. I deserve it.

' – but shouldn't you be looking after your customers?'

'I wanted to find you,' said Ann. 'So I came out – '

'I thought I was the one who tried to do that,' Gwen sighed. 'At quite the wrong time and place. Don't you think you'd better come in again? Will they let you?' Gwen glanced anxiously at a sign that said 'No Re-Admissions'.

'It's all right, I've got an exhibitor's pass. Gwen –' Ann felt horribly shy, but Gwen had taken a risk so why shouldn't she?

'What?'

'How about dinner tonight?'

Buck Castle had been right to say that he and his colleagues – all, like himself, senior aides to Lindbergh Stanley – had come along just in time. Daphne did not know what had nearly come over her.

It was the heat, she supposed. And the threats of the beggar. She had become quite confused.

She had been disappointed to discover that the second man in the car was not Lindbergh Stanley himself. But she was thrilled to know that he was, at this very moment, on his way from the airport. He had been touring a neighbouring state and was going out of his way to be present at her first course.

So we will meet at last, Mr Stanley, she thought. *Lindbergh? Lindy? No. Formality will be maintained, the more enjoyably to break it down. You have played me like a fish and you have caught me. I have your message loud and clear. No one leaves START Selling to compete with it. I am the best. You would not have chosen me otherwise. You have caught me. You think. We shall see, when we meet.*

This was the big time. Daphne had always known how to win admiration, affection. Alistair, Teresa, had been too easy. She wanted to be admired and loved – yes, she admitted it, loved – by one greater than herself. One who had proved himself greater. She had regretted impersonating Teresa. Of course she regretted it. The Daphne Barclays of this world do not impersonate people. They do not need to. The Daphne Barclays? She laughed. There was only one.

She was welcomed to Stalton International House, shaken by the hand, introduced to officials. She hardly heard their names. There was only one name she wanted to hear. On the matter of the nappy rash cream, she held her tongue. It was probably all right in this climate. Was Lindbergh Stanley's first impression of her to be as a person talking about nappy rash cream?

'Your delegates are waiting, Miss Barclay.' She was escorted along a cool corridor towards a small theatre.

'What about Mr Stanley?'

'Mr Stanley has been delayed. You are to start without him. He will watch you from the projection room when he gets here, so that you won't be disturbed.'

So Lindbergh Stanley did not want to disturb her. His first impression of her would be as a person who talked while he listened.

Daphne walked out briskly on to the stage. Her delegates waited, quiet and too well-mannered to meet her eyes. She would soon let them know that they could look at her without fear. Daphne Barclay saw neither black nor white; she saw only saleswomen.

She smiled. She was looking at the curtained window at the back of the theatre. Were shadows playing tricks, or did she see a figure move, take its place, wait? Daphne lifted up her chin and breathed in from her diaphragm. 'I would like you,' she said,'to give yourselves a round of applause for being here.'

Zoe Fairbairns

HERE TODAY

She always knew men wanted her, as wife, secretary or lover. What if they don't?

Antonia's life had been perfect – temp of the year at the Here Today agency and a happy marriage to come home to. Suddenly all that has changed. Her husband doesn't want her and nor, it seems, do the increasingly-automated offices of London. Her home and her health are under threat, and so is her knowledge of who she is.

Antonia's search for answers also becomes the search for Samantha, another office worker and a rumoured victim of sexual assault. Pursuing the truth about Samantha provides Antonia with answers to questions about herself she didn't even know she was asking . . .

'Her most successful novel so far – racy, crisp and yes, very thrilling'
Tribune

'Witty, provocative, ironic and, above all, lots of fun'
Sara Maitland, *New Statesman*

Valerie Miner

MOVEMENT

Movement captures ten years of changes in Susan Campbell's life. Expatriate, leftist activist, journalist, committed feminist – all these are part of her passage through the seventies. Travelling from the USA to Canada, Africa and Britain, we follow her search for self-knowledge in a decade of challenge and re-examination. Valerie Miner's skills as a storyteller and insights as a reflective feminist have never been stronger.

'I liked the form of *Movement* very much – it is indeed a novel of movement, political, personal movement from country to country and subculture to subculture . . . vignettes and stories out of Susan's life, but never episodic, always carrying her development as a person and as a political personage a step further'
Marge Piercy

'This is a compelling book, invigorated by Susan's idealism and enthused with her deep passion for life'
Publishers Weekly

Michèle Roberts

THE WILD GIRL

In the parched soil of Provence, a fifth gospel has been discovered, Mary Magdalene's account of Jesus' teaching and her relationship with him. It is a book of revelation, for it unveils a new Christianity, one which embraces the female equally with the male and acknowledges and celebrates women's spirituality. It is also a passionate story of love and search, of separation and rebirth, centred on Mary as the wellspring of womanhood.

Michèle Roberts' novel offers a brilliant and moving vision that is also startlingly modern in its conclusions. It confirms her stature as one of Britain's most talented and exciting new writers.

'Bold and moving'
> *The Guardian*

'Michèle Roberts is intelligent and passionate; by her rich use of symbols and metaphor she transforms feminist cliché into something alive and moving'
> *Times Literary Supplement*

'An assured tour de force of passion ... the power with which it reclaims spiritual and sexual strength for women cannot be ignored'
> *Time Out*

Jenny Diski

NOTHING NATURAL

'*Nothing Natural* centres with illuminating precision on a sadomasochistic relationship. Rachel is in her thirties, a single parent admired by her friends for her self-sufficiency . . . But when she meets the compelling, sinister Joshua she discovers another side to herself . . . In a sense which horrifies her, she has found herself . . . An outstandingly well-written novel.'

New Statesman

Jenny Diski writes with an admirable lack of sensationalism about a difficult subject . . . an honest and startling look at the angry face of sex'

Cosmopolitan

'Its efficiency and its loathsomeness are about equal'

Anthony Thwaite, *Observer*

'Absolutely terrifying'

Margaret Drabble

'Chillingly clever. Jenny Diski is a writer to follow.'

Robert Nye, *Guardian*

'Galvanizing reading'

Women's Review

'Her combination of searching intelligence and remorseless, writerly precision is remarkable'

The Listener

Julia Voznesenskaya

THE WOMEN'S DECAMERON

'Ten women, who . . . have all just given birth in a Leningrad clinic, are unexpectedly quarantined together for ten days. Each night each woman undertakes to tell a story on some previously chosen subject: first love, rape, revenge, jealousy, money, betrayal, happiness, noble deeds or sex in absurd situations . . . It is an intimate world, startlingly frank about personal and social relationships and, as such, reveals more about Soviet life than anything to be read in a newspaper.'

Sheila MacLeod, *New Statesman*

'Now here is a robust, spicy saga of adultery, jealousy and betrayal . . . a sharp and savage review of Soviet life'
Sunday Telegraph

'Vigorous, funny, appealing and appalling tales'
Books & Bookmen

'Lively tales about women getting by, even getting some fun, however grim, out of life in the Soviet Union'
Hilary Spurling, *Guardian*

'Plain, simple, fine . . . useful, important and oddly cheering . . . a veritable riot of local colour, a very warm and funny book'
City Limits

'An extraordinary account of what life is like for modern Russian women'

Literary Review

'A remarkable book'
London Review of Books

Women's Writing from Methuen

While every effort is made to keep prices low, it is sometimes necessary to increase prices at short notice. Methuen Paperbacks reserves the right to show new retail prices on covers which may differ from those previously advertised in the text or elsewhere.

The prices shown below were correct at the time of going to press.

☐	413 41360 8	**Oroonoko and Other Stories**	Aphra Behn	£3.95
☐	413 41840 5	**Men Have all the Fun**	Gwynneth Branfoot	£3.95
☐	413 59180 8	**The Juniper Tree**	Barbara Comyns	£3.50
☐	413 40490 0	**Nothing Natural**	Jenny Diski	£2.50
☐	413 54660 8	**Londoners**	Maureen Duffy	£2.95
☐	413 60470 5	**I Want To Go To Moscow**	Maureen Duffy	£3.50
☐	413 57930 1	**Here Today**	Zoë Fairbairns	£1.95
☐	413 57550 0	**The Border**	Elaine Feinstein	£2.95
☐	413 54630 6	**The Riding Mistress**	Harriett Gilbert	£2.95
☐	413 59940 X	**Necessary Treasons**	Maeve Kelly	£3.95
☐	413 60230 3	**Non-Combatants and Others**	Rose Macaulay	£3.95
☐	413 57040 1	**Axioms**	Sheila MacLeod	£3.50
☐	413 59750 4	**Daddy Was a Number Runner**	Louise Meriwether	£3.50
☐	413 57940 9	**Movement**	Valerie Miner	£3.50
☐	413 14010 5	**The Women of Brewster Place**	Gloria Naylor	£3.95
☐	413 55230 6	**The Wild Girl**	Michèle Roberts	£2.95
☐	413 42100 7	**Death of an Ex-Minister**	Nawal El Saadawi	£2.95
☐	413 51970 8	**Sassafrass, Cypress & Indigo**	Ntozake Shange	£2.95
☐	413 60100 5	**Broderie Anglaise**	Violet Trefusis	£3.50
☐	413 14710 X	**The Women's Decameron**	Julia Voznesenskaya	£3.95
☐	413 41830 8	**Prisons of Glass**	Elizabeth Wilson	£3.95

All these books are available at your bookshop or newsagent, or can be ordered direct from the publisher. Just tick the titles you want and fill in the form below.

Methuen Paperbacks, Cash Sales Department,
PO Box 11, Falmouth,
Cornwall TR10 109EN.

Please send cheque or postal order, no currency, for purchase price quoted and allow the following for postage and packing:

UK	62p for the first book, 22p for the second book and 14p for each additional book ordered to a maximum charge of £1.75.
BFPO and Eire	62p for the first book, 22p for the second book and 14p for each next seven books, thereafter 8p per book.
Overseas Customers	£1.64 for the first book plus 25p per copy for each additional book.

NAME (Block Letters) ....

ADDRESS...

....